OXFORD WORLD'S CLASSICS

# JONATHAN WILD

HENRY FIELDING was born in Sharpham Park in Somerset on 22 April 1707. He was educated at Eton, and in the late 1720s settled in London, where he embarked on a career writing comedies, burlesques, and satires for the stage. His satires became more pointed in the heated political atmosphere of the mid-1730s, to the extent that they helped to prompt the passing of the Licensing Act in 1737, which introduced the censorship of stage plays and effectively terminated Fielding's career as a dramatist. He began to train as a lawyer, and turned his attention first to political journalism (notably through the *Champion* 1739–41, but he continued to engage in journalism through the 1740s), and then to prose fiction, beginning with *Shamela* (1741) and continuing with *Joseph Andrews* (1742), *Jonathan Wild* (1743), *Tom Jones* (1749), and *Amelia* (1751). His famous heroines Sophia Western and Amelia Booth were both said to be closely based on his first wife Charlotte Cradock, whom he married in 1734; after her death he married her maid Mary Daniel. In 1748 he was made Justice of the Peace for Westminster; he worked for legal reforms, and instituted the first organized police force in London. His health, which had been poor since the early 1740s, was placed under further strain by his hard work as Justice. In 1754 he travelled to Lisbon in an attempt to improve his health; he died in nearby Junqueira on 8 October.

LINDA BREE is Publisher, Literature, at Cambridge University Press. She is author of *Sarah Fielding* (1996) and editor of Sarah Fielding's *The Adventures of David Simple* (2002), as well as editor of Jane Austen's *Persuasion* (2000).

CLAUDE RAWSON is the Maynard Mack Professor of English at Yale University. He is author of a wide range of books, including *Henry Fielding and the Augustan Ideal under Stress* (1972), *Satire and Sentiment, 1660–1830: Stress Points in the English Augustan Tradition* (1994, corrected paperback edition 2000), and, most recently, *God, Gulliver, and Genocide: Barbarism and the European Imagination, 1492–1945* (Oxford University Press, 2001).

## OXFORD WORLD'S CLASSICS

*For over 100 years Oxford World's Classics have brought
readers closer to the world's great literature. Now with over 700
titles—from the 4,000-year-old myths of Mesopotamia to the
twentieth century's greatest novels—the series makes available
lesser-known as well as celebrated writing.*

*The pocket-sized hardbacks of the early years contained
introductions by Virginia Woolf, T. S. Eliot, Graham Greene,
and other literary figures which enriched the experience of reading.
Today the series is recognized for its fine scholarship and
reliability in texts that span world literature, drama and poetry,
religion, philosophy and politics. Each edition includes perceptive
commentary and essential background information to meet the
changing needs of readers.*

OXFORD WORLD'S CLASSICS

HENRY FIELDING

*The Life of*
# Mr Jonathan Wild
*the Great*

*Text edited by*
HUGH AMORY

*Edited with an Introduction by*
CLAUDE RAWSON
*and Notes by*
LINDA BREE

OXFORD
UNIVERSITY PRESS

# OXFORD
### UNIVERSITY PRESS

Great Clarendon Street, Oxford OX2 6DP

Oxford University Press is a department of the University of Oxford.
It furthers the University's objective of excellence in research, scholarship,
and education by publishing worldwide in

Oxford New York

Auckland Bangkok Buenos Aires Cape Town Chennai
Dar es Salaam Delhi Hong Kong Istanbul Karachi Kolkata
Kuala Lumpur Madrid Melbourne Mexico City Mumbai Nairobi
São Paulo Shanghai Taipei Tokyo Toronto

Oxford is a registered trade mark of Oxford University Press
in the UK and in certain other countries

Published in the United States
by Oxford University Press Inc., New York

Text © Hugh Amory 1997
Introduction © Claude Rawson 2003
Editorial matter © Linda Bree 2003

The moral rights of the author have been asserted

Database right Oxford University Press (maker)

First published 2003
First published as an Oxford World's Classics paperback 2003
Reissued 2008

British Library Cataloguing in Publication Data

Data available

Library of Congress Cataloging in Publication Data

Data available

ISBN 978–0–19–954975–7

5

Typeset in Ehrhardt
by RefineCach Limited, Bungay, Suffolk
Printed in Great Britain by
Clays Ltd, St Ives plc

# CONTENTS

# ACKNOWLEDGEMENTS

WE owe our greatest debt to the editors of *Miscellanies: Volume Three* in the Wesleyan edition of the Works of Henry Fielding, Bertrand A. Goldgar and the late Hugh Amory. In addition, we would like to thank Ros Ballaster, Mrs Angela Cottrell Dormer, Cynthia Ingram, Ananya Kabir, Thomas Keymer, James McLaverty, David McKitterick, W.R. Owens, Peter Sabor, and Kathryn Sutherland for offering help, guidance, and information on points of detail. The staffs of the Cambridge University Library, the British Library, and the Beinecke Library at Yale University have been helpful throughout.

L.J.B.
C.R.

# INTRODUCTION

HENRY FIELDING (1707–54) was born in Somerset. His family was related to the earls of Denbigh and claimed descent from the Habsburgs. The claim was fanciful, but the historian Gibbon, who appeared to accept it, said that 'the romance of *Tom Jones*, that exquisite picture of human manners, [would] outlive . . . the Imperial Eagle of the house of Austria'. The Earl's family spelt its name Feilding, which led the novelist to remark that his own branch was 'the first that knew how to spell'. Fielding's branch was an impoverished one. The combination of financial embarrassment and aristocratic caste is emblematic of the whole atmosphere of his life, and is variously reflected in his writings. He grew up in straitened circumstances, and most of his adult life was a struggle against debt, so that he had to write for a living, like any low scribbler or party hack. He sneered at the type, in the approved lordly accents of Augustan satirical rhetoric, but belonged to it himself, as his lowlier opponents were fond of pointing out.

Fielding went to Eton and, briefly in 1728–9, to the University of Leiden. His first play, *Love in Several Masques*, was published in 1728, and between 1728 and 1737 he wrote over twenty comedies and burlesques, including *The Author's Farce* (1730), *The Tragedy of Tragedies: or, The Life and Death of Tom Thumb the Great* (1731), *Pasquin* (1736), *Eurydice, The Historical Register for the Year 1736*, and *Eurydice Hiss'd* (1737). By that time, he was established as England's leading playwright. Although Fielding's relations with the Prime Minister Sir Robert Walpole were at most periods highly ambiguous, his later plays contained outspoken attacks on Walpole's government, and helped to precipitate the Licensing Act of 1737. This made dramatic performances subject to government censorship and remained in force until 1968 (in its later period the Act was more often concerned with moral than with political censorship).

## Fielding and the Augustan Tradition

Fielding is the only one among the important early novelists whose origins were patrician, and the only one also whose style and cultural loyalties were closely tied to the tradition we sometimes call Augustan. The term refers not to all writers of the period 1660–1790, but to those of a classicizing and patrician subculture within it, including Dryden and Gibbon, as well as Fielding, but not Defoe, Richardson, or Blake. The dominant representatives in Fielding's lifetime were Swift and Pope. Early in his career he sometimes called himself Scriblerus Secundus, after their famous coterie the Scriblerus Club. He published a poem, *The Masquerade* (1728), purporting to be by Lemuel Gulliver, Poet Laureate of Lilliput. He thus early signalled his allegiance to a particular style and ethos, although his personal and political relations with the leading Scriblerians were never close and sometimes hostile. One of his earliest poems was an unpublished mock-*Dunciad* against them, discovered some years ago among the papers of his cousin Lady Mary Wortley Montagu. Fielding seems to have been playing on Lady Mary's hostility to Pope and his friends, and may have hoped through her influence to secure the patronage of the Prime Minister, Walpole. There was no love lost between Walpole and the Scriblerians either, and Fielding's fluctuating attitudes to them are sometimes inverse indicators of where Fielding stood (or wanted to stand) with Walpole.

Nevertheless, his literary tastes and his cultural outlook were extensions of theirs, even when personal ties or political allegiance pulled the other way. Even his political allegiances were in fact more often and more publicly against Walpole than not. His praise of Swift's writings, and his sense of Swift as one of his own great literary masters, along with (and perhaps surpassing) Aristophanes, Lucian, Rabelais, and Cervantes, was strong. In return, Swift is said to have admired Fielding's wit and to have confessed that one of the only two occasions in his life when he remembered having laughed was 'at the circumstance of Tom Thumb's killing the ghost'. That occurs, as it happens, in one of the plays to which Fielding attached a mock-commentary by Scriblerus Secundus, modelled mainly on Pope's *Dunciad*, not very long after his mock-*Dunciadic* attack on Pope and Swift themselves. The remarkable thing, however, was not so much that Fielding appropriated specific routines from the Scriblerian masters, as that he later extended his deep assimilation of their stylistic manner into his novels: into a genre, that is, whose defining characteristics might have been thought outside the range of their literary sympathies and even antithetical to them.

It is a recurrent phenomenon in the history of literary forms, and especially perhaps of the novel, that an anti-form quickly resolves itself into a member of the class it is subverting. Fielding brought to novel-writing a manner shaped for other purposes by the Augustan satirists, urbanely interventionist rather than self-effacing, and designed to indicate authorial management rather than induce an illusion of unmediated reality. The formal structurings and closures of his periods and paragraphs, his highly personal blend of hauteur, irony, and fervour, his parodic set-pieces and inventive grotesqueries, contributed to the establishment of a rival narrative mode, more dedicated to displaying a controlling authorial personality than that of Fielding's two main novelist predecessors, Daniel Defoe (1660–1731) and Samuel Richardson (1689–1761). The style, though partly derived from non-fictional models, helped to turn Fielding into the principal inventor of the English comic novel and an early practitioner of the kind of fiction that is concerned, self-consciously and on a substantial scale, with the writing of itself.

His first two works of prose fiction, *Shamela* (1741) and *Joseph Andrews* (1742), were in fact triggered by his dislike of Samuel Richardson's first novel-in-letters, *Pamela* (1740), and both treated its author as a low vulgarian, in a manner plainly derived from the older satirists' treatment of the dunces and Grub Street hacks. One of the piquancies of the case was that the patrician Fielding picked up his lordly accents, to some extent at least, from authors who were themselves non-patrician. He was known for hard drinking and womanizing as well as improvidence, and lived up to a lordly stereotype of free manners and generous insouciance, contemptuous of the narrowness, rigidity, and prudentialism of burgherly aspirants to gentility. He sometimes professed a preference for the frankly 'low', for the demotic energies and coarse speech of popular entertainments, over the pseudo-politeness and merchant morality of the middle ranks, a not uncommon patrician stance affected at a later time by W. B. Yeats.

The Licensing Act effectively ended Fielding's dramatic career. He turned to three alternative employments which were to occupy him to the end of his life, and which interacted with each other in various ways: the law, political journalism, and novel-writing. He began his legal studies in 1737, was called to the Bar in 1740, and in 1748 became Justice of the Peace for Westminster, eventually

extending his jurisdiction to the whole of Middlesex. He created the
force which eventually became the Metropolitan Police, and in his
later years as a magistrate wrote a number of tracts on socio-legal
issues. His judicial philosophy, as expressed in these, was relatively
hard-line, but his novels, and especially *Amelia*, show an angry
awareness of the malpractices and injustices of the law and a compassionate feeling for its victims: the plight of good persons driven by
poverty into petty crime and punished by corrupt and unfeeling
magistrates is a recurrent preoccupation. A tension between the
claims of strict justice, and those of a larger perspective on the whole
human case, seems to have exercised Fielding throughout his legal
and fiction-writing career. The compassionate focus on legal
injustice is especially evident in the fiction, from 'A Journey from
this World to the Next' (1743) to *Tom Jones* (1749) and *Amelia* (1751).

## Fielding and the Novel

Fielding is one of a small group of eighteenth-century writers whom
we think of as the early masters of English fiction. Together with
Defoe and Richardson, two contemporaries of very different style
and outlook, he is an inaugural figure who helped to shape the English, and indeed the European, novel as we know it today. They were
not the first writers of prose fiction, and the writing of each was
partially formed by predecessors and contemporaries, whether from
classical antiquity, or Renaissance Europe, or the more immediate
context of English, French, and Spanish fictions of their own time,
and of the preceding decades. Behind Fielding stands the great
formative figure of Cervantes (1547–1616), author of *Don Quixote*
(1605–15).

The novels for which Fielding is best known, *Joseph Andrews*
(1742) and *Tom Jones* (1749), are examples of a style of fiction in
which the author is always visible as a manager of the narrative and
as a commentator on human life. He is not concerned to create an
'illusion of life', in which the author aims to be invisible, or to induce
in the reader a feeling that the story is not a story, but life itself. The
latter ambition is deeply embedded in an alternative fictional tradition which includes writers as various as Richardson, Flaubert,
Conrad, and Ford Madox Ford. It was one to which Fielding was
unsympathetic by temperament and social conditioning, and which,

in its Richardsonian form, he despised. So far was he from wishing the reader to forget that the story is a story, with an author in charge, that he built into the fabric of his narrative a continuous authorial commentary not only on the events, but on the composition, of this narrative. His writing is partly about the writing itself, about its style and structure, about what the author chooses to include or exclude, about his expectations of his readers, and his opinion of those who fulfil or fail to fulfil these expectations. In that sense, his two best-known fictions are early classics of a mode of writing which, from Sterne's *Tristram Shandy* (1759–67) to the many twentieth-century exemplars of the self-conscious or 'reflexive' novel, is strongly preoccupied with the processes of its own composition.

Fielding's authorial voice is of course concerned with life as well as letters, and the panoramas of the English social scene in *Joseph Andrews*, and especially *Tom Jones*, are filtered through a genial perspective of sharply observant reportage that has left an unmistakable stamp on the English comic novel. These are, however, not Fielding's only novels, nor do they represent his only style. His last novel, *Amelia* (1751), belongs to a period of darkened outlook, and is an uneven achievement. Though for the most part a work in the domestic-sentimental mode which Fielding never mastered, it has an opening of great power. Set in Newgate prison, it projects a world whose surreal injustices and radically incomprehensible surprises of behaviour and circumstance anticipate the more painful absurdist perspectives of modern times. The novel is also powerfully innovative in sketching out a serious rather than parodic parallelism between its 'modern' story and Virgil's *Aeneid*, in something like the way James Joyce was to structure *Ulysses* (1922) on the *Odyssey* of Homer.

Similar things may be said about *Jonathan Wild*, which may have been Fielding's first novel, as *Amelia* was his last, though it appeared the year after *Joseph Andrews* in the third volume of his *Miscellanies*, a three-volume collection of poems, essays, and fictional and dramatic pieces, which appeared in April 1743. Like *Amelia*, it has a darker theme than the two better-known books, anticipates Joycean parallels between past and present, and contains a sentimental subplot not wholly under Fielding's control. It is of interest that both the first and last of his important fictions should have a comparable element of adventurous experimentation, and some insecurities of style which seem to combine pessimistic perspectives with a compensating penchant for sentimental portrayals of virtuous characters in distress. Both works deserve to be seen as flawed masterpieces, whose interest and appeal are in some ways richer and less predictable than those of *Joseph Andrews* and *Tom Jones*, for all the buoyancy and managerial command of these better-known books.

Of all Fielding's extended fictions of modern life, *Jonathan Wild* is perhaps the least like a novel in the conventional sense. Its drumming emphasis on an upside-down allegory of Greatness (criminal wickedness, often praised as 'admirable') and Goodness (honest virtue, often referred to in mock-contempt as 'low', 'foolish', 'weak', or 'silly'), the harshly distorting sarcasm of its mock-heroic formula, remove it from the broadly realistic mode which Fielding, in the Preface to *Joseph Andrews*, liked to describe as 'exactest copying of Nature', and which he professed (not entirely convincingly, even in that novel) to be his way of writing. There is an argument for regarding *Jonathan Wild* as a prose poem in the mock-heroic mode, whose counterparts in verse are Dryden's *Mac Flecknoe* (1682) and especially Pope's *Dunciad* (1728–43), the latter a work of which Fielding was unremittingly aware during his career as a playwright in the 1730s, and whose final version appeared, after fifteen years of successive revisions, in the same year as *Jonathan Wild* itself. *Jonathan Wild* is in various other ways a remarkably modern work, whose formula of likening criminal malefactors to national leaders derives from Gay's *Beggar's Opera* (1728) and looks forward to Bertolt Brecht's satirical plays on the same theme, *The Threepenny Opera* (1928) and *The Resistible Rise of Arturo Ui* (1941, first performed 1958), the latter an amalgam of a gangster in the Al Capone mould and Hitler, revived in New York in October 2002 with Al Pacino as Ui and with allusions to George W. Bush. Although Brecht also wrote a 'Wildian' novel, *The Threepenny Novel* (1934), the principal analogues of *Jonathan Wild* are not novels.[1] But *Jonathan Wild* too, in some unexpected ways, and against superficial appearances, has an intimate place in the story of the novel form, touched by its incipient tendencies as well as contributing to its evolution.

---

[1] For fuller discussion of the relation of *The Beggar's Opera* and *Jonathan Wild* to the writings of Brecht, see Claude Rawson, *Henry Fielding and the Augustan Ideal under Stress* (London: Routledge and Kegan Paul, 1972; corrected paperback edn., Atlantic Highlands, NJ: Humanities Press, 1991), 111–12, 124, 209 ff.

Analogies or equations of criminals with national leaders, of gang-sters with conquerors and tyrants, or vice versa, are not new. What is perhaps 'modern' is making them the central theme of a work, and indeed turning the practice into something of a literary genre in its own right. If *The Beggar's Opera* inaugurates the formula, which Brecht's *Threepenny Opera* adapted to a twentieth-century perspec-tive in the bicentenary of Gay's play, *Jonathan Wild*, which alludes to and develops some of Gay's ironies, is the first important example in prose fiction, with Brecht's *Threepenny Novel* as one of its most powerful twentieth-century descendants.

A principal irony of this formula is expressed by Brecht's Mac-heath, when he asks in *The Threepenny Opera*, 'What is the burgling of a bank to the founding of a bank?' (III. iii). The moral of Gay's opera had been 'that the lower Sort of People have their Vices in a degree as well as the Rich: And that they are punish'd for them' (*Beggar's Opera*, III. xvi). A striking example, only three years earlier, was the fact that in the same week that the real-life Jonathan Wild was condemned to death, technically for a sum of 10 guineas,[2] the Lord Chancellor, the Earl of Macclesfield, was being tried for bribery and embezzlement of public funds amounting to £100,000 (several million in modern money), and got off with a fine. Gay's Macheath is reprieved because 'an Opera must end happily', and the crimes of Brecht's Macheath are on such a large scale that he is not only reprieved but ennobled, and granted a castle and £10,000 a year, in 1928 money, worth millions today.

Fielding rejected the debonair flourish of Gay's happy ending, and made sure his Jonathan Wild was hanged, as the real-life original had been. Gay's irony that the poor get punished while the powerful go free applies in a qualified way to Fielding's novel, in the sense that an analogy is conducted between Wild's behaviour and that of his political counterpart the Prime Minister, Sir Robert Walpole, who was not hanged, but (like Brecht's Macheath) ennobled, though fallen from power. In the hanging chapter (IV. xv), Fielding remarks that it is Fortune who decides whether 'you shall be hanged or be a Prime Minister'. But at the same time, Fielding's Wild is made out

---

[2] Not £10, as stated by some modern authorities (see Howson, 6; John Gay, *Dramatic Works*, ed. John Fuller, 2 vols. (Oxford: Clarendon Press, 1983), ii. 383 n.: for the correct sum, see *Mist's Weekly Journal*, 22 May 1725; *Select Trials*, ii. 224–5; and below, App. 1, p. 217.

to be a dangerously powerful figure in his own right, like Brecht's Macheath, who does go free. Wild terrorizes over the innocent Heartfrees, and generally behaves so ruthlessly that no sympathy is wasted on him as an underdog unjustly discriminated against. That this too is an oversimplification, and that Fielding's Wild has an engaging side, is part of a peculiar chemistry of this novel, about which there will be more to say.

The real-life Jonathan Wild (*c.*1682–1725) was a notorious pro-tection-racketeer and 'thief-taker' who ran a profitable business in the interface between crime and the policing authorities. He con-trolled a network of thieves, receivers, and informers, and was brought to trial and executed in 1725. He was sufficiently notorious to have generated a number of posthumous accounts, including two lives insecurely attributed to Daniel Defoe.[3] (One of these is reprinted as Appendix 1 in the present edition.) Fielding said he was not greatly interested in portraying the historical Wild, and the design of his story, while reflecting some actual circumstances of his career, has a fictional agenda which partly revolves around the analogy between 'great' men in crime and in politics.

Fielding also professed, in impish disclaimers, that his analogy should not be taken to reflect on any specific politicians, but on the roguery of highly placed persons in general (below, Appendices 2 and 3). It is hard to take these disclaimers at face value. In satirical and polemical writings of the time, it was a well-established conven-tion to use Wild's name when referring to Sir Robert Walpole, the Prime Minister. 'Great Man', though capable of being applied to others, was also a familiar sobriquet for Walpole, and references to the Prime Minister in the text corroborate the connection.[4] The editors of the excellent Wesleyan Edition of this novel, whose text has been used in this volume, have recently argued that the 'Great Man' analogue was indeed, as Fielding professed, a generic rather

---

[3] *The Life of Jonathan Wild*, by 'H.D.' (1725: see App. 1, below), and *The True and Genuine Account of the Life and Actions of the Late Jonathan Wild* (1725). For their attribution to Defoe, see J. R. Moore, *A Checklist of the Writings of Daniel Defoe* (2nd edn., Hamden, Conn., 1971), 196–8, Nos. 471, 473; for de-attribution, P. N. Furbank and W. R. Owens, *Defoe De-Attributions: A Critique of J. R. Moore's Checklist* (London: Hambledon, 1994), 138–9 (Nos. 471, 473, keyed to Moore's *Checklist*).

[4] For examples of the multiple equations of Wild, Walpole, 'Great Man', and 'Prime Minister', see *M3*, pp. xxvii ff., xxxi, 21 n., 48 n.

than specific figure.[5] This view runs counter to most readings of the book from its own time to ours, as well as being undermined by its declared relationship to *The Beggar's Opera*, whose principal target was acknowledged to be the Prime Minister, and whose *dramatis personae* draw directly on the criminal fraternity of Wild and his associates.

This is not to say that either work is restricted to personal allegory, in the mode of Barbara Garson's *MacBird* (1966), about Lyndon Johnson at the time of the Kennedy assassination and the Vietnam War, or Philip Roth's satiric novel about Richard Nixon, *Our Gang (Starring Tricky and his Friends)* (1971). Both *The Beggar's Opera* and *Jonathan Wild* have a wide general reach, as an anatomy of the relationship between crime and government, or gangsters, thieves, despots, and conquerors. But this wider reach is experienced by way of, rather than in competition with, or exclusion of, the personal application. Without this, both works would have a disembodied quality. Much of their stinging commentary on the larger issues derives force and flavour from a sense that specific political contexts are in play, even for readers with only a slight knowledge of the historical particulars.

In both *The Beggar's Opera* and *Jonathan Wild* the core comparison has unexpected ramifications. Gay's play offers a scabrous view of mercenary political manoeuvring, but its hero Macheath is a genial and charming figure, attractive to women, and blessed with the attractions of a musical-comedy lead. The festive ending, because 'an Opera must end happily', gives the lie to those who, like Swift, chose to see the play as portraying 'Vices of all Kinds in the strongest and most odious Light'.[6] It is Brecht's festive ending whose charge of sarcasm made the final reward of Mackie the Knife an exposure of society's corrupt values. In *Polly*, Gay's sequel to *The Beggar's Opera*, Macheath is transported to America and finally hanged, a gloomier version closer in character to Fielding's Wild, who is also hanged.[7] But it is possible that *Jonathan Wild* should not be conventionally read as Swift read *The Beggar's Opera*, as a portrait of unrelieved viciousness deservedly punished. When Byron said the

[5] See *M3*, 'General Introduction', pp. xxvii–xxxv, 'Textual Introduction', 197–208; for some arguments against this opinion, see the review by Claude Rawson, *Times Literary Supplement*, 27 Feb. 1998, pp. 4–6.

[6] Jonathan Swift, review of *The Beggar's Opera*, in *Intelligencer*, No. 3, 25 May 1728, Jonathan Swift and Thomas Sheridan, *The Intelligencer*, ed. James Woolley (Oxford: Clarendon Press, 1992), 63.

[7] On these matters, see Rawson, 123–6, esp. 124.

book exposed the 'littleness of the great', he seems to have meant that it attacked inequality and disparaged those in high places.[8] But the book is also, in some ways, a study of a 'littleness' in 'Great Men', which it treats with unexpected sympathy, alongside the contempt. The fact partly reflects real-life complexities in Fielding's relations with Walpole, and partly a feeling for the fictional Wild as one whose 'littleness' has a pluckily vulnerable humanity and truth to self.

## Heroes and Hero-Worship

At the heart of *Jonathan Wild* is an anxiety about 'heroes', and what we call, in praise or otherwise, the heroic. Both national leadership and the exploits of gangsters are implicated in this issue. Wild is throughout sarcastically described as 'heroic' or 'our hero'. He was himself, we are told, 'a passionate Admirer of Heroes', an admiration which goes back to his schooldays. In such a context, 'heroes' were, in the first instance, the warrior protagonists of the great epic poems of classical antiquity, chiefly Homer's *Iliad* and Virgil's *Aeneid*. These poems were traditionally viewed as the highest poetic expression humanity had achieved or was capable of achieving. They cele-brated, in a grandly elevated style, the great events of the Greek warlords and the national origins of the Romans. These included military victories, usually portrayed as brilliant set-pieces of valour by individual warriors, in single or successive man-to-man combat. Homer's Achilles and Virgil's Aeneas, both of whom are important points of reference in *Jonathan Wild*, were perhaps the two most celebrated epic exemplars of martial prowess. Another virtue, espe-cially in Greek epic, was cunning or guile, mainly associated with the Homeric Odysseus, the capacity to outwit the enemy without necessarily resorting to armed force.

We would not expect a mobster like Wild to be a fan of the ancient classics, but we learn that he was in fact very impressed by their valorization of coercive force and trickery. Without troubling to mas-ter the 'learned Languages', and getting his information at second hand, the schoolboy Wild 'was wonderfully pleased with that Pas-sage in the Eleventh *Iliad*, where *Achilles* is said to have bound two Sons of *Priam* upon a Mountain, and afterwards released them for a

---

[8] Byron, 'Detached Thoughts', Nov. 1821, in Claude Rawson (ed.), *Henry Fielding: A Critical Anthology* (Harmondsworth: Penguin, 1973), 244.

Sum of Money' (I. iii).[9] He was similarly impressed by, or took a connoisseur's interest in, feats of cattle-rustling in both Homer and Virgil.[10] Of the first episode, which Homer represented in a context of accepted conventions of ransom, and of ritual exchanges of the spoils of war, and which Wild not implausibly reinterpreted as kidnapping for gain, Wild commented that it was 'alone sufficient to refute those who affected a Contempt for the Wisdom of the Ancients' (I. iii).

This remark would have a powerfully witty resonance for many of Fielding's readers, for whom the old issue of the relative merit of ancient and modern cultures was still a matter of live debate. For partisans of the ancients, the status of epic was especially sensitive, since this highest of poetic forms was increasingly seen to be in conflict with Christian values, a progressive increase in anti-war sentiment, and a growing demand, on the part of an ever-widening bourgeois readership, for narratives dealing with the lives of ordinary people rather than the battlefield exploits of chieftains. The 'realist' novel was partly the result of the cultural readjustments which were simultaneously challenging the status of epic. Indeed, the two earliest major novelists in English, Defoe and Richardson, expressed outright distaste both for the subject matter and moral values of the old heroic poems.

For Fielding to attribute classical sympathies to Wild, and for such openly disreputable reasons, would seem to align him with the pro-modern, anti-Homeric position expressed by Defoe and Richardson. In fact, he was for the most part a loyalist of the ancients. All his novels are saturated with a sense of live relationship to the poems of Homer and Virgil, whether in the affectionate mock-heroic idiom of *Joseph Andrews* and *Tom Jones*, or in the more sombre relationship of *Amelia* to the *Aeneid*, which, as I mentioned, prefigures Joyce. *Jonathan Wild* is itself a mock-heroic work, in a mode developed into serious art precisely during the period when epics were still thought of as the highest form, but recognized to be out of tune with the times. Writers with epic aspirations, including Dryden (1631–1700) and Pope (1688–1745), never completed their projected epics, but executed important translations of Virgil and Homer, as it were by proxy, and elsewhere filtered their epic interests through

---

[9] *Iliad*, 11. 104–6.
[10] *Iliad*, 11, 670 ff.; *Aeneid*, 8. 185–225.

ironic parody. The mock-heroic of Dryden and Pope is a form of
parody which does not attack what it parodies. It instead exposes a
lowered modern reality by presenting it as unworthy of the heroic
pretensions implied by the style. The epic accents of *The Rape of the
Lock* bring out the triviality of a social group, not the shortcomings
of ancient poets. The same is true of the *Dunciad*'s treatment of
Pope's literary contemporaries.

Mock-heroic was nevertheless an expression of split purposes.
Dryden said that its mock-majesties retained something of the original grandeurs, so that satire itself might become a form of heroic
poetry.[11] By the same token, irony is a two-edged weapon, capable of
undermining what it defends as well as what it attacks. For all their
epic loyalties, the partisans of the ancients were defensive about the
epic's celebration of brutal warfare, eliminating such subject matter
from mock-heroic poems, softening Homer in translation (as Pope
did), and making strenuous distinctions between the greatness of
the poems and the brutality of the times they were written in, or
about. Achilles was said by Addison to be 'Morally Vicious, and only
Poetically Good'.[12]

In *Jonathan Wild* these incompletely resolved sympathies are
brought out with an invigorated recognition of the differences
between admired poems and the moral values and historical realities
they reflected. We can be sure that Wild's admiration for Homer and
Virgil is different from Fielding's, but all the evidence we have suggests that Wild's approval cannot simply be translated into his
author's disapproval. The primary implication is not that Wild is
wrong to admire Homer and Virgil, but that he admires them for the
wrong reasons. On the other hand, Fielding does suggest, more
boldly than previous practitioners of loyal mock-heroic, including
Pope, that the disreputable aspects of the heroic poems may indeed
be as disreputable as it takes for a scoundrel like Wild to approve of
them. The schoolboy enthusiasms of Wild do not misdescribe what
occurs in the poems. The reader is forced to balance his or her
antipathy to Wild against the fact that Wild's perception that the

---

[11] John Dryden, *A Discourse Concerning the Original and Progress of Satire* (1693), in
*Of Dramatic Poesy and Other Critical Essays*, ed. George Watson, 2 vols. (London:
Everyman, 1962), ii. 149.
[12] *Spectator*, No. 548, 28 Nov. 1712, ed. Donald F. Bond (Oxford: Oxford University
Press, 1965), iv. 464; for a similar comment by Dryden about Achilles, see Bond's
editorial note.

admired poets are celebrating kidnapping and cattle-rustling, the successful exercise of force and deception, is indeed sustainable.

If this is so, Fielding has, at least in this passage, gone beyond the traditional mock-heroic formula, which purports to suggest that the present is a lowered version of a noble past, to a more ambiguous suggestion that, while this may be true, it is not wholly true. If Homer and Virgil celebrate thuggery and deception, then the past, however grander than the present in other ways, is also very much like it. The sense of a two-way valuation, destabilized of its textbook certainties, is gaining a foothold. Joyce's idea of Homer's *Odyssey* not as a heroic contrast to modern life, but as a comprehensively non-heroic prototype, is some way away, but the germ of it is detectable. Certainly a two-way valuation of the past as a repository of lost grandeurs, and also as a prototype of modern depravities, which we take for granted in Eliot's *Waste Land*, exists here in a gingerly form.

The momentary emergence of a destabilized perspective on the icons of the classical past is striking. But Fielding normally uses another method, closer to the manoeuvres of Pope, for disengaging the epic poems from the bad doings they celebrate. Immediately after the account of Wild's enthusiasm for the scabrous deeds of epic heroes, Fielding announces that Wild 'was a passionate Admirer of Heroes, particularly *Alexander* the Great, between whom and the late King of *Sweden* he would frequently draw Parallels'. It seems superficially a natural transition, but it marks an abrupt change, from poetic to historical examples. The tactic is a signature of the book. It flirts with epic precedents, but the gravamen of its charge is that the mobsters are evil because they resemble the real-life villains of history, Alexander the Great and Charles XII (1682–1718).

Both had reputations as ruthless conquerors, admired by some, detested (from antiquity onwards) by others. Charles XII was especially reviled by many in England because, though a Protestant king, he had, for geopolitical reasons, been complicit in a Jacobite plot against George I. This would not have endeared him to Fielding, but the main charge against him, like that against Alexander, was his insatiable military ruthlessness. Since the historical Wild was probably the same age as Charles, the latter's military victories are unlikely to have impressed Wild in his schooldays (though Charles became King at 14 and was fighting wars at 17). Fielding changed

Wild's birth year to 1665, for special reasons unrelated to Charles, actually making schoolboy awareness of Charles impossible for the Wild of the story. Fielding's account is fictive, of course, and he may have forgotten the anachronism, or perhaps was projecting Wild's supposed later view into the imagined schooldays. Either way, the anachronism is a sign of Fielding's determination to implicate Charles in his indictment of military villainy. Fielding had recently translated from the French the *Military History of Charles XII* (1740) by Gustavus Adlerfeld, and was familiar with Voltaire's *History of Charles XII* (1731). Both are admiring portraits, which may lend an edge to Fielding's denunciations of historians who praise villainous despots, though it also seems evident that Fielding admired Voltaire's work.

The switch from poetic to historical villains is abrupt and striking. It serves to intimate a disconnection between epics and history, poems and real life, which helped to disinfect the poems from the taint of slaughter. In fact, the harshest mock-heroic sarcasms in *Jonathan Wild*, which border on the anti-heroic, are those which denounce historical tyrants, Alexander, Caesar, Louis XIV of France, Charles XII. The uncoupling is pointed, but it depends on an initial coupling. The Homeric and Virgilian examples had to be mentioned first in order to become an issue, requiring adjustment. And behind the names of Alexander and Charles was a chain of connection of which many readers would have been aware at the time. Charles XII had developed a schoolboy admiration, almost a hero-worship, of Alexander, when learning Latin as a boy. He is said never to have wanted to read about anything or anyone else (except sometimes Caesar, another hero of Wild's), and he aspired to and achieved the reputation of an 'Alexander of the North'.[13] Alexander himself had from childhood formed a similar emulative admiration for Homer's Achilles, and carried a version of the *Iliad* on his expeditions, calling it a handbook of military art. These facts were part of the common lore about him, reported by all the historians and

---

[13] Voltaire, *History of Charles XII*, trans. from the French, 6th edn. (1735), 9, 25, 102, 128, 176, 318; Adlerfeld, *Military History of Charles XII*, 3 vols. (1740), i. 2–3 n.; Fielding's translation, possibly with collaborators. Fielding added, as footnotes to the original, freshly translated extracts from Voltaire's history, including the account cited here of Charles's early reading about Alexander, which seems to have been a source for the schoolboy chapter of *Jonathan Wild* (I. iii).

biographers, Diodorus Siculus, Quintus Curtius, Plutarch, Arrian, whom Fielding knew and possessed in his library.[14]

An even more striking example of an epic analogue offered, and then incompletely withdrawn, or neutralized, by a historical replacement, occurs in III. iv, when the character of Fireblood is introduced: 'The Name of this Youth, who will hereafter make some Figure in this History, being the *Achates* of our *Æneas*, or rather the *Hæphestion* of our *Alexander* was *Fireblood*'. The corrective readjustment from poetry to history is fraught with secondary ironies. Achates was the loyal friend of Aeneas, often named in Virgil with the identifying epithet of *fidus* (faithful), while Fireblood becomes the lover of his master's wife (III. vii, IV. xi). No sooner is Fireblood's epic connection introduced than our attention is redirected. He is, as if in retraction, converted from the friend of an epic hero to the henchman of a historical thug. The name Fireblood puns on the name Hephaestion (Hephaestus was the god of fire, and the name Hephaestion, probably not a straightforward diminutive, might suggest 'dear to' or 'similar to' Hephaestus). Once again, the transition is conspicuous, while the original epic analogue, having been stated, cannot wholly be unsaid. Indeed, a further chain of epic connection exists subtextually beneath the disconnection itself. Hephaestion appears in the biographies as a figure whom Alexander loved as Achilles loved Patroclus, and Homeric precedents, self-consciously cultivated by the historical Alexander, keep epic reminders discreetly in play even as they are being ostensibly contradicted.[15]

It is remarkable that Jonathan Wild's schooldays play such a prominent part in establishing the elusive epic presence in the mock-heroic scheme, even as the latter, in its specialized way, seems to turn *anti*-heroic. Mock-heroic, as I have suggested, is usually loyal, but Fielding's partial trick of collapsing differences between epic and history goes some way to subverting this loyalty. In Blake, and in Byron, we later find a willingness to ignore the distinction, and to say

---

[14] Diodorus Siculus, *Library*, 17. 97. 3; Quintus Curtius, *History of Alexander*, summaries to Books 1 and 2 (Loeb, i. 11, 19, 38), 4. 6. 30, 8. 4. 26; Plutarch, *Life of Alexander*, 8. 2, 15. 8–9, 26. 1–2; Plutarch, 'On the Fortune or the Virtue of Alexander', *Moralia*, 327. 4, 331. 10; Arrian, *Anabasis of Alexander*, 1. 12. 1–2, 7. 14. 3–5. For Fielding's familiarity with, and ownership of, these writings, see Frederick G. and Anne R. Ribble, *Fielding's Library: An Annotated Catalogue* (Charlottesville: Bibliographical Society of the University of Virginia, 1996), D18, C60, P31–3, A41.

[15] Quintus Curtius, 2 (summary) [Loeb, i. 38]; Arrian, 1. 12. 1–2, 7. 14. 3–5, 16. 8.

that ancient epics, whether you like them (Byron) or not (Blake), are really about the same thing as modern wars.[16] Fielding does not take that step. Perhaps the schoolboy setting in which the analogy is first raised helps to blunt the impact. There is an old connection between epics and schoolboys, one of whose implications, which is the subject of jokes by the Roman satirists Persius and Juvenal, is that epic poems, and the historical rampages of Alexander or Hannibal, survive mainly as exercises for schoolboy recitation.[17] W. B. Yeats put it nostalgically rather than satirically in 'The Song of the Happy Shepherd':

> Where are now the warring kings?
> An idle word is now their glory,
> By the stammering schoolboy said.

When Fielding introduced Wild's schooldays, he was expressing an intuition wider and deeper than Juvenal's dismissal of schoolboy recitations. He was sketching out an analogy, later explored with a fuller self-awareness by W. H. Auden and Christopher Isherwood, between the world of schoolboy gangs and intrigues, the thuggeries of epic and saga, and the behaviour of totalitarian states in Europe in the 1930s. They too did so with a certain nostalgia. Isherwood wrote about Auden in 1937:

The saga-world is a schoolboy world, with its feuds, its practical jokes, its dark threats conveyed in puns and riddles and understatements . . . I once remarked to Auden that the atmosphere of *Gisli the Outlaw* very much reminded me of our schooldays. He was pleased with the idea: and, soon after this, he produced his first play, *Paid on Both Sides*, in which the two worlds are so inextricably confused that it is impossible to say whether the characters are really epic heroes or only members of a school O.T.C.[18]

And Auden, who elsewhere said about the Nazis' admiration for the sagas: 'I love the sagas, but what a rotten society they describe, a society with only the gangster virtues,' said of his own *The Orators*: The central theme of *The Orators* seems to be Hero-worship, and we all

---

[16] William Blake, 'On Homer's Poetry' (*c.* 1820), and see the entries on Homer and Virgil in S. Foster Damon, *A Blake Dictionary*, rev. edn. (Hanover, NH: University Press of New England, 1988), 187–9, 435–6; Byron, e.g. on the Siege of Ismail, *Don Juan*, VII and VIII, *passim*.

[17] For Persius on heroic pretensions, or schoolboy recitations, or both, see *Satires*, 1. 3–5, 28–30, 50–1, 69–97, 121–3; 3. 44–7; 5. 7; 6. 9–11. Juvenal, *Satires*, 7. 158 ff., 10. 166 ff., and *passim*.

[18] Christopher Isherwood, *Exhumations* (Harmondsworth: Penguin, 1969), 31, cited Rawson, 173. For fuller discussion of Auden and Isherwood, as well as Jarry's *Ubu* plays, and the schoolboy theme in general, see Rawson, 171–227.

know what that can lead to politically. . . . I realise that it is precisely the schoolboy atmosphere and diction which act as a moral criticism of the rather ugly emotions and ideas they are employed to express. By making the latter juvenile, they make it impossible to take them seriously. In one of the Odes I express all the sentiments with which his followers hailed the advent of Hitler, but these are rendered, I hope, innocuous by the fact that the Führer so hailed is a new-born baby and the son of a friend.[19]

These are provocative connections, and since the 1890s and the *Ubu* plays of Alfred Jarry, our imaginations have become accustomed to strange interconnections between schoolboy gangs, tyrannical pedagogues, and grimmer forms of political despotism.

Fielding's insight into such associations is a powerful one, similar to Auden's, without the revelation of personal nostalgia. He too realizes that the analogy may be ugly, but that the phenomenon is in some ways childish, 'juvenile . . . impossible to take . . . seriously'. Wild must be taken seriously, but in some ways, beginning with the strutting, hero-worshipping, lumpenbookishness of his schoolboy enthusiasms, he is also in a special sense 'impossible to take seriously'. That special sense is partly conveyed, without the schoolboy accoutrements, in the Hitler of Charlie Chaplin's *The Great Dictator* (1940). Chaplin was a favourite of Brecht, and it is also found in Brecht's 'charismatically loutish' Arturo Ui, the gangsterized version of Hitler, who takes elocution and deportment lessons, as the real-life Wild and his subordinates were said to do. Ui's recitations, like the heroics of Jarry's Ubu, are from Shakespeare's plays rather than the ancient epics, and Ui's speech tutor is a dilapidated Shakespearian actor. Shakespeare seems in modern times to have become the common, and indeed international, source, or repository of choice, for an awareness of 'heroic' styles and behaviour, replacing the classical epics (and not invariably sharing their endorsement of the heroic ethos). Thus Garson's *MacBird* is a parody of *Macbeth*, and, like the Ubu cycle, is permeated with allusions to the other plays, and Roth's Nixon novel, *Our Gang*, includes an occupation, or 'liberation', of Hamlet's Elsinore by American troops.[20]

[19] W. H. Auden, *The Orators*, 3rd edn. (London: Faber, 1966), 7–8.

[20] For 'charismatically loutish' see the review of the 2002 production of Brecht's play by Ben Brantley, *New York Times*, 22 Oct. 2002; 'H.D.', *The Life of Jonathan Wild* (1725), 33 (below, Appendix 1, p. 200); on Ui, see Rawson, 209–11; Barbara Garson, *MacBird* (New York: Grassy Knoll Press, 1966); Philip Roth, *Our Gang (Starring Tricky and His Friends)* (New York: Random House, 1971), 88–9, 122–8.

For all the harping on his diabolical villainy and insatiable ruthlessness, Wild remains a small-time operator, and also, in a broader sense, a 'little man'. The wealthy big-time mobster reported by H.D.'s biography (see Appendix 1) turns into a bully who fights an accomplice for spoils of no more than eighteen pence (I. xiv).[21] He is outwitted by his enemies and deceived by his women. He is, notwithstanding Fielding's brassy assertion to the contrary, a repeated failure in crime and in love. His resilience is that of the human automaton who, again like Charlie Chaplin, bounces back every time he is put down. He is the prisoner of his own compulsiveness, unable to stop his pockets being picked because his hands are employed in the pockets of others. He makes a preposterously 'heroic' speech lamenting the vulnerability of the Great, from which ordinary men who don't pick pockets are protected (II. iv), as common citizens, in 'serious' examples of such flights of oratory, are spared the tribulations of kings.

## Devil Incarnate or Small-Time Crook?

Readers have been so mesmerized by the harping assertions of Wild's wickedness, and by the unrelenting pressure of the upside-down ironies of Greatness and Goodness, that they have usually taken Wild to be, in the words of Sir Walter Scott, 'a picture of complete vice, unrelieved by any thing of human feeling, and never by any accident even deviating into virtue'.[22] What Fielding presents bears a certain relation to this, but it exists in a totally different atmosphere. This can best be seen in close-up in the 'operatic' finale of Wild's execution: operatic not in Gay's sense, that 'an Opera must end happily', which Fielding had already made a point of dissociating himself from in an earlier context (IV. vi), but in the crowded and animated montage of the scene at Tyburn, with a mob worthy of Cecil B. De Mille hurling missiles and execrations at him.

---

[21]  The episode opens Book II. At the end of the previous Book (I. xiv), the narrative had spoken of 'no considerable booty'. The second edition (1754) adds to the emphasis by saying that the booty was no 'more than two shillings' (of which Wild's share of three-quarters was eighteen pence; for Wild's habit of extorting three-quarters rather than his due of half the booty, see also the close of I. viii). But the original version already seems concerned to signal 'Eighteen pence' as a marker of Wild's financial horizons (I. vi).

[22]  Scott, 'Prefatory Memoir to Fielding', 25 Oct. 1820, *The Novelist's Library*, vol. i (1824), in Rawson, *Henry Fielding: A Critical Anthology*, 232.

It is his moment of Glory, on the 'Tree of Glory'. It is the fate for which he was born. He even escaped drowning in a shipwreck during an energetic attempt to rape Mrs Heartfree (II. x), in evident conformity with the proverb that he who was born to be hanged shall never be drowned. So there is a Justice superior to Gay's, and a superior 'Conservation of Character'. This 'conservation' refers variously to Wild's sustaining his character to the end, to Fortune's determination to see that he gets his due deserts, and to the book's achievement of truth in both respects. It is a tribute to truth to life, to poetic justice and the fitness of things, and, since the author is in control of both, to the management of the story. If 'Conservation of Character' means that the character has remained consistent, and earns a jokey boast for the author, it also offers a somewhat deeper sense of the character's fidelity to his own nature than the author perhaps knew.

The episode is conducted with an appropriate parade of mock-heroic bombast, repeatedly referring to the hero's 'Apotheosis', 'Completion of GREATNESS', 'Completion of Glory'. The execration, and the hurling of 'Stones, Brickbats, Dirt, and all Manner of mischievous Weapons', are part of the sleazy grandeur, every bit as much as the gross material rewards of Brecht's Macheath on his reprieve. The hostile members of the crowd 'endeavoured to prevent' this completion, not from any wish to spare him, but, 'by knocking him on the Head as he stood under the Tree', in order to abort the grand finale of the hanging. But the 'Completion of Glory' was not to be stopped.

All the sleazy pomp and circumstance may seem designed to suggest the mighty doom of an unregenerate malefactor, bold and unrepentant. Wild remains unmoved by all the expressions of hatred, and uncowed by the volley of missiles. This is not, however, the brazen courage of the diabolical Machiavel, but a low-grade effrontery supported by drink and drugs. It is not the dignity of a great anti-hero, but an altogether lesser composure, not in its way unimpressive, and partly akin to the resilient impassivity of a puppet or clown. This is just as much part of his 'Conservation of Character' as the inflated glories of the magniloquent montage.

A careful reading of the hanging chapter shows the consistent survival of a plucky low-level resilience. In prison beforehand, having given up hope of survival, he showed not dejection or contrition, but 'rather infused more Confidence and Assurance into his Looks'. He drank to keep his spirits up and when he was 'asked, whether he was afraid to die, he answered, *D——n me, it is only a Dance without Music*'. When someone said he hoped 'he would die like a Man, he cocked his Hat in Defiance, and cried out greatly, *Zounds! who's afraid?*' The next paragraph but one shows a final meeting with his wife, the faithless Laetitia, as quarrelsome an exchange of insults and recriminations as all their previous dialogues. Both the seeming consistency and the cockiness retain a shabby dignity, even in indignity.

The supreme revelation of truth to self, in this particular sense of 'Conservation of Character', on which Fielding expressly insists, occurs at the moment of hanging:

We must not however omit one Circumstance, as it serves to shew the most admirable Conservation of Character in our Hero to his last Moment, which was, that whilst the Ordinary was busy in his Ejaculations, *Wild*, in the midst of the Shower of Stones, *&c.* which played upon him, applied his Hands to the Parson's Pocket, and emptied it of his Bottle-Screw, which he carried out of the World in his Hand. (IV. xv)

This is not the triumphal exit of an arch-villain, but the last dexterity of a small-time crook. It is also compulsive behaviour. That it happens at such a moment has a strutting stylishness. It would not be wrong to think of it as a schoolboy prank, almost endearing in its skill, its instinctive expression of character, and its essential harmlessness. This 'Conservation of Character' is the 'Apotheosis' of the little man, vulnerable, cocky, and slightly absurd. This littleness of moral stature has its poetry, whose proper place is prose fiction. In this spotlight on a shabby endearing figure, a 'survivor' even in the moment of death, not only 'admirable' in the vocabulary of Fielding's mock-heroic, but actually admired as ordinary humanity, *Jonathan Wild* makes its most unexpected, least noticed, but perhaps most significant contribution to the evolution of the novel. This is independent of the interesting fact that Joyce may have remembered the 'corkscrew cross', hanging on the end of 'a rosary of corks', in the phantasmagoria of His Eminence, Simon Stephen Cardinal Dedalus, Primate of All Ireland, in the Circe episode of *Ulysses*.[23]

It was said that prisoners on the gallows made faces at the Ordinary of Newgate, the prison's officiating parson, and an episode is

---

[23] James Joyce, *Ulysses* (London: Bodley Head, 1955), 497.

reported in 1728 of his pocket being picked at a hanging (see the note on this passage, pp. 293–4). In view of the novel's preoccupation with Charles XII of Sweden, and Wild's obsessive admiration of that monarch, it is possible that Fielding was remembering an anecdote about Charles's death. Voltaire's *History of Charles XII* (1731), which Fielding owned and admired, describes how, on the battlefield in Norway, after a cannon ball hit the King's head, 'He was dead the moment he received this; but he had the force in that instant to put his hand by a natural motion to the guard of his sword'.[24] This reflex manifests the King's warrior instinct, his natural combativeness and steely nerve, of which Voltaire was an admirer. If Fielding was remembering this conservation of character at the moment of death, his transformation of it into the cocky allure of Wild's last exploit on the gallows is the studied exercise of a brilliant comic genius.

Fielding referred in *Tom Jones* (VIII. i) to 'what the dramatic Critics call Conservation of Character', as a combination of truth to life or probability, and of consistency. There he again speaks of it as an author's gift, requiring 'a very extraordinary Degree of Judgment, and a most exact Knowledge of Human Nature'. As we have seen, the resonances of the phrase in *Jonathan Wild* are broader, and include in a special sense Wild's truth to his own character. They also include the fitness of things, which ensures that a character like Wild gets the fate he deserves, an expression of poetry's or fiction's obligations to the moral order. Playful fuss is made of Fortune's determination to see the execution through, and of the vanity of struggling 'against this Lady's Decrees'. Whether 'she hath determined you shall be hanged or be a Prime Minister, it is in either case lost Labour to resist'. This is similar to Gay's comment that the vices of low and high people are the same, but that the poor are punished. In Brecht's adaptation, Macheath's reprieve and elevation to high honours is the equivalent of 'or be a Prime Minister' in Fielding's alternative scenario.

'Prime Minister' expressly evokes Sir Robert Walpole, who had been associated with Wild in polemical writings and satirical tracts from the 1720s onwards. By the time the book was published,

---

[24] Voltaire, *History of Charles XII*, 6th edn. (London, 1735), 316; 7th edn. (1740), 316; on the other hand, the 3rd edn. (1732), 362, among other variants omits the words 'by a natural motion', which correspond to 'par un mouvement naturel' in at least some versions of the French text, thus *Histoire de Charles XII*, 3rd edn. ('Basle', 1732), 358.

Walpole had fallen (February 1742). Sometime before then, he and Fielding seem to have reached a permanent accommodation. Walpole is genially treated in Fielding's pamphlet *The Opposition* (December 1741), and there is recent evidence that Walpole had bought Fielding off in some 'final' way in December 1741.[25] The relations between them had in any case been fluctuating, and Fielding's outspoken attacks on Walpole in his plays and political journalism seem to have been punctuated by not always edifying efforts at accommodation. When Fielding's *Miscellanies* were put up for subscription, Walpole paid 20 guineas for ten sets on royal paper.

These facts may not be consistent with the view of *Jonathan Wild* as a vitriolic attack on the Prime Minister, and might seem to support the recent argument that Walpole was not the satire's prime target. This view rests on a supposition that the work is indeed a vitriolic attack, whereas the fictional reality seems to be that the portrayal of Wild is a nuanced one, with elements of a covert and almost affectionate admiration. If Walpole bought Fielding off, or if Fielding turned friendly towards him, neither would expect that a fiction about Wild, with pointed political parallels, could be sustained without a strong residue of earlier hostile polemics, in which Fielding had played a notorious role. Nor is it thinkable that a political satire on Wild would fail to bring Walpole to mind among readers of the time. That being so, any accommodation with Walpole, if the work was to be published at all, had to be a broad-minded one. The traditional view in need of revision concerns not the centrality of Walpole to the satire, but the idea of Wild's unrelieved villainy. The editors of the Wesleyan edition, who contend that Walpole is not central, also believe that the work was written shortly before publication, and after *Joseph Andrews*. The most usual view is that *Jonathan Wild* was put together from a variety of earlier writings, some of them dating back to the 1730s. There is no conclusive evidence at present for deciding either way.

Problems of tone and structure exist, including the apparent incongruity of the 'sentimental' Heartfree plot, and the bizarre

---

[25] Frederick G. Ribble, 'Fielding's Rapprochement with Walpole in Late 1741', *Philological Quarterly*, 80 (2001), 71–81, esp. 74–5. The whole article is a sane reappraisal of Fielding's fluctuating and ambivalent relations with both Walpole and the Opposition. Detailed accounts of these matters may be found in the Wesleyan volume of Fielding's *Contributions to the Champion and Related Writings*, ed. W. B. Coley (Oxford: Clarendon Press, 2003).

digression about Mrs Heartfree's travels. In a somewhat experi-
mental work written with conflicting purposes and some uncer-
tainties of mood, and in a mode of irony palpably different from
Fielding's usual ironic style, this does not necessarily argue against
integrated composition. The same things might be said of his last
novel *Amelia*, whose composition does not appear to have been a
fragmented one. The Heartfree plot seems to some readers not
entirely successful, though it has persuasive defenders. Something
like it was doubtless necessary to provide innocent victims of Wild's
villainy, and to show the virtuous obverse of the depravities that go
under the names of 'Greatness', the 'Heroic', and the 'Admirable'.
The mirror-reversal which redefines the virtuous innocence of the
Heartfrees as 'weak' and 'silly', may, however, sometimes appear as
a clumsy device, defeated by its own overemphasis.

There are times indeed when the gullible meekness of the Heartfrees comes over as implausibly unworldly, so that the ironic jargon
of 'weak' and 'silly' backfires into literalness. Some academic readers
of the last half-century or so have argued that Fielding's design was
to expose the inadequacies of the Heartfrees' virtue. They draw
attention to the discussion of greatness and goodness in the Preface
to the first volume of *Miscellanies*, which makes the sensible and
obvious point that innocent persons are easily deceived, and that the
highest combination of human qualities is to be found in the rare
category of the Great and Good.[26] This Fielding calls 'the *true Sublime* in Human Nature', found in 'the highest Degree' only in a few
choice spirits, '*Socrates* and *Brutus*; and perhaps in some among us'
(*M1*, 12). By the latter, Fielding is clearly pointing to some favourite
highly placed figures, George Lyttelton or Lord Chesterfield, perhaps, whose praises are sung, in the same volume of *Miscellanies*, in
the poems 'Of True Greatness', 'Of Good-nature', 'Liberty', and
elsewhere.[27] Fielding's Great and Good comes close in this context
to the present-day conception of the Great and the Good in British
society.

The argument that the Heartfrees fall short of this standard is
equivalent to saying that Tom Jones is condemned for not being
Socrates. The discussion of the Great and Good in the Preface to
*Miscellanies* is a broad meditation in moral philosophy, not an

[26] For a summary of the debate, see General Introduction of *M3*, pp. xxxviii–xxxix.
[27] *M1*, 29, 35, 36, 126, 138, 152; see Rawson, 230–7, esp. 231.

invitation to read the novel in a reductively schematic way. The idea that Fielding is proposing a human norm somewhere between Wild and Heartfree is like the view that Swift's favoured type of person falls somewhere between the Houyhnhnms and the Yahoos: totally obvious as a matter of common sense about human affairs, and largely irrelevant, as a supposed thematic force, to the fiction's atmosphere and sympathies. Both are the result of a mania for middle ways, golden means, and the schematic ironing-out of literary works, which afflicted the academic culture of the mid-twentieth century, and has not been entirely exorcized to this day. The Heartfrees stand for virtue, as Wild stands for vice, though in a less nuanced way. Passive innocence is hard to make interesting, and the Heartfrees suffer from that. They are small merchants, affectionately portrayed by Fielding, but possibly remaining life-less under a benign patrician gaze more disposed to be responsive to the low and the high, than to the modest genteel virtues, and to their victimizing by an engaging and resourceful rogue.

# NOTE ON THE TEXT

THE text of *Jonathan Wild* reproduced here is that established by Hugh Amory for *Miscellanies, Volume 3*, in the Wesleyan Fielding (1997). It is based on the first edition published on 7 April 1743. Most of the substantial number of changes made for the 1754 edition, which became the basis for nearly all subsequent editions of the text, have not been incorporated. The differences between the 1743 and 1754 editions are discussed in more detail in the Textual Notes section. The very small number of occasions when the present editors have not followed Amory's text are noted in the Explanatory Notes.

A degree sign (°) indicates an editorial note at the back of the book.

# SELECT BIBLIOGRAPHY

## Editions

*The Wesleyan Edition of the Works of Henry Fielding*, ed. William B. Coley and others (Oxford: Clarendon Press, 1967– ), 11 volumes to date, includes all the prose fiction except *Shamela*. *Jonathan Wild* is published in *Miscellanies, Volume Three*, ed. Bertrand A. Goldgar and Hugh Amory (1997). The other useful modern edition of *Jonathan Wild* was edited by Douglas Brooks and published with *The Journal of a Voyage to Lisbon* (London: Dent, 1973).

There are several modern editions of *Shamela* (1741) and *Joseph Andrews* (1742) (often published together, as in the Everyman's Library edition, ed. Arthur Humphreys and David Campbell, with introduction by Claude Rawson, 1998, and the Oxford World's Classics edition, ed. Douglas Brooks-Davies, rev. Thomas Keymer, 1999), and *Tom Jones* (1749). There is currently no paperback edition of *Amelia* in print; an edition ed. Linda Bree (Peterborough, Ont.: Broadview Press) is forthcoming.

A useful collection of Fielding's critical writings can be found in Ioan Williams (ed.), *The Criticism of Henry Fielding* (London: Routledge, 1970). Claude Rawson (ed.), *Henry Fielding: A Critical Anthology* (Harmondsworth: Penguin, 1973), contains extracts from Fielding's work.

Henry Fielding's letters have been published in Martin C. Battestin and Clive T. Probyn, *The Correspondence of Henry and Sarah Fielding* (Oxford: Clarendon Press, 1993).

## Bibliographical and Related Studies

Hahn, H. George, *Henry Fielding: An Annotated Bibliography* (Metuchen, NJ: Scarecrow Press, 1979).

Morrissey, L. J., *Henry Fielding: A Reference Guide* (Boston: G. K. Hall, 1980).

Ribble, Frederick G., and Ribble, Anne G., *Fielding's Library: An Annotated Catalogue* (Charlottesville: Bibliographical Society of the University of Virginia, 1996).

Stoler, John A., 'Henry Fielding: A Partly Annotated Bibliography of Criticism, 1978–1992', *Bulletin of Bibliography*, 50 (1993), 83–101.

—— and Fulton, Richard D., *Henry Fielding: An Annotated Bibliography of Twentieth-Century Criticism, 1900–1977* (New York: Garland, 1980).

*Biographical Studies*

Battestin, Martin, with Ruthe R. Battestin: *Henry Fielding: A Life* (London: Routledge, 1989; repr. 1993).

Cross, Wilbur L., *The History of Henry Fielding*, 3 vols. (New Haven: Yale University Press, 1918).

Dudden, F. Holmes, *Henry Fielding: His Life, Works, and Times*, 2 vols. (Oxford: Clarendon Press, 1952).

Pagliaro, Harold, *Henry Fielding: A Literary Life* (Basingstoke: Macmillan, 1998).

Paulson, Ronald, *The Life of Henry Fielding* (Oxford: Blackwell, 2000).

Rogers, Pat, *Henry Fielding: A Biography* (London: Elek, 1979).

Thomas, Donald, *Henry Fielding* (London: Weidenfeld, 1990).

*Critical Studies of* Jonathan Wild *and of Fielding and his Work*

Alter, Robert, *Fielding and the Nature of the Novel* (Cambridge: Harvard University Press, 1968).

Campbell, Jill, *Natural Masques: Gender and Identity in Fielding's Plays and Novels* (Stanford, Calif.: Stanford University Press, 1995).

Cleary, Thomas, *Henry Fielding: Political Writer* (Waterloo, Ont.: Wilfrid Laurier University Press, 1984).

Goldgar, Bertrand A., 'The *Champion* and the Chapter on Hats in *Jonathan Wild*', *Philological Quarterly*, 72 (1993), 443–50.

—— 'Fielding on Fiction and History', *Eighteenth-Century Fiction*, 7 (Apr. 1995), 279–92.

Hatfield, Glenn W., *Henry Fielding and the Language of Irony* (Chicago: University of Chicago Press, 1968).

Hunter, J. Paul, *Occasional Form: Henry Fielding and the Chains of Circumstance* (Baltimore: Johns Hopkins University Press, 1975).

Irwin, William Robert, *The Making of Jonathan Wild: A Study in the Literary Method of Henry Fielding* (New York: Columbia University Press, 1941).

McKeon, Michael, *The Origins of the English Novel, 1600–1740* (Baltimore: Johns Hopkins University Press, 1987).

McRea, Brian, *Henry Fielding and the Politics of Mid-Eighteenth-Century England* (Athens: University of Georgia Press, 1981).

Miller, Henry Knight, *Essays on Fielding's Miscellanies: A Commentary on Volume One* (Princeton: Princeton University Press, 1961).

Paulson, Ronald (ed.), *Henry Fielding: A Collection of Critical Essays* (Englewood Cliffs, NJ: Prentice Hall, 1962).

—— and Lockwood, Thomas (eds.), *Henry Fielding: The Critical Heritage* (London: Routledge & Kegan Paul, 1969).

Rawson, Claude (ed.), *Henry Fielding: A Critical Anthology* (Harmondsworth: Penguin, 1973).

—— *Henry Fielding and the Augustan Ideal under Stress* (London: Routledge & Kegan Paul, 1972, repr. Atlantic Highlands, NJ: Humanities Press, 1991).

—— *Order from Confusion Sprung: Studies in Eighteenth-Century Literature from Swift to Cowper* (London: Allen & Unwin, 1985; repr. Atlantic Highlands, NJ: Humanities Press, 1992).

Ribble, Frederick G., 'Fielding's Rapprochement with Walpole in Late 1741', *Philological Quarterly*, 80 (2001), 71–81.

Rinehart, Hollis, 'The Role of Walpole in Fielding's *Jonathan Wild*', *English Studies in Canada*, 5/4 (Winter 1979), 420–31.

Rivero, Albert J. (ed.), *Critical Essays on Henry Fielding* (New York: G. K. Hall, 1998).

Smallwood, Angela J., *Fielding and the Woman Question: The Novels of Henry Fielding and the Feminist Debate, 1700–1750* (Hemel Hempstead: Harvester Wheatsheaf, 1989).

Varey, Simon, *Henry Fielding* (Cambridge: Cambridge University Press, 1986).

Watt, Ian, *The Rise of the Novel: Studies in Defoe, Richardson and Fielding* (London: Chatto & Windus, 1957).

Wells, John Edwin, 'Henry Fielding and the History of Charles XII', *Journal of English and Germanic Philology*, 9 (1912), 603–13.

—— 'Fielding's Political Purpose in *Jonathan Wild*', *Publications of the Modern Language Association of America*, 28 (1913), 1–55.

## Useful Background Works

Beattie, J. M., *Policing and Punishment in London, 1660–1750: Urban Crime and the Limits of Terror* (Oxford: Oxford University Press, 2001).

Cockburn, J. S. (ed.), *Crime in England 1550–1800* (London: Methuen, 1977).

Faller, Lincoln B., *Turned to Account: The Forms and Functions of Criminal Biography in Late Seventeenth- and Early Eighteenth-Century England* (Cambridge: Cambridge University Press, 1987).

Goldgar, Bertrand A., *Walpole and the Wits: The Relation of Politics to Literature, 1722–1742* (Lincoln: University of Nebraska Press, 1976).

Hay, Douglas, 'Property, Authority and the Criminal Law', in Douglas Hay et al., *Albion's Fatal Tree: Crime and Society in Eighteenth-Century England* (London: Allen Lane, 1975; London: Peregrine Books 1977, repr. 1988), 17–63.

Howson, Gerald, *Thief-Taker General: The Rise and Fall of Jonathan Wild* (London: Hutchinson, 1970).

Moore, Lucy (ed.), *Conmen and Cutpurses: Scenes from the Hogarthian Underworld* (London: Allen Lane, 2000).

Paulson, Ronald, *Satire and the Novel in Eighteenth-Century England* (New Haven: Yale University Press, 1967).

Plumb, J. H., *Sir Robert Walpole*, 2 vols. (London, 1956, 1960).

*Further Reading in Oxford World's Classics*

Defoe, Daniel, *Moll Flanders*, ed. G. A. Starr.

Defoe, Daniel, *Roxana*, ed. John Mullan.

Fielding, Henry, *Joseph Andrews and Shamela*, ed. Tom Keymer.

—— *Tom Jones*, ed. John Bender and Simon Stern.

Pope, Alexander, *Selected Poetry*, ed. Pat Rogers.

Richardson, Samuel, *Pamela*, ed. Tom Keymer and Alice Wakely.

# A CHRONOLOGY OF HENRY FIELDING

1707      22 April: HF born at his maternal grandfather's house, Sharpham Park, near Glastonbury, Somerset

1710      8 November: Sarah, the third of HF's four sisters, born at the family estate at East Stour, Dorset

1718      14 April: death of Sarah Gould Fielding, HF's mother. Within a year Edmund Fielding, HF's father, remarries and an acrimonious battle with Lady Gould, the children's maternal grandmother, for the custody of the children begins

1719–24      Education at Eton. Among his fellow students is George Lyttelton, a friend and patron in HF's later life

1721      16 September: HF's half-brother John, who later worked with HF and succeeded him as magistrate at Bow Street, born

1722      Lady Gould wins the court case for custody of the Fielding children. Robert Walpole (born 26 August 1676), having already held various offices of state, comes to power as head of government

1725      February: Jonathan Wild arrested and sent to Newgate. Wild was tried in April and hanged at Tyburn on 24 May

1728      29 January: *The Masquerade* (first published poem) published; first performance of *The Beggar's Opera*. 16 February: *Love in Several Masques* (first play) performed. 16 March: HF registers at the University of Leiden as a student of literature. 18 May: Publication of the *Dunciad* in three books

1729      Return to London from Leiden

1730–7      Highly successful career as a playwright. More than twenty often political comedies, satires, and burlesques including *The Author's Farce* (1730), *The Tragedy of Tragedies; or, The Life and Death of Tom Thumb the Great* (1731), *Pasquin* (1736), and *The Historical Register of 1736* (1737)

1734      28 November: marriage to Charlotte Cradock at Charlcombe, just outside Bath, following an elopement

1737      Passing of Licensing Act, partly to silence HF's political satires. The new law effectively ends HF's career as a playwright. He becomes a law student in the Middle Temple

1739–41      Edits the *Champion*, a paper which forms part of the political opposition to Walpole

1740    20 June: called to the Bar. 6 November: Samuel Richardson's
        novel *Pamela* published. December: beginning of the War of
        Austrian Succession, which continues until 1748

1741    4 April: *An Apology for the Life of Mrs. Shamela Andrews*, HF's
        parody of *Pamela*, published anonymously. HF seems to break
        with the Opposition and to side with Walpole's government

1742    Walpole forced out of office, retires from politics and is created
        Earl of Orford. 22 February: *The History of the Adventures of
        Joseph Andrews, And of his Friend Mr. Abraham Adams. Written
        in Imitation of the Manner of Cervantes* published. Death of
        HF's daughter Charlotte and severe illness of HF's wife

1743    12 April: *Miscellanies* published in three volumes, including
        poems, plays, essays, the lengthy allegory 'A Journey from this
        World to the Next' and, occupying the whole of the third
        volume, *The History of the Life of Mr Jonathan Wild the Great*.
        29 October: Publication of the *Dunciad* in four books

1744    4 May: Sarah Fielding's *The Adventures of David Simple* pub-
        lished. Second edition published in July, including HF's Pre-
        face and revisions. November: death of HF's wife Charlotte.
        December, several of his patrons including Lyttelton receive
        appointments in the new government

1745    'The Forty Five', the invasion by the 'Young Pretender' Prince
        Charles Edward Stuart attempting to restore the long-exiled
        Stuart monarchy with the aid of Jacobite supporters in Britain.
        November 1745 to June 1746: HF edits *The True Patriot*, a
        pro-Hanoverian paper opposing the rebellion

1746    April: final defeat of the Jacobites at Culloden

1747    Sarah Fielding's *Familiar Letters between the Characters in
        David Simple and Others* published, with a Preface and some
        other contributions from HF. November, marries Mary Daniel,
        formerly his first wife's maid, now pregnant with his child.
        December 1747–November 1748: edits the *Jacobite's Journal*.
        December 1747: the first part of Richardson's novel *Clarissa*
        published

1748    January: reviews *Clarissa* favourably in the *Jacobite's Journal*.
        April, December: the remaining part of *Clarissa* published.
        Autumn: privately circulates copies of Books I–VI of *Tom
        Jones*. October: becomes Justice of the Peace for Westminster
        (his jurisdiction was later extended to cover the whole of
        Middlesex, and the appointment was due largely to Lyttelton
        and also to John Russell, Duke of Bedford)

1749      February: *The History of Tom Jones: A Foundling* published. A second edition published before the end of February, a third in April, and a fourth revised edition in December

1750      February: the opening of the Universal Register Office, a clearing house for employment, sales, exchange, and property transactions, managed by HF and his half-brother John. In a six-month period three of HF's four sisters die in London

1751      January: *An Enquiry into the Causes of the late Increase of Robbers*, an important legal-sociological work reflecting HF's views on crime and the ways in which it could be controlled, published. December: *Amelia* published (dated 1752)

1752      January–November, edits *Covent-Garden Journal*

1753      January: *A Proposal for making an Effectual Provision for the Poor, for Amending their Morals, and for Rendering them useful Members of the Society* published

1754      March 1754: revised edition of *Jonathan Wild* published. HF's health, poor for several years, deteriorates to the extent that he has to resign his office as magistrate. June–August: travels to Lisbon in hopes the Portuguese air would improve his health. 8 October: dies at Junqueira near Lisbon

1755      February: *The Journal of A Voyage to Lisbon* published

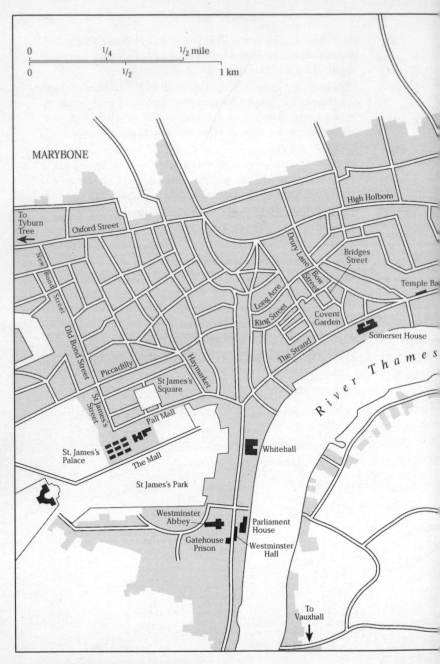

London in the early eighteenth century

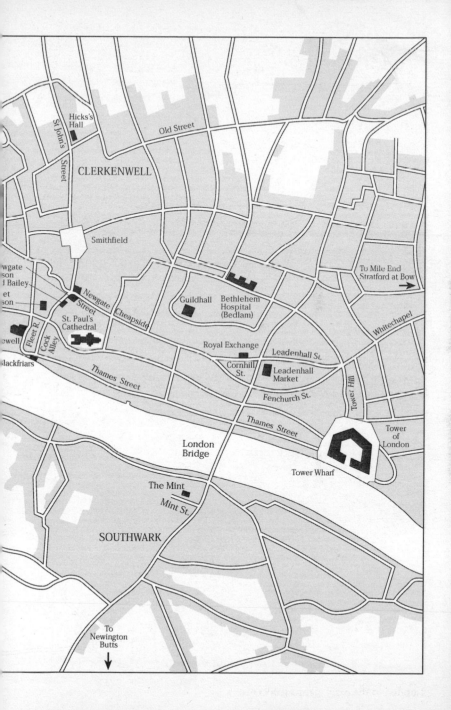

# MISCELLANIES.

## THE
## LIFE
### OF
## M: JONATHAN WILD
### THE GREAT.

## VOL. III.

## By HENRY FIELDING, Esq;

*LONDON,*

Printed for the AUTHOR; and fold by A. MIL-
LAR, oppofite to *Catharine-ftreet* in the *Strand.*
MDCCXLIII.

# CONTENTS

## BOOK I

## BOOK IV

# THE
# LIFE
OF
# Mr. JONATIIAN WILD
THE GREAT.°

## BOOK I

### CHAPTER I

*Shewing the wholesome Uses drawn from recording the*
*Atchievements of those wonderful Productions of Nature called*
GREAT MEN.°

As it is necessary that all great and surprizing Events, the Designs of
which are laid, conducted, and brought to Perfection by the utmost
Force of human Invention and Art, should be managed by great and
eminent Men, so the Lives of such may be justly and properly styled
the Quintessence of History. In these, when delivered to us by sensible Writers, we are not only most agreeably entertained, but usefully
instructed;° for besides the attaining hence a consummate Knowledge
of human Nature in general; its secret Springs, various Windings,
and perplexed Mazes;° we have here before our Eyes, lively Examples
of whatever is amiable or detestable, worthy of Admiration or
Abhorrence, and are consequently taught, in a Manner infinitely
more effectual than by Precept, what we are eagerly to imitate or
carefully to avoid.

But besides the two obvious Advantages of surveying as it were in
a Picture, the true Beauty of Virtue, and Deformity of Vice, we may
moreover learn from *Plutarch, Nepos, Suetonius,*° and other Biographers this useful Lesson, not too hastily nor in the gross to
bestow either our Praise or Censure: Since we shall often find such a
Mixture of Good and Evil in the same Character, that it may require
a very accurate Judgment and elaborate Inquiry to determine which

Side the Ballance turns: for tho' we sometimes meet with an *Aristides* or a *Brutus*, a *Lysander* or a *Nero*,° yet far the greater Number are of the mixt Kind; neither totally good nor bad; their greatest Virtues being obscured and allayed by their Vices, and those again softened and coloured over by their Virtues.

Of this Kind was the illustrious Person whose History we now undertake; who, as he was embellished with many of the greatest and noblest Endowments, so these could not well be said to be absolutely pure and without Allay. If we view one Side of his Character only, he must be acknowledged equal, if not superior to most of the Heroes of Antiquity: But if we turn the Reverse, it must be confessed our Admiration will be a little abated, and his Character will savour rather of the Weakness of modern than the uniform Greatness of ancient Heroes.°

We would not therefore be understood to affect giving the Reader a perfect or consummate Pattern of human Virtue; but rather by faithfully recording the little Imperfections which somewhat darkened the Lustre of his great Qualities, to teach the Lesson we have above mentioned, and induce our Reader with us to lament the Frailty of human Nature, and to convince him that no Mortal, after a thorough Scrutiny, can be a proper Object of our Adoration.

But before we enter on this great Work, we must endeavour to remove some Errors of Opinion which Mankind have by the Disingenuity of Writers contracted: For those from their Fear of attacking or contradicting the obsolete Doctrines of a Set of simple Fellows called, in Derision, Sages or Philosophers, have endeavoured as much as possible, to confound the Ideas of Greatness and Goodness, whereas no two Things can possibly be more distinct from each other. For Greatness consists in bringing all Manner of Mischief on Mankind, and Goodness in removing it from them.° Now, tho' the Writer, if he will confine himself to Truth, is obliged to draw a perfect Picture of the former in all the Actions which he records of his Hero, yet to reconcile his Work with those absurd Doctrines above-mentioned, he is ever guilty of interspersing Reflections in Reality to the Disadvantage of that great Perfection, Uniformity of Character; for Instance, in the Histories of *Alexander* and *Cæsar*, we are frequently reminded of their Benevolence and Generosity. When the former had with Fire and Sword overrun a whole Empire, and destroyed the Lives of Millions of innocent People, we are told as an

Example of his Benevolence, that he did not cut the Throat of an old
Woman, and ravish her Daughters whom he had before undone: And
when the mighty *Cæsar* had with wonderful Greatness of Mind
destroyed the Liberties of his Country, and gotten all the Power into
his own Hands, we receive, as an Evidence of his Generosity, his
Largesses to his Followers and Tools, by whose Means he had
accomplished his Purpose, and by whose Assistance he was to
establish it.°

Now who doth not see that such sneaking Qualities as these are
rather to be bewailed as Imperfections than admired as Ornaments
in those Great Men, rather obscuring their Glory and holding them
back in their Race to Greatness, and unworthy the End for which
they seem to have come into the World, *viz.* of perpetrating vast and
mighty Mischief?

We hope our Reader will have Reason justly to acquit us of any
such confounding Ideas in the following Pages, in which, as we are to
record the Actions of a Great Man,° so we have no where mentioned
any Spark of Goodness which hath discovered itself either faintly in
him, or more glaringly in any other Person, but as a Meanness and
Imperfection, disqualifying them for Undertakings which lead to
Honour and Esteem among Men.

As our Hero had as little as perhaps is to be found of that Meanness, indeed only enough to make him Partaker of the Imperfection
of Humanity, and not the Perfection of *Dæmonism*, we have ventured
to call him THE GREAT; nor do we doubt but our Reader will, when
he hath perused his Story, concur with us in allowing him that Title.

CHAPTER II

*Giving an Account of as many of our Hero's Ancestors as can be
gathered out of the Rubbish of Antiquity, which hath been
carefully sifted for that Purpose.°*

MR. *Jonathan Wild*, or *Wyld* (for he himself did not always agree in
one Method of spelling his Name)° was descended from the Great
*Wolfstan Wild*, who came over with *Hengist*, and distinguished himself very eminently at that famous Festival where the *Britons* were so
treacherously murdered by the *Saxons*; for when the Word was

given, *i.e. Nemet eour Saxes, Take out your Swords*, this Gentleman being a little hard of hearing, mistook the Sound for *Nemet her Sacs, Take out their Purses*;° instead therefore of applying to the Throat, he immediately applied to the Pocket of his Guest, and contented himself with taking all that he had, without attempting his Life.

The next Ancestor of our Hero, who was remarkably eminent, was *Wild*, surnamed *Langfanger* or *Longfinger*. He flourished in the Reign of *Henry* III. and was strictly attached to *Hubert de Burgh*, whose Friendship he was recommended to by his great Excellence in an Art, of which *Hubert* was himself the Inventor:° He could, without the Knowledge of the Proprietor, with great Ease and Dexterity draw forth a Man's Purse from any Part of his Garment where it was deposited, and hence he derived his Surname. This Gentleman was the first of his Family who had the Honour to suffer for the Good of his Country: On whom a Wit of that Time made the following Epitaph.

> *O Shame o' Justice*, Wild *is hang'd,*
> *For that'n hath a Pocket fang'd,*
> *While safe old* Hubert, *and his Gang,*
> *Doth the Pocket of the Nation fang.*

*Langfanger* left a Son named *Edward*, whom he had carefully instructed in the Art for which he himself was so famous. This *Edward* served as a Voluntier under the famous Sir *John Falstaffe*, and by his gallant Demeanor so recommended himself to his Captain, that he would have certainly been promoted by him, had *Harry* the Fifth kept his Word with his old Companion.°

After the Death of *Edward*, the Family remained in some Obscurity down to the Reign of *Charles* the First, when *James Wild* distinguished himself on both Sides the Question in the Civil Wars,° passing from one to t'other, as Heaven seemed to declare itself in Favour of either Party. At the End of the Wars, *James*, not being rewarded according to his Merits, as is usually the Case of such impartial Persons, he associated himself with a brave Man of those Times, whose Name was *Hind*,° and declared open War with both Parties. He was successful in several Actions, and spoiled many of the Enemy; till at length, being over-powered and taken, he was, contrary to the Law of Arms, put basely and cowardly to death, by a Combination between twelve Men of the Enemy's Party, who after some Consultation unanimously agreed on the said Murder.°

This *James*° took to Wife *Rebecca*, the Daughter of the abovementioned *John Hind* Esq; by whom he had Issue *John, Edward, Thomas* and *Jonathan*, and three Daughters, namely, *Grace, Charity* and *Honour*. *John* followed the Fortunes of his Father, and suffering with him, left no Issue. *Edward* was so remarkable for his compassionate Temper, that he spent his Life in soliciting the Causes of the distressed Captives in *Newgate*,° and is reported to have held a strict Friendship with an eminent Divine, who solicited the spiritual Causes of the said Captives.° He married *Editha*, Daughter and Coheiress of *Geoffry Snap* Gent. who long enjoyed an Office under the High Sheriff of *London* and *Middlesex*, by which with great Reputation he acquired a handsome Fortune;° by her he had no Issue. *Thomas* went very young abroad to one of our *American* Colonies,° and hath not been since heard of. As for the Daughters, *Grace* was married to a Gentleman of *Yorkshire*, who dealt in Horses.° *Charity* took to Husband an eminent Broker of *Change-Alley*:° And *Honour*, the youngest, died unmarried. She lived many Years in this Town, was a great frequenter of Plays, and used to be remarkable for distributing Oranges to all who would accept of them.°

*Jonathan* married *Elizabeth*, Daughter of *Ralph Hollow* Esq; and by her had *Jonathan*, who is the illustrious Subject of these Memoirs.


CHAPTER III

*The Birth, Parentage, and Education of Mr.* Jonathan Wild
*the Great.*


IT is observable that Nature seldom produces any one who is afterwards to act a notable Part on the Stage of Life, but she gives some Warning of her Intention; and as the dramatic Poet generally prepares the Entry of every considerable Character, with a solemn Narrative, or at least a great Flourish of Drums and Trumpets; so doth this our *Alma Mater*° by some shrewd Hints, pre-admonish us of her Intention. Thus *Astyages*, who was the Grandfather of *Cyrus*, dreamed that his Daughter was brought to bed of a Vine whose

Branches over-spread all *Asia*;° and *Hecuba*, while big with *Paris*, dreamed that she was delivered of a Firebrand that set all *Troy* in Flames;° so did the Mother of our Great Man, while she was with child of him, dream that she was enjoyed in the Night by the Gods *Mercury*, and *Priapus*. This Dream puzzled all the learned Astrologers of her Time, seeming to imply in it a Contradiction; *Mercury* being the God of Ingenuity, and *Priapus* the Terror of those who practised it. What made this Dream the more wonderful, and perhaps the true Cause of its being remembred, was a very extra-ordinary Circumstance, sufficiently denoting something preter-natural in it; for tho' she had never heard even the Name of either of these Gods, she repeated these very Words in the Morning, with only a small Mistake of the Quantity of the latter, which she chose to call *Priăpus* instead of *Priāpus*; and her Husband swore that tho' he might possibly have named *Mercury* to her, for he had heard of such an Heathen God, he never in his Life could have any wise put her in Mind of that other Deity, with whom he had no Acquaintance.°

Another remarkable Incident was, that during her whole Preg-nancy, she constantly longed for every thing she saw; nor could be satisfied with her Wish unless she injoyed it clandestinely; and as Nature by true and accurate Observers is remarked to give us no Appetites without furnishing us with the Means of gratifying them; so had she at this Time a most marvellous glutinous Quality attend-ing her Fingers, to which as to Birdlime, every thing closely adhered that she handled.

To omit other Stories, some of which may be perhaps the Growth of Superstition, we proceed to the Birth of our Hero, who made his first Appearance on this Great Theatre, the very Day when the Plague first broke out in 1665.° Some say his Mother was delivered of him in an House of an orbicular or round Form in *Covent-Garden*;° but of this we are not certain. He was some Years afterwards baptized by the famous Mr. *Titus Oates*.°

Nothing very remarkable past in his Years of Infancy, save, that as the Letters *Th* are the most difficult of Pronunciation, and the last which a Child attains to the Utterance of, so they were the first that came with any Readiness from young Master *Wild*.° Nor must we omit the early Indications which he gave of the Sweetness of his Temper; for tho' he was by no Means to be terrified into Compli-ance, yet might he by a Sugar-plumb be brought to your Purpose:

Indeed, to say the Truth, he was to be bribed to any thing, which made many say, he was certainly born to be a Great Man.

He was scarce settled at School before he gave Marks of his lofty and aspiring Temper; and was regarded by all his School-Fellows with that Deference which Men generally pay to those superior Genius's who will exact it of them. If an Orchard was to be robb'd, *Wild* was consulted, and tho' he was himself seldom concerned in the Execution of the Design, yet was he always Concerter of it, and Treasurer of the Booty; some little Part of which he would now and then, with wonderful Generosity, bestow on those who took it. He was generally very secret on these Occasions: But if any offered to plunder of his own Head,° without acquainting Master *Wild* and making a Deposite of the Booty, he was sure to have an Information against him lodged with the School-Master, and to be severely punished for his Pains.

He discovered so little Attention to School-Learning, that his Master, who was a very wise and worthy Man, soon gave over all Care and Trouble on this Account, and acquainting his Parents that their Son proceeded extremely well in his Studies, he permitted his Pupil to follow his own Inclinations; perceiving they led him to nobler Pursuits than the Sciences, which are generally acknowledged to be a very unprofitable Study, and greatly to hinder the Advancement of Men in the World: But tho' Master *Wild* was not esteemed the readiest at making his Exercise,° he was universally allowed to be the most dextrous at stealing it of all his School-Fellows: Being never detected in such furtive Compositions, nor indeed in any other Exercitations of his great Talents, which all inclined the same Way, but once, when he had laid violent Hands on a Book called *Gradus ad Parnassum*, i.e. *A Step towards Parnassus*;° on which Account his Master, who was a Man of most wonderful Wit and Sagacity, is said to have told him, he wished it might not prove in the Event, *Gradus ad Patibulum*, i.e. *A Step towards the Gallows*.°

But tho' he would not give himself the Pains requisite to acquire a competent Sufficiency in the learned Languages, yet did he readily listen with Attention to others, especially when they translated the Classical Authors to him;° nor was he in the least backward at all such Times, to express his Approbation. He was wonderfully pleased with that Passage in the Eleventh *Iliad*, where *Achilles* is said to have bound two Sons of *Priam* upon a Mountain, and afterwards released them for a Sum of Money.° This was, he said, alone sufficient to refute those who affected a Contempt for the Wisdom of the Ancients, and an undeniable Testimony of the great Antiquity of *Priggism.° He was ravished with the Account which *Nestor* gives in the same Book, of the rich Booty which he bore off (*i.e.* stole) from the *Eleans.° He was desirous of having this often repeated to him, and at the End of every Repetition, he constantly fetched a deep Sigh, and said, *It was a glorious Booty*.

When the Story of *Cacus* was read to him out of the Eighth *Æneid*, he generously pitied the unhappy Fate of that Great Man, to whom he thought *Hercules* much too severe:° One of his School-Fellows commending the Dexterity of drawing the Oxen backward by their Tails into his Den, he smiled, and with some Disdain said, *He could have taught him a better Way*.

He was a passionate Admirer of Heroes, particularly *Alexander* the Great, between whom and the late King of *Sweden* he would frequently draw Parallels.° He was much delighted with the Accounts of the *Czar's* Retreat from the latter, who carried off the Inhabitants of great Cities to people his own Country.° *This*, he said, *was not once thought of by* Alexander; but added, *perhaps he did not want them*.

Happy had it been for him, if he had confined himself to this Sphere; but his chief, if not only Blemish, was that he would sometimes, from an Humility in his Nature, too pernicious to true Greatness, condescend to an Intimacy with inferior Things and Persons. Thus the Spanish *Rogue* was his favourite Book, and the *Cheats of* Scapin his favourite Play.°

The young Gentleman being now at the Age of seventeen, his Father, from a foolish Prejudice to our Universities, and out of a false, as well as excessive Regard to his Morals, brought his Son to Town, where he resided with him till he was of an Age to travel. Whilst he was here, all imaginable Care was taken of his Instruction, his Father endeavouring his utmost to inculcate Principles of Honour and Gentility into his Son.

* Thievery.

CHAPTER IV

*Mr*. Wild's *first Entrance into the World. His Acquaintance with Count* La Ruse.

AN Accident happened soon after his Arrival in Town, which almost saved him his whole Labour on this Head, and provided Master *Wild* a better Tutor than any Care or Expence could have furnished him with. The old Gentleman, it seems, was a FOLLOWER of the For-tunes of Mr. *Snap*, Son of Mr. *Geoffry Snap*, whom we have before mentioned to have enjoyed a reputable Office under the Sheriff of *London* and *Middlesex*, whose Daughter, the Sister of this Gentleman, had inter-married with the *Wilds*. Mr. *Snap*, being thereto well *war-ranted*,° had laid violent Hands on, or, as the Vulgar express it, arrested one Count *La Ruse*,° a Man of considerable Figure in those Days, and had confined him to his own House, till he could find two Seconds° who would in a formal Manner give their Words that the Count should, at a certain Day and Place appointed, answer all that one *Thomas Thimble* a Taylor had to say to him; which *Thomas Thimble*, it seems, alledged that the Count had, according to the Law of the Realm, made over his Body to him as a Security for some Suits of Cloaths to him delivered by the said *Thomas Thimble*. Now, as the Count, tho' perfectly a Man of Honour, could not immediately find these Seconds, he was obliged for some Time to reside at Mr. *Snap's* House; for it seems the Law of the Land is, that whoever owes another 10 *l*. may be on the Oath of that Person, immediately taken up and carried away from his own House and Family, and kept abroad till he is made to owe 50 *l*. whether he will or no; for which he is, perhaps, afterwards obliged to lie in Gaol; and all this without any Trial had, or any other Evidence of the Debt than the abovesaid Oath, which if untrue, as it often happens, you have no Remedy against the Perjurer; he was, forsooth! mistaken.°

But tho' Mr. *Snap* would not (as perhaps by the nice Rules of Honour he was obliged) discharge the Count on his Parole;° yet did he not (as by the strict Rules of Law he was enabled) confine him to his Chamber. The Count had his Liberty of the whole House, and Mr. *Snap*, using only the Precaution of keeping his Doors well lock'd and barr'd, took his Prisoner's Word that he would not go out.

Mr. *Snap* had by his Second Lady two Daughters, who were now in the Bloom of their Youth and Beauty. These young Ladies, like Damsels in Romance, compassionated the captive Count, and endeavoured by all Means to make his Confinement less irksome to him; which, tho' they were both very beautiful, they could not attain by any other Way so effectually, as by engaging with him at Cards, in which Contentions, as will appear hereafter, the Count was greatly skilful.

As Whisk and Swabbers° was the Game then in the chief Vogue, they were oblig'd to look for a fourth Person, in order to make up their Parties. Mr. *Snap* himself would sometimes relax his Mind, from the violent Fatigues of his Employment, by these Recreations; and sometimes a neighbouring young Gentleman, or Lady, came in to their Assistance: But the most frequent Guest was young Master *Wild*, who had been educated from his Infancy with the Miss *Snaps*, and was, by all the Neighbours, allotted for the Husband of Miss *Tishy*, or *Lætitia*, the younger of the two; for though, being his Cousin-German,° she was perhaps, in the Eye of a strict Conscience, somewhat too nearly related to him; yet the old People on both Sides, tho' sufficiently scrupulous in nice Matters, agreed to overlook this Objection.

Men of great Genius as easily discover one another as Free-Masons can.° It was therefore no Wonder that the Count soon conceived an Inclination to an Intimacy with our young Hero, whose vast Abilities could not be concealed from one of the Count's Discernment; for though this latter was so expert at his Cards, that he was proverbially said, to *play the whole Game*, he was no Match for Master *Wild*, who, inexperienced as he was, notwithstanding all the Art, the Dexterity, and often the Fortune of his Adversary, never failed to send him away from the Table with less in his Pocket than he brought to it; for indeed *Langfanger* himself could not have extracted a Purse with more Ingenuity than our young Hero.

His Hands made frequent Visits to the Count's Pocket, before the latter had entertained any Suspicion of him, imputing the several Losses he sustained rather to the innocent and sprightly Frolick of Miss *Doshy*, with which, as she indulged him with little innocent Freedoms about her Person in Return, he thought himself obliged to be contented; but one Night, when *Wild* imagined the Count asleep, he made so unguarded an Attack upon him, that the other caught him in the Fact:° However, he did not think proper to acquaint him with the Discovery he had made; but, preventing him from any Booty at that Time, he only took Care for the future to button his Pockets, and pack the Cards° with double Industry.

So far was this Detection from causing any Quarrel between these two *Prigs*,° that these and many other such Instances of his Ingenuity, operated so violently on the Count, that, notwithstanding the Disparity which Age, Title, and above all Dress, had set between them, he resolved to enter into an Acquaintance, which soon produced a perfect Intimacy, and that a Friendship which had a longer Duration than is common to that Passion between Persons, who only propose to themselves the common Advantages of eating, drinking, whoring, or borrowing Money; which Ends as they soon fail, so doth the Friendship founded upon them.

CHAPTER V

*A Dialogue between young Master* Wild *and Count* La Ruse, *which, having extended to the Rejoinder, had a very quiet, easy, and natural Conclusion.*

ONE Evening after the Miss *Snaps* were retired to Rest, the Count thus addressed himself to young *Wild*: 'You cannot, I apprehend, Mr. *Wild*, be such a Stranger to your own great Capacity, as to be surprized when I tell you, I have often viewed, with a Mixture of Astonishment and Concern, your shining Qualities confined to a Sphere, where they can never reach the Eyes of those who would introduce them properly into the World, and raise you to an Eminence, where you may blaze out to the Admiration of all Men. I assure you I am pleased with my Captivity, when I reflect, I am likely to owe to it an Acquaintance, and I hope Friendship, with the greatest Genius of my Age; and, what is still more, when I indulge my Vanity with a Prospect of drawing from Obscurity (pardon the Expression) such Talents as were, I believe, never before like to have been buried in it; for I make no Question, but, at my Discharge from Confinement, which will now soon happen, I shall be able to introduce you into Company, where you may reap the Advantage of your superior Parts.

'I will bring you acquainted, Sir, with those, who, as they are capable of setting a true Value on such Qualifications, so they will have it both in their Power and Inclination to prefer you for them. Such an Introduction is the only Advantage you want, without which your Merit might be your Misfortune; for those Abilities which would entitle you to Honour and Profit in a superior Station, may render you only obnoxious to Danger and Disgrace in a lower.'

Mr. *Wild* answered: 'Sir, I am not insensible of my Obligations to you, as well for the Overvalue you have set on my small Abilities, as the Kindness you express in offering to introduce me among my Superiours. I must own, my Father hath often persuaded me to push myself into the Company of my betters; but to say the Truth, I have an aukward Pride in my Nature, which is better pleased with being at the Head of the lowest Class, than at the bottom of the highest. Permit me to say, tho' the Idea may be somewhat coarse, I had rather stand on the Summit of a Dunghil, than at the bottom of a Hill in Paradise; I have always thought it signifies little into what Rank of Life I am thrown, provided I make a great Figure therein; and should be as well satisfied with exerting my Talents well at the Head of a small Party or Gang, as in the Command of a mighty Army; for I am far from agreeing with you, that great Parts are often buried in Oblivion; on the contrary, I am convinced it is impossible they should be so. I have often persuaded myself that there were not fewer than a thousand in *Alexander's* Troops capable of performing what *Alexander* himself did.°

'But because such Spirits were not elected or destined to an Imperial Command, are we therefore to imagine they came off without a Booty? Or that they contented themselves with the Share in common with their Comrades? Surely, no. In *Civil* Life, doubtless, the same Genius, the same Indowments have often composed the Statesman and the *Prig*, for so we call what the Vulgar name a *Thief*.° The same Parts, the same Actions often promote Men to the Head of superior Societies, which raise them to the Head of lower; and where is the essential Difference if the one ends on *Tower-Hill*, and the other at *Tyburn*?° Hath the Block any Preference to the Gallows, or the Ax to the Halter, but what is given them by the ill-guided Judgment of Men? You will pardon me therefore if I am not so hastily enflamed with the common Out-side of things, nor join the general Opinion in preferring one State to another. A Guinea is as valuable in a Leathern as in an embroidered Purse; and a Codshead is a Codshead still, whether in a Pewter or a Silver Dish.'°

The Count replied as follows: 'What you have now said doth not lessen my Idea of your Capacity; but confirms my Opinion of the ill Effects of bad and low Company. Can any Man doubt, whether it is better to be a prime Minister,° or a common Thief? I have often heard that the Devil used to say, where, or to whom, I know not, *that it was better to reign in Hell, than be a* Valet de Chambre *in Heaven*,° and perhaps he was in the right; but sure if he had had the Choice of both, he would have chosen better. The Truth therefore is, that, by low Conversation, we contract a greater Awe for high Things than they deserve. We decline great Pursuits not from Contempt, but Despair. The Man who prefers the Highroad° to a more reputable Way of making his Fortune, doth it because he imagines the one easier than the other: But you yourself have asserted, and with undoubted Truth, that the same Abilities qualify you for undertaking, and the same Means will bring you to your End in both Journies; as, in Musick, it is the same Tune whether you play it in a higher or a lower Key. To instance in some Particulars: Is it not the same Qualification which enables *this* Man to hire himself as a Servant, and get into the Confidence and Secrets of his Master, in order to rob him, and *that* to undertake Trusts of the highest Nature with a Design to break and betray them? Is it less difficult, by false Tokens, to deceive a Shopkeeper into the Delivery of his Goods, which you afterwards run away with, than to impose upon him by outward Splendour and the Appearance of Fortune, into a Credit, by which you gain, and he loses twenty times as much? Doth it not require more Dexterity in the Fingers to draw out a Man's Purse from his Pocket, or to take a Lady's Watch from her Side, without being perceived of any, an Excellence in which, without Flattery, I am persuaded you have no Superior, than to cog a Die, or shuffle a Pack of Cards?° Is not as much Art, as many excellent Qualities, required to make a pimping Porter at a common Bawdy-House, as would enable a Man to prostitute his own or his Friend's Wife or Child? Doth it not ask as good a Memory, as nimble an Invention, as steady a Countenance, to forswear yourself in *Westminster-Hall*,° as would furnish out a complete Ministerial Tool, or perhaps a prime Minister himself? It is needless to particularize every Instance; in all we shall find, that there is a nearer Connection between high and low Life than is generally imagined, and that a Highwayman is entitled to more Favour with the Great than he usually meets with.° If therefore, as I think I have proved, the same Parts which qualify a Man for Eminence in a low Sphere, qualify him likewise for Eminence in a higher, sure it can be no Doubt in which he should chuse to exert them. Ambition, without which no one can be a great Man, will immediately instruct him, in your own Phrase, to prefer a Hill in Paradise to a Dunghil; nay, even Fear, a Passion the most repugnant to Greatness, will shew him how much more safely he may indulge himself in the full and free Exertion of his mighty Abilities in the higher, than the lower Rank: Since Experience teaches him, that there is a Crowd oftner in one Year at *Tyburn*, than on *Tower-Hill* in a Century.'

Mr. *Wild* rejoined: 'That the same Capacity which qualifies a \**Millken*, a †*Bridle-cull*, or a ‡*Buttock* and *File*, to arrive at any Degree of Eminence in his Profession, would likewise raise a Man in what the World esteem a more honourable Calling, I do not deny; nay, in many of your Instances it is evident, that more Ingenuity, more Art are necessary to the lower, than the higher Proficients. If therefore you had only contended, that every *Prig* might be a Statesman if he pleased, I had readily agreed to it; but when you conclude, that it is his Interest to be so, that Ambition would bid him take that Alternative; in a Word, that a Statesman is greater or happier than a *Prig*, I must deny my Assent. But, in comparing these two together, we must carefully avoid being misled by the vulgar erroneous Estimation of Things; for Mankind err in Disquisitions of this Nature, as Physicians do, who, in considering the Operations of a Disease, have not a due Regard to the Age and Complexion of the Patient. The same Degree of Heat which is common in this Constitution, may be a Fever in that; in the same manner, that which may be Riches or Honour to me, may be Poverty or Disgrace to another; for all these things are to be estimated by Relation to the Person who possesses them. A Booty of 10 *l.* looks as great in the Eye of a *Bridle-cull*, and gives as much real Happiness to his Fancy, as that of as many thousands to the Statesman; and doth not the former lay out his Acquisitions in Whores and Fiddles, with much greater Joy and Mirth, than the latter in Palaces and Pictures?° What are the Flattery,

---

\* A Housebreaker.
† A Highwayman.
‡ A Shoplifter, Terms used in the *Cant Dictionary*.°

the false Compliments of his Gang to the Statesman, when he himself must condemn his own Blunders, and is obliged against his Will to give Fortune the whole Honour of his Success; what is the Pride resulting from such sham Applause, compared to the secret Satisfaction which a *Prig* enjoys in his Mind, in reflecting on a well-contrived and well-executed Scheme? Perhaps indeed the greater Danger is on the Prig's Side; but then you must remember, that the greater Honour is so too. When I mention Honour, I mean that which is paid them by their Gang; for that weak Part of the World, which is vulgarly called THE WISE, see *both* in a disadvantageous and disgraceful Light: And as the *Prig* enjoys (and merits too) the greater Degree of Honour from his Gang, so doth he suffer the less Disgrace from the World, who think his Misdeeds, as they call them, sufficiently at least punished with a Halter, which at once puts an End to his Pain and Infamy; whereas the other is not only hated in Power, but detested and contemned at the Scaffold; and future Ages vent their Malice on his Fame, while the other sleeps quiet and forgotten. Besides, let us a little consider the secret Quiet of their Consciences; how easy is the Reflection of having taken a few Shillings or Pounds from a Stranger, without any Breach of Confidence, or perhaps any great Harm to the Person who loses it, compared to that of having betrayed a publick Trust, and ruined the Fortunes of thousands? How much braver is an Attack on the Highway, than at a Gaming-Table; and how much innocenter the Character of a B——y-House than a C——t Pimp?"° He was eagerly proceeding when, casting his Eyes on the Count, he perceived him to be fast asleep, wherefore having gently jogged him, in order to take his Leave, and promised to return to him the next Morning to Breakfast, they separated; the Count retired to Rest, and Master *Wild* to a Night-Cellar.


CHAPTER VI

*Further Conferences between the Count and Master* Wild, *with other Matters of the* GREAT *Kind.*


BEING met the next Morning, the Count (who, though he did not agree with the whole of his Friend's Doctrine, was, however, highly pleased with his Argument) began to bewail the Misfortune of his

Captivity, and the Backwardness of Friends to assist each other in their Necessities; but what vexed him, he said, most, was the Cruelty of the Fair; for he entrusted *Wild* with the Secret of his having had an Intrigue with Miss *Theodosia,* the eldest of the Miss *Snaps*, ever since his Confinement, tho' he could not prevail with her to set him at Liberty. *Wild* answered, with a Smile: 'It was no Wonder a Woman should wish to confine her Lover, where she might be sure of having him entirely to herself;' but added, 'he believed he could tell him a Method of certainly procuring his Escape.' The Count eagerly besought him to acquaint him with it. *Wild* told him: 'Bribery was the surest Means, and advised him to apply to the Maid.' The Count thanked him, but returned: 'That he had not a Farthing left besides one Guinea, which he had then given her to change.' To which *Wild* said: 'He must make it up with Promises, which he supposed he was Courtier enough to know how to put off.' The Count greatly applauded the Advice, and said, he hoped he should be able in Time to persuade him to condescend to be a Great Man, for which he was so perfectly well qualified.

This Method being concluded on, the two Friends sat down to Cards, a Circumstance which I should not have mentioned, but for the sake of observing the prodigious Force of Habit; for, though the Count knew, if he won never so much of Mr. *Wild*, he should not receive a Shilling, yet could he not refrain from packing the Cards; nor could *Wild* keep his Hands out of his Friend's Pockets, though he knew there was nothing in them.

When the Maid came home, the Count began to put it to her; offered her all he had, and promised Mountains *in futuro*,° but all in vain, the Maid's Honesty was impregnable. She said, 'She would not break her Trust for the World; no, not if she could gain a Million of Money by it.' Upon which *Wild* stepping up, and telling her: 'She need not fear losing her Place, for it would never be found out; that they could throw a Pair of Sheets into the Street, by which it might appear he got out at Window; that he himself would swear he saw him descending; that the Money would be so much Gains in her Pocket; that, besides his Promises, which she might depend on being performed, she would receive from him twenty Shillings and Nine-pence in ready Money, (for she had only laid out Three-pence in plain *Spanish*)° and that besides his Honour, the Count should leave a Pair of Gold Buttons (which afterwards turned out to be Brass) of great Value in her Hands as a further Pawn; and, lastly, that he himself would lend his Friend Eighteen pence, being all he had about him, to deposite *in præsenti*.'°

These Arguments at length prevailed with the Maid, who had always the Reputation of a very honest Servant; and she promised faithfully in the Evening to open the Door to the Count.

Thus did our young Hero not only lend his Rhetorick, which few People care to do without a Fee, but his Money too, Eighteen pence, a Sum which many a good Man would have made eighteen Excuses before he would have parted with, to his Friend, and procured him his Liberty.

But it would be highly derogatory from the GREAT Character of *Wild*, should the Reader imagine he lent such a Sum as eighteen pence to a Friend without the least View of serving himself. As, therefore, he may easily account for it in a manner more advantageous to our Hero's Reputation, by concluding that he had some interested View in the Count's Enlargement, we hope he will judge with Charity, especially as the Sequel makes it not only reasonable but necessary to suppose he had some such View.

A long Intimacy and Friendship subsisted between the Count and Mr. *Wild*, who, being by the Advice of the Count dressed in good Cloaths, was by him introduced into the best Company. They constantly frequented the Assemblies, Auctions, Gaming-Tables, and Play-Houses; at which last they saw two Acts every Night, and then retired without paying, this being, it seems, an immemorial Privilege which the Beaus of the Town prescribe to themselves.° This, however, did not suit *Wild's* Temper, who called it a Cheat, and objected against it, as requiring no Dexterity but what every Blockhead might put in Execution. He said it was a Custom very much savouring of the *Sneaking-Budge*,° but neither so honourable nor so ingenious.

*Wild* now made a considerable Figure, and passed for a Gentleman of great Fortune in the Funds.° Women of Quality treated him with great Familiarity, young Ladies began to spread their Charms for him, when an Accident happened that put a Stop to his Continuance in a Way of Life too insipid and inactive to afford Employment for those great Talents, which were designed to make a much more considerable Figure in the World, than attends the Character of a Beau° or a pretty Gentleman.

### CHAPTER VII

*Master* Wild *sets out on his Travels, and returns home again. A*
*very short Chapter, containing infinitely more Time and less*
*Matter than any other in the whole Story.*

WE are sorry we cannot indulge our Reader's Curiosity with a full
and perfect Account of this Accident; but as there are such various
Accounts, one of which only can be true, and possibly, and indeed
probably, none; instead of following the general Method of Historians, who in such Cases set down the various Reports, and leave to
your own Conjecture which you will chuse, we shall pass them all
over.

Certain it is, that whatever this Accident was, it determined our
Hero's Father to send his Son immediately abroad, for seven Years;
and, which may seem somewhat remarkable, to his Majesty's Plan-
tations in *America*.° That Part of the World being, as he said, freer
from Vices than the Courts and Cities of *Europe*, and consequently
less dangerous to corrupt a young Man's Morals. And as for the
Advantages, the old Gentleman thought they were equal there with
those attained in the politer Climates; for travelling, he said, was
travelling in one Part of the World as well as another: It consisted in
being such a Time from home, and in traversing so many Leagues;°
and appealed to Experience, whether most of our Travellers in
*France* and *Italy*, did not prove at their Return, that they might have
been sent as profitably to *Norway* and *Greenland*?

According to these Resolutions of his Father, the young Gentleman went aboard a Ship, and with a great deal of good Company set
out for the *American* Hemisphere.° The exact Time of his Stay is
somewhat uncertain; most probably longer than was intended: But
howsoever long his Abode there was, it must be a Blank in this
History; as the whole Story contains not one Adventure worthy the
Reader's Notice; being indeed, a continued Scene of whoring,
drinking, and removing from one Place to another.

To confess a Truth, we are so ashamed of the Shortness of this
Chapter, that we would have done a Violence to our History, and
have inserted an Adventure or two of some other Traveller: To
which Purpose we borrowed the Journals of several young Gentlemen who have lately made the Tour of *Europe*; but to our great

Sorrow could not extract a single Incident strong enough to justify the Theft to our Consciences.

When we consider the ridiculous Figure this Chapter must make, being the History of no less than eight Years, our only Comfort is, that the History of some Mens Lives, and perhaps of some Men who have made a Noise in the World, are in Reality as absolute Blanks as the Travels of our Hero. As, therefore, we shall make sufficient Amends in the Sequel for this Inanity, we shall hasten on to Matters of true Importance, and immense Greatness. At present we content ourselves with setting down our Hero where we took him up, after acquainting our Reader that he went abroad, staid seven Years, and then came home again.

CHAPTER VIII

*An Adventure where* Wild, *in the Division of the Booty, exhibits an astonishing Instance of* GREATNESS.

THE Count was one Night very successful at the Hazard-Table,° where *Wild*, who was just returned from his Travels, was then present; as was likewise a young Gentleman whose Name was *Bob Bagshot*,° an Acquaintance of Mr. *Wild's*, and of whom he entertained a great Opinion; taking therefore Mr. *Bagshot* aside, he advised him to provide himself (if he had them not about him) with a Case of Pistols,° and to attack the Count, in his Way home, promising to plant himself near with the same Arms, as a *Corps de Reserve*, and to come up on Occasion.° This was accordingly executed, and the Count obliged to surrender to savage Force what he had in so genteel and civil a Manner taken at Play.

And as it is a wise and philosophical Observation, that one Misfortune never comes alone,° the Count had hardly passed the Examination of Mr. *Bagshot*, when he fell into the Hands of Mr. *Snap*, who, in Company with Mr. *Wild* the elder, and one or two more Gentlemen, being it seems thereto well *warranted*, laid hold of the unfortunate Count, and conveyed him back to the same House from which, by the Assistance of his good Friend he had formerly escaped.

Mr. *Wild* and Mr. *Bagshot* went together to the Tavern, where Mr. *Bagshot*, generously (as he thought) offered to share the Booty, and having divided the Money into two unequal Heaps, and added a golden Snuff-Box° to the lesser Heap, he desired Mr. *Wild* to take his Choice.

Mr. *Wild* immediately conveyed the larger Share of the Ready into his Pocket, according to an excellent Maxim of his: *First secure what Share you can, before you wrangle for the rest:*° And then, turning to his Companion, he asked him, with a stern Countenance, whether he intended to keep all that Sum to himself? Mr. *Bagshot* answered, with some Surprize, that he thought Mr. *Wild* had no Reason to complain; for it was surely fair, at least on his Part, to content himself with an equal Share of the Booty, who had taken the whole. 'I grant you took it,' replied *Wild*, 'but, pray who proposed or counselled the taking it? Can you say, that you have done more than executed my Scheme, and might not I, if I had pleased, have employed another? since you well know there was not a Gentleman in the Room but would have taken the Money, if he had known how conveniently and safely to do it.' 'That is very true (returned *Bagshot*) but did not I execute the Scheme, did not I run the whole Risque? Should not I have suffered the whole Punishment if I had been taken, and is not the Labourer worthy of his Hire?'° 'Doubtless (says *Jonathan*) he is so, and your Hire I shall not refuse you, which is all that the Labourer is entitled to, or ever enjoys. I remember when I was at School to have heard some Verses, which for the Excellence of their Doctrine, made an Impression on me, purporting that the Birds of the Air, and the Beasts of the Field, work not for themselves.° It is true, the Farmer allows Fodder to his Oxen, and Pasture to his Sheep; but it is for his own Service, not theirs. In the same manner the Plowman, the Shepherd, the Weaver, the Builder and the Soldier, work not for themselves but others; they are contented with a poor Pittance (the Labourer's Hire) and permit us the GREAT to enjoy the Fruits of their Labours. *Aristotle*, as my Master told us, hath plainly proved, in the first Book of his *Politicks*, that the low, mean, useful Part of Mankind, are born Slaves to the Wills, and for the Use of their Superiors, as well as the Cattle.° It is well said of us, the higher Order of Mortals, that we are born only to devour the Fruits of the Earth;° and it may be as well said of the lower Class, that they are born only to produce them for us. Is not the Battle gained by the Sweat and Danger of the common Soldier, is not the Honour and Fruit of the Victory the General's who laid the Scheme? Is not the

House built by the Labour of the Carpenter, and the Bricklayer? Is it not built for the Profit only of the Architect, and for the Use of the Inhabitant, who could not easily have placed one Brick upon another? Is not the Cloth, the Silk, wrought into its Form, and variegated with all the Beauty of Colours, by those who are forced to content themselves with the coarsest and vilest Part of their Work, while the Profit and Enjoyment of their Labours fall to the Share of others? Cast your Eye abroad, and see who is it lives in the most magnificent Buildings, feasts his Palate with the most luxurious Dainties, his Eyes with the most beautiful Sculptures and delicate Paintings, and cloathes himself in the finest and richest Apparel; and tell me if all these do not fall to his Lot, who had not any the least Share in producing all these Conveniencies, nor the least Ability so to do? Why then should the State of a *Prig* differ from all others? Or why should you, who are the Labourer only, the Executor of my Scheme, expect a Share in the Profit? Be advised, therefore, deliver the whole Booty to me, and trust to my Bounty for your Reward.' Mr. *Bagshot* was some Time silent, and looked like a Man Thunderstruck: But at last recovering himself from his Surprize, he thus began. 'If you think, Mr. *Wild*, by the Force of your Arguments to get the Money out of my Pocket, you are greatly mistaken. What is all this Stuff to me? D——n me, I am a Man of Honour, and tho' I can't talk as well as you, by G—— you shall not make a Fool of me, and if you take me for one, I must tell you, you are a Rascal.' At which Words, he laid his Hand to his Sword. *Wild*, perceiving the little Success the great Strength of his Arguments had met with, and the hasty Temper of his Friend, gave over his Design for the present, and told *Bagshot*, he was only in Jest. But this Coolness had rather the Effect of Oil than Water thrown on the Flames of the other, who replied, in a Rage, 'D——n me, I don't like such Jests; I see you are a pitiful Rascal, and a Scoundrel.' *Wild*, with a Philosophy worthy of great Admiration, returned. 'As for your Abuse, I have no Regard to it; but to convince you, I am not afraid of you, let us lay the whole Booty on the Table, and let the Conqueror take it all.' And having so said, he drew out his shining Sword, whose glittering so dazzled the Eyes of *Bagshot*, that in a Tone entirely altered, he said, 'No, he was contented with what he had already; that it was mighty ridiculous in them to quarrel among themselves; that they had common Enemies enough abroad, against whom they should unite their common

Force; that if he had mistaken *Wild*, he was sorry for it, and as for a
Jest, he could take a Jest as well as another.' *Wild*, who had a wonderful Knack of discovering and applying to the Passions of Men,
beginning now to have a little Insight into his Friend, and to conceive
what Arguments would make the quickest Impression on him, cried
out in a loud Voice, 'That he had bullied him into drawing his
Sword, and since it was out, he would not put it up without Satisfaction.' 'What Satisfaction would you have?' (answered the other.)
'Your Money or the Sword,' said *Wild*. 'Why lookye, Mr. *Wild* (said
*Bagshot*) if you want to borrow a little of my Part, since I know you
to be a Man of Honour, I don't care if I lend you:—For tho' I am not
afraid of any Man living, yet rather than break with a Friend, and as
it may be necessary for your Occasions—' *Wild*, who often declared
that he looked upon borrowing to be as good a Way of *taking* as any,
and as he called it, the genteelest Kind of *Sneaking-Budge*, putting
up his Sword, and shaking his Friend by the Hand, told him, he had
hit the Nail on the Head; it was really his present Necessity only that
prevailed with him against his Will; for that his Honour was concerned to pay a considerable Sum the next Morning. Upon which,
contenting himself with one Half of *Bagshot's* Share, so that he had
three Parts in four of the whole, he took leave of his Companion, and
retired to rest.

CHAPTER IX

Wild *pays a Visit to Miss* Lætitia Snap. *A Description of
that lovely young Creature, and the successless Issue of Mr.*
Wild's *Addresses.*

THE next Morning when he waked, he began to think of paying a
Visit to Miss ~~Fishy~~ Snap; for tho' she was really a Woman of Merit,
and great Generosity, yet Mr. *Wild* found a Present was ever most
welcome to her, as being a Token of Respect in her Lover. He therefore went directly to a Toy-Shop,° and there purchased a genteel
Snuff-Box, with which he waited upon his Mistress; whom he found
in the most beautiful Deshabille.° Her lovely Hair hung wantonly
over her Forehead, being neither white with, nor yet free from Powder; a neat double Clout, which seemed to have been worn a few

Times only, was pinned under her Chin; some Remains of that Art which Ladies improve Nature with, shone on her Cheeks. Her Body was loosely attired, without Stays or Jumps, so that her Breasts had uncontroulled Liberty to display their beauteous Orbs, which they did as low as her Girdle; a thin Covering of a rumpled Muzlin Handkerchief almost hid them from the Eyes, save in a few Parts where a good-natured Hole gave Opportunity to the naked Breast to appear, and put us in Mind by its Whiteness of the Fault in the Handkerchief, which might have otherwise past unobserved. Her Gown was a Sattin of a whitish Colour, with about a dozen little Silver Spots upon it, so artificially interwoven, that they looked as if they had fallen there by Chance. This flying open, discovered a fine white Petticoat beautifully edged round the Bottom with a narrow Piece of half Gold-Lace, beneath this appeared another Petticoat stiffened with Whalebone, vulgarly called a Hoop, which was six Inches at least below the other; and under this again appeared a red Stuff. She likewise displayed two pretty Feet covered with Silk, and adorned with Lace, and tied the right with a handsome Piece of blue Ribband; the left, as more unworthy, with a Piece of red Stuff, which seemed to have been a Strip of her Under-Petticoat.° Such was the lovely Creature whom Mr. *Wild* attended. She received him at first with some Coldness, which Women of strict Virtue by a commendable, tho' sometimes painful Restraint, enjoin themselves to their Lovers. The Snuff-Box being produced, was at first civilly, and indeed, gently refused: But on a second Application accepted. The Tea-Table was soon called for,° at which a Discourse passed between these young Lovers, which could we set down with any Accuracy, would be very edifying as well as entertaining to our Reader; let it suffice then that the Wit, together with the Beauty of this young Creature, so inflamed the Passion of *Wild*, which, tho' an honourable Sort of a Passion, was at the same Time extremely violent, that it transported him to Freedoms too offensive to the nice Chastity of *Lætitia*, who was, to confess the Truth, more indebted to her own Strength for the Preservation of her Virtue, than to the awful Respect or Backwardness of her Lover; for he was indeed so very urgent in his Addresses, that had he not with many Oaths promised her Marriage, we could scarce have been justified in calling his Passion strictly honourable; but he was so remarkably attached to Decency, that he never offered any Violence to a young Lady without the most earnest Promises of that kind, being, he said, a Ceremonial due to their Modesty, and which was so easily performed, that the Omission could arise from nothing but the mere Wantonness of Brutality. The lovely *Lætitia*, either out of Prudence, or perhaps Religion, of which she was a liberal Professor, was deaf to all his Promises, and luckily invincible by his Force; for though she had not learnt the vulgar Art of clenching her Fist, Nature had not, however, left her defenceless; for at the Ends of her Fingers she wore Arms, which she used with such admirable Dexterity, that the hot Blood of Mr. *Wild* soon began to appear in several little Spots on his Face, and his full-blown Cheeks to resemble that Part which Modesty forbids a Boy to turn up any where but in publick School, after some Pedagogue, strong of Arm, hath exercised his Talents thereon. *Wild* now retreated from the Conflict, and the victorious *Lætitia*, with becoming Triumph and noble Spirit, cried out, 'D——n you, if this be your Way of shewing your Love, I'll warrant I gives you enough on't.' She then proceeded to talk of her Virtue, which *Wild* bid her carry to the Devil with her;° and thus our Lovers parted.

### CHAPTER X

*A Discovery of some Matters concerning the chaste* Lætitia, *which must wonderfully surprize, and perhaps affect our Reader.*

MR. *Wild* was no sooner departed, than the fair Conqueress opening the Door of a Closet, called forth a young Gentleman, whom she had there enclosed at the Approach of the other. The Name of this Gallant was *Tom Smirk*. He was Apprentice to a Tallow-Chandler, and was indeed the greatest Beau, and the greatest Favourite of the Ladies, at the End of the Town where he lived. As we take Dress to be the Characteristic or efficient Quality of a Beau, we shall, instead of giving any Character of this young Gentleman, content ourselves with describing his Dress only to our Readers.° He wore, then, a Pair of white Stockings on his Legs, and Pumps on his Feet; his Buckles were a large Piece of *Pinchbeck* Plate, which almost covered his whole Foot. His Breeches were of red Plush, which hardly reached his Knees; his Wastecoat was a white Dimity richly embroidered with yellow Silk, over which he wore a blue Plush coat with Metal Buttons, a smart Sleeve, and a Cape reaching half way down his Back. His Wig was of a brown Colour, covering almost half his Pate, on which was hung on one Side a little laced Hat, but cocked with great Smartness. Such was the accomplished *Smirk*, who, at his issuing forth from the Closet, was received with open Arms by the amiable *Lætitia*. She addressed him by the tender Name of Dear *Tommy*; and told him she had dismist the odious Creature whom her Father intended for her Husband, and had now nothing to interrupt her Happiness with him.

Here, Reader, thou must pardon us if we stop a while to lament the Capriciousness of Nature in forming this charming Part of the Creation, designed to complete the Happiness of Man; with their soft Innocence to allay his Ferocity, with their Sprightliness to sooth his Cares, and with their constant Friendship to relieve all the Troubles and Disappointments which can happen to him. Seeing, then, that this is universally certain, that these are the Blessings chiefly sought after, and generally found in every Wife, how must we lament that Disposition in these lovely Creatures, which leads them to prefer in their Favour those Individuals of the other Sex, who do not seem intended by Nature as her greatest Master-piece. For surely, however useful they may be in the Creation, as we are taught, that nothing, not even a Louse, is made in vain; yet these Beaus, even that most splendid and honoured Part, which, in this our Island, Nature loves to distinguish in Red,° are not, as some think, the noblest Part of the Creation. For my own Part, let any Man chuse to himself two Beaus, let them be Captains or Colonels, as well dressed Men as ever lived, really, as fine Men, I would venture to oppose a single Sir *Isaac Newton*, a *Shakespear*, a *Milton*,° or perhaps some few others to both these Beaus; nay, and I very much doubt, whether it had not been better for the World in general, that neither of these Beaus had ever been born, than that it should have wanted the Benefit arising to it from the Labour of any one of those Persons.

If this be true, how melancholy must be the Consideration, that any single Beau, especially if he have but half a Yard of Ribbon in his Hat,° shall weigh heavier, in the Scales of female Affection, than twenty Sir *Isaac Newtons*. How must our Reader, who perhaps had wisely accounted for the Resistance which the chaste *Lætitia* had made to the violent Addresses of the ravished (or rather ravishing) *Wild* from that Lady's impregnable Virtue, how must he blush, I say, to perceive her quit the Strictness of her Carriage,° and abandon herself to those loose Freedoms which she indulged to *Smirk*. But, alas! when we discover all, as, to preserve the Fidelity of our History, we must, when we relate that every Familiarity had past between them, and that the FAIR *Lætitia* (for we must, in this single Instance, imitate *Virgil*, where he drops the *pius* and the *pater*,° and drop our favourite Epithet of *chaste*) the FAIR *Lætitia* had, I say, made *Smirk* as happy as *Wild* desired to be, what must then be our Reader's Confusion? We will, therefore, draw a Curtain over this Scene, from that Philogyny which is in us, and proceed to Matters, which, instead of dishonouring the human Species, will greatly raise and ennoble it.

CHAPTER XI

*Containing as great and as noble Instances of human*
GREATNESS *as are to be met with in ancient or modern*
*History. Concluding with some wholesome Hints to the gay*
*Part of Mankind.*

*WILD* no sooner parted from the chaste *Lætitia*, than recollecting that his Friend the Count was returned to his Lodgings in the same House, he resolved to visit him; for he was none of those half-bred Fellows, who are ashamed to see their Friends when they have plundered and betrayed them: From which base and pitiful Temper many monstrous Cruelties have been transacted by Men, who have sometimes carried their Modesty so far as to the Murther, or utter Ruin of those against whom their Consciences have suggested to them, that they have committed some small Trespass, either by the debauching a Wife or Daughter, belying or betraying, or some other such trifling Instance. In our Hero there was nothing not truly GREAT: He could, without the least Abashment, drink a Bottle with the Man who knew he had the Moment before picked his Pocket; and, when he had stript him of every thing he had, never desired to do him any further Mischief; for he carried Good-nature to that wonderful and uncommon Height, that he never did a single Injury to Man or Woman, by which he himself did not expect to reap some Advantage.

Our Hero found the captive Count not basely lamenting his Fate, nor abandoning himself to Despair, but, with due Resignation, employing himself in preparing several Packs of Cards for future Exploits. The Count, little suspecting that *Wild* had been the sole Contriver of the Misfortune which had befallen him, rose up, and eagerly embraced him; and *Wild*, who well knew the whole, returned his Embrace with equal Warmth. They were no sooner seated than *Wild* took an Occasion, from seeing the Cards lying on the Table, to inveigh against Gaming, and, with an usual° and highly commendable Freedom, after first exaggerating the distrest Circumstances in which the Count was then involved, imputed all his Misfortunes to that cursed Itch of Play, which, he said, he concluded had brought his present Confinement upon him, and must unavoidably end in his Destruction. The other, with great Alacrity, defended his favourite Amusement (or rather Employment) and having told him the great Success he had after his unluckily quitting the Room, acquainted him with the Accident which followed, and which the Reader, as well as Mr. *Wild*, hath had some Intimation of before; adding, however, one Circumstance not hitherto mentioned, *viz.* that he had defended his Money with the utmost Bravery, and had dangerously wounded at least two of the three Men who had attacked him. This Behaviour *Wild*, who not only knew the extreme Readiness with which the Booty had been delivered, but also the constant Frigidity of the Count's Courage, highly applauded, and wished he had been present to assist him. The Count then proceeded to animadvert on the Carelessness of the Watch,° and the Scandal it was to the Laws, that People could not walk the Streets in Safety, and, after expatiating some Time on that Subject, he asked Mr. *Wild* if he ever saw so prodigious a Run of Luck (for so he chose to call his Winning, though he knew *Wild* was well acquainted with his having loaded Dice in his Pocket). The other answered, it was indeed prodigious, and almost sufficient to justify any Person, who did not know him better, in suspecting his fair Play. 'No Man, I believe, dares call that in Question,' replied he. 'No, surely,' says *Wild*, 'you are well known to be a Man of more Honour: But pray, Sir,' continued he, 'did the Rascals rob you of all?' 'Every Shilling,' cries the other with an Oath; 'they did not leave me a single Stake.'

While they were thus discoursing, Mr. *Snap*, with a Gentleman who followed him, introduced Mr. *Bagshot* into the Company. It seems Mr. *Bagshot*, immediately after his Separation from Mr. *Wild*, returned to the Gaming-Table, where, he having trusted to Fortune that Treasure which he had procured by his Industry, the faithless Goddess committed a Breach of Trust, and sent Mr. *Bagshot* away with as empty Pockets as are to be found in any laced Coat in the Kingdom. Now as that Gentleman was walking to a certain reputable House or Shed in *Covent-Garden* Market, he fortuned to meet with Mr. *Snap*, who had just returned from conveying the Count to his Lodgings, and was then walking to and fro before the Gaming-House Door; for you are to know, my good Reader, if you have never been a Man of Wit and Pleasure about Town, that as the voracious Pike lieth snug under some Weed before the Mouth of any of those little Streams which discharge themselves into a large River, waiting for the small Fry which issue thereout;° so hourly before the Door or Mouth of these Gaming-Houses doth Mr. *Snap*, or some other Gentleman of his Occupation, attend the issuing forth of the small Fry of young Gentlemen, to whom they deliver little Slips of Parchment, containing Invitations of the said Gentlemen to their Houses, together with one Mr. *John Doe*, a Person whose Company is in great Request.° Mr. *Snap*, among many others of these Billets, happened to have one directed to Mr. *Bagshot*, being at the Suit or Solicitation of one Mrs. *Anne Sample*, Spinster, at whose House the said *Bagshot* had lodged several Months, and whence he had inadvertently departed without taking a formal Leave; on which Account Mrs. *Anne* had taken this Method of *speaking with* him.

Mr. *Snap's* House being now very full of good Company, he was obliged to introduce Mr. *Bagshot* into the Count's Apartment, it being, as he said, the only Chamber he had to *lock up* in. Mr. *Wild* no sooner saw his Friend than he ran to embrace him, and immediately presented him to the Count, who received him with great Civility.

*Further Particulars relating to Miss* Tishy, *which perhaps
may not greatly surprize after the former. The Description
of a very fine Gentleman. And a Dialogue between* Wild
*and the Count, in which public Virtue is just hinted at,
with &c.*

MR. *Snap* had turned the Key a very few Minutes before a Servant
of the Family called Mr. *Bagshot* out of the Room, telling him, there
was a Person below who desired to speak with him; and this was no
other than Miss *Lætitia Snap*, whose Admirer Mr. *Bagshot* had long
been, and in whose tender Breast his Passion had raised a more
ardent Flame than that of any of his Rivals had been able to raise.
Indeed she was so extremely fond of this Youth, that she often
confessed to her female Confidents, if she could ever have listened to
the Thought of living with any one Man, Mr. *Bagshot* was he. Nor
was she singular in this Inclination, many other young Ladies being
her Rivals in this Lover, who had all the great and noble Qualifications necessary to form a true Gallant, and which Nature is seldom
so extremely bountiful as to indulge to any one Person. We will
endeavour, however, to describe them all with as much Exactness as
possible. He was, then, six Feet high, had large Calves, broad Shoul-
ders, a ruddy Complexion, with brown curled Hair, a modest Assurance, and clean Linen. He had indeed, it must be confest, some small
Deficiencies to counterbalance these heroic Qualities, for he was the
silliest Fellow in the World, could neither write nor read, nor had he
a single Grain or Spark of Honour, Honesty, or Good-nature in his
whole Composition.

As soon Mr. *Bagshot* had quitted the Room, the Count, taking
*Wild* by the Hand, told him he had something to communicate to
him of very great Importance; he then proceeded to inform him, he
was very well convinced that *Bagshot* was the Person who robbed
him. *Wild* started with great seeming Amazement at this Discovery,
and told the Count with a most serious Countenance, he advised him
to take Care how he cast any such Reflections on a Man of Mr.
*Bagshot's* nice Honour; for he was certain he would not bear it.
'D——n his Honour,' quoth the enraged Count, 'nor can I bear
being robbed; I will apply to a Justice of Peace.'° *Wild* replied with

great Indignation, since he durst entertain such a Suspicion against his Friend, he would henceforth disclaim all Acquaintance with him; that he knew Mr. *Bagshot* was a Man of Honour, and his Friend, and consequently it was impossible he should be guilty of a bad Action; with much more to the same purpose, which had not the expected Weight with the Count; for the latter seemed still certain as to the Person, and resolute in applying for Justice, which, he said, he thought he owed to the Public, as well as to himself. *Wild* then changed his Countenance into a kind of Derision, and spoke as follows: 'Suppose it should be possible that Mr. *Bagshot* had, in a Frolic, (for I will call it no other) taken this Method of borrowing your Money, what will you get by prosecuting him? Not your Money again; for you hear he was stript at the Gaming-Table;' (of which *Bagshot* had, during their short Confabulation, informed them) 'you will get then an Opportunity of being still more out of Pocket by the Prosecution. Another Advantage you may promise yourself is the being blown up at every Gaming-House in Town, for that I will assure you of; and then much Good may it do you to sit down with the Satisfaction of having discharged what it seems you owe the Public. I am ashamed of my own Discernment, when I mistook you for a great Man. Would it not be better for you to receive Part (perhaps all) of your Money again by a wise Concealment; for however *seedy*° Mr. *Bagshot* may be now, if he hath really plaid this Frolic with you, you may believe he will play it with others, and when he is in Cash, you may depend on a Restoration; the Law will be always in your Power, and that is the last Remedy which a brave or a wise Man would resort to. Leave the Affair therefore to me; I will examine *Bagshot*, and if I find he hath plaid you this Trick, I will engage my own Honour, you shall in the End be no Loser.' The Count answered: 'If I was sure to be no Loser, Mr. *Wild*, I apprehend you have a better Opinion of my Understanding than to imagine I would prosecute a Gentleman for the sake of the Public. These are foolish Words of Course, which we learn a ridiculous Habit of speaking, and will often break from us without any Design or Meaning. I assure you all I desire is a Reimbursement, and if I can, by your Means, obtain that, the Public may ——' concluding with a Phrase too coarse to be inserted in a History of this kind.

They were now informed that Dinner° was ready, and the

Company assembled below Stairs, whither the Reader may, if he please, attend these Gentlemen.

There sat down at the Table Mr. *Snap*, and the two young Ladies his Daughters, Mr. *Wild* the elder, Mr. *Wild* the younger, the Count, Mr. *Bagshot*, and a grave Gentleman, who had formerly had the Honour of carrying Arms in a Regiment of Foot, and now engaged in the Office (perhaps a more reputable° one) of assisting or following Mr. *Snap* in the Execution of the Laws of his Country.

Nothing very remarkable passed at Dinner. The Conversation (as is usual in polite Company) rolled° chiefly on what they were then eating, and what they had lately eaten. In which the military Gentleman, who had served in *Ireland*, gave them a very particular Account of a new manner of roasting Potatoes,° and others gave an Account of other Dishes. In short, an indifferent By-stander would have concluded from their Discourse, that they had all come into this World for no other purpose, than to fill their Bellies; and indeed if this was not the chief, it is probable it was the most innocent Design Nature had in their Formation.

As soon as *the Dish* was removed, and the Ladies retired, the Count proposed a Game at Hazard, which was immediately assented to by the whole Company, and the Dice being immediately brought in, the Count took up the Box, and demanded who would set him:° To which no one made any Answer, imagining perhaps the Count's Pockets to be more empty than they were; for, in Reality, that Gentleman (notwithstanding what he had heartily swore to Mr. *Wild*) had since his Arrival at Mr. *Snap's*, conveyed a Piece of Plate to pawn, by which Means he had furnished himself with ten Guineas. The Count, therefore, perceiving this Backwardness in his Friends, and probably somewhat guessing at the Cause of it, took the said Guineas out of his Pocket, and threw them on the Table; when lo! (such is the Force of Example) all the rest began to produce their Funds, and immediately a considerable Sum glittering in their Eyes, the Game began.

## CHAPTER XIII

*A Chapter, of which we are extremely vain, and which indeed
we look on as our* Chef d'Oeuvre, *containing a wonderful
Story concerning the Devil, and as nice a Scene of Honour as
ever happened.*

MY Reader, I believe, even if he be a Gamester, would not thank me
for an exact Relation of every Man's Success; let it suffice then that
they played till the whole Money vanished from the Table; and
whether the Devil himself carried it away, I will not determine; but
very surprizing it was, that every Person protested he had lost, nor
could any one guess who, but the Devil, had won.

But though very probable it is, that this Arch-Fiend had some
Share in the Booty, it is likely he had not all; Mr. *Bagshot* being
imagined to be a considerable Winner, notwithstanding his Assertions to the contrary; for he was seen by several to convey Money
often into his Pocket, and what is still a little stronger Presumption
is, that the grave Gentleman whom we have mentioned to have
served his Country in two honourable Capacities, not being willing
to trust alone to the Evidence of his Eyes, had frequently dived into
the said *Bagshot's* Pocket, whence tho' he might extract a few Pieces,
he was very sensible he had left many behind.

The Gentleman had long indulged his Curiosity in this Way
before Mr. *Bagshot*, in the Heat of Gaming, had perceived him: But
as he was now leaving off Play, he discovered this ingenious Feat of
Dexterity; upon which, leaping up from his Chair in a violent Passion, he cried out, 'I thought I had been among Gentlemen, and
Men of Honour, but, d——n me, I find we have a Pickpocket in
Company.' The scandalous Sound of this Word extremely alarmed
the whole Board, nor did they all shew less Surprize than the
*Conv——n* (whose not sitting of late is much lamented) would
express at hearing there was an *Atheist* in the Room:° But it more
particularly affected the Gentleman; who likewise started from his
Chair, and with a fierce Countenance and Accent, said, 'Do you
mean Me? D——n your Eyes, you are a Rascal and a Scoundrel.'
Those Words would have been immediately succeeded by Blows, had
not the Company interposed, and with strong Arm withheld the two
Antagonists from each other. It was, however, a long Time before

they could be prevailed on to sit down, which being at last happily brought about, Mr. *Wild* the elder, who was a well-disposed old Man, advised them to shake Hands and be Friends; but the Gentleman, who had received the first Affront, absolutely refused it, and swore, *He would have the Villain's Blood.* Mr. *Snap* highly applauded the Resolution, and affirmed that the Affront was by no Means to be put up by any who bore the Name of a Gentleman, and that unless his Friend resented it properly,° he would never execute another Warrant in his Company; that he had always looked upon him as a Man of Honour, and doubted not but he would prove himself so; and that if it was his own Case, nothing should persuade him to put up such an Affront without proper Satisfaction. The Count likewise spoke on the same Side, and the Parties themselves muttered several short Sentences, purporting their Intentions. At last, Mr. *Wild* our Hero, rising slowly from his Seat, and having fixed the Attention of all present, began as follows. 'I have heard, with infinite Pleasure, every Thing which the two Gentlemen who spoke last have said, with Relation to Honour, nor can any Man possibly entertain a higher and nobler Sense of that Word, nor a greater Esteem of its inestimable Value than myself. If we have no Name to express it by in our Cant Dictionary, it were well to be wished we had. It is indeed the essential Quality of a Gentleman, and which no Man who ever was great in the Field, or on the Road (as others express it)° can possibly be without. But alas! Gentlemen, what Pity is it, that a Word of such sovereign Use and Virtue should have so uncertain and various an Application, that scarce two People mean the same Thing by it.° Do not some by Honour mean Good-Nature and Humanity, which weak Minds call Virtues? How then! Must we deny it to the Great, the Brave, the Noble, to the Sackers of Towns, the Plunderers of Provinces, and the Conquerors of Kingdoms? Were not these Men of Honour? And yet they scorned those pitiful Qualities I have mentioned. Again, some few (or I am mistaken) include the Idea of Honesty in their Honour. And shall we then say, that no Man who withholds from another what Law or Justice perhaps calls his own, or who GREATLY and boldly deprives him of such Property, is a Man of Honour? G—— forbid I should say so in this, or indeed, in any other good Company. Is Honour Truth? No. It is not in the Lie's going from us, but in its coming to us our Honour is injured.° Doth it then consist in what the Vulgar call Cardinal Virtues?° It would be an

Affront to your Understandings to suppose it, since we see every Day so many Men of Honour without any. In what then doth the Word Honour consist? Why in itself alone. A Man of Honour is he that is called a Man of Honour; and while he is so called, he so remains, and no longer. Think not any Thing a Man commits can forfeit his Honour. Look abroad into the World, the PRIG while he flourishes is a Man of Honour; when in Gaol, at the Bar, or the Tree, he is so no longer. And why is this Distinction? Not from his Actions; for those are often as well known in his flourishing Estate,° as they are afterwards; but because Men call him a Man of Honour in the former, and cease to call him so in the latter Condition. Let us see then, how hath Mr. *Bagshot* injured the Gentleman's Honour? Why, he hath called him a Pick-pocket, and that probably, by a severe Construction and a long roundabout Way of Reasoning, may seem a little to derogate from his Honour, if considered in a very nice Sense. Admitting it, therefore, for Argument's Sake, to be some small Imputation on his Honour, let Mr. *Bagshot* give him Satisfaction; let him doubly and triply repair this oblique Injury by directly asserting, that he believes he is a Man of Honour.' The Gentleman answered, he was content to refer it to Mr. *Wild*, and whatever Satisfaction he thought sufficient, he would accept. 'Let him give me my Money again first,' said *Bagshot*, 'and then I will call him a Man of Honour with all my Heart.' The Gentleman then protested he had not any, which *Snap* seconded, declaring he had his Eyes on him all the while; but *Bagshot* remained still unsatisfied, till *Wild*, rapping out a hearty Oath, swore he had not taken a single Farthing, adding that whoever asserted the contrary gave him the Lie, and he would resent it. And now, such was the Ascendency of this GREAT MAN, that *Bagshot* immediately acquiesced, and performed the Ceremonies required: And thus, by the exquisite Address of our Hero, this Quarrel, which had so fatal an Aspect, and which between two Persons so extremely jealous of their Honour, would most certainly have produced very dreadful Consequences, was happily concluded.

Mr. *Wild* was indeed a little interested in this Affair, as he himself had set the Gentleman to work, and had received the greatest Part of the Booty, and as to Mr. *Snap's* Deposition in his Favour, it was the usual Height to which the Ardour of that worthy Person's Friendship too frequently hurried him. It was his constant Maxim, That he was a pitiful Fellow who would stick at a little \**Rapping*° for his Friend.

## CHAPTER XIV

*In which the History of* GREATNESS *is continued.*

MATTERS being thus reconciled, and the gaming over, from Reasons before hinted, the Company proceeded to drink about with the utmost Chearfulness and Friendship, drinking Healths, shaking Hands, and professing the most perfect Affection for each other. All which were not in the least interrupted by some Designs which they then agitated in their Minds, and which they intended to execute as soon as the Liquor had prevailed over some of their Understandings. *Bagshot* and the Gentleman intending to rob each other; Mr. *Snap* and Mr. *Wild* the elder, meditating what other Creditors they could find out, to charge the Gentlemen then in Custody with; the Count hoping to renew the Play, and *Wild* our Hero, laying a Design to put *Bagshot* out of the Way, or as the Vulgar express it, to hang him with the first Opportunity. But none of these great Designs could at present be put in Execution, for Mr. *Snap* being soon after summoned abroad on Business of great Moment, which required likewise the Assistance of Mr. *Wild* the elder and his other Friend, and as he did not care to trust to the Nimbleness of the Count's Heels, of which he had already had some Experience, he declared he must *lock up* for that Evening. And now, Reader, if thou pleasest, as we are in no great Haste, we will stop and make a Simile. As when their Lap is finished, the cautious Huntsman to their Kennel gathers the nimble-footed Hounds, they with lank Ears and Tails slouch sullenly on, whilst he with his Whippers-in,° follows close at their Heels, regardless of their dogged Humour, till having seen them safe within the Door, he turns the Key, and then retires to whatever Business or Pleasure calls him thence: So with louring Countenance, and reluctant Steps mounted the Count and *Bagshot* to their Chamber, or rather Kennel, whither they were attended by *Snap*, and those who followed him, and where *Snap* having seen them deposited, very

---

\* *Rapping*, is a Cant Term for Perjury.

contentedly locked the Door and departed. And now, Reader, if you please we will, in Imitation of the truly laudable Custom of the World, leave these our good Friends to deliver themselves as they can, and pursue the thriving Fortunes of *Wild* our Hero, who with that great Aversion to Satisfaction and Content, which is inseparably incident to GREAT Minds, began to enlarge his Views with his Prosperity:° For this restless amiable Disposition, this noble Avidity which encreases with Feeding,° is the first Principle or constituent Quality of these our GREAT MEN, to whom, in their Passage on to Greatness, it happens as to a Traveller over the *Alps*, or if this be a too far fetched Simile, to one who travels over the Hills near *Bath*, where the Simile was indeed made.° He sees not the End of his Journey at once; but passing on from Scheme to Scheme, and from Hill to Hill, with noble Constancy, resolving still to attain the Summit on which he hath fixed his Eye, however dirty the Roads may be through which he struggles, he at length arrives at—some vile Inn, where he finds no Kind of Entertainment nor Conveniency for Repose. I fancy, Reader, if thou hast ever travelled in these Roads, one Part of my Simile is sufficiently apparent, (and indeed, in all these Illustrations one Side is generally much more apparent than the other) but believe me, if the other doth not so evidently appear to thy Satisfaction, it is from no other Reason than because thou art unacquainted with these GREAT MEN, and hast not had sufficient Instruction, Leisure, or Opportunity to consider what happens to those who pursue what is generally understood by GREATNESS: For surely if thou hadst animadverted not only on the many Perils to which GREAT MEN are daily liable while they are in their Progress, but hadst discerned as it were through a Microscope (for it is invisible to the naked Eye) that diminutive Speck of Happiness which they attain even in the Consummation of their Wishes, thou wouldst lament with me the unhappy Fate of these GREAT GENIUS'S on whom Nature hath set so superior a Mark, that the rest of Mankind are born for their Use and Emolument only, and be apt to cry out, 'It is Pity that THOSE for whose Pleasure and Profit Mankind are to labour and sweat, to be hacked and hewed, to be pillaged, plundered, and every Way destroyed, should reap so LITTLE Advantage from all the Miseries they occasion to others.' For my Part, I own myself of that humble Kind of Mortals who consider themselves born for the Behoof of some GREAT Man or other, and could I behold his Happiness carved out of the Labour and Ruin of a thousand such Reptiles as myself, I might with Satisfaction exclaim, *Sic, sic juvat*:° But when I behold one GREAT MAN starving with Hunger and freezing with Cold in the Midst of fifty thousand, who are suffering the same Evils for his Diversion;° when I see another whose own Mind is a more abject Slave to his own Greatness, and is more tortured and wrecked° by it than those of all his Vassals:° Lastly, when I consider whole Nations extirpated only to bring Tears into the Eyes of a GREAT MAN, that he hath no more Nations to extirpate,° then indeed I am almost inclined to wish that Nature had spared us this her MASTER-PIECE, and that no GREAT MAN had ever been born into the World.°

But to proceed with our History, which will, we hope, produce much better Lessons and more instructive than any we can preach: *Wild* was no sooner retired to a Night-Cellar, than he began to reflect on the Sweets he had that Day enjoyed from the Labours of others, *viz*. First, from Mr. *Bagshot*, who had for his Use robbed the Count; and Secondly, from the Gentleman, who for the same good Purpose had picked the Pocket of *Bagshot*. He then proceeded to reason thus with himself. 'The Art of Policy is the Art of Multiplication; the Degrees of GREATNESS being constituted by those two little Words *More* and *Less*. Mankind are first properly to be considered under two grand Divisions, those that use their Hands, and those who employ Hands. The Former are the Base and Rabble; the latter, the genteel Part of the Creation. The mercantile Part of the World, therefore, wisely use the Term *Employing of Hands*, and justly prefer each other, as they employ more or fewer; for thus one Merchant says he is greater than another, because he employs more Hands. And now indeed the Merchant should seem to challenge some Character of GREATNESS, did we not necessarily come to a second Division, *viz*. Of those who employ Hands for the Use of the Community in which they live, and of those who employ Hands merely for their own Use, without any Regard to the Benefit of Society.° Of the former Sort are the Yeoman, the Manufacturer, the Merchant, and, perhaps, the Gentleman. The first of these being to manure and cultivate his native Soil, and to employ Hands to pro-duce the Fruits of the Earth. The second being to improve them by employing Hands likewise, and to produce from them those useful Commodities, which serve as well for the Conveniencies as Neces-saries of Life. The third is to employ Hands for the Exportation of the Redundance of our own Commodities, and to exchange them with the Redundancies of foreign Nations, that thus every Soil and every Climate may enjoy the Fruits of the whole Earth. The Gentleman is, by employing Hands likewise, to embellish his Country with the Improvement of Arts and Sciences, with the making and executing good and wholesome Laws for the Preservation of Property and the Distribution of Justice, and in several other Manners to be useful to Society. Now we come to the second Part of this Division, *viz.* Of those who employ Hands for their own Use only: And this is that noble and GREAT Part, who are generally distinguished into *Conquerors, absolute Princes, Prime Ministers*, and *Prigs*. Now all these differ from each other in GREATNESS only, as they employ *more* or *fewer* Hands. And *Alexander* the Great was only *greater* than a Captain of one of the *Tartarian* or *Arabian Hords*, as he was at the Head of a larger Number. In what then is a single *Prig* inferior to any other GREAT Man, but because he employs his own Hands only; for he is not on that Account to be levelled with the Base and Vulgar, because he employs his Hands for his own Use only. Now, suppose a *Prig* had as many Tools as any Prime Minister ever had, would he not be as GREAT as any Prime Minister whatsoever? Undoubtedly he would. What then have I to do in the Pursuit of GREATNESS, but to procure a Gang, and to make the Use of this Gang center in myself?° This Gang shall rob for me only, receiving very moderate Rewards for their Actions; out of this Gang I will prefer to my Favour the boldest and most iniquitous (as the Vulgar express it;) the rest I will, from Time to Time, as I see Occasion, transport and hang at my Pleasure; and thus (which I take to be the highest Excellence of a *Prig*) convert those Laws which are made for the Benefit and Protection of Society, to my single Use.'

Having thus pre-conceived his Scheme, he saw nothing wanting to put it in immediate Execution, but that which is indeed the Beginning as well as End of all human Devices: I mean Money. Of which Commodity he was possessed of no more than sixty-five Guineas, being all that remained from the double Benefits he had made of *Bagshot*, and which did not seem sufficient to furnish his House, and every other Convenience necessary for so grand an Undertaking. He resolved therefore to go immediately to the Gaming-House, which was then sitting, not so much with an Intention of trusting to Fortune, as to play the surer Card of attacking the Winner in his Way home. On his Arrival, however, he thought he might as well try his Success at the Dice, and reserve the other Recourse as his last Expedient. He accordingly sat down to play, and as Fortune no more than others of her Sex, is observed to distribute her Favours with strict Regard to great mental Endowments, so our Hero lost every Farthing in his Pocket. He then resolved to have immediate Recourse to his surer Stratagem; and casting his Eyes round the Room, he soon perceived a Gentleman sitting in a disconsolate Posture, who seemed a proper Instrument or Tool for his Purpose. In short (to be as concise as possible in these least shining Parts of our History) he accosted him, sounded him, found him fit to execute, proposed the Matter, received a ready Assent, and having fixed on the Person who seemed that Evening the greatest Favourite of Fortune, they posted themselves in the most proper Place to surprize the Enemy as he was retiring to his Quarters, where he was soon attacked, subdued and plundered, but indeed of no considerable Booty; for it seems this Gentleman played on a common Stock, and had deposited his Winnings at the Scene of Action.°

This was so cruel a Disappointment to *Wild*, and so sensibly affects us, as no doubt it will the Reader; that, as it must disqualify us both from proceeding any farther at present, we will now take a little Breath; and therefore we shall here close this Book.

# BOOK II

## CHAPTER I

*Characters of silly People, with the proper Uses for which such are designed.*

ONE Reason why we chose to end our first Book as we did with the last Chapter, was that we are now obliged to produce two Characters of a Stamp entirely different from what we have hitherto dealt in. These Persons are of that pitiful Order of Mortals, who are in Contempt called *Good-natured*;° being indeed sent into the World by Nature, with the same Design as Men put little Fish into a Pike-Pond, in order to be devoured by that voracious Water-Hero.

But to proceed with our History, *Wild* having shared the Booty in much the same Manner as before, *i.e.* taken three Fourths of it, amounting to eighteen Pence, was now retiring to rest, in no very happy Mood, when by Accident he met a young Fellow, who had formerly been his School-Fellow. This Person had a Regard for our Hero, as he had more than once, for a small Reward, taken a Fault on himself, for which the other, who had more Regard for his Skin than *Wild*, was to have been whipp'd. He therefore accosted *Wild* in the most friendly Manner, and invited him home with him to Breakfast, it being now near Nine in the Morning, which our Hero with no great Difficulty consented to. This young Man, who was about *Wild's* Age, had some Time before set up in the Trade of a *Jeweller*,° in the Materials or Stock for which, he had laid out the greatest Part of a little Fortune, and had married a very agreeable Woman for Love, by whom he then had two Children. As our Reader is to be more acquainted with this Person, it may not be improper to open somewhat of his Character, especially as it will serve as a Kind of Foil to the noble and GREAT Disposition of our Hero,° and as the one seems sent into this World as a proper Object on which the GREAT Talents of the other were to be displayed with a proper and just Success.

Mr. *Thomas Heartfree* then (for that was his Name) was of an honest and open Disposition. He was of that Sort of Men, whom

Experience only, and not their own Natures, must inform that there are such things as Deceit and Hypocrisy in the World;° and who, consequently, are not at five and twenty as difficult to be imposed upon as the oldest and most subtile. He was possessed of several great Weaknesses of Mind; being good-natured, friendly, and generous to a great Excess. He had indeed too little Regard to common Justice, for he had forgiven some Debts to his Acquaintance, only because they could not pay him; and had entrusted a Bankrupt on his setting up a second time, from having been convinced, that he had dealt in his Bankruptcy with a fair and honest Heart, and that it was owing to Misfortune, and not to Neglect or Imposture. He was withal so silly a Fellow that he never took the least Advantage of the Ignorance of his Customers, and contented himself with very moderate Gains on his Goods; which he was the better enabled to do, notwithstanding his Generosity, because his Life was extremely temperate, his Expenses being solely confined to the cheerful Entertainment of his Friends at Home, and now and then a moderate Glass of Wine, in which he indulged himself in the Company of his Wife, who was a mean-spirited, poor, domestic, low-bred Animal, who confined herself mostly to the Care of her Family, placed her Happiness in her Husband and her Children; followed no expensive Fashions or Diversions, and indeed rarely went abroad, unless to return the Visits of a few plain Neighbours, and twice a Year at furthest afforded herself in Company with her Husband the Diversion of a Play, where she never sat in a higher Place than the Pit.°

To this silly Woman did this silly Fellow introduce the GREAT *WILD*, informing her at the same Time of their former Acquaintance, and the Obligations he had received from him; for, as it often happens, that he who confers the Obligation, forgets the Price paid for it, so it sometimes, but very seldom, falls out with him who receives it. This simple Woman no sooner heard her Husband had been obliged to her Guest, than her Eyes sparkled on him with a Benevolence which is an Emanation from the Heart, and of which GREAT and NOBLE MINDS, whose Hearts never swell but with an Injury, can have no very adequate Idea; it is therefore no Wonder that our Hero should misconstrue as he did, the poor, innocent, and simple Affection of Mrs. *Heartfree* towards her Husband's Friend, for that great and generous Passion, which fires the Eyes of a modern Heroine, when the Colonel is so kind as to indulge his City

Creditor with partaking of his Table to Day, and of his Bed to Morrow. *Wild* therefore instantly returned the Compliment, as he understood it, with his Eyes, and presently after bestowed many Encomiums on her Beauty, with which perhaps she, who was a Woman, though a good one, and misapprehended the Design, was not displeased any more than the Husband.

When Breakfast was ended, and the Wife retired to her houshold Affairs, *Wild*, who had a quick Discernment into the Weaknesses of Men, and who, besides the Knowledge of his good (or foolish) Disposition when a Boy, had now discovered several Sparks of Goodness, Friendship, and Generosity in his Friend, began to discourse over the Accidents which had happened in their Childhood, and took frequent Occasions of reminding him of those Favours which we have before mentioned his having conferred on him; he then proceeded to the most vehement Professions of Friendship, and to the most ardent Expressions of Joy in this Renewal of their Acquaintance. He at last told him with great seeming Pleasure, that he believed he had an Opportunity of serving him by the Recommendation of a Gentleman to his Custom, who was then on the Brink of Marriage, 'and, if not already engaged, I will,' says he, 'endeavour to prevail on him to furnish his Lady with Jewels at your Shop.'

*Heartfree* was not backward in Thanks to our Hero, and, after many earnest Solicitations to Dinner, which were refused, they parted for the first Time.

But here, as it occurs to our Memory, that our Readers may be surprized (an Accident which sometimes happens in Histories of this kind) how Mr. *Wild* the elder, in his present Capacity, should have been able to maintain his Son at a reputable School, as this appears to have been, it may be necessary to inform him, that Mr. *Wild* himself was then a Tradesman in good Business; but, by Misfortunes in the World, to wit, Extravagance and Gaming, he had reduced himself to that honourable Occupation which we have formerly mentioned.

Having cleared up this Doubt, we will now pursue our Hero, who forthwith repaired to the Count, and having first settled preliminary Articles concerning Distributions, he acquainted him with the Scheme which he had formed against *Heartfree*; and after consulting proper Methods to put it in Execution, they began to concert

Measures for the Enlargement of the Count; on which the first and indeed only Point to be considered, was to raise Money, not to pay his Debts, for that would have required an immense Sum, and was contrary to his Inclination, or Intention, but to procure him Bail; for as to his Escape, Mr. *Snap* had taken such Precautions that it appeared absolutely impossible.

CHAPTER II

*Great Examples of* GREATNESS *in* Wild, *shewn as well by*
*his Behaviour to* Bagshot, *as in a Scheme laid first to*
*impose on* Heartfree *by Means of the Count, and then to*
*cheat the Count of the Booty.*

*WILD* undertook, therefore, to extract some Money from *Bagshot*, who, notwithstanding the Depredations made on him, had carried off a pretty considerable Booty from their Engagement at Dice the preceding Day. He found Mr. *Bagshot* in Expectation of his Bail, and, with a Countenance full of Concern, which he could at any Time, with wonderful Art, put on, told him, that all was discovered; that the Count knew him, and intended to prosecute him for the Robbery, 'had not I exerted,' said he, 'my utmost Interest, and with great Difficulty prevailed on him in Case you refund the Money—' 'Refund the Money!' cry'd *Bagshot*, 'that is in your Power; for you know what an inconsiderable Part of it fell to my Share.' 'How!' reply'd *Wild*, 'is this your Gratitude to me for saving your Life? For your own Conscience must convince you of your Guilt, and with how much Certainty the Gentleman can give Evidence against you.' ' Marry come up,'° quoth *Bagshot*, 'I believe my Life alone will not be in Danger. I know those who are as guilty as myself. Do you tell me of Conscience?' 'Yes, Sirrah!'° answered our Hero, taking him by the Collar, 'and since you dare threaten me, I will shew you the Difference between committing a Robbery, and conniving at it, which is all I can charge myself with.° I own indeed I suspected when you shewed me a Sum of Money, that you had not come honestly by it.' 'How,' says *Bagshot*, frightened out of one half of his Wits, and amazed out of the other, 'can you deny?' 'Yes, you Rascal,' answered *Wild*, 'I do deny every thing, and do you find a Witness to prove it; and, to shew you how little Apprehension I have of your Power to hurt me, I will have you apprehended this Moment.'—At which Words he offered to break from him; but *Bagshot* laid hold of his Skirts,° and, with an altered Tone and Manner, begged him not to be so impatient. 'Refund then, Sirrah,' cries *Wild*, 'and perhaps I may take pity on you.' 'What must I refund?' answered *Bagshot*. 'Every Farthing in your Pocket,' replied *Wild*; 'then I may have some Compassion on you, and not only save your Life, but, out of an Excess of Generosity, may return you something.' At which Words *Bagshot* seeming to hesitate, *Wild* pretended to make to the Door, and rapt out an Oath of Vengeance with so violent an Emphasis, that his Friend no longer presumed to ballance, but suffered *Wild* to search his Pockets, and draw forth all he found, to the Amount of twenty one Guineas and an half, which last Piece our generous Hero returned him again; telling him, he might now sleep secure, but advised him for the future never to threaten his Friends.

Thus did our Hero execute the greatest Exploits with the utmost Ease imaginable, by Means of those transcendent Qualities which Nature had indulged him with, *viz.* a bold Heart, a thundering Voice, and a steddy Countenance.

*Wild* now returned to the Count, and informed him that he had got ten Guineas of *Bagshot*; for with great and commendable Prudence, he sunk the other eleven in his own Pocket; and told him with that Money he would procure him Bail, which he after prevailed on his Father and another Gentleman of the same Occupation to become° for two Guineas each; so that he made lawful Prize of six more; for such were his great Abilities, and so vast the Compass of his Understanding, that he never made any Bargain without overreaching (or, in the vulgar Phrase, cheating) the Person with whom he dealt.

The Count being, by these Means, enlarged, the first thing they did, in order to procure Credit from Tradesmen, was the taking a handsome House ready furnished in one of the new Streets, in which, as soon as the Count was settled, they proceeded to furnish him with Servants and Equipage, and all the *Insignia* of a large Estate proper to impose on poor *Heartfree*.° These being all obtained, *Wild* made a second Visit to his Friend, and, with much Joy in his Countenance, acquainted him that he had succeeded in his Endeavours, and that the Gentleman had promised to deal with him for the Jewels which he intended to present his Bride, and which were designed to be very splendid and costly; he therefore appointed him to go to the Count the next Morning, and bring with him a Set of the richest and most beautiful Jewels he had, giving him at the same Time some Hints of the Count's Ignorance of that Commodity, and that he might extort what Price of him he pleased; but *Heartfree* told him, not without some Disdain, that he scorned to take any such Advantage; and, after expressing much Gratitude to his Friend for his Recommendation, he promised to carry the Jewels at the Hour, and to the Place appointed.

I am sensible that the Reader, if he hath but the least Notion of GREATNESS, must have such a Contempt for the extreme Folly of this Fellow, that he will be very little concerned at any Misfortunes which befal him in the Sequel; for, to have no Suspicion that an old School-fellow, with whom he had, in his tenderest Years, contracted a Friendship, and who, on the accidental renewing their Acquaintance, had professed the most passionate Regard for him, should be very ready to impose on him; in short, to conceive that a Friend should, of his own Accord, without any View to his own Interest, endeavour to do him a Service; must argue such Weakness of Mind, such Ignorance of the World, and such an artless, simple, undesigning Heart, as must render the Person possessed of it the lowest Creature, and the properest Object of Contempt imaginable, in the Eyes of every Man of Understanding and Discernment.

*Wild* remembered that his Friend *Heartfree's* Faults were rather in his Heart than his Head; that tho' he was an abject mean Fellow, and never capable of laying a Design to injure any human Creature, yet was he by no Means a Fool, nor liable to any gross Imposition, unless where his Heart betrayed him. He therefore instructed the Count to take only one of his Jewels at the first Interview, and to reject the rest as not fine enough, and order him to provide some richer. He said, this Management would prevent *Heartfree* from expecting ready Money for the Jewel he brought with him, which the Count was presently to dispose of, and by Means of that Money, and his great Abilities at Cards and Dice, to get together as large a Sum as possible, which he was to pay down to *Heartfree* at the Delivery of the Set of Jewels, who would be thus void of all manner of Suspicion, and would not fail to give him Credit for the Residue.

By this Contrivance it will appear in the Sequel, that *Wild* did not only propose to make the Imposition on *Heartfree* void of all Suspicion, but to rob the Count himself of this Sum; this double Method of cheating the very Tools who are their Instruments to cheat others, is the superlative Degree of GREATNESS, and is probably, as far as any Spirit crusted over with Clay can carry it, falling very little short of *Dæmonism* itself.

This Method was immediately put in Execution, and the Count, the first Day, took only a single Brilliant, worth about five hundred Pounds, and ordered a Necklace, Ear-rings, and Solitaire of the Value of four thousand Pounds, to be prepared by that Day Sevennight.

This Interval was employed by *Wild* in prosecuting his Scheme of raising a Gang, in which he met with such Success, that within a few Days he had levied several bold and resolute Fellows, fit for any Enterprize, how dangerous or GREAT, *i.e.* villainous soever.

We have before remarked, that the truest Mark of GREATNESS is Insatiability. *Wild* had covenanted with the Count to receive threefourths of the Booty, and had, at the same time, covenanted with himself to secure the other fourth Part likewise, for which he had formed a very GREAT and noble Design; but he now saw with Concern, that Sum, which was to be received in Hand by *Heartfree*, in Danger of being absolutely lost. In order, therefore, to possess himself of that likewise, he contrived, that the Jewels should be brought in the Afternoon, and that *Heartfree* should be detained before the Count could see him; that the Night should overtake him in his Return, when two of his Gang were ordered to attack and plunder him.

### CHAPTER III

*Containing Scenes of Softness, Love, and Honour, all in the* GREAT *Style.*

THE Count had disposed of his Jewel for four hundred Pounds, which he had, by Dexterity, raised to a thousand Pounds; and that Sum he paid down to *Heartfree*, promising him the rest within a Month. His House, his Equipage, his Appearance, but, above all, a certain Plausibility in his Voice and Behaviour would have deceived

any but one whose GREAT and wise Heart had dictated to him something within, which would have secured him from any Danger of
Imposition. *Heartfree* therefore did not in the least scruple giving
him Credit, but as he had, in Reality, procured those Jewels of
another, his own little Stock not being able to furnish any thing so
valuable, he begged the Count would be so kind to give his Note° for
the Money, payable at the time he mentioned, which that Gentleman
did not in the least scruple; so he paid him the thousand Pound in
*Specie*, and gave his Note for four thousand five hundred Pounds
more to *Heartfree*,° who burnt with Gratitude to *Wild*, for the noble
Customer he had recommended to him.

As soon as *Heartfree* was departed, *Wild*, who waited in another
Room, came in, and received the Casket from the Count, it having
been agreed between them, that it should be deposited in his Hands,
as he was the original Contriver of the Scheme, and was to have
the largest Share. *Wild* having received the Casket, offered to meet
the Count late that Evening to come to a Division; but such was the
latter's Confidence in the Honour of our Hero, that, he said, if it was
any Inconvenience to him, the next Morning would do altogether as
well. This was more agreeable to *Wild*, and accordingly an Appointment being made for that purpose, he set out in haste to pursue
*Heartfree* to the Place where the two Gentlemen were ordered to
meet and attack him. Those Gentlemen, with noble Resolution, executed their Purpose; they attacked and spoiled the Enemy of the
whole Sum he had received from the Count.

As soon as the Engagement was over and *Heartfree* left sprawling
on the Ground, our Hero, who wisely declined trusting the Booty in
his Friends Hands, tho' he had good Experience of their Honour,
made off after the Conquerors; at length they being all at a Place of
Safety, *Wild*, according to a previous Agreement, received nine
tenths of the Booty; the subordinate Heroes did indeed profess some
little Unwillingness (perhaps more than was strictly consistent with
Honour) to perform their Contract; but *Wild*, partly by Argument,
but more by Oaths and Threatnings, prevailed with them to fulfil
their Promise.

Our Hero having thus with wonderful Address brought this
GREAT and glorious Action to a happy Conclusion, resolved to
relax his Mind after his Fatigue, in the Conversation of the Fair.
He therefore set forwards to his lovely *Lætitia;* but in his Way,

accidentally met with a young Lady of his Acquaintance, Miss *Molly Straddle*,° who was taking the Air in *Bridges-Street*.° Miss *Molly* seeing Mr. *Wild*, stopp'd him, and with a Familiarity peculiar to a genteel Town Education, tapp'd or rather slapp'd him on the Back, and asked him to treat her with a Pint of Wine, at a neighbouring Tavern. The Hero, tho' he loved the chaste *Lætitia* with excessive Tenderness, was not of that low sniveling Breed of Mortals who, as it is generally expressed, *tie themselves to a Woman's Apron-Strings*; in a Word, who are tainted with that mean, base, low Vice, of Constancy; he therefore immediately consented, and attended her to a Tavern famous for excellent Wine, known by the Name of the *Rummer* and *Horshoe*,° where they retired to a Room by themselves. *Wild* was very vehement in his Addresses, but to no Purpose; the young Lady declared she would grant no Favour till he had made her a Present; this was immediately complied with, and the Lover made as happy as he could desire.

The immoderate Fondness which *Wild* entertained for his dear *Lætitia*, would not suffer him to waste any considerable Time with Miss *Straddle*. Notwithstanding, therefore, all the Endearments and Caresses of that young Lady, he soon made an Excuse to go down Stairs, and thence immediately set forward to *Lætitia*, without taking any formal Leave of Miss *Straddle*, or indeed of the Drawer, with whom the Lady was afterwards obliged to come to an Account for the Reckoning.

Mr. *Wild*, on his Arrival at Mr. *Snap's*, found only Miss *Doshy* at home; that young Lady being employed alone, in Imitation of *Penelope*, with her Thread or Worsted; only with this Difference, that whereas *Penelope* unravelled by Night what she had knit, or wove, or spun by Day, so what our young Heroine unravelled by Day, she knit again by Night.° In short, she was mending a Pair of blue Stockings with red Clocks;° a Circumstance which, perhaps, we might have omitted, had it not served to shew that there are still some Ladies of this Age, who imitate the Simplicity of the Ancients.

*Wild* immediately asked for his Beloved, and was informed, that she was not at Home. He then enquired, where she was to be found, and declared, he would not depart till he had seen her; nay, not till he had married her; for, indeed, his Passion for her was truly honourable, in other Words, he had so ungovernable a Desire for her Person, that he would go any Lengths to satisfy it. He then pulled out the Casket, which he swore was full of the finest Jewels, and that he would give them all to her, with other Promises; which so prevailed on Miss *Doshy*, who had not the common Failure of Sisters in envying, and often endeavouring to disappoint each other's Happiness; that she desired Mr. *Wild* to sit down a few Minutes, whilst she endeavoured to find her Sister, and to bring her to him. The Lover thanked her, and promised to stay till her Return; and Miss *Doshy*, leaving Mr. *Wild* to his Meditations, fastened him in the Kitchen by barring the Door (for most of the Doors in this Mansion were made to be bolted on the outside) and then slapping to the Door of the House with great Violence, without going out at it, she stole softly up Stairs, where Miss *Lætitia* was engaged in close Conference with Mr. *Bagshot*. Miss *Letty*, being informed by her Sister in a Whisper of what Mr. *Wild* had said, and what he had produced, told Mr. *Bagshot*, that a young Lady was below to visit her, whom she would dispatch with all imaginable Haste, and return to him. She desired him therefore to stay with Patience for her in the mean Time, and that she would leave the Door unlocked, tho' her Papa would never forgive her if he should discover it. *Bagshot* promised on his Honour, not to step without his Chamber; and the two young Ladies went softly down Stairs; when pretending first to make their Entry into the House, they repaired to the Kitchen, where not even the Presence of the chaste *Lætitia* could restore that Harmony to the Countenance of her Lover, which Miss *Theodosia* had left him possessed of; for during her Absence he had discovered the Absence of that Purse which had been taken from Mr. *Heartfree*, and which, indeed, Miss *Straddle* had in the Warmth of his amorous Caresses, unperceived, drawn from him. However, as he had that perfect Mastery of his Temper, or rather of his Muscles, which is as necessary to form a GREAT Character as to personate it on the Stage,° he soon conveyed a Smile into his Countenance, and concealing as well his Misfortune as his Chagrin at it, began to pay honourable Addresses to Miss *Letty*. This young Lady, amongst many other good Ingredients, had three very predominant Passions,° to wit, Vanity, Wantonness, and Avarice. To satisfy the first of these, she applied° Mr. *Smirk* and Comp.,° to the second, Mr. *Bagshot* and Comp., and our Hero had the Honour and Happiness of solely engrossing the third. Now, these three Sorts of Lovers she had very different Ways of entertaining. With the first, she was all gay and coquette;° with the second, all fond and rampant; and with the last, all cold and reserved. She, therefore, told Mr. *Wild*, with a most composed Aspect, that she was glad he had repented of his Manner of treating her at their last Interview, where his Behaviour was so monstrous, that she had resolved never to see him any more; that she was afraid her own Sex would hardly pardon her the Weakness she was guilty of in receding from that Resolution, which she was persuaded she never should have prevailed with herself to do, had not her Sister, who was there to confirm what she said, (as she did with many Oaths) betrayed her into his Company, by pretending it was another Person to visit her: But however, as he now thought proper to give her more convincing Proofs of his Affection (for he had now the Casket in his Hand) and since she perceived his Designs were no longer against her Virtue, but were such as a Woman of Honour might listen to, she must own—and then she feign'd an Hesitation, when *Theodosia* began. 'Nay, Sister, I am resolved you shall counterfeit no longer. I assure you, Mr. *Wild*, she hath the most violent Passion for you in the World; and if you offer to go back, since I plainly see Mr. *Wild's* Designs are honourable, I will betray all you have ever said.' 'How, Sister, (answered *Lætitia*) I protest you will drive me out of the Room: I did not expect this Usage from you.' *Wild* then fell on his Knees, and taking hold of her Hand, repeated a Speech which, as the Reader may easily suggest it to himself, I shall not here minutely set down. He then offered her the Casket, but she gently rejected it; and on a second Offer, with a modest Countenance and Voice, desired to know what it contained. *Wild* then open'd it, and took forth (with Sorrow I write it, and with Sorrow will it be read) one of those beautiful Necklaces, with which at the Fair of *Bartholomew*, they deck the well whitened Neck of *Thalestris* Queen of the *Amazons*, *Anna Bullen*, Queen *Elizabeth*, or some other High Princess in *Drollic* Story.° It was indeed composed of that Paste, which *Derdæus Magnus*,° an ingenious Toyman, doth at a very moderate Price dispose of to the second Rate Beaus of the Metropolis. For, to open a Truth, which we ask our Reader's Pardon for having concealed from him so long; the sagacious Count, wisely fearing, lest some Accident might prevent Mr. *Wild's* Return at the appointed Time, had carefully conveyed the Jewels which Mr. *Heartfree* had brought with him, into his own Pocket; and in their Stead had placed in the Casket these artificial Stones, which, tho' of equal Value to a Philosopher, and perhaps of a much greater to a true Admirer of the Compositions of Art, had not however the same Charms in the Eyes of Miss *Letty*; who had indeed some Knowledge of Jewels: For Mr. *Snap*, with great Reason considering how valuable a Part of a young Lady's Education it would be to have his Daughter instructed in these Things, in an Age when young Ladies learn little more than how to dress themselves, had in her youth, placed Miss *Letty* as the Hand-maid (or House-maid, as the Vulgar call it) of an eminent Pawn-broker. The Lightning, therefore, which should have flashed from the Jewels, flashed from her Eyes, and Thunder immediately followed from her Voice. She be-knaved, be-rascalled, be-rogued the unhappy Hero, who stood silent, confounded with Astonishment, but more with Shame and Indignation, at being thus outwitted and over-reached. At length, he recovered his Spirits, and throwing down the Casket in a Rage, he snatched the Key from the Table; and without making any Answer to the Ladies, who both very plentifully open'd upon him, or taking any leave of them, he flew out at the Door, and repaired with the utmost Expedition to the Count's Habitation.

## CHAPTER IV

*In which* Wild, *after many fruitless Endeavours to discover his Friend, moralizes on his Misfortune in a Speech, which may be of Use (if rightly understood) to some other considerable Speech-Makers.*

Not the highest-fed Footman of the highest-bred Woman of Quality knocks with more Impetuosity, than *Wild* did at the Count's Door, which was immediately opened by a well-drest Livery Man, who answered, his Master was not at Home. *Wild*, not satisfied with this, searched the House, but to no purpose; he then ransacked all the Gaming-Houses in Town, but found no Count: Indeed that Gentleman had taken Leave of his House the same Instant Mr. *Wild* had turned his Back, and, equipping himself with Boots and a Post-horse, without taking with him either Servant, Clothes, or any Necessaries, for the Journey of a great Man, made such mighty

Expedition that he was now upwards of twenty Miles on his Way to *Harwich*.°

*Wild*, finding his Search ineffectual, resolved to give it over for that Night; he then retired to his Seat of Contemplation, a Night-Cellar, where, without a single Farthing in his Pocket, he called for a Sneaker of Punch, and, placing himself on a Bench by himself, he softly vented the following Soliloquy:

'How vain is human GREATNESS!° What avail superiour Abilities, and a noble Defiance of those narrow Rules and Bounds which confine the Vulgar; when our best concerted Schemes are liable to be defeated! How unhappy is the State of PRIGGISM! How impossible for human Prudence to foresee and guard against every Circumvention! It is even as a Game of *Chess*, where, while the Rook, or Knight, or Bishop, is busied in forecasting some great Enterprize, a worthless Pawn interposes, and disconcerts his Scheme. Better had it been for me to have observed the simple Laws of Friendship and Morality, than thus to ruin my Friend for the Benefit of others. I might have commanded his Purse to any degree of Moderation, I have now disabled him from the Power of serving me. Well! but that was not my Design. If I cannot arraign my own Conduct, why should I, like a Woman or a Child, sit down and lament the Disappointment of Chance! But can I acquit myself of all Neglect? Did I not misbehave in putting it into the Power of others to outwit me? But this is impossible to be avoided. In this a *Prig* is more unhappy than any other: A cautious Man may, in a Crowd, preserve his own Pockets by keeping his Hands in them; but while he employs his Hands in another's Pocket, how shall he be able to defend his own? Indeed in this Light what can be imagined more miserable than a *Prig*? How dangerous are his Acquisitions! how unsafe, how unquiet his Possessions! Why then should any Man wish to be a *Prig*, or where is his GREATNESS? I answer, in his Mind: 'Tis the inward Glory, the secret Consciousness of doing great and wonderful Actions, which can alone support the truly GREAT Man, whether he be a CONQUEROR, a TYRANT, a MINISTER, or a PRIG. These must bear him up against the private Curse and public Imprecation, and while he is hated and detested by all Mankind, must make him inwardly satisfied with himself. For what but some such inward Satisfaction as this could inspire Men possessed of Wealth, of Power, of every human Blessing, which Pride, Avarice, or Luxury could desire, to forsake their

Homes, abandon Ease and Repose, and, at the Expence of Riches, Pleasures, at the Price of Labour and Hardship, and at the Hazard of all that Fortune hath liberally given them, could send them at the Head of a Multitude of *Prigs*, called an Army, to molest their Neighbours; to introduce Rape, Rapine, Bloodshed, and every kind of Misery on their own Species? What but some such glorious Appetite of Mind could inflame Princes, endowed with the greatest Honours, and enriched with the most plentiful Revenues, to desire maliciously to rob those Subjects, who are content to sweat for their Luxury, and to bow down their Knees to their Pride, of their Liberties, and to reduce them to an absolute Dependence on their own Wills, and those of their brutal Successors! What other Motive could seduce a Subject, possest of great Property in his Community, to betray the Interest of his Fellow-Subjects, of his Brethren, and his Posterity, to the wanton Disposition of such Princes! Lastly, what less Inducement could persuade the *Prig* to forsake the Methods of acquiring a safe, an honest, and a plentiful Livelihood, and, at the Hazard of even Life itself and what is mistakenly called Dishonour, to break openly and bravely through the Laws of his Country, for uncertain, unsteddy, and unsafe Gain! Let me then hold myself contented with this Reflection, that I have been wise, though unsuccessful, and am a GREAT, though an unhappy Man.'

His Soliloquy and his Punch concluded together; for he had at every Pause comforted himself with a Sip. And now it came first into his Head, that it would be more difficult to pay for it, than it was to swallow it, when, to his great Pleasure, he beheld, at another Corner of the Room, one of the Gentlemen whom he had employed in the Attack on *Heartfree*, and who, he doubted not, would readily lend him a Guinea or two; but he had the Mortification, on applying to him, to hear that the Gaming-Table had stript him of all the Booty which his own Generosity had left in his Possession. He was therefore obliged to pursue his usual Method on such Occasions; so, cocking his Hat fiercely, he marched out of the Room without making any Excuse, or any one daring to make the least Demand.

## CHAPTER V

*Containing many surprizing Adventures, which our Hero, with*
GREAT GREATNESS, *atchieved.*

WE will now leave our Hero to take a short Repose, and return to
Mr. *Snap's*, where, at Wild's Departure, the fair *Theodosia* had again
betaken herself to her Stocking, and Miss *Letty* had retired up Stairs
to Mr. *Bagshot;* but that Gentleman had broken his Parole, and,
having conveyed himself below Stairs behind a Door, he took the
Opportunity of *Wild's* Sally to make his Escape. We shall only
observe, that Miss *Letty's* Surprize was the greater, as she had, notwithstanding her Promise to the contrary, taken the Precaution to
turn the Key; but, in her Hurry, she did it ineffectually. How
wretched must have been the Situation of this young Creature, who
had not only lost a Lover, on whom she perfectly doated, but was
exposed to the Rage of an injured Father, tenderly jealous of his
Honour, which was deeply engaged to the Sheriff of *London* and
*Middlesex*, for the safe Custody of the said *Bagshot*, and for which
two very good responsible Friends had given not only their Words
but their Bonds.

But let us remove our Eyes from this melancholy Object, and
survey our Hero, who, after a successless Search for Miss *Straddle*,
with wonderful GREATNESS of Mind, and Steddiness of Countenance, went early in the Morning to visit his Friend *Heartfree*, at a
Time when the common Herd of Friends would have forsaken and
avoided him. He entered the Room with a chearful Air, which he
presently changed into Surprize on seeing his Friend in a Night-
Gown, with his wounded Head bound about with Linen, and looking extremely pale from a great Profusion of Blood. When *Wild* was
informed by *Heartfree* what had happened, he first expressed great
Sorrow, and afterwards suffered as violent Agonies of Rage against
the Robbers to burst from him. This latter, in Compassion to the
deep Impressions his Misfortune seemed to make on his Friend,
endeavoured to lessen it as much as possible, at the same Time
exaggerating the Obligation he owed to *Wild*, in which his Wife
likewise seconded him; and they breakfasted with more Comfort
than was reasonably to be expected after such an Accident. *Heartfree*
expressing great Satisfaction that he had put the four thousand

Pound Note° in another Pocket-Book, adding, that such a Loss would have been fatal to him; 'for, to confess the Truth to you, my dear Friend,' said he, 'I have had some Losses lately, which have greatly perplexed my Affairs, and though I have many Debts due to me from People of great Fashion, I assure you I know not where to be certain of getting a Shilling.' *Wild* greatly felicitated him on the lucky Accident of preserving his Note, and then proceeded, with much Acrimony, to inveigh against the Barbarity of People of Fashion, who kept Tradesmen out of their Money.

While they amused themselves with Discourses of this kind, *Wild*, meditating within himself whether he should borrow or steal from his Friend, or indeed whether he could not effect both, the Apprentice brought a Bank-Note in to *Heartfree*, which, he said, a Gentlewoman in the Shop, who had been looking at some Jewels, desired him to exchange. *Heartfree* looking at the Back of it, immediately perceived the Count's Endorsement, and presently recollected it to be one of those he had been robbed of. With this Discovery he acquainted *Wild*, who, with the notable Presence of Mind, and unchanged Complexion, so essential to a GREAT Character, advised him to proceed cautiously; and offered (as Mr. *Heartfree* himself was, he said, too much flustered to examine the Woman with sufficient Art) to take her into a Room in his House alone. He would, he said, personate the Master of the Shop, would pretend to shew her some Jewels, and would undertake to get sufficient Information out of her to secure the Rogues, and most probably all their Booty. This Proposal was readily and thankfully accepted by *Heartfree*. *Wild* went immediately up Stairs into the Room appointed, whither the Apprentice, according to Appointment, conducted the Lady.

The Apprentice was ordered down Stairs the Moment the Lady entered the Room; and *Wild*, having shut the Door, approached her with great Ferocity in his Looks, and began to expatiate on the complicated Baseness of the Crime she had been guilty of; but though he uttered many good Lessons of Morality, as we doubt whether from a particular Reason they may work any very good Effect on our Reader, we shall omit his Speech, and only mention his Conclusion, which was by asking her, what Mercy she could now expect from him? The young Lady, who had had a good Education, and had been more than once present at the *Old Baily*,° very confidently denied the whole Charge, and said, she had receiv'd the

Note from a Friend. *Wild* then, raising his Voice, told her, she should
be immediately committed, and she might depend on being convicted; 'but,' added he, changing his Tone, 'as I have a violent Affection for thee, my dear *Straddle*, if you will follow my Advice, I
promise you on my Honour, to forgive you, nor shall you be ever
called in Question on this Account.' 'Why, what would you have me
to do, Mr. *Wild?*' replied the young Lady, with a pleasanter Aspect.
'You must know then,' said *Wild*, 'the Money you picked out of my
Pocket (nay, by G——d you did, and if you offer to flinch,° you shall
be convicted of it) I won at Play of a Fellow who, it seems, robbed my
Friend of it; you must, therefore, give an Information on Oath°
against one *Thomas Fierce*, and say, that you received the Note from
him, and leave the rest to me. I am certain, *Molly*, you must be
sensible of your Obligations to me, who return Good for Evil to you
in this manner.' The Lady readily consented; and Mr. *Wild* and she
embraced and kissed each other in a very tender and passionate
Manner.

*Wild*, having given the Lady a little further Instruction, desired
her to stay a few Minutes behind him; then returned to his Friend,
and acquainted him that he had discovered the whole Roguery, that
the Woman had confessed from whom she had received the Note,
and had promised to give an Information before a Justice of Peace;
adding, he was concerned he could not attend him thither, being
obliged to go to the other End of the Town to receive thirty Pounds,
which he was to pay that Evening. *Heartfree* said that should not
prevent him of his Company,° for he could easily lend him such a
Trifle: Which was accordingly done and accepted, and *Wild*, *Heartfree*, and the Lady went to the Justice together.

The Warrant being granted, and the Constable being acquainted
by the Lady, who received her Information from *Wild*, of Mr.
*Fierce's* Haunts, he was easily apprehended, and, being confronted
with Miss *Straddle*, who swore positively to him, though she
had never seen him before; he was committed to *Newgate*, where
he immediately conveyed an Information to *Wild* of what had
happened, and in the Evening received a Visit from him.

*Wild* affected great Concern for his Friend's Misfortune, and as
great Surprize at the Means by which it was brought about. However, he said, he must certainly be mistaken in that Point, of his
having had no Acquaintance with her; that, as for the Note, he had

himself paid it away to a Shopkeeper, and would endeavour, by all
safe Means, to enquire into the Secrets of the Matter; that he
would find out Miss *Straddle*, and endeavour to take off her Evidence; which, he observed, did not come home enough to endanger
him; besides he would secure him Witnesses of an *Alibi*, and five or
six to his Character;° so that he need be under no Apprehension,
for his Confinement till the Sessions would be his only
Punishment.

*Fierce*, who was greatly comforted by these Assurances of his
Friend, returned him many Thanks, and both shaking each other
very earnestly by the Hand, with a very hearty Embrace they
separated.

The Hero considered with himself, that the single Evidence of
Miss *Straddle* would not be sufficient to convict *Fierce*, whom he
resolved to hang, as he was the Person who had principally refused to
deliver him the stipulated Share of the Booty; he therefore went in
Quest of Mr. *James Sly*, the Gentleman who had assisted in the
Exploit; and found, and acquainted him with the apprehending of
*Fierce*. *Wild* then intimating his Fear, lest *Fierce* should impeach *Sly*,
advised him to be beforehand, and go directly to a Justice of Peace,
and offer himself as an Evidence.° *Sly* approved Mr. *Wild's* Opinion,
went directly to a Magistrate, and was by him committed to the
*Gate-house*,° with a Promise of being admitted Evidence against his
Companion.

*Fierce* was, in a few Days, brought to his Trial at the *Old Baily*,
when, to his great Confusion, his old Friend *Sly* appeared against
him, as did Miss *Straddle*. His only Hopes were now in the Assistance which our Hero had promised him. These unhappily failed
him: So that the Evidence being plain against him, and he making no
Defence, the Jury convicted him, the Court condemned him, and
Mr. *Ketch*° executed him.

With such infinite Address, did this truly GREAT MAN know to
play with the Passions of Men, and to set them at Variance with each
other, and to work his own Purposes out of those Jealousies and
Apprehensions, which he was wonderfully ready at creating, by
Means of those great Arts, which the Vulgar call Treachery, Dis-
sembling, Promising, Lying, Falshood, &c. but which are by GREAT
MEN summed up in the collective Name of Policy, or Politicks, or
rather *Pollitricks*;° an Art of which, as it is the highest Excellence of

Human Nature, so perhaps, was our GREAT MAN the most eminent
Master.

## CHAPTER VI

### Of Hats.°

HE had now got together a very considerable Gang, composed of
undone Gamesters, ruined Bailiffs, broken Tradesmen, idle Apprentices, and loose and disorderly Youth, who being born to no Fortune,
nor bred to no Trade or Profession, were willing to live luxuriously
without Labour. As these Persons wore different *Principles*, i.e. *Hats*,
frequent Dissentions grew among them. There were particularly two
Parties, *viz.* those who wore Hats *fiercely* cocked, and those who
preferr'd the *Nab* or Trencher Hat, with the Brim flapping over their
Eyes; between which, Jars and Animosities almost perpetually arose.
*Wild*, therefore, having assembled them all at an Alehouse on the
Night after *Fierce's* Execution, and perceiving evident Marks of their
Misunderstanding,° from their Behaviour to each other, addressed
them in the following gentle, but forcible Manner\*.° 'Gentlemen, I am
ashamed to see Men embarked in so GREAT and glorious an Undertaking, as that of robbing the Publick, so foolishly and weakly dis-
senting among themselves. Do you think the first Inventors of Hats,
or at least of those Distinctions between them, really conceived that

---

\* There is something very mysterious in this Speech,° which probably that Chapter
written by *Aristotle* on this Subject, which is mentioned by a *French* Author, might have
given some Light into; but that is unhappily among the lost Works of that Philosopher.° It
is remarkable, that *Galerus* which is *Latin* for a *Hat*, signifies likewise a Dog-fish,° as the
*Greek* Word Κυνέη doth the Skin of that Animal, of which I suppose the Hats or
Helmets of the Ancients were composed, as ours at present are of the Beaver or Rabbit.
*Sophocles* in the latter End of his *Ajax*, alludes to a Method of cheating in Hats, and the
Scholiast on the Place tells us of one *Cresphontes*, who was a Master of the Art.° It is
observable likewise, that *Achilles*, in the first *Iliad* of *Homer*, tells *Agamemnon*, in Anger,
that he had Dog's Eyes.° Now, as the Eyes of a Dog are handsomer than those of almost
any other Animal; this could be no Term of Reproach. He must therefore mean, that he
had a Hat on, which, perhaps, from the Creature it was made of, or from some other
Reason, might have been a Mark of Infamy. This superstitious Opinion may account for
that Custom, which hath descended through all Nations, of shewing Respect by pulling
off this Covering; and that no Man is esteemed fit to converse with his Superiors with it
on. I shall conclude this learned Note with remarking, that the Term *Old Hat*,° is at
present used by the Vulgar, in no very honourable Sense.

one Form of Hats should inspire a Man with Divinity, another with Law, another with Learning, or another with Bravery? No, they meant no more by these outward Signs, than to impose on the Vulgar, and instead of putting GREAT MEN to the Trouble of acquiring or maintaining the Substance, to make it sufficient that they condescend to wear the Type or Shadow of it. You do wisely, therefore, when in a Crowd, to amuse the Mob by Quarrels on such Accounts, that while they are listening to your Jargon, you may with the greater Ease and Safety, pick their Pockets: But surely to be in earnest, and privately to keep up such a ridiculous Contention among yourselves, must argue the highest Folly and Absurdity. When you know you are all *Prigs*, what Difference can a broad or a narrow Brim create? Is a *Prig* less a *Prig* in one Hat than in another? If the Public should be weak enough to interest themselves in your Quarrels, and to prefer one Pack to the other, while both are aiming at their Purses; it is your Business to laugh at, not imitate their Folly. What can be more ridiculous than for Gentlemen to quarrel about Hats, when there is not one among you, whose Hat is worth a Farthing? What is the Use of a Hat, further than to keep the Head warm, or to hide a bald Crown from the Public? It is the Mark of a Gentleman to move° his Hat on every Occasion; and in Courts and noble Assemblies, no man ever wears one. Let me hear no more therefore of this Childish Disagreement, but all toss up your Hats together with one Accord, and consider that Hat as the best, which will contain the largest Booty.' He thus ended his Speech, which was followed by a murmuring Applause, and immediately all present tossed their Hats together, as he had commanded them.

### CHAPTER VII

*Shewing the Consequences which attended* Heartfree's *Adventures with* Wild; *all natural, and common enough to little Wretches who deal with* GREAT MEN; *together with some Precedents of Letters, being the different Methods of answering a Dun.*

LET us now return to *Heartfree*, to whom the Note of four thousand five hundred Pound which he had paid away, was returned, with an Account that the Drawer was not to be found, and that on enquiring after him, they had heard he was run away, and consequently the Money was now demanded of the Endorser.° The Apprehension of such a Loss would have affected any Man of Business, but much more one whose unavoidable Ruin it must prove. He expressed so much Concern and Confusion on this Occasion, that the Proprietor° of the Note was frightned, and resolved to lose no Time in securing what he could. So that in the Afternoon of the same Day, Mr. *Snap* was commissioned to pay *Heartfree* a Visit, which he did with his usual Formality, and conveyed him to his own House.

Mrs. *Heartfree* was no sooner informed of what had happened to her Husband, than she raved like one distracted; but after she had vented the first Agonies of her Passion in Tears and Lamentations, she applied herself to all possible Means to procure her Husband's Liberty. She hastened to beg her Neighbours to secure Bail for him. But as the News had arrived at their Houses before her, she found none of them at home, except an honest *Quaker*, whose Servants durst not tell a Lie. However, she succeeded no better with him, for unluckily he had made an Affirmation the Day before, that he would never be Bail for any Man.° After many fruitless Efforts of this Kind, she repaired to her Husband to comfort him, at least with her Presence. She found him sealing the last of several Letters, which he had dispatched to his Friends and Creditors. The Moment he saw her, a sudden Joy sparkled in his Eyes, which, however, had a very short Duration; for Despair soon clouded them again; nor could he help bursting into some passionate Expressions of Concern for her and their little Family; which she, on her Part, did her utmost to lessen, by endeavouring to mitigate the Loss, and raise in him Hopes from the Count, who might, she said, be possibly, only gone into the Country. She comforted him likewise, with the Expectation of Favour from his Acquaintance, especially those whom he had in a particular Manner obliged and served. Lastly, she conjured him, by all the Value and Esteem he professed for her, not to endanger his Health, on which alone depended her Happiness, by too great an Indulgence of Grief; assuring him that no State of Life could appear unhappy to her with him, unless his own Sorrow or Discontent made it so.

In this manner did this weak, poor-spirited Woman attempt to relieve her Husband's Pains, which it would have rather become her to aggravate, by not only painting out his Misery in the liveliest

Colours imaginable, but by upbraiding him with that Folly and Confidence which had occasioned it, and by lamenting her own hard Fate, in being obliged to share his Sufferings.

*Heartfree* returned this Goodness (as it is called) of his Wife, with the warmest Gratitude, and they past an Hour in a Scene of Tenderness, too low and contemptible to be recounted to our GREAT Readers. We shall therefore omit all such Relations, as they tend only to make human Nature low and ridiculous.

Those Messengers who had obtained any Answers to his Letters now returned. We shall here copy a few of them, as they may serve for Precedents to others who have an Occasion, which happens commonly enough in genteel Life, to answer the Impertinence of a Dun.

### LETTER I

MR. HEARTFREE,

My Lord commands me to tell you, he is very much surprized at your Assurance in asking for Money, which you know hath been so little while due; however, as he intends to deal no longer at your Shop, he hath ordered me to pay you as soon as I shall have Cash in Hand, which, considering many Disbursements for Bills long due, &c. can't possibly promise any Time, &c. at present. And am

> your humble Servant,
> ROGER MORECRAFT.

### LETTER II

DEAR SIR,

The Money, as you truly say, hath been three Years due, but upon my Soul I am at present incapable of paying a Farthing; but as I doubt not, very shortly, not only to content° that small Bill, but likewise to lay out very considerable further Sums at your House, hope you will meet with no Inconvenience by this short Delay in, dear Sir,

> Your most sincere
> humble Servant
> CHA. COURTLY.

### LETTER III

MR. HEARTFREE,

I beg you would not acquaint my Husband of the trifling Debt between us; for as I know you to be a very good-natured Man, I will

trust you with a Secret; he gave me the Money long since, to discharge it, which I had the ill Luck to lose at play. You may be assured
I will satisfy you the first Opportunity, and am, Sir,

Your very humble Servant
CATH. RUBBERS.°

Please to present my Service to Mrs. *Heartfree*.

### LETTER IV

MR. THOMAS HEARTFREE, SIR,
Your's received; but as to Sum mentioned therein, doth not suit at
present

Your humble Servant
PETER POUNCE.°

### LETTER V

SIR,
I am sincerely sorry it doth not at present suit me to comply with
your Request, especially after so many Obligations received on my
Side, of which I shall always entertain the most grateful Memory. I
am very greatly concerned at your Misfortunes, and would have
waited upon you in Person, but am not at present very well, and
besides, am obliged to go this Evening to *Vaux-hall*.° I am, Sir,

Your most obliged humble Servant
CHA. EASY.°

There were more Letters to much the same Purpose; but we proposed giving our Reader a Taste only. Of all these, the last was
infinitely the most grating to poor *Heartfree*, as it came from one to
whom, when in Distress, he had himself lent a considerable Sum,
and of whose present flourishing Circumstances he was well assured.

### CHAPTER VIII

*In which our Hero carries* GREATNESS *to an immoderate Height*.

LET us remove, therefore, as fast as we can this detestable Picture of
Ingratitude, and present the much more agreeable Portrait of that
Assurance to which the *French* very properly annex the Epithet of

*Good.*° *Heartfree* had scarce done reading his Letters, when our Hero appeared before his Eyes, not with that Aspect with which a pitiful Parson meets his Patron, after having opposed him at an Election,° or which a Doctor wears, when sneaking away from a Door, where he is informed of his Patient's Death; not with that down-cast Countenance which betrays the Man, who, after a strong Conflict between Virtue and Vice, hath surrendered his Mind to the latter, and is discovered in his first Treachery; but with that noble, bold, GREAT Confidence with which a Prime Minister assures his Dependent, that the Place he promised him was disposed of before.° And such Concern and Uneasiness as he expresses in his Looks on those Occasions did *Wild* testify on the first Meeting of his Friend. And as the said Prime Minister chides you for Neglect of your Interest, in not having asked in Time, so did our Hero attack *Heartfree* for his giving Credit to the Count, and, without suffering him to answer a Word, proceeded in a Torrent of Words to overwhelm him with Abuse; which, however friendly its Intention might be, was scarce to be outdone by an Enemy. By these Means *Heartfree*, who might perhaps otherwise have vented some little Concern for that Recommendation which *Wild* had given him to the Count, was totally prevented from any such Endeavour, and, like an invading Prince, when attacked in his own Dominions, forced to recall his whole Strength to defend himself at home. This indeed he did so well by insisting on the Figure and outward Appearance of the Count and his Equipage, that *Wild* at length grew a little more gentle, confessing that he had the least Reason of all Mankind to censure another for an Imprudence of this Nature, as he was himself the most easily to be imposed upon, and indeed had been so by this Count, who, if he was insolvent, had, he said, cheated him of five hundred Pounds. 'But, for my own Part,' said he, 'I will not yet despair, nor would I have you. Many Men have found it convenient to retire, or abscond for a while, and afterwards have paid their Debts, or at least handsomely compounded them. This I am certain of, should a Composition° take place, which is the worst can be apprehended, I shall be the only Loser; for I shall think myself obliged in Honour to repair your Loss, even though you must confess it was principally owing to your own Folly. Z——ds!° had I imagined it necessary, I would have cautioned you; but I thought the Part of the Town where he lived, sufficient Caution not to trust

*goodness as an adherence to character under all crimes*

him.—And such a Sum—The Devil must have been in you
certainly!'

Mrs. *Heartfree*, who had before vented the most violent Execrations on *Wild*, was now thoroughly satisfied of his Innocence, and
begged him not to insist any longer on what he perceived so deeply
affected her Husband. She said, Trade could not be carried on without Credit, and surely he was sufficiently justified in giving it to such
a Person as the Count appeared to be. Besides, she said, Reflections
on what was past and irretrievable would be of little Service; that
their present Business was to consider how to prevent the evil Consequences which threatened, and first to endeavour to procure her
Husband his Liberty. 'Why doth he not procure Bail?' said *Wild*.
'Alas! Sir,' said she, 'we have applied to many of our Acquaintance in
vain; we have met with Excuses even where we could least expect
them.' 'Not Bail!' answered *Wild*, in a Passion, 'he shall have Bail, if
there is any in the World. It is now very late, but trust me to procure
him Bail to Morrow Morning.'

Mrs. *Heartfree* received these Professions with Tears, and told
*Wild* he was a Friend indeed. She then proposed to stay that Evening
with her Husband; but he would not permit her, on account of his
little Family,° whom he would not agree to trust to the Care of
Servants in this Time of Confusion.

A Hackney Coach was then sent for, but without Success; for
these, like Hackney Friends, always offer themselves in the Sun-
shine, but are never to be found when you want them. And as for
a Chair, Mr. *Snap* lived in a Part of the Town which Chairmen
very little frequent. The good Woman was therefore obliged to
walk home, whither the gallant *Wild* offered to attend her as a
Protector. This Favour was thankfully accepted, and the Husband
and Wife having taken a tender Leave of each other, the former
was locked in, and the latter lock'd out by the Hands of Mr. *Snap*
himself.

As this Visit of Mr. *Wild's* to *Heartfree* may seem one of those
Passages in History, which Writers, *Drawcansir*-like, introduce only
*because they dare*;° indeed as it may seem somewhat contradictory to
the GREATNESS of our Hero, and may tend to blemish his Character
with an Imputation of that kind of Friendship, which savours too
much of Weakness and Imprudence; it may be necessary therefore to
account for this Visit, especially to our more sagacious Readers,

whose Satisfaction we shall always consult in the most especial
Manner. They are to know then, that at the first Interview with Mrs.
*Heartfree*, Mr. *Wild* had conceived that Passion, or Affection, or
Friendship, or Desire for that handsome Creature, which the
Gentlemen of this our Age agree to call LOVE;° and which is indeed
no other than that Friendship which, after the Exercise of the
Dominical Day° is over, a lusty Divine is apt to conceive for the well-
drest Sirloin, or handsome Buttock,° which the well-edified 'Squire,
in Gratitude, sets before him, and which, so violent is his Love, he is
desirous to devour. Not less ardent was the hungry Passion of our
Hero, who, from the Moment he had cast his Eyes on that charming
Dish, cast about in his Mind by what Method he might come at it.
This, as he perceived, might most easily be effected after the Ruin of
*Heartfree*, which, for other Considerations, he had intended. So he
postponed all Endeavours for this purpose, till he had first effected
what, by Order of Time, was particularly to precede this latter
Design; with such Regularity and true GREATNESS did this our
Hero conduct all his Schemes, and so truly superiour was he to all
the Efforts of Passion, which so often disconcert and disappoint the
noblest Views of others.

CHAPTER IX

*More* GREATNESS *in* Wild. *A low Scene between Mrs.* Heartfree
*and her Children, and a Scheme of our Hero, worthy the highest
Admiration, and even Astonishment.*

WHEN first he conducted his Flame (or rather his Dish, to continue
our Metaphor) from the Proprietor, he had projected a Design of
conveying her to one of those Eating-Houses in *Covent-Garden*,
where female Flesh is deliciously drest, and served up to the greedy
Appetites of young Gentlemen;° but fearing lest she should not come
readily enough into his Wishes, and that, by too eager and hasty a
Pursuit, he should frustrate his future Expectations, and luckily at
the same Time a noble Hint suggesting itself to him, by which he
might almost inevitably secure his Pleasure, together with his Profit,
he contented himself with waiting on Mrs. *Heartfree* home, and,
after many Protestations of Friendship and Service to her Husband,

took his Leave, and promised to visit her early in the Morning, and conduct her back to Mr. *Snap's.*

*Wild* now retired to a Night-Cellar, where he found several of his Acquaintance, with whom he spent the remaining Part of the Night in revelling; nor did the least Compassion for *Heartfree's* Misfortunes disturb the Pleasure of his Cups.° So truly GREAT was his Soul, that it was absolutely composed, save that an Apprehension of Miss *Tishy's* making some Discovery° (as she was then in no good Temper towards him) a little ruffled and disquieted the perfect Serenity he would otherwise have enjoyed. As he had, therefore, no Opportunity of seeing her that Evening, he wrote her a Letter full of ten thousand Protestations of honourable Love, and (which he more depended on) containing as many Promises, in order to bring the young Lady into good Humour, without acquainting her in the least with his Suspicion, or giving her any Caution: For it was his constant Maxim, Never to put it into any one's Head to do you a Mischief, by acquainting them that it is in their Power.

We must now return to Mrs. *Heartfree*, who past a sleepless Night in as great Agonies and Horrour for the Absence of her Husband, as a fine well-bred Woman would feel at the Return of her's from a long Voyage or Journey. In the Morning the Children being brought to her, the eldest asked, *Where dear Papa was?* At which she could not refrain from bursting into Tears. The Child perceiving it, said, *Don't cry, Mamma, I am sure Papa would not stay abroad, if he could help it.* At which Words she caught the Child in her Arms, and throwing herself into the Chair, in an Agony of Passion, cried out, *No, my Child, nor shall all the Malice of Hell keep us long asunder.*

These are Circumstances which we should not, for the Amusement of six or seven Readers only, have inserted, had they not served to shew, that there are Weaknesses in vulgar Life, which are commonly called *Tenderness;* to which GREAT MINDS are so entirely Strangers, that they have not even an Idea of them; and, secondly, by exposing the Folly of this low Creature, to set off and elevate that GREATNESS, which we endeavour to draw a true Portrait of in this History.

*Wild* entering the Room, found the Mother with one Child in her Arms, and the other at her Knee. After paying her his Compliments, he desired her to dismiss the Children and Servant, for that he had something of GREAT Moment to impart to her.

She immediately complied with his Request, and, the Door being shut, asked him with great Eagerness if he had succeeded in his Intentions of procuring the Bail. He answered, he had not endeavoured at it yet; for a Scheme had entered into his Head, by which she might certainly preserve her Husband, herself, and her Family. In order to which he advised her instantly to remove with the most valuable Jewels she had to *Holland*, before any Statute of Bankruptcy issued to prevent her;° that he would himself attend her thither, and place her in Safety, and then return to deliver her Husband, who would be easily able to satisfy his Creditors. He added, that he was that Instant come from *Snap's*, where he had communicated the Scheme to *Heartfree*, who had greatly approved it, and desired her to put it in Execution without Delay, concluding that a Moment was not to be lost.

The Mention of her Husband's Approbation left no Doubt in this poor Woman's Breast, she only desired a Moment's Time to pay him a Visit, in order to take her Leave. But *Wild* peremptorily refused; he said by every Moment's Delay she risqued the Ruin of her Family; that she would be absent only a few Days from him; adding, that if she had not Resolution enough to execute the Commands he brought her from her Husband, his Ruin would lie at her Door, and, for his own Part, he must give up any further meddling in his Affairs.

She then proposed to take her Children with her; but *Wild* would not permit it, saying, they would only retard their Flight, and that it would be properer for her Husband to bring them. He at length absolutely prevailed on this poor Woman, who immediately packed up the most valuable Effects she could find, and, after taking a tender Leave of her Infants, earnestly commended them to the Care of a very faithful Servant. Then they called a Hackney-Coach, which conveyed them to an Inn, where they were furnished with a Chariot and six,° in which they set forward for *Harwich*.

*Wild* rode with an exulting Heart; secure, as he now thought himself, of the Possession of that lovely Woman, together with a rich Cargo. In short, he enjoyed in his Mind all the Happiness which unbridled Lust and rapacious Avarice could promise him. As to the poor Creature, who was to satisfy these Passions, her whole Soul was employed in reflecting on the Condition of her Husband and Children. A single Word scarce escaped her Lips; while a Flood of Tears gushed from her brilliant Eyes, which, if I may use a coarse

Expression, served only as delicious Sauce to heighten the Appetite
of *Wild*.


### CHAPTER X

*Sea-Adventures very new and surprizing.*

WHEN they arrived at *Harwich*, they found a Vessel, which had put
in there, just ready to depart for *Rotterdam*. So they went immediately on board, and sailed with a fair Wind; but they had hardly
proceeded out of Sight of Land, when a sudden and violent Storm
arose, and drove them to the South West; so that the Captain apprehended it impossible to avoid the *Goodwin* Sands,° and he and all his
Crew gave themselves for lost. Mrs. *Heartfree*, who had no other
Apprehensions from Death, but those of leaving her dear Husband
and Children, fell on her Knees to beseech the Almighty's Favour,
when *Wild*, with a Contempt of Danger truly GREAT, took a
Resolution as worthy to be admired perhaps as any recorded of the
bravest Hero, ancient or modern. He saw the Tyrant Death ready to
rescue from him his intended Prey, which he had yet devoured only
in Imagination. He therefore swore he would prevent him, and
immediately attacked the poor Wretch, who was in the utmost
Agonies of Despair, first with Solicitation, and afterwards with
Force.

   Mrs. *Heartfree*, the Moment she understood his Meaning, which,
in her present Temper of Mind, and in the Opinion she held of him,
she did not immediately, rejected him with all the Repulses which
Indignation and Horrour could animate: But when he attempted
Violence, she filled the Cabin with her Shrieks, which were so vehe-
ment, that they reached the Ears of the Captain, the Storm at this
Time luckily abating. This Man, who was a Brute rather from his
Education, and the Element he inhabited, than from Nature, ran
hastily down to her Assistance, and finding her struggling on the
Ground with our Hero, he presently rescued her from her intended
Ravisher; who was soon obliged to quit the Woman, in order to
engage with her lusty Champion, who spared neither Pains nor
Blows in the Assistance of his fair Passenger.

   When the short Battle was over, in which our Hero, had he not

been overpowered with Numbers, who came down on their Captain's Side, would have been victorious; the Captain rapped out a
hearty Oath, and asked *Wild, If he had no more Christianity in him
than to ravish a Woman in a Storm!* To which the other GREATLY and
sullenly answered: *It was very well; but d———n him, if he had not
Satisfaction the Moment they came on Shore.* The Captain replied,
*Kiss ——— &c.*° and then, turning *Wild* out of the Cabin, he, at Mrs.
*Heartfree's* Request, locked her into it, and returned to the Care of
his Ship.

The Storm was now entirely ceased, and nothing remained but
the usual ruffling of the Sea after it, when one of the Sailors spied a
Sail at a Distance, which the Captain wisely apprehended might be a
Privateer° (for we were then engaged in a War with *France*°) and
immediately ordered all the Sail possible to be crowded;° but his
Caution was in vain; for the little Wind which then blew, was directly
adverse; so that the Ship bore down upon them, and soon appeared
to be what the Captain had feared, a *French* Privateer. He was in no
Condition of Resistance, and immediately struck° on her firing the
first Gun. The Captain of the *Frenchman*, with several of his Hands,
came on board the *English* Vessel; which they rifled of every thing
valuable, and, amongst the rest, poor Mrs. *Heartfree's* whole Cargo,
and then taking the Crew, together with the two Passengers, aboard
his own Ship, he determined as the other would be only a Burthen to
him, to sink her, she being very old and leaky, and not worth going
back with to *Dunkirk*. He preserved, therefore, nothing but the Boat,°
as his own was none of the best, and then pouring a Broad-side into
her, he sent her to the bottom.

The *French* Captain, who was a very young Fellow, and a Man of
Gallantry, was presently enamoured to no small Degree with his
beautiful Captive; and imagining *Wild*, from some Words he dropt,
to be her Husband, notwithstanding the ill Affection towards him
which appeared in her Looks, he asked her, if she understood
*French?* She answered in the Affirmative, for indeed she did perfectly
well.° He then asked her, how long she and that Gentleman (pointing
to *Wild*) had been married? She answered with a deep Sigh, and
many Tears, that she was married indeed, but not to that Villain,
who was the sole Cause of all her Misfortunes. That Appellation
raised a Curiosity in the Captain, and he importuned her in so
pressing, but gentle a manner to acquaint him with the Injuries she

complained of, that she was at last prevailed on to recount to him the whole History of her Afflictions. This so moved the Captain, who had too little Notions of GREATNESS, and so incensed him against our Hero, that he resolved to punish him; and, without Regard to the Laws of War,° he immediately ordered out his shattered Long-boat, and, making *Wild* a Present of half-a-dozen Biscuits to prolong his Misery, he put him therein, and then committing him to the Mercy of the Sea, proceeded on his Cruize.

### CHAPTER XI

*The* GREAT *and wonderful Behaviour of our Hero in the Boat.*

IT is probable, that a Desire of ingratiating himself with his charming Captive, or rather Conqueror, had no little Share in promoting this extraordinary Act of illegal Justice; for he had conceived the same Sort of Passion, or Hunger, which *Wild* himself had felt, and was as much resolved, by some Means or other, to satisfy it. We will leave him, however, at present, in the Pursuit of his Wishes, and attend our Hero in his Boat; since it is in Circumstances of Distress, that true GREATNESS appears most wonderful. For, that a Prince in the midst of his Courtiers, all ready to compliment him with his favourite Character, or Title; or that a Conqueror, at the Head of an hundred thousand Men, all prepared to execute his Will, how ambitious, wanton, or cruel soever, should, in the Giddiness of his Pride, elevate himself many Degrees above those his Tools, seems not difficult to be imagined, or indeed accounted for. But that a Man in Chains, in Prisons, nay, in the vilest Dungeon, should with persevering Pride and obstinate Dignity, discover that vast Superiority in his own Nature over the rest of Mankind, who, to a vulgar Eye, seem much happier than himself; nay, that he should discover Heaven and Providence (whose peculiar Care, it seems, he is) at that very Time at work for him; this is among the *Arcana* of GREATNESS, to be perfectly understood only by an Adept in that Science.

What could be imagined more miserable than the Situation of our Hero at this Season, floating in a little Boat on the open Seas, without Oar, without Sail, and at the Mercy of the first Wave to overwhelm him; which was indeed a much more eligible Fate than that

Alternative, which threatened him with almost unavoidable Certainty, *viz.* Starving with Hunger, the sure Consequence of a Continuance of the Calm.

Our Hero finding himself in this Condition, began to ejaculate a Round of Blasphemies, which the Reader, without being overpious, might be offended at seeing repeated. He then accused the whole Female Sex, and the Passion of Love (as he called it) particularly that which he bore to Mrs. *Heartfree*, as the unhappy Occasion of his present Sufferings. At length, finding himself descending too much into the Language of Meanness and Complaint, he stopp'd short, and soon after broke forth as follows. 'D——n it, a Man can die but once, what signifies it! Every Man must die, and when it is over it is over. I never was afraid of any thing yet, nor I won't begin now; no, d——n me, won't I. What signifies Fear? I shall die whether I am afraid or no: Who's afraid then, d——n me?' At which Words he looked extremely fierce, but recollecting that no one was present to see him, he abated the Terror of his Countenance, and pausing a little, repeated the Word, *D——n!* 'Suppose I should be d——ned at last, when I never thought a Syllable of the Matter! I have often laughed and made a Jest about it, and yet it may be so, for any Thing which I know to the contrary. If there should be another World it will go hard with me, that is certain. I shall never escape for what I have done to *Heartfree*. The Devil must have me for that undoubtedly. The Devil! Pshaw! I am not such a Fool to be frightned at him neither. No, no; when a Man's dead, there is an End of him. I wish I was certainly satisfied of it tho'; for there are some Men of Learning of a different Opinion. It is but a bad Chance methinks I stand. If there be no other World, why I shall be in no worse Condition than a Block or a Stone: But if there should,—D——n me, I will think no longer about it.—Let a Pack of cowardly Rascals be afraid of Death, I dare look him in the Face. But shall I stay and be starved!—No, I will eat up the Biscuits the *French* Son of a Whore bestowed on me, and then leap into the Sea for Drink, since the unconscionable Dog hath not allowed me a single Dram.' Having thus said, he proceeded immediately to put his Purpose in Execution, and as his Resolution never failed him, he had no sooner dispatched the small Quantity of Provision, which his Enemy had with no vast Liberality presented him, than he cast himself headlong into the Sea.

### CHAPTER XII

### *Of* PROVERBS. *A Chapter full of very cunning and curious Learning.*°

HERE, Reader, we cannot omit an Opportunity of commending the vast Usefulness of that Learning, which is to be collected from those Funds of Knowledge, called PROVERBS: Being short *Aphorisms*, in which Men of Great Genius have wrapt up some egregious Discovery, either in Nature or Science, making it thus easily portable for the Memory, which is apt to fail under the Burthen of voluminous Erudition. Next, therefore, to the Merit of those Sages who first drop'd these inestimable Pearls, are we obliged to their Care and Industry, who have collected them together. And here, as it would be needless to add to the Encomiums given to *Erasmus* on this Occasion,° I shall pass on to the incomparable Publisher of Joe Miller's *Jests;* whether he be the lamentable *Elijah Jenkins* Esq; or the facetious *Edmundus de Crull* Esq; is not very material.° *In these*, as the learned Lord *Bacon* says of the *Proverbs* of *Solomon, We see not a few profound and excellent Cautions, Precepts, Positions, extending to much Variety of Occasions, whereupon we will stay a while offering to Consideration some Number of Examples.*°

### PROVERB I

The GREATEST MEN may sometimes overshoot themselves, but their very Mistakes are so many Lessons of Instruction. *To teach others the Art of over-reaching.*

### PROVERB II

A good Outside is the best Sir *Clement Cotterel* in a strange Place.° *Here is noted, Sir* Clement Cotterel *doth with excellent Address usher Persons into a strange Place.*

### PROVERB III

Were we to believe nothing but what we can comprehend, every Man upon the Face of the Earth would be an Atheist. *Nothing being so easy as to believe that Proportion is the Effect of Chance, nor any Proposition so comprehensible, as that dead Matter should of its own Accord produce Life, Thought,* &c.

### PROVERB IV

Arguments among Men are like Bones among Dogs; serve to set them together by the Ears. *Ergo, an Argument is called a Bone of Contention.*

### PROVERB V

The Chimney and the Garret are related, and therefore Taylors and Chimney-Sweepers are Cousin-Germans. *This is not to be understood literally but metaphorically. Taylors are in very great Contempt among the English, nine of them being said to make only one Man;° and in the Play-House the Public express their Contempt of your Judgment by calling you a Taylor.° Some imagine this to proceed from the ancient Britons going naked, and consequently never using this Mechanic: But I rather apprehend the Reason to be from the Moderns using him so much that they are never out of his Books.°*

### PROVERB VI

The sick Man doth ill for himself, who makes his Physician his Heir. *Here Caution is given, that it is not adviseable to make it that Man's Interest to hurt you, who hath the Power.*

### PROVERB VII

The sensible Man and the silent Woman are the best Conversation. *Here is noted that a Woman talks best who says nothing.*

### PROVERB VIII

He who rises from Table without saying Grace, may be said to go away without paying his Ordinary. *Here is noted, that he who hath no Chaplain at his Table will not pay his Dues to the* ORDINARY,° i.e. *Bishop.*

### PROVERB IX

A young Fellow who falls in Love with a Whore, may be said to fall asleep in a Hogstye. *Here is observed the likeness or Resemblance between a Whore and a Hogstye.*

### PROVERB X

Our Carts are never worse employed than when waited on by Coaches. *i.e. When they carry Rogues to* Tyburn.

PROVERB XI

Five of the most agreeable Things on a Journey, are Money in one's Pocket, a good Road, a wholsome Bed, fine Weather, and a kind Landlady; if she be handsome too, 'tis so much the better. *Here are five excellent Things brought together in the Compass of two or three Lines.*

PROVERB XII

Debauching a Member of the House of Commons from his Principles, and creating him a Peer, is not much better than making a Woman a Whore, and afterwards marrying her.° *Here a Member of the House of Commons is set forth in the lovely State of virgin Simplicity and Innocence, and it is insinuated that if you first debauch him from that State of Purity and make him a Rogue, he remains a Rogue still, notwithstanding a subsequent Peerage; as a Woman who is debauched remains a Whore still, notwithstanding a subsequent Marriage. And this the Proverb would say further, notwithstanding the World calls the former* RIGHT HONOURABLE, *and the latter an* HONEST *Woman.*°

Thus having (to use the Words of that noble Author once more) *staid somewhat longer on these Sentences than is agreeable to the Proportion of an Example,*° and perhaps offended some, who will direct the Force of this Chapter (if it have any) where it was little meant; I now return to our Hero, who, to the Surprise, I apprehend, of the Reader, exemplified the Truth of one Proverb, *viz. He that is born to be hang'd will never be drowned*; which, as *Shakespear* phrases it, may be somewhat *musty*;° but I am convinced never had so pregnant an Example of its Veracity before.

CHAPTER XIII

*The strange and yet natural Escape of our Hero.*

OUR Hero having with wonderful Resolution thrown himself headlong into the Sea, as we have mentioned, was miraculously within two Minutes after replaced in his Boat; and this without the Assistance of a Dolphin or Sea-Horse, or any other Fish or Animal, who are always as ready at Hand when a Poet or Historian pleases to call for them to carry a Hero through a Sea; as any Chairman at a Coffee-House Door near St. *James's*,° to convey a Beau over a Street, and preserve his white Stockings. The Truth is, we do not chuse to have any Recourse to Miracles, from the strict Observance we pay to that Rule of *Horace*,

> *Nec Deus intersit nisi dignus vindice nodus.*

The Meaning of which is, *Do not bring in a supernatural Agent when you can do without him;*° and indeed, we are much deeper read in natural than supernatural Causes. We will therefore endeavour to account for this extraordinary Event from the former of these; and in doing this it will be necessary to disclose some profound Secrets to our Reader, extremely well worth his knowing, and which may serve him to account for many Occurrences of the Phænomenous Kind which have lately appeared in this our Hemisphere.°

Be it known then, that the Great *Alma Mater* Nature is of all other Females the most obstinate, and tenacious of her Purpose. So true is that Observation,

> *Naturam expellas furca licet, usque recurret.*

Which I need not render in *English*, it being to be found in a Book which most fine Gentlemen read.° Whatever Nature, therefore, purposes to herself, she never suffers any Reason, Design or Accident, to frustrate. Now, tho' it may seem to a shallow Observer, that some Persons were designed by Nature for no Use or Purpose whatever; yet certain it is, that no Man is born into the World without his particular Allotment; *viz.* some to be Kings, some Statesmen, some Embassadors,° some Bishops, some Generals, and so on. Of these there be two Kinds, those to whom Nature is so generous to give some Endowment, qualifying them for the Parts she intends them afterwards to act on this Stage; and those whom she uses as Instances of her unlimited Power; and for whose Preferment to such and such Stations, *Solomon* himself could have invented no other Reason than that Nature designed them so.° These latter some great Philosophers have, to shew them to be the Favourites of Nature, distinguished by the honourable Appellation of NATURALS. Indeed the true Reason of the general Ignorance of Mankind on this Head seems to be this; That as Nature chuses to execute these her Purposes by certain second Causes or Tools, and as many of these second Causes seem so totally foreign to her Design, the Wit of Man, which like his Eye, sees best directly forward and very little and imperfectly, what is oblique, is not able to discern the End by the Means.° Thus, how a handsome Wife or Daughter should contribute to execute her original Designation of a General; or how Flattery should denote a Judge, or Impiety and Atheism, a Bishop, he is not capable of comprehending. And indeed, we ourselves, wise as we are, are forced to reason *ab effectu*, and if we were asked what Nature had intended such Men for, before she herself had by the Event demonstrated her Purpose, it is possible we might be sometimes puzzled to declare; for it must be confessed, that at first Sight, and to a Man uninspired, great Fortitude of Mind with a vast Capacity and Knowledge, might induce a Belief in the Beholder, that such Endowments were by Nature designed for Power and Honour rather than the reverse; whereas daily Experience convinces us of the contrary, and drives us as it were into the Opinion I have here disclosed.

Now, Nature having originally intended our GREAT MAN for that final Exaltation,° which as it is the most proper and becoming End of all GREAT MEN, it were heartily to be wished they might all arrive at; would by no Means be diverted from her Purpose. She therefore no sooner spied him in the Water, than she softly whispered in his Ear to attempt the Recovery of his Boat; which Call he immediately obeyed, and being a good Swimmer with great Facility accomplished it.

Thus we think this Passage in our History, at first so greatly surprising, is very naturally accounted for; and our Relation rescued from the *Prodigious* which, tho' it often occurs in Biography, is not to be encouraged nor much commended on any Occasion, unless when absolutely necessary to prevent the History's being at an End. Secondly, We hope our Hero is justified from that Imputation of want of Resolution, which must be fatal to the GREATNESS of his Character.

CHAPTER XIV

*The Conclusion of the Boat Adventure, and the End of the*
*second Book.*

OUR Hero past the Remainder of the Evening, the Night, and the next Day, in a Condition not much to be envied by any Passion of the human Mind, unless by Ambition; which, provided it can only entertain itself with the most distant Music of Fame's Trumpet, can disdain all the Pleasures of the Sensualist, and those more solemn, tho' quieter Comforts, which a good Conscience suggests to a Christian Philosopher.

He spent his Time in Contemplation, that is to say, in blaspheming, cursing, and sometimes singing and whistling. At last, when Cold and Hunger had almost subdued his native Fierceness, it being a good deal past Midnight, and extremely dark, he thought he beheld a Light at a Distance, which the Cloudiness of the Sky prevented his mistaking for a Star; This Light, however, did not seem to approach him, at least it approached by such imperceptible Degrees, that it gave him very little Comfort, and at length totally forsook him. He then renewed his Contemplation as before, in which he continued till the Day began to break; when, to his inexpressible Delight, he beheld a Sail at a very little Distance, and which luckily seemed to be making towards him. He was likewise soon espied by those in the Vessel, who wanted no Signals to inform them of his Distress, and as it was almost a Calm, and their Course lay within five hundred Yards of him, they hoisted out their Boat and fetched him aboard.

The Captain of this Ship was a *Frenchman;* she was laden with Deal from *Norway,* and had been extremely shattered in the late Storm. This Captain was of that kind of Men, who are actuated by a general Humanity, and whose Compassion can be raised by the Distress of a Fellow-Creature, though of a Nation whose King had quarrelled with the Monarch of their own. He therefore commiserating the Circumstances of *Wild,* who had drest up a Story proper to impose on such a silly Fellow; told him, that, as himself well knew, he must be a Prisoner on his Arrival in *France,* but that he would endeavour to procure his Redemption; for which our Hero greatly thanked him. But as they were making very slow Sail (for they had lost their Main-mast in the Storm) *Wild* saw a little Vessel at a Distance, they being within a few Leagues of the *English* Shore, which, on Enquiry, he was informed was probably an *English* Fishing-Boat. And, it being then perfectly calm, he promised, that if they would accommodate him with an Oar, he could get within Reach of the Boat, at least near enough to make Signals to her; and he preferred any Risque to the certain Fate of being a Prisoner. As his Courage was somewhat restored by the Provisions (especially

Brandy) with which the *Frenchman* had supplied him, he was so earnest in his Entreaties, that the Captain, after many Persuasions, at length complied; and he was furnished with an Oar, with some Bread, Pork, and a Bottle of Brandy. Then, taking Leave of his Preservers, he again betook himself to his Boat, and rowed so heartily, that he soon came within the Sight of the Fisherman, who immediately made towards him, and took him aboard.

No sooner was *Wild* got safe on board the Fisherman, then he begged him to make the utmost Speed into *Deal*;° for that the Vessel, which was still in Sight, was a distressed *Frenchman*, bound for *Havre de Grace*,° and might easily be made a Prize, if there was any Ship ready to go in Pursuit of her. So nobly and GREATLY did our Hero neglect all Obligations conferred on him by the Enemies of his Country, that he would have contributed all he could to the taking his Benefactor, to whom he owed both his Life and his Liberty.

The Fisherman took his Advice, and soon arrived at *Deal*, where the Reader will, I doubt not, be as much concerned as *Wild* was, that there was not a single Ship prepared to go on the Expedition.

Our Hero now saw himself once more safe on *Terra firma*; but unluckily at some Distance from that City where Men of Ingenuity can most easily supply their Wants without the Assistance of Money. However, as his Talents were superiour to every Difficulty, he framed so dextrous an Account of his being a Merchant, having been taken and plundered by the Enemy, and of his great Effects in *London*, that he was not only heartily regaled by the Fisherman at his House; but made so handsome a Booty by way of Borrowing, a Method of taking which we have before mentioned to have his Approbation,° that he was enabled to provide himself with a Place in the Stage-Coach;° which ( as GOD permitted it to perform the Journey°) brought him, at the appointed time, to an Inn in the Metropolis.

And now, Reader, as thou canst be in no Suspence for the Fate of our GREAT MAN, since we have returned him safe to the principal Scene of his Glory, we will a little look back on the Fortunes of Mr. *Heartfree*, whom we left in no very pleasant Situation, especially as the Behaviour of this poor Wretch will considerably serve to set off the GREAT and exemplary Conduct of our Hero; but of this we shall treat in the next Book.

# BOOK III

*The low and pitiful Behaviour of* Heartfree; *and the foolish Conduct of his Apprentice.*

HIS Misfortunes did not entirely prevent *Heartfree* from closing his Eyes. On the contrary, he slept several Hours the first Night of his Confinement. However, he perhaps paid too severely dear both for his Repose, and for a sweet Dream which accompanied it, and represented his little Family in one of those tender Scenes, which had frequently past in the Days of his Happiness and Prosperity, when the Provision they were making for the future Fortunes of their Children used to be one of the most agreeable Topics of Discourse, with which he and his Wife entertained themselves. The Pleasantness of this Vision, therefore, served only, on his awakening, to set forth his present Misery with additional Horrour, and to heighten the dreadful Ideas which now crowded on his Mind.

He had spent a considerable Time after his first rising from the Bed on which he had, without undressing, thrown himself, and now began to wonder at Mrs. *Heartfree's* long Absence; but as Men are apt (and perhaps wisely too) to draw comfortable Conclusions from malign Events; so he hoped the longer her Stay was, the more certain was his Deliverance. At length his Impatience prevailed, and he was just going to dispatch a Messenger to his own House, when his Apprentice came to pay him a Visit, and, on his Enquiry, informed him, that his Wife had departed in Company with Mr. *Wild* many Hours before, and had carried all his most valuable Effects with her; adding at the same time, that she had acquainted him she had her Husband's Orders for so doing.

It is the Observation of many wise Men, who have studied the Anatomy of the human Soul with more Attention than our young Physicians generally bestow on that of the Body; that great and violent Surprize hath a different Effect from that which is wrought in a good Housewife by perceiving any Disorders in her Kitchen; who, on such Occasions, commonly spreads the Disorder, not only over her whole Family, but the Neighbourhood. Now, these great Calamities, especially when sudden, tend to stifle and deaden all the Faculties, instead of elevating them; and accordingly one *Herodotus* tells us a Story of *Cræsus*, King of *Lydia*, who, on beholding his Servants and Courtiers led captive, wept bitterly; but when he saw his Wife and Children in that Condition, stood stupid and motionless;° so stood poor *Heartfree* on this Relation of his Apprentice, nothing moving but his Colour, which entirely forsook his Countenance.

The Apprentice, who had not in the least doubted the Veracity of his Mistress, perceiving the Surprize which too visibly appeared in his Master, became speechless likewise, and both remained silent some Minutes, gazing with Astonishment and Horrour at each other. At last *Heartfree* cry'd out in an Agony: 'My Wife deserted me in my Misfortunes!' 'GOD forbid, Sir,' answered the other. 'And what is become of my poor Children?' replied *Heartfree*. 'They are at home, Sir,' said the Apprentice. 'GOD be praised, she hath forsaken them too,' cries *Heartfree*: 'Fetch them hither this Instant. Go, my dear *Jack*, bring hither my little All which remains now: Fly, Child,° if thou dost not intend likewise to forsake me in my Afflictions.' The Youth answered he would die sooner than entertain such a Thought, and, begging his Master to be comforted, instantly obeyed his Orders.

*Heartfree*, the Moment the young Man was departed, threw himself on his Bed in an Agony of Despair; but, recollecting himself after he had vented the first Sallies of his Passion, he began to question the Infidelity of his Wife, as a Matter impossible. He ran over in his Thoughts the uninterrupted Tenderness which she had always shewn him, and, for a Minute, blamed the Rashness of his Belief against her; 'till the many Circumstances of her having left him so long, and neither writ nor sent to him since her Departure with all his Effects, and with *Wild*, of whom he was not before without Suspicion; and lastly and chiefly, her false Pretence to his Commands,° entirely turned the Scale, and convinced him of her Disloyalty.

While he was in these Agitations of Mind, the good Apprentice, who had used the utmost Expedition, brought his Children to him. He embraced them with the most passionate Fondness, and imprinted numberless Kisses on their little Lips. The little Girl flew to him with almost as much Eagerness as he himself exprest at her Sight, and cry'd out: 'O Papa, why did you not come home to poor Mamma all this while; I thought you would not have left your little *Nanny*° so long.' After which he asked for her Mother, and was told she had kiss'd them in the Morning, and cried very much for his Absence. All which brought a Flood of Tears into the Eyes of this weak, silly Man, who had not GREATNESS sufficient to conquer these low Efforts of Tenderness and Humanity.

He then proceeded to enquire of the Maid-servant, who acquainted him, that she knew no more than that her Mistress had taken Leave of her Children in the Morning with many Tears and Kisses, and had recommended them in the most earnest manner to her Care; which, she said, she had promised faithfully to do, and would, while they were entrusted to her, fulfil. For which Profession *Heartfree* expressed much Gratitude to her; and, after indulging himself with some little Fondnesses, which we shall not relate, he delivered his Children into the good Woman's Hands, and dismissed her.

CHAPTER II

*A Soliloquy of* Heartfree's, *full of low and base Ideas, without a Syllable of* GREATNESS.

BEING now alone, he sat some short Time silent, and then burst forth into the following Soliloquy:°

'What shall I do? Shall I abandon myself to a dispirited Despair, or fly in the Face of the Almighty! Surely both are unworthy of a wise Man; for what can be more vain than weakly to lament my Fortune, if irretrievable, or, if Hope remains, to offend that Being, who can most strongly support it: But are my Passions then voluntary? Am I so absolutely their Master, that I can resolve with myself, *so far only will I grieve?* Certainly, no. Reason, however we flatter ourselves, hath not such despotic Empire in our Minds, that it can, with imperial Voice, hush all our Sorrow in a Moment. Where then is its Use? for either it is an empty Sound, and we are deceived in thinking we have Reason, or it is given us to some End, and hath a Part assigned it by the All-wise Creator. Why, what can its Office be, other than justly to weigh the Worth of all Things, and to direct us to that Perfection of human Wisdom, which proportions our Esteem of every Object by its real Merit, and prevents us from over or under-valuing whatever we hope for, we enjoy, or we lose. It doth not foolishly say to us, *Be not glad*, or *Be not sorry*, which would be as vain and idle, as to bid the purling River cease to run, or the raging Wind to blow. It prevents us only from exulting, like Children, when we receive a Toy, or from lamenting when we are deprived of it. Suppose then I have lost the Enjoyments of this World, and my Expectation of future Pleasure and Profit is for ever disappointed; what Relief can my Reason afford! What, unless it can shew me I had fixed my Affections on a Toy; that what I desired was not, by a wise Man, eagerly to be affected, nor its Loss violently deplored; for there are Toys adapted to all Ages, from the Rattle to the Throne.° And perhaps the Value of all is equal to their several Possessors; for if the Rattle pleases the Ears of the Infant, what can the Flattery of Syco-phants do more to the Prince? The latter is as far from examining into the Reality and Source of his Pleasure as the former; for if both did, they must both equally despise it. And surely if we consider them seriously, and compare them together, we shall be forced to conclude all those Pomps and Pleasures, of which Men are so fond, and which, through so much Danger and Difficulty, with such Violence and Villany they pursue, to be as worthless Trifles as any exposed to Sale in a Toyshop. I have often noted my little Girl viewing, with eager Eyes, a jointed Baby;° I have marked the Pains and Solicitations she hath used, till I have been prevailed on to indulge her with it. At her first obtaining it, what Joy hath sparkled in her Countenance! with what Raptures hath she taken the Posses-sion; but how little Satisfaction hath she found in it! What Pains to work out her Amusement from it! Its Dress must be varied; the Tinsel Ornaments which first caught her Eyes, produce no longer Pleasure; she endeavours to make it stand and walk in vain, and is constrained herself to supply it with Conversation. In a Day's time it is thrown by and neglected, and some less costly Toy preferred to it. How like the Situation of this Child is that of every Man! What Difficulties in the Pursuit of his Desires! What Inanity in the Posses-sion of most, and Satiety in those which seem more real and substan-tial! The Delights of most Men are as childish and as superficial as that of my little Girl; a Feather or a Fiddle are their Pursuits and their Pleasures through Life, even to their ripest Years, if such Men may be said to attain any Ripeness at all. But let us survey those whose Understandings are of a more elevated and refined Temper, how empty do they soon find the World of Enjoyments worth their Desire or attaining! How soon do they retreat to Solitude and Contemplation, to Gardening and Planting, and such rural Amusements, where their Trees and they enjoy the Air and the Sun in common, and both vegetate with very little Difference between them. But suppose (which neither Honesty nor Wisdom will allow) we could admit something more valuable and substantial in those Blessings, would not the Uncertainty of their Possession be alone sufficient to lower their Price? How mean a Tenure is that at the Will of Fortune, which Chance, Fraud, and Rapine are every Day so likely to deprive us of, and the more likely, by how much the greater Worth our Possessions are of! Is it not to place our Affections on a Bubble in the Water, or a Picture in the Clouds! What Mad-man would build a fine House, or frame a beautiful Garden on Land in which he held so uncertain an Interest! But again, was all this less undeniable, did Fortune, like the Lady of a Manor, lease to us for our Lives; of how little Consideration must even this Term appear? For admitting that these Pleasures were not liable to be torn from us; how certainly must we be torn from them! Perhaps To-morrow,—Nay or even sooner: For as the excellent Poet says,

> *Where is To-morrow?—In the other World.*
> *To thousands this is true, and the Reverse*
> *Is sure to none.*°

But if I have no further Hope in this World, can I have none beyond it? Surely those laborious Writers, who have taken such infinite Pains to destroy or weaken all the Proofs of Futurity, have not so far succeeded as to exclude us from Hope. That active Principle in Man, which with such Boldness pushes on through every Labour and Difficulty, to attain the most distant and most improbable Event in this World, will not surely deny us a little flattering Prospect; which, if it could be chimerical, must be allowed the loveliest which can entertain the Eye of Man;° and which, if we understand the Road rightly, hath so little Labour and Fatigue, so few Thorns and Briers in its Way.° If the Proofs of a supreme Being be as strong as I imagine them, surely enough may be deduced from that Ground only to comfort and support the most miserable Man in his Afflictions. And this I think my Reason tells me, that if the Professors and Propagators of Infidelity are in the right, the Losses which Death brings to the Virtuous are not worth their lamenting; but if they are, as certainly they seem, in the wrong, the Blessings it procures them are not sufficiently to be coveted and rejoiced at.

'On my own Account then, I have no cause for Sorrow, but on my Children's—! Why, the same Being to whose Goodness and Power I entrust my own Happiness, is likewise as able and as willing to procure theirs. Nor matters it what State of Life they are allotted, whether to procure Bread with their own Labour, or to eat it at the Sweat of others. Perhaps, if we consider the Case with proper Attention, or resolve it with due Sincerity; the former is the sweetest. The Hind may be more happy than the Lord; for his Desires are fewer, and those such as are attended with more Hope and less Fear. I will do my utmost to lay the Foundations of their Happiness, I will carefully avoid educating them in a Station superior to their Fortune, and for the Event trust to that Being in whom whoever rightly confides, must be superior to all worldly Sorrows.'

In this low Manner, did this poor Wretch proceed to argue, till he had worked himself up into an Enthusiasm,° which by Degrees soon became invulnerable to every human Attack; so that when Mr. *Snap* acquainted him with the Return of the Writ,° and that he must carry him to *Newgate*, he received the Message as *Socrates* did the News of the Ship's Arrival, and that he was to prepare for Death.°

### CHAPTER III

*Wherein our Hero proceeds in the Road to* GREATNESS.

BUT we must not detain our Reader too long with these low Stories. He is doubtless as impatient as the Audience at the Theatre, till the principal Figure returns on the Stage; we will therefore indulge his Inclination, and pursue the Actions of the GREAT WILD.

There happened to be in the Stage-Coach, in which Mr. *Wild* travelled from *Dover*, a certain young Gentleman who had sold an Estate in *Kent*, and was going to *London* to receive the Money. There was likewise a handsome young Woman who had left her Parents at

*Canterbury*, and was proceeding to the same City, in order (as she informed her Fellow Travellers) to make her Fortune. With this Girl the young Spark was so much enamoured, that he publickly acquainted her with the Purpose of his Journey, and offered her a considerable Sum in Hand and a Settlement, if she would consent to return with him into the Country, where she would be at a safe Distance from her Relations. Whether she accepted this Proposal or no, we are not able with any tolerable Certainty to deliver: But *Wild*, the Moment he heard of this Money, began to cast about in his Mind by what Means he might become Master of it. He entred into a long Harangue about the Methods of carrying Money safely on the Road, and said, he had at that Time two Bank Bills of a hundred Pounds each sowed in his Stock;° 'which,' added he, 'is so safe a Way, that if I met never so many Highwaymen it is almost impossible I should be in any Danger of being robbed.'

The Gentleman, who was no Descendant of *Solomon's*, greatly approved *Wild's* Ingenuity, and thanking him for his Information, declared he would follow his Example when he returned into the Country: By which Means he proposed to save the Premium commonly taken for the Remittance.° *Wild* had then no more to do but to inform himself rightly of the Time of the Gentleman's Journey, which he did with great Certainty, before they separated.

At his Arrival in Town, he fixed on two whom he regarded as the most resolute of his Gang for this Enterprize; and accordingly having summoned the principal or most desperate, as he imagined him, of these two (for he never chose to communicate in the Presence of more than one) he proposed to him the robbing and murthering this Gentleman.

Mr. *Marybone*° (for that was the Gentleman's Name to whom he applied) readily agreed to the Robbery; but he hesitated at the Murther. He said, as to *Robbery*, he had, on much weighing and considering the Matter, very well reconciled his Conscience to it; for tho' that noble Kind of Robbery which was executed on the Highway, was from the Cowardice of Mankind less frequent, yet the baser and meaner Species sometimes called Cheating, but more commonly known by the Name of *Robbery within the Law*, was in a Manner universal. He did not therefore pretend to the Reputation of being so much honester than other People; but could by no Means satisfy himself in the Commission of Murther, which was a Sin of the most heinous Nature, and so immediately prosecuted by God's Judgment, that it never passed undiscovered or unpunished.°

*Wild*, with the utmost Disdain in his Countenance, answered as follows. 'Art thou he whom I have selected out of my whole Gang for this glorious Undertaking, and dost thou cant of *God's Revenge against Murther*?° You have, it seems, reconciled your Conscience (a pretty Word) to Robbery from its being so common. Is it then the Novelty of Murther which deters you? Do you imagine that Guns, and Pistols, and Swords, and Knives, are the only Instruments of Death? Look into the World and see the Numbers whom broken Fortunes and broken Hearts bring untimely to the Grave. To omit those glorious Heroes, who, to their immortal Honour, have massacred whole Nations, what think you of private Persecution, Treachery, and Slander, by which the very Souls of Men are in a Manner torn from their Bodies? Is it not more generous, nay, more Good-natured to send a Man to his rest; than after having plundered him of all he hath, or from Malice or Malevolence deprived him of his Character, to punish him with a languishing Death, or what is worse, a languishing Life? Murther, therefore, is not so uncommon as you weakly conceive it, tho', as you said of Robbery, that more noble Kind, which lies within the Paw of the Law, may be so. But this is the most innocent in him who doth it, and the most eligible to him who is to suffer it. Believe me, Lad, the Tongue of a Viper is less hurtful than that of a Slanderer,° and the gilded Scales of a Rattle-Snake less dreadful than the Purse of the Oppressor.° Let me therefore hear no more of your Scruples; but consent to my Proposal without further Hesitation, unless like a Woman you are afraid of blooding your Cloaths, or like a Fool are terrified with the Apprehensions of being hanged in Chains. Take my Word for it, you had better be an honest Man than half a Rogue. Do not think of continuing in my Gang without abandoning yourself absolutely to my Pleasure; for no Man shall ever receive a Favour at my Hands, who sticks at any thing, or is guided by any other Law than that of my Will.'

*Wild* thus ended his Speech, which had not the desired Effect on *Marybone:* He agreed to the Robbery, but would not undertake the Murther, as *Wild* (who feared that by *Marybone's* demanding to search the Gentleman's Neck,° he might hazard Suspicion himself) insisted. *Marybone* was immediately entered by *Wild* in his

*Black-Book,*° and was presently after impeached and executed, as a Fellow on whom his Leader could not place sufficient Dependence.

CHAPTER IV

*In which a young Hero, of wonderful good Promise, makes his first Appearance, with many other* GREAT MATTERS.

OUR Hero next applied himself to another of his Gang, who instantly received his Orders, and instead of hesitating at a single Murther, asked if he should blow out the Brains of all the Passengers, Coachman and all. But *Wild*, whose Moderation we have before noted, would not permit him; and therefore having given him an exact Description of the devoted Person, with his other necessary Instructions, he dismissed him, with strictest Orders to avoid, if possible, doing hurt to any other Person.

The Name of this Youth, who will hereafter make some Figure in this History, being the *Achates* of our *Æneas*, or rather the *Hæphestion* of our *Alexander* was *Fireblood.*° He had every Qualification to make a Second-Rate GREAT MAN; or in other Words, he was completely equipped for the Tool of a Real or First-Rate GREAT MAN. We shall therefore (which is the properest Way of dealing with this Kind of GREATNESS) describe him negatively, and content ourselves with telling our Reader what Qualities he had not: In which Number were Humanity, Modesty, and Fear, not one Grain of any of which was mingled in his whole Composition.

We will now leave this Youth, who was esteemed the most promising of the whole Gang, and whom *Wild* often declared to be one of the prettiest Lads he had ever seen, of which Opinion, indeed, were most other People of his Acquaintance; we will however leave him at his Entrance on this Enterprize, and keep our Attention fixed on our Hero, whom we shall observe taking large Strides towards the Summit of human Glory.

*Wild*, immediately at his Return to Town, went to pay a Visit to Miss *Lætitia Snap*; for he had that Weakness of suffering himself to be enslaved by Women, so naturally incident to Men of Heroic Disposition;° to say the Truth, it might more properly be called a Slavery to his own Appetite; for could he have satisfied that, he had not cared three Farthings what had become of the little Tyrant for whom he profest so violent a Regard. Here he was informed that Mr. *Heartfree* had been conveyed to *Newgate* the Day before, the Writ being then returnable. He was somewhat concerned at this News; not from any Compassion for the Misfortunes of *Heartfree*, whom he hated with such Inveteracy, that one would have imagined he had suffered the same Injuries from him which he had done towards him. His Concern therefore had another Motive: In Fact, he was uneasy at the Place of Mr. *Heartfree's* Confinement, as it was to be the Scene of his future Glory, and where consequently he should be frequently obliged to see a Face which Hatred and not Shame, made him detest the Sight of.

To prevent this, therefore, several Methods suggested themselves to him. At first, he thought of removing him out of the Way by the ordinary Method of Murther, which he doubted not but *Fireblood* would be very ready to execute; for that Youth had at their last Interview, sworn, *D——n his Eyes, he thought there was no better Pastime than blowing a Man's Brains out*. But besides the Danger of this Method, it did not look horrible nor barbarous enough for the last Mischief which he should do to *Heartfree*. Considering, therefore, a little farther with himself, he at length came to a Resolution to hang him if possible, the very next Sessions.°

Now, tho' the Observation, *How apt Men are to hate those they injure*, or *how unforgiving they are of the Injuries they do themselves*,° be common enough, yet I do not remember to have ever seen the Reason of this strange *Phænomenon*, as at first it appears. Know therefore, Reader, that with much and severe Scrutiny we have discovered this Hatred to be founded on the Passion of Fear, and to arise from an Apprehension that the Person whom we have ourselves greatly injured, will use all possible Endeavours to revenge and retaliate the Injuries we have done him. An Opinion so firmly established in bad and Great Minds (and those who confer Injuries on others, have seldom very good, or mean ones) that no Benevolence nor even Beneficence on the injured Side, can eradicate it. On the contrary they refer all these Acts of Kindness to Imposture and Design of lulling their Suspicion, till an Opportunity offers of striking a surer and severer Blow; and thus while the good Man who hath received it, hath truly forgotten the Injury, the evil Mind which did it, hath it in lively and fresh Remembrance.

As we scorn to keep any such Discoveries secret from our Readers, whose Instruction as well as Diversion, we have greatly considered in this History, we have here digressed somewhat to communicate the following short Lesson to those who are simple, and well inclined; *Tho' as a Christian thou art obliged, and we advise thee to forgive thy Enemy;* NEVER TRUST THE MAN WHO HATH REASON TO SUSPECT THAT YOU KNOW HE HATH INJURED YOU.

### CHAPTER V

*More and more* GREATNESS, *unparalleled in History or Romance.*

IN order to accomplish this great and noble Scheme, which the vast Genius of *Wild* had contrived, the first necessary Step seemed to be to regain the Confidence of *Heartfree.* He determined therefore to undertake it, how impossible soever it appeared. The chief Requisite on this Occasion, was that steady Countenance in which he was superior to all Mankind. He went to *Newgate*, and burst resolutely into the Presence of *Heartfree*, whom he eagerly embraced and kissed; and then, first arraigning his own Rashness, and afterwards lamenting his unfortunate want of Success, he acquainted him with the Particulars of what had happened; concealing only that single Incident of his Attack on the other's Wife, the Lies he had told her concerning her Husband's Commands; and his Motive to the Undertaking, which he assured *Heartfree* was a Desire to preserve his Effects from a Statute of Bankruptcy.°

The frank Openness of this Declaration, with the Composure of Countenance with which it was delivered; his seeming only ruffled by the Concern for his Friend's Misfortune; the Probability of Truth attending it, joined to the Boldness and disinterested Appearance of this Visit, together with his many Professions of immediate Service, at a Time when he could not have the least visible Motive from Self-Love; and above all, his offering him Money, the last and surest Token of Friendship, rushed with such united Force on the well-disposed Heart, as it is vulgarly called, of this simple Man, that they instantly staggered and soon subverted all the Determination he had before made in Prejudice of *Wild:* Who perceiving the Ballance to be turning in his Favour, presently threw in a hundred Imprecations on his own Folly and ill-advised Forwardness to serve his Friend, which had thus unhappily produced his Ruin; he added as many Curses on the Count, whom he vowed to pursue with Revenge all over *Europe*: Lastly, he cast in some Grains of Comfort, assuring *Heartfree* that his Wife was fallen into the gentlest Hands, that she would be carried no farther than *Dunkirk*, whence she might be very easily redeemed.

*Heartfree*, to whom the lightest Presumption of his Wife's Fidelity would have been more delicious than the absolute Restoration of all his Jewels, and who, indeed, had with the utmost Difficulty been brought to entertain the slightest Suspicion of her Inconstancy, immediately abandoned all Distrust of both her and his Friend, whose Sincerity (luckily for *Wild's* Purpose) seemed to him to depend on the same Evidence. He then embraced our Hero, who had in his Countenance all the Symptoms of the deepest Concern, and begged him to be comforted; saying, that the Intentions rather than the Actions of Men conferred Obligations; that as to the Event of human Affairs, it was governed either by Chance or some superior Agent, that Friendship was concerned only in the Direction of it. And suppose it failed of Success, or produced an Event never so contrary to its Design, the Merit of a good Intention was not in the least lessened, but was rather entitled to Compassion.

*Wild* having thus, with admirable and truly laudable Conduct, atchieved the first Step, began to discourse on the Badness of the World; and particularly to blame the Severity of Creditors, who seldom or never attended to any unfortunate Circumstances, but without Mercy inflicted Confinement on the Debtor, whose Body the Law, with very unjustifiable Rigour, delivered into their Power. He added, that for his Part, he looked on this Restraint to be as heavy a Punishment as any appointed by Law for the greatest Offenders. That the Loss of Liberty was, in his Opinion, equal to, if not worse, than the Loss of Life; that he had always determined, if by any Accident or Misfortune he had been subjected to the former, he would run the greatest Risque of the latter to rescue himself from it; which he said, if Men did not want Resolution, was always easy enough to do; for that it was ridiculous to conceive that two or three Men could confine two or three hundred, unless the Prisoners were either Fools or Cowards, especially when they were neither chained nor fettered. He went on in this Manner, till perceiving the utmost Attention in *Heartfree*, he ventured to propose to him an Endeavour to make his Escape, which he said might easily be executed; that he would himself raise a Party in the Prison, and that, if a Murther or two should happen in the Attempt, he (*Heartfree*) might keep free from any Share either in the Guilt or in the Danger.

There is one Misfortune which attends all great Men and their Schemes, *viz.* That in order to carry them into Execution, they are obliged in proposing their Purpose to their Tools, to discover themselves to be of that Disposition, in which certain little Writers have advised Mankind to place no Confidence: An Advice which hath been sometimes taken. Indeed many Inconveniencies arise to the said GREAT MEN from these Scriblers publishing without Restraint their Hints or Alarms to Society; and many great and glorious Schemes have been thus frustrated; wherefore it were to be wished that in all well-regulated Governments, such Liberty should be by some wholesome Laws restrained; and all Writers inhibited from venting any other Instructions to the People than what should be first approved and licensed by the said GREAT MEN, or their proper Instruments or Tools; by which Means nothing would ever be published but what made for the advancing their most noble Projects.°

*Heartfree*, whose Suspicions were again raised by this Advice, viewing *Wild* with inconceivable Disdain, spoke as follows. 'There is one thing, the Loss of which I should deplore infinitely beyond that of Liberty and of Life also, I mean that of a good Conscience, a Blessing which he who possesses can never be thoroughly unhappy; for the bitterest Portion of Life is by this so sweetened, that it soon becomes palatable; whereas without it, the most delicate Enjoyments quickly lose all their Relish, and Life itself grows insipid, or rather nauseous to us. Would you then lessen my Misfortunes by robbing me of what hath been my only Comfort under them, and on which I place my Dependence of being relieved from them? I have read that *Socrates* refused to save his Life by breaking the Laws of his Country, and departing from his Prison, when it was open.° Perhaps my Virtue would not go so far; but God forbid Liberty should have such Charms, to tempt me to the Perpetration of so horrid a Crime as Murther. As to the poor Evasion of committing it by other Hands, it might be useful indeed to those who seek only the Escape from temporal Punishment; but can be of no Service to excuse me to that Being whom I chiefly fear offending; nay, it would greatly aggravate

my Guilt by so impudent an Endeavour to impose upon him, and by
so wickedly involving others in my Crime. Give me therefore no
more Advice of this Kind; for this is my great Comfort in all my
Afflictions, that it is in the Power of no Enemy to rob me of my
Conscience, nor will I ever be so much my own Enemy to destroy it.'

Though our Hero heard all this with proper Contempt, he made
no direct Answer; but endeavoured to evade his Proposal as much as
possible, and promising to use all honest Means for his Service, since
he was so scrupulous, he took his Leave of his Friend for the present.
*Heartfree*, having indulged himself an Hour with his Children,
repaired to Rest, which he enjoyed quiet and undisturbed; whilst
*Wild*, disdaining Repose, sat up all Night, consulting how he might
bring about the final Destruction of his Friend, without being
beholden to any Assistance from himself; which he now despaired of
procuring. With the Result of these Consultations we shall acquaint
our Reader in good time; but at present we have Matters of much
more Consequence to relate to him.

### CHAPTER VI

*The Event of* Fireblood's *Adventure, and a Treaty of*
*Marriage, which might have been concluded either at*
Smithfield *or* St. James's.°

*FIREBLOOD* returned from his Enterprize unsuccessful. The
Gentleman happened to go home another Way than he had intended;
so that the whole Design miscarried. *Fireblood* had indeed robbed
the Coach, and wantonly discharged a Pistol into it, which slightly
wounded one of the Passengers in the Arm. The Booty he met with
was not very considerable, tho' much greater than that with which he
acquainted *Wild;* for, of eleven Pounds in Money, two Silver-
watches, and a Wedding-Ring, he produced no more than two
Guineas and the Ring, which he protested with numberless Oaths
was his whole Booty. However, when an Advertisement of the
Robbery was published, with a Reward promised for the Ring and
the Watches, *Fireblood* was obliged to confess the whole, and to
acquaint our Hero where he had pawned the latter; which he, taking
the full Value of them for his Pains, restored to the right Owner.

He did not fail catechizing his young Friend on this Occasion. He said, he was sorry to see any of his Gang guilty of a Breach of Honour; that without Honour *Priggery* was at an End; that if a *Prig* had but Honour, he would overlook every Vice in the World. But, nevertheless, he said, he would forgive him this time, as he was a hopeful Lad, and wished never afterwards to find him delinquent in this grand Point.

*Wild* had now brought his Gang to great Regularity: He was obeyed and feared by them all. He had likewise established an Office where all Men, who were robbed, paying the Value only (or a little more) of their Goods might have them again.° This was of notable Use to several Persons who had lost Pieces of Plate they had received from their Grandmothers; to others who had a particular Value for certain Rings, Watches, Heads of Canes, Snuff-Boxes, &c. for which they would not have taken twenty times as much as they were worth, either because they had them a long time, or that somebody else had had them before, or from some other such excellent Reason, which often stamps a greater Value on a Toy, than the great *Bubble-boy* himself° would have the Impudence to set upon it.

By these Means he seemed in so promising a Way of procuring a Fortune, and was regarded in so thriving a Light by all the Gentlemen of his Acquaintance, as by the Keeper and Turnkeys of *Newgate*,° by Mr. *Snap*, and others of his Occupation; that Mr. *Snap* one Day, taking Mr. *Wild* the elder aside, very seriously proposed what they had often lightly talked over, a strict Union between their Families, by marrying his Daughter *Tishy* to our Hero. This Proposal was very readily accepted by the old Gentleman, who promised to acquaint his Son with it.

On the Morrow, on which this Message was to be delivered, our Hero, little dreaming of the Happiness which, of its own Accord, was advancing so near towards him, had called *Fireblood* to him, and, after informing him of the Violence of his Passion for the young Lady, and assuring him what Confidence he reposed in him and his Honour, to which the other answered, he would be sure to discharge whatever he entrusted to him, with the utmost Fidelity; he dispatched him to Miss *Tishy* with the following Letter, which we here insert, not only as we take it to be extremely curious, but to be a much better Pattern for that Epistolary kind of Writing, which is generally called LOVE-LETTERS, than any to be found in the

*Academy of Compliments,*° and which we challenge all the Beaus of our Time to equal either in Matter or Spelling.

   Most Deivine and adwhorable Creture,
I dout not but those IIs, briter than the Son, which have kindled such a Flam in my Hart, have likewise the Faculty of seeing it. It would be the hiest Preassumption to imagin you eggnorant of my Loav. No, Maddam, I sollemly purtest, that, of all the Butys in the unaversal Glob, there is none kapable of hateracting my IIs like you. Corts and Pallaces would be to me Deserts without your Kumpany, and with it a Wilderness would have more Charms than Haven itself. For I hop you will beleve me when I sware every Place in the Univarse is a Haven with you. I am konvinced you must be sinsibel of my violent Passion for you, which, if I endevored to hid it, would be as impossible as for you, or the Son to hide your Butys. I assure you I have not slept a Wink since I had the Hapness of seeing you last; therefore hop you will, out of Kumpassion, let me have the Honour of seeing you this Afternoon; for I am, with the greatest Adwhoration,

                    Most Deivine Creeture,
                    *Iour most pessionate Amirer,*
                    *Adwhorer, and Slave,*
                    JOHANATAN WYLD.

   If the spelling of this Letter be not so strictly orthographical, the Reader will be pleased to remember, that such a Defect might be worthy of Censure in a low and scholastic Character; but can be no Blemish in that sublime GREATNESS, of which we endeavour to raise a complete Idea in this History. In which kind of Composition, Spelling, or indeed any kind of human Literature, hath never been thought a necessary Ingredient; for if these sort of GREAT Personages can but complot and contrive their noble Schemes, and hack and hew Mankind sufficiently, there will never be wanting fit and able Persons who can spell, to record their Praises. Again, if it should be observed that the Style of this Letter doth not exactly correspond with that of our Hero's Speeches, which we have here recorded, we answer, <u>it is sufficient</u> if in these the <u>Historian adheres faithfully to the Matter</u>, though <u>he embellishes the Diction</u> with some Flourishes of his own Eloquence, without which the excellent Speeches recorded in ancient Historians (particularly in *Sallust*) would have scarce been found in their Writings.° Nay, even amongst the Moderns, famous as they are for Elocution, it may be doubted whether those inimitable Harangues (published in the Monthly *Magazines*) came literally from the Mouths of the Hurgos, &c. as they are there inserted, or whether we may not rather suppose some Historian of great Eloquence hath borrowed the Matter only, and adorned it with those Rhetorical Flowers for which many of the said Hurgos are not so extremely eminent.°

CHAPTER VII

*Matters preliminary to the Marriage between Mr.* Jonathan Wild *and the chaste* Lætitia.

BUT to proceed with our History: *Fireblood* having received this Letter, and promised on his Honour, as we have before hinted, to discharge his Embassy faithfully, went to visit the fair *Lætitia*. Having opened the Letter, and read it, she put on an Air of Disdain, and told Mr. *Fireblood*, she could not conceive what Mr. *Wild* meant by troubling her with his Impertinence; she begged him to carry the Letter back again, saying, had she known from whom it came, she would have been d——d before she had opened it. Moreover, she said, she was not angry with him, nay, she was sorry so pretty a young Man should be employed in such an Errand. She accompanied these Words with so tender an Accent, and so wanton a Leer, that *Fireblood*, who was no backward Youth, began to take her by the Hand, and proceeded so warmly, that, to imitate his Actions with the Rapidity of our Narration, he in a few Minutes ravished this fair Creature, or at least would have ravished her, if she had not, by a timely Compliance, prevented him.

*Fireblood*, after he had ravished as much as he could, returned to *Wild*, and acquainted him as far as any wise Man would, with what had past; concluding with many Praises of the young Lady's Beauty, with whom, he said, if his Honour would have permitted him, he should himself have fallen in Love; but, d——n him, if he would not sooner be torn in Pieces by wild Horses, than even think of injuring his Friend. And if he could be of any Service, he might command him to go to *Lætitia* when, and as often as he pleased.

Thus constituted were the Love-Affairs of our Hero, when his Father brought him Mr. *Snap's* Proposal. The Reader must know very little of Love, or indeed of any thing else, if he requires any Information concerning the Reception which this Proposal met with. *Not guilty* never sounded sweeter in the Ears of *Culprit*,° nor a Reprieve to the Prisoner condemned, than did every Word of the old Gentleman in the Ears of our Hero. He gave his Father full Power to treat in his Name, and desired nothing more than Expedition.

The old People now met, and *Snap*, who had Information from his Daughter of the violent Passion of her Lover, endeavoured to improve it to the best Advantage, and would have not only declined giving her any Fortune himself, but attempted to cheat her of what she owed to the Liberality of her Relations, particularly of a Pint Silver Caudle Cup,° the Gift of her Grandmother. However, the young Lady herself afterwards took Care to prevent him. As to old Mr. *Wild*, he did not sufficiently attend to all the Designs of *Snap*, as his Faculties were busily employed in Designs of his own, to over-reach (or, as others express it, to cheat) the said Mr. *Snap*, by pre-tending to give his Son a whole Number for a Chair, when in Reality he was intitled to a third only.°

While Matters were thus settling between the old Folks, the young Lady agreed to admit Mr. *Wild's* Visits; and, by Degrees, began to entertain him with all the Shew of Affection, which the great natural Reserve of her Temper, and the greater artificial Reserve of her Educa-tion would permit. At length every thing being agreed between their Parents, Settlements made, and the Lady's Fortune (to wit, Seventeen Pounds and nine Shillings in Money and Goods) paid down, the Day for their Nuptials was fixed, and they were celebrated accordingly.

Most Histories as well as Comedies end at this Period; the His-torian and the Poet both concluding they have done enough for their Hero when they have married him; or intimating rather, that the rest of his Life must be a dull Calm of Happiness, very delightful indeed to pass through, but somewhat insipid to relate: And Matrimony in general must, I believe, without any Dispute, be allowed to be this State of tranquil Felicity, so little concerned with Variety, that, like *Salisbury* Plain, it affords only one Prospect, a very pleasant one it must be confest, but the same.°

Now there was all the Probability imaginable, that this Contract would have proved of such happy Note, both from the great Accomplishments of the young Lady, and the truly ardent Passion of Mr. *Wild*; but whether it was that Nature and Fortune had great Designs for him to execute, and would not suffer his vast Abilities to be lost and sunk in the Arms of a Wife, or whether neither Nature nor Fortune had any Hand in the Matter, is a Point I will not determine. Certain it is that this Match did not produce that serene State we have mentioned above, but resembled the most turbulent and ruffled, rather than calm Sea.

I cannot here omit a Conjecture ingenious enough of a Friend of mine, who had a long Intimacy in the *Wild* Family. He hath often told me he fancied one Reason of the Dissatisfactions which afterwards fell out between *Wild* and his Lady, arose from the Number of Gallants, to whom she had before Marriage granted Favours; 'for,' says he, and indeed very probable it is too, 'the Lady might expect from her Husband, what she had before received from several, and being angry not to find one Man as good as ten, she had, from that Indignation, taken those Steps which we cannot perfectly justify.'

From this Person I received the following Dialogue, which, he assured me, he had overheard, and taken down *verbatim*. It passed on the Day Fortnight after they were married.

### CHAPTER VIII

*A Dialogue matrimonial,*° *which passed between* JONATHAN WILD, *Esquire, and* LÆTITIA *his Wife, on the Morning of the Day Fortnight on which his Nuptials were celebrated; which concluded more amicably than those Debates generally do.*

#### *Jonathan*

MY Dear, I wish you would lie a little longer in Bed this Morning.

#### *Lætitia*

Indeed I cannot: I am engaged to breakfast with Sir *John*.

#### *Jonathan*

I don't know what Sir *John* doth so often at my House. I assure you I am uneasy at it; for though I have no Suspicion of your Virtue, yet it may injure your Reputation in the Opinion of my Neighbours.

### *Lætitia*

I don't trouble my Head about my Neighbours; and they shall no more tell me what Company I am to keep than my Husband shall.

### *Jonathan*

A good Wife would keep no Company which made her Husband uneasy.

### *Lætitia*

You might have found one of those good Wives, Sir, if you had pleased, I had no Objection to it.

### *Jonathan*

I thought I had found one in you.

### *Lætitia*

You did! I am very much obliged to you for thinking me so poor-spirited a Creature; but I hope to convince you to the contrary. What, I suppose you took me for a raw, senseless Girl, who knew nothing what other married Women do!

### *Jonathan*

No Matter what I took you for: I have taken you for better and worse.°

### *Lætitia*

And at your own Desire too? For, I am sure, you never had mine. I should not have broken my Heart if Mr. *Wild* had thought proper to bestow himself on any other more happy Woman.—Ha, ha.

### *Jonathan*

I hope, Madam, you don't imagine that was not in my Power, or that I married you out of any kind of Necessity.

### *Lætitia*

O no, Sir, I am convinced there are silly Women enough. And far be it from me to accuse you of any Necessity for a Wife, I believe you could have very well been contented with the State of a Batchelor; but that, you know, a Woman cannot tell beforehand.

### *Jonathan*

I can't guess what you would insinuate; for I believe no Woman had ever less Reason to complain of her Husband's Want of Fondness.

### *Lætitia*

Then some, I am certain, have great Reason to complain of the Price they give for them.—But I know better things. *(These Words to be spoken with a very great Air, and Toss of the Head.)* ✳ characters – characters + not actually real people

### *Jonathan*

Well, my Sweeting, I will make it impossible for you to wish me more fond.—

### *Lætitia*

Pray, Mr. *Wild*, none of this nauseous Behaviour, nor those odious Words.—I wish you were fond!—I assure you—I don't know what you would pretend to insinuate of me.—I have no Wishes which misbecome a virtuous Woman—No, nor should not, if I had married for Love.—And especially now when no body, I am sure, can suspect me of any such thing.—

### *Jonathan*

If you did not marry for Love, why did you marry?

### *Lætitia*

Because it was convenient, and my Parents forced me.

### *Jonathan*

I hope, Madam, at least, you will not tell me to my Face, you have made your Convenience of me.°

### *Lætitia*

I have made nothing of you; nor do I desire the Honour of making any thing of you.

### *Jonathan*

Yes, you have made a Husband of me.

### *Lætitia*

No, you made your self so; for I repeat once more, It was not my Desire but your own.

### *Jonathan*

You should think yourself obliged to me for that Desire.

### *Lætitia*

La! Sir, you was not so singular in it. I was not in Despair.—I have had other Offers, and better too.

### *Jonathan*

I wish you had accepted them with all my Heart.

### *Lætitia*

I must tell you, Mr. *Wild*, this is a very brutish Manner of treating a Woman, to whom you have such Obligations; but I know how to despise it, and to despise you too for shewing it me. Indeed I am well enough paid for the foolish Preference I gave to you. I flattered myself that I should at least have been used with good Manners. I thought I had married a Gentleman; but I find you every way contemptible, and below my Concern.

### *Jonathan*

D——n you, Madam, have not I more Reason to complain, when you tell me you married me for your Convenience only?

### *Lætitia*

Very fine, truly. Is it Behaviour worthy a Man to swear at a Woman? Yet why should I mention what comes from a Wretch whom I despise!

### *Jonathan*

Don't repeat that Word so often. I despise you as heartily as you can me. And, to tell you a Truth, I married you for my Convenience likewise, to satisfy a Passion which I have now satisfied, and you may be d——d for any thing I care.

### *Lætitia*

The World shall know how barbarously I am treated by such a Villain.

### *Jonathan*

I need take very little Pains to acquaint the World what a B——ch you are,° your Actions will demonstrate it.

### *Lætitia*

Monster, I would advise you not to depend too much on my Sex, and provoke me too far; for I can do you a Mischief, and will, if you dare use me so, you Villain!

### *Jonathan*

Begin whenever you please, Madam; but, assure yourself, the Moment you lay aside the Woman, I will treat you as such no longer; and if the first Blow is yours, I promise you the last shall be mine.

### *Lætitia*

Use me as you will; but d——n me if ever you shall use me as a Woman again; for, may I be cursed, if ever I enter your Bed more.

### *Jonathan*

May I be cursed if that Abstinence be not the greatest Obligation you can lay upon me; for, I assure you faithfully, your Person was all I had ever any Regard for; and that I now loath and detest, as much as ever I liked it.

### *Lætitia*

It is impossible for two People to agree better; for I always detested your Person; and, as for any other Regard, you must be convinced I never could have any for you.

### *Jonathan*

Why, then, since we are come to a right Understanding, as we are to live together, suppose we agreed, instead of quarrelling and abusing, to be civil to each other.

### *Lætitia*

With all my Heart.

### *Jonathan*

Let us shake Hands then, and henceforwards never live like Man and Wife; that is, never be loving, nor never quarrel.

### *Lætitia*

Agreed.—But pray, Mr. *Wild*, why B——ch? Why did you suffer such a Word to escape you?

### *Jonathan*

It is not worth your Remembrance.

### *Lætitia*

You agree I shall converse with° whomsoever I please?

### *Jonathan*

Without Controul. And I have the same Liberty?

### *Lætitia*

When I interfere, may every Curse you can wish attend me.

### *Jonathan*

Let us now take a Farewell-Kiss; and may I be hang'd if it is not the sweetest you ever gave me.

### *Lætitia*

But why, B——ch?—Methinks I should be glad to know why B——ch?

At which Words he sprang from the Bed, d——ing her Temper heartily. She returned it again with equal Abuse, which was continued on both Sides while he was dressing. However, they agreed to continue stedfast in this new Resolution; and the Joy arising on that Occasion at length dismissed them pretty amicably from each other, though *Lætitia* could not help concluding with the Words, WHY B——CH?

### CHAPTER IX

*Observations on the foregoing Dialogue, together with a
base Design on our Hero, which must be detested by every
Lover of* GREATNESS.

THUS did this Dialogue (which tho' we have termed it matrimonial,
had indeed very little Savour of the Sweets of Matrimony° in it)
produce at last a Resolution more wise than strictly pious, and
which, if they could have rigidly adhered to it, might have prevented
some unpleasant Moments as well to our Hero as to his Serene
Consort;° but their Hatred was so very great and unaccountable, that
they never could bear to see the least Composure in one another's
Countenance, without attempting to ruffle it. This set them on so
many Contrivances to plague and vex one another, that as their
Proximity afforded them such frequent Opportunities of executing
their malicious Purposes, they seldom past one easy or quiet Day
together.

And this, Reader, and no other is the Cause of those many
Inquietudes, which thou must have observed to disturb the Repose
of some married Couples, who mistake implacable Hatred for Indifference; for why should *Corvinus*, who lives in a Round of Intrigue,
and seldom doth, and never willingly would, dally with his Wife,
endeavour to prevent her from the Satisfaction of an Intrigue in her
Turn? Why doth *Camilla*° refuse a more agreeable Invitation abroad,
only to expose her Husband at his own Table at home? In short, to
mention no more Instances, whence can all the Quarrels, and Jealousies, and Jars, proceed, in People who have no Love for each other,
unless from that noble Passion abovementioned, that Desire, according to my Lady *Betty Modish*, of *curing each other of a Smile?*°

We thought proper to give our Reader a short Taste of the
domestic State of our Hero, the rather to shew him that GREAT MEN
are subject to the same Frailties and Inconveniencies in ordinary
Life, with little Men, and that Heroes are really of the same Species
with other human Creatures, notwithstanding all the Pains they
themselves, or their Flatterers take to assert the contrary; and that
they differ chiefly in the Immensity of their GREATNESS, or as the
Vulgar erroneously call it, Villainy. Now therefore, that we may not
dwell too long on low Scenes, in a History of this sublime Kind, we

shall return to Actions of a higher Note, and more suitable to our Purpose.

When the Boy *Hymen* had with his lighted Torch driven the Boy *Cupid* out of Doors;° that is to say, in common Phrase, when the Violence of Mr. *Wild's* Passion (or rather Appetite) for the chaste *Lætitia*, began to abate, he returned to visit his Friend *Heartfree*, who was now in the Liberties of the *Fleet*,° and had appeared to the Commission of Bankruptcy against him,° where he met with a less cold Reception than he himself had apprehended. *Heartfree* had long entertained Suspicions of *Wild*, but these Suspicions had from time to time been confounded with Circumstances, and principally smothered with that amazing Confidence, which was indeed the most striking Virtue in our Hero. He was unwilling to condemn him, without certain Evidence, and laid hold on every probable Semblance to acquit him; but the Proposal made at his last Visit had so totally blackned his Character in this poor Man's Opinion, that it entirely fixed the wavering Scale, and he no longer doubted but that our Hero was one of the greatest Villains in the World.

Circumstances of great Improbability often escape Men who devour a Story with greedy Ears; the Reader therefore cannot wonder that *Heartfree*, whose Passions were so variously concerned, first for the Fidelity, and secondly for the Safety of his Wife; and lastly, who was so distracted with Doubt concerning the Conduct of his Friend, should at his first Relation pass unobserved the Incident of his being committed to the Boat by the Captain of the Privateer, which he had not at the time of his telling it in the least accounted for; but now when *Heartfree* came to reflect on the whole, and with a high Prepossession against *Wild*, the Absurdity of this Fact glared in his Eyes, and struck him in the most sensible Manner. At length a Thought of great Horror suggested itself to his Imagination, and this was, Whether the whole was not a Fiction, and *Wild*, who was, as he had learn'd from his own Mouth, equal to any Undertaking how black soever, had not spirited away, robbed and murthered his Wife.

Intolerable as this Apprehension was, he not only turned it round and examined it carefully in his own Mind, but acquainted young *Friendly* with it at their next Interview. *Friendly*, who detested *Wild* (from that Envy, probably, with which these GREAT CHARACTERS naturally inspire low Fellows) encouraged these Suspicions so much, that *Heartfree* resolved to attach° our Hero and carry him before a Magistrate.

This Resolution had been some time taken, and *Friendly* with a Warrant and a Constable had with the utmost Diligence, searched several Days for our Hero; but to no Purpose, whether it was that in Compliance with modern Custom, he had retired to spend the Honey-Moon° with his Bride, the only Moon indeed in which it is fashionable or customary for the married Parties to have any Affection for each other; or perhaps his Habitation might for particular Reasons be usually kept a Secret: Like those of some few GREAT MEN, whom unfortunately the Law hath left out of that reasonable as well as honourable Provision, which it hath made for the Security of most GREAT MEN's Persons.°

But *Wild* resolved to perform Works of Supererogation° in the Way of Honour, and, tho' no Hero is obliged to answer the Challenge of my Lord Chief Justice, or indeed, of any other Magistrate; but may with unblemished Reputation slide away from it; yet such was the Bravery, such the GREATNESS, the Magnanimity of *Wild*, that he appeared in Person to it.

Indeed Envy may say one Thing, which may lessen the Glory of this Action, namely, that the said Mr. *Wild* knew nothing of the said Warrant or Challenge; and as thou may'st be assured, Reader, that the malicious Fury° will omit nothing which can any ways sully so great a Character, so she hath endeavoured to account for this second Visit of our Hero to his Friend *Heartfree*, from a very different Motive than that of asserting his own Innocence.

### CHAPTER X

*Mr.* Wild, *with unprecedented Generosity, visits his Friend* Heartfree, *and the ungrateful Reception he met with.*

IT hath been said then, that Mr. *Wild*, not being able on the strictest Examination to find in a certain Spot of human Nature called his own Heart, the least Grain of that pitiful low Quality called Honesty, had resolved, perhaps a little too generally, that there was no such thing. He therefore imputed the Resolution with which Mr. *Heartfree* had so positively refused to concern himself in Murther, either to a Fear of bloodying his Hands, or the Apprehension of a Ghost,° or lest he should make an additional Example in that excellent Book called, *God's Revenge against Murther;*° and doubted not but he would (at least in his present Necessity) agree without Scruple to a simple Robbery, especially where any considerable Booty should be proposed, and the Safety of the Attack plausibly made appear; which, if he could prevail on him to undertake, he would immediately afterwards get him impeached, convicted, and hanged. He no sooner therefore had discharged his Duties to *Hymen*, and heard that *Heartfree* had procured himself the Liberties of the *Fleet*, than he resolved to visit him, and propose a Robbery with all the Allurements of Profit, Ease and Safety.

This Proposal was no sooner made, than it was answered by *Heartfree* in the following Manner.

'I might have hoped the Answer which I gave to your former Advice would have prevented me from the Danger of receiving a second Affront of this Kind. An Affront I call it, and surely if it be so to call a Man a Villain, it can be no less to shew him you suppose him one. Indeed it may be wondered how any Man can arrive at the Boldness, I may say Impudence, of first making such an Overture to another; surely it is seldom done, unless to those who have previously betrayed some Symptoms of their own Baseness. If I have therefore shewn you any such, these Insults are more pardonable; but I assure you, if such appear, they discharge all their Malignance outwardly, and reflect not even a Shadow within; for to me, Baseness seems inconsistent with this Rule, OF DOING NO OTHER PERSON AN INJURY FROM ANY MOTIVE OR ON ANY CONSIDERATION WHATEVER. This, Sir, is the Rule by which I am determined to walk, nor can that Man justify disbelieving me, who will not own, he walks not by it himself. But whether it be allowed to me or no, or whether I feel the good Effects of its being practised by others, I am resolved to maintain it: For surely no Man can reap a Benefit from my pursuing it equal to the Comfort I myself enjoy: For what a ravishing Thought! how replete with Extasy must the Consideration be, that the Goodness of God is engaged to reward me!° How indifferent must such a Persuasion make a Man to all the Occurrences of this Life! What Trifles must he represent to himself both the Enjoyments and the Afflictions of this World! How easily must he acquiesce under missing the former, and how patiently will he submit to the

latter, who is convinced that his failing of a transitory imperfect
Reward here, is a most certain Argument of his obtaining one permanent and complete hereafter! Dost thou think then, thou little,
paltry, mean Animal, (with such Language did he treat our truly
GREAT MAN) that I will forego such comfortable Expectations for
any pitiful Reward which thou canst suggest or promise to me; for
that sordid Lucre for which all Pains and Labour are undertaken by
the Industrious, and all Barbarities and Iniquities committed by the
Vile; or for a worthless Acquisition which such as thou art can possess, can give or can rob me of?' The former Part of this Speech
occasioned much yawning in our Hero, but the latter roused his
Anger; and he was collecting his Rage to answer, when *Friendly* and
the Constable,° who had been summoned by *Heartfree*, on *Wild's* first
Appearance, entred the Room, and seized the GREAT MAN just as
his Wrath was bursting from his Lips.

The Dialogue which now ensued, is not worth relating, *Wild* was
soon acquainted with the Reason of this rough Treatment, and presently conveyed before a Magistrate.

Notwithstanding the Doubts raised by Mr. *Wild's* Lawyer on his
Examination, he insisting that the Proceeding was improper; for that
a Writ *de Homine Replegiando* should issue, and on the Return of that
a *Capias in Withernam*,° the Justice inclined to commitment, so that
*Wild* was driven to other Methods for his Defence. He therefore
acquainted the Justice, that there was a young Man likewise with him
in the Boat, and begged that he might be sent for, which Request was
accordingly granted, and the faithful *Achates* (Mr. *Fireblood*) was
soon produced to bear Testimony for his Friend, which he did with
so much becoming Zeal, and went through his Examination with
such Coherence (tho' he was forced to collect his Evidence from the
Hints given him by *Wild* in the Presence of the Justice and the
Accusers,) that, as here was direct Evidence against mere Presumption, our Hero was most honourably acquitted, and poor *Heartfree*
was charged by the Justice, the Audience, and all others, who afterwards heard the Story, with the blackest Ingratitude, in attempting
to take away the Life of a Man, to whom he had such eminent
Obligations.

Lest so vast an Effort of Friendship as this of *Fireblood's* should
too violently surprize the Reader in this degenerate Age; it may be
proper to inform him, that besides the Ties of Engagement in the

same Employ, another nearer and stronger Alliance subsisted between our Hero and this Youth, which latter was just departed from the Arms of the lovely *Lætitia*, when he received her Husband's Message: An Instance which may also serve to justify those strict Intercourses of Love and Acquaintance, which so commonly subsist in modern History between the Husband and Gallant, displaying the vast Force of Friendship, contracted by this more honourable than legal Alliance, which is thought to be at present one of the strongest Bonds of Amity between GREAT MEN, and the most reputable as well as easy Way to Preferment.

Four Months had now passed since *Heartfree's* first Confinement, and his Affairs had begun to wear a more benign Aspect; but they were a good deal injured by this Attempt on *Wild* (so dangerous is any Attack on a GREAT MAN) several of his Neighbours, and particularly one or two of his own Trade, industriously endeavouring, from their bitter Animosity against such Kind of Iniquity, to spread and exaggerate his Ingratitude as much as possible; not in the least scrupling, in the violent Ardour of their Indignation, to add some small Circumstances of their own Knowledge of the many Obligations conferred on *Heartfree* by *Wild*. To all these Scandals he quietly submitted, comforting himself in the Consciousness of his own Innocence, and confiding in Time, the sure Friend of Justice, to acquit him.

CHAPTER XI

*A Scheme so deeply laid that it shames all the Politics of this our Age; with Digression and Sub-digression.°*

*WILD* having now, to the Hatred he bore *Heartfree* on Account of those Injuries he had done him, an additional Spur from this Injury received (for so it appeared to him, who no more than the most ignorant, considered how truly he deserved it) applied his utmost Industry to accomplish the Ruin of one whose very Name sounded odious in his Ears; when luckily a Scheme arose in his Imagination, which not only promised to effect it securely; but (which pleased him most) by Means of the Mischief he had already done him; and which would at once load him with the Imputation of having committed what he himself had done for him, and would bring on him the severest Punishment for a Fact, of which he was not only innocent, but had already so greatly suffered by. And this was no other than to charge him with having conveyed away his Wife, with his most valuable Effects, in order to defraud his Creditors.

He no sooner started this Thought than he immediately resolved on putting it in Execution. What remained to consider was only the *Quomodo*, and the Person or Tool to be employed; for the Stage of the World differs from that in *Drury-Lane* principally in this;° that whereas on the latter, the Hero, or chief Figure, is almost continually before your Eyes, whilst the Under-actors are not seen above once in an Evening; now, on the former, the Hero, or GREAT MAN, is always behind the Curtain, and seldom or never appears, or doth any thing in his own Person. He doth indeed, in this *grand Drama*, rather perform the Part of the *Prompter*, and instructs the well-drest Figures, who are strutting in public on the Stage, what to say and do. To say the Truth, a Puppet-show will illustrate our Meaning better, where it is the Master of the Show (the GREAT MAN) who dances and moves every thing; whether it be the King of *Muscovy*, or whatever other Potentate, *alias* Puppet, which we behold on the Stage; but he himself wisely keeps out of Sight; for should he once appear, the whole Motion would be at an End. Not that any one is ignorant of his being there, or supposes that the Puppets are not mere Sticks of Wood, and he himself the sole Mover; but as this (tho' every one knows it) doth not appear visibly, *i.e.* to their Eyes, no one is ashamed of consenting to be imposed upon; of helping on the *Drama*, calling the several Sticks or Puppets by the Names which the Master hath allotted to them, and assigning to each the Character which the GREAT MAN is pleased they shall move in, or rather in which he himself is pleased to move them.°

It would be to suppose thee, gentle Reader, one of very little Knowledge in this World, to imagine thou hast never seen some of these Puppet-Shews, which are so frequently acted on the GREAT Stage; but though thou shouldst have resided all thy Days in those remote Parts of this Island, which GREAT Men seldom visit; yet, if thou hast any Penetration, thou must have had some Occasions to admire both the Solemnity of Countenance in the Actor, and the Gravity in the Spectator, while some of those Farces are carried on, which are acted almost daily in every Village in the Kingdom. He must have a very despicable Opinion of Mankind indeed, who can conceive them to be imposed on as often as they appear to be so. The Truth is, they are in the same Situation with the Readers of *Romances*; who, though they know the whole to be one entire Fiction, nevertheless agree to be deceived; and as these find Amusement, so do the others find Ease and Convenience in this Concurrence. But this being a Sub-digression, I return to my Digression.

A GREAT MAN ought to do his Business by others; to employ Hands, as we have before said, to his Purposes, and keep himself as much behind the Curtain as possible; and though it must be acknowledged that two very GREAT Men, whose Names will be both recorded in History, did, in former Times, come forth themselves on the Stage; and did hack and hew, and lay each other most cruelly open to the Diversion of the Spectators;° yet this must be mentioned rather as an Example of Avoidance, than Imitation, and is to be ascribed to the Number of those Instances which serve to evince the Truth of these Maxims: *Nemo mortalium omnibus horis sapit.*° *Ira furor brevis est,*° *&c.*

### CHAPTER XII

*Elogiums on Constables, &c. And new Instances of*
Friendly's *Folly.*

To return to my History, which, having rested itself a little, is now ready to proceed on its Journey: *Fireblood* was the Person chosen by *Wild* for this Service. He had, on the late Occasion, experienced the Talents of this Youth for a good round Perjury. He immediately, therefore, found him out, and proposed it to him, and, receiving his instant Assent, they consulted together, and soon framed an Evidence, which, being communicated to one of the most bitter and severe Creditors of *Heartfree*, by him laid before a Magistrate, and attested by the Oath of *Fireblood*, the Justice granted his Warrant; and *Heartfree* was accordingly apprehended and brought before him.

When the Officers came for this poor Wretch, they found him meanly diverting himself with his little Children, the youngest of whom sat on his Knees, and the eldest was playing at a little Distance from him with *Friendly*. The Constable, who was a very good sort of a Man, but one very laudably severe in his Office, after acquainting *Heartfree* with his Errand, bad him come along and be d——d, and leave those little Bastards; for so, he said, he supposed they were, for a Legacy to the Parish.° *Heartfree* was much surprized at hearing there was a Warrant for Felony against him;° but he shewed less Concern than *Friendly* did in his Countenance. The eldest Daughter, when she saw the Constable lay hold on her Father, immediately quitted her Play, and, running to him, and bursting into Tears, cry'd out: *You shall not hurt poor Papa*. One of the other Ruffians offered to take the little one rudely from his Knees; but *Heartfree* started up, and, catching the Fellow by the Collar, dashed his Head so violently against the Wall, that, had he had any Brains, he might possibly have lost them by the Blow.

The Constable, like most of those heroic Spirits who insult Men in Adversity, had some Prudence mixt with his Zeal for Justice. Seeing, therefore, this rough Treatment of his Companion, he began to pursue more gentle Methods, and very civilly desired Mr. *Heartfree* to go with him, seeing he was an Officer, and obliged to execute his Warrant; that he was sorry for his Misfortune, and hoped he would be acquitted. The other answered, he should patiently submit to the Laws of his Country, and would attend him whither he was ordered to conduct him; then, taking Leave of his Children with a tender Kiss, he recommended them to the Care of *Friendly*; who promised to see them safe Home, and then to attend him at the Justice's, whose Name and Abode he had learnt of the Constable.

This latter arrived at the Magistrate's House, just as he had signed the *Mittimus*° against his Friend; for the Evidence of *Fireblood* was so clear and strong, and the Justice was so incensed against *Heartfree*, and so convinced of his Guilt, that he would hardly hear him speak in his own Defence, which the Reader perhaps, when he hears the Evidence against him, will be less inclined to censure: For this Witness deposed, 'that he had been, by *Heartfree* himself, employed to carry the Orders of Embezzling to *Wild*, in order to be delivered to his Wife; that he had been afterwards present with *Wild* and her at the Inn, when they took Coach for *Harwich*, where she shewed him the Casket of Jewels, and desired him to tell her Husband, that she had fully executed his Command.'

When *Friendly* found the Justice obdurate, and that all he could say had no Effect, nor was it any way possible for *Heartfree* to escape being committed to *Newgate*, he resolved to accompany him thither: Where, when they arrived, the Keeper would have confined *Heartfree* (he having no Money) amongst the common Felons; but *Friendly* would not permit it, and advanced every Shilling he had in his Pocket, to procure a Room in the *Press-Yard* for his Friend.°

They spent that Day together, and, in the Evening, the Prisoner dismissed his Friend, desiring him, after many Thanks for his Fidelity, to be comforted on his Account. 'I know not,' says he, 'how far GOD may permit the Malice of my Enemies to prevail; but whatever my Sufferings are, I am convinced my Innocence will somewhere be rewarded. If, therefore, any fatal Accident should happen to me, (for he who is in the Hands of Perjury, may apprehend the worst) my dear *Friendly*, be a Father to my poor Children,' at which Words the Tears gushed from his Eyes. The other begged him not to admit any such Apprehensions; for that he would employ his utmost Diligence in his Service, and doubted not but to subvert any villainous Design laid for his Destruction, and to make his Innocence appear to the World as white as it was in his own Opinion.

We cannot help mentioning a Circumstance here, though we doubt it will appear very unnatural and incredible to our Reader; which is, that, notwithstanding the former Character and Behaviour of *Heartfree*, this Story of his embezzling was so far from surprizing his Neighbours, that many of them declared they expected no better from him. Some were assured he could pay forty Shillings in the Pound, if he would.° Others had overheard Hints formerly pass between him and Mrs. *Heartfree*, which had given them Suspicions. And, what is most astonishing of all is, that many of those who had before censured him for an extravagant heedless Fool, now no less confidently abused him for a cunning, tricking, avaricious Knave.

CHAPTER XIII

*Something concerning* Fireblood, *which will surprize; and somewhat touching one of the Miss* Snaps, *which will greatly concern the Reader.*

HOWEVER, notwithstanding all those Censures abroad, and in Despight of all his Misfortunes at home, *Heartfree* in *Newgate*

enjoyed a quiet, undisturbed Repose; while our Hero, nobly disdaining Rest, lay sleepless all Night; partly from the Apprehensions of
Mrs. *Heartfree's* Return before he had executed his Scheme; and
partly from a Suspicion lest *Fireblood* should betray him; of whose
Infidelity he had, nevertheless, no other Cause to maintain any Fear,
but from his knowing him to be an accomplished Rascal, as the
Vulgar term it, a complete GREAT Man in our Language. And
indeed, to confess the Truth, these Doubts were not without some
Foundation; for the very same Thought unluckily entred the Head
of that noble Youth, who considered, whether he might not possibly
sell himself for some Advantage to the other Side, as he had yet no
Promise from *Wild*; but this was, by the Sagacity of the latter, prevented in the Morning with a Profusion of Promises, which shewed
him to be of the most generous Temper in the World, with which
*Fireblood* was extremely well satisfied; and made use of so many
Protestations of his Faithfulness, that he convinced *Wild* of the
Injustice° of his Suspicions.

At this Time an Accident happened, which, though not immediately affecting our Hero, we cannot avoid relating, as it occasioned
great Confusion in his Family, as well as in the Family of *Snap*. It is
indeed a Calamity highly to be lamented, when it stains untainted
Blood, and happens to an honourable House. An Injury never to be
repaired. A Blot never to be wiped out. A Sore never to be healed.° To
detain my Reader no longer: Miss *Theodosia Snap* was now safely
delivered of a Male-Infant, the Product of an Amour which that
beautiful (O that I could say, virtuous) Creature had with the Count.

Mr. *Wild* and his Lady were at Breakfast, when Mr. *Snap*, with all
the Agonies of Despair both in his Voice and Countenance, brought
them this melancholy News. Our Hero, who had (as we have said)
wonderful Good-nature when his GREATNESS or Interest was not
concerned, instead of reviling his Sister-in-Law, asked with a Smile:
'Who was the Father?' But the chaste *Lætitia*, we repeat *the chaste*,
for well did she now deserve that Epithet;° received it in another
Manner. She fell into the utmost Fury at the Relation, reviled her
Sister in the bitterest Terms, and vowed she would never see nor
speak to her more. Then burst into Tears, and lamented over her
Father, that such a Dishonour should ever happen to him and herself. At length she fell severely on her Husband, for the light Treatment which he gave this fatal Accident. She told him, he was

unworthy of the Honour he enjoyed, of marrying into a chaste Family. That she looked on it as an Affront to her Virtue. That if he had married one of the naughty Hussies of the Town, he could not have behaved to her in a worse Manner. She concluded with desiring her Father to make an Example of the Slut, and turn her out of Doors; for that she would not otherwise enter his House, being resolved never to set her Foot within the same Threshold with the Trollop, whom she detested so much the more, because (which was perhaps true) she was her own Sister.

So violent, and indeed so outragious was this chaste Lady's Love of Virtue, that she could not forgive a single Slip (indeed the only one *Theodosia* had ever made) in her own Sister, in a Sister who loved her, and to whom she owed a thousand Obligations.

Perhaps the Severity of Mr. *Snap*, who greatly felt the Injury done to the Honour of his Family, would have relented, had not the Parish-Officers been extremely pressing on this Occasion, and, for want of Security, conveyed the unhappy young Lady to a Place, the Name of which, for the Honour of the *Snaps*, to whom our Hero was so nearly allied, we bury in eternal Oblivion;° where she suffered so much Correction for her Crime, that the good-natured Reader of the Male kind may be inclined to compassionate her, at least to imagine she was sufficiently punished for a Fault, which, with Submission to the chaste *Lætitia*, and all other strictly virtuous Ladies, it should be either less criminal in a Woman to commit, or more so in a Man to solicit her to it.°

But to return to our Hero, who was a living and strong Instance, that human GREATNESS and Happiness are not always inseparable. He was under a continual Alarm of Frights, and Fears, and Jealousies. He thought every Man he beheld wore a Knife for his Throat, and a Pair of Scissars for his Purse.° As for his own Gang particularly, he was throughly convinced there was not a single Man amongst them, who would not, for the Value of five Shillings, bring him to the Gallows.° These Apprehensions so constantly broke his Rest, and kept him so assiduously on his Guard, to frustrate and circumvent any Designs which might be forming against him; that his Condition, to any other than the glorious Eye of Ambition, might seem rather deplorable, than the Object of Envy or Desire.

*In which our Hero makes a Speech well worthy to be celebrated;
and the Behaviour of one of the Gang, perhaps more unnatural
than any other Part of this History.*

THERE was in the Gang a Man named *Blueskin*;° one of those
Merchants who trade in dead Oxen, Sheep, &c. in short, what the
Vulgar call a *Butcher*. This Gentleman had two Qualities of a GREAT
Man, *viz.* undaunted Courage, and an absolute Contempt of those
ridiculous Distinctions of *Meum* and *Tuum*.° The common Forms of
exchanging Property by Trade seemed to him too tedious; he therefore resolved to quit the mercantile Profession, and, falling
acquainted with some of Mr. *Wild's* People, he provided himself
with Arms, and enlisted of the Gang. In which he behaved for some
time with great Decency and Order, and submitted to accept such
Share of the Booty with the rest, as our Hero allotted him.

But this Subserviency agreed ill with his Temper; for we should
have before remembered a third heroic Quality, namely, Ambition,
which was no inconsiderable Part of his Composition. One Day,
therefore, having robbed a Gentleman at *Windsor* of a Gold-Watch;
which, on its being advertised in the News-Paper, with a considerable Reward, was demanded of him by *Wild*, he peremptorily refused
to deliver it.

'How, Mr. *Blueskin*!' says *Wild*, 'you will not deliver the Watch?'
'No, Mr. *Wild*,' answered he; 'I have taken it, and will keep it; or, if I
dispose of it, I will dispose of it myself, and keep the Money for
which I sell it.' 'Sure,' replied *Wild*, 'you have not the Assurance to
pretend you have any Property or Right in this Watch?' 'I am certain,' returned *Blueskin*, 'whether I have any Right in it or no, you
can prove none.' 'I will undertake,' cries the other, 'to shew I have an
absolute Right to it, and that by the Laws of our Gang, of which I am
providentially at the Head.' 'I know not who put you at the Head of
it,' cries *Blueskin*; 'but those who did, certainly did it for their own
Good, that you might conduct them the better in their Robberies,
inform them of the richest Booties, prevent Surprizes,° pack Juries,
bribe Evidence, and so contribute to their Benefit and Safety; and
not to convert all their Labour and Hazard to your own Benefit and
Advantage.' 'You are greatly mistaken, Sir,' answered *Wild*; 'you are

talking of a legal Society, where the chief Magistrate is always chosen for the public Good, which, as we see in all the legal Societies of the World, he constantly consults, daily contributing, by his superiour Skill, to their Prosperity, and not sacrificing their Good to his own Wealth, or Pleasure, or Humour:° But in an illegal Society or Gang, as this of ours, it is otherwise; for who would be at the Head of a Gang, unless for his own Interest? And without a Head, you know, you cannot subsist.° Nothing but a Head, and Obedience to that Head, can preserve a Gang a Moment from Destruction. It is absolutely better for you to content yourselves with a moderate Reward, and enjoy that in Safety at the Disposal of your Chief, than to engross the whole with the Hazard to which you will be liable without my Protection. And surely there is none in the whole Gang, who hath less Reason to complain than you; you have tasted of my Favours; witness that Piece of Ribbon you wear in your Hat, with which I dubbed you Captain.—Therefore pray, Captain, deliver the Watch.'

'D——n your cajoling,' says *Blueskin:* 'Do you think I value myself on this Bit of Ribband, which I could have bought myself for six-pence, and wore without your Leave? Do you imagine I think myself a Captain, because you, whom I know not empowered to make one, call me so? The Name of Captain is but a Shadow: The Men and the Salary are the Substance: And I am not to be bubbled with a Shadow. I will be called Captain no longer, and he who flatters me by that Name, I shall think affronts me, and I will knock him down, I assure you.'

'Did ever Man talk so unreasonably?' cries *Wild.* 'Are you not respected as a Captain by the whole Gang since my dubbing you so? But it is the Shadow only, it seems; and you will knock a Man down for affronting you, who calls you Captain! Might not a Man as reasonably tell a Minister of State: *Sir, you have given me the Shadow only. The Ribbon, or the Bawble, that you give me, implies that I have either signalized myself, by some great Action, for the Benefit and Glory of my Country; or at least that I am descended from those who have done so. I know myself to be a Scoundrel, and so have been those few Ancestors I can remember, or have ever heard of. Therefore I am resolved to knock the first Man down, who calls me Sir, or Right Honourable.*° But all GREAT and wise Men think themselves sufficiently repaid by what procures them Honour and Precedence in the Gang, without enquiring into Substance; nay, if a Title, or a Feather,° be equal to this Purpose, they are Substance, and not mere Shadows; but I have not Time to argue with you at present, so give me the Watch without any more Deliberation.' 'I am no more a Friend to Deliberation than yourself,' answered *Blueskin*, 'and so I tell you once for all, By G—— I never will give you the Watch, no, nor will I ever hereafter surrender any Part of my Booty. I won it, and I will wear it. Take your Pistols yourself, and go out on the Highway, and don't lazily think to fatten yourself with the Dangers and Pains of other People.' At which Words he departed in a fierce Mood, and repaired to the Tavern used by the Gang, where he had appointed to meet some of his Acquaintance, whom he informed of what had passed between him and *Wild*, and advised them all to follow his Example; which they all readily agreed to, and Mr. *Wild's* D——tion was the universal Toast: In drinking Bumpers to which, they had finished a large Bowl of Punch, when a Constable, with a numerous Attendance, and *Wild* at their Head, entered the Room, and seized on *Blueskin*, whom his Companions, when they saw our Hero, did not dare attempt to rescue. The Watch was found upon him, which, together with *Wild's* Information,° was more than sufficient to commit him to *Newgate*.

In the Evening, *Wild*, and the rest of those who had been drinking with *Blueskin*, met at the Tavern, where nothing was to be seen but the profoundest Submission to their Leader. They vilified and abused *Blueskin* as much as they had before abused our Hero, and now repeated the same Toast, only changing the Name of *Wild* into that of *Blueskin*. All agreeing with *Wild*, that the Watch found in his Pocket, and which must be a fatal Evidence against him, was a just Judgment on his Disobedience and Revolt.

Thus did this GREAT Man, by a resolute and timely Example (for he went directly to the Justice when *Blueskin* left him) quell one of the most dangerous Conspiracies which could possibly arise in a Gang; and which, had it been permitted one Day's Growth, would inevitably have ended in his Destruction; so much doth it behoove GREAT Men and *Prigs* to be eternally on their Guard, and expeditious in the Execution of their Purposes; while none but weak and honest Men can indulge themselves in Remissness or Repose.

The *Achates*, *Fireblood*, had been present at both these Meetings; but though he had a little too hastily concurred in cursing his

Friend, and vowing his Perdition; yet now he saw all that Scheme dissolved, he returned to his Integrity; of which he gave an incontestable Proof, by informing *Wild* of the Measures which had been concerted against him. In which, he said, he had pretended to acquiesce, in order the better to betray them; but this, as he afterwards confessed on his Death-Bed, *i.e.* in the Cart at *Tyburn,*° was only a Copy of his Countenance;° for that he was, at that Time, as sincere and hearty in his Opposition to *Wild* as any of his Companions.

Our Hero, however, desired him to keep this a severe Secret;° for, he said, as they had seen their Errors, and repented, nothing was more noble than Forgiveness. But though he was pleased modestly to ascribe this to his Lenity, it really arose from much more noble and political Principles. He considered that it would be dangerous to attempt the Punishment of so many; besides, he flattered himself that Fear would keep them in Order; and indeed he concluded, that *Fireblood* had told him nothing more than he knew before, *viz.* that they were all complete *Prigs*, whom he was to govern by their Fears, and in whom he was to place no more Confidence than was necessary, and to watch them with the utmost Caution and Circumspection; for a Rogue, he wisely said, was like Gunpowder, which, whoever uses, must do it very cautiously, lest it blow up himself, instead of executing his mischievous Purpose against some other Person or Animal.

We will now repair to *Newgate*, it being the Place where most of the GREAT Men of this History are hastening as fast as possible; and, to confess the Truth, it is a Castle° very far from being an improper, or misbecoming Habitation for any GREAT Man whatever. And as this Scene will continue during the Residue of our History, we shall open it with a new Book; and shall, therefore, take this Opportunity of closing our third.

# BOOK IV

## CHAPTER I

*A Sentiment of the Ordinary's, worthy to be written in Letters of Gold; a very extraordinary Instance of Folly in* Friendly; *and a dreadful Accident which befel our Hero.*

*HEARTFREE* had not been long in *Newgate* before his frequent Conversation with his Children, and other Instances of a good Heart, which betrayed themselves in his Actions and Conversation, possessed° all about him that he was one of the silliest Fellows in the Universe. The Ordinary himself, a very sagacious as well as worthy Person,° declared that he was a cursed Rogue, but no Conjurer.°

What indeed might induce the former, *i.e.* the roguish Part of this Opinion in the Ordinary was a wicked Sentiment which *Heartfree* one Day disclosed in Conversation, and which we, who are truly Orthodox, will not pretend to justify, *viz. That he believed a sincere* Turk *would be saved.*° To this the good Man, with becoming Zeal and Indignation, answered, *I know not what may become of a sincere* Turk, *but if this be your Persuasion, I pronounce it impossible you should be saved. No, Sir, so far from a sincere* Turk's *being within the Pale of Salvation, neither will any sincere* Presbyterian, Anabaptist, *nor* Quaker *whatever, be saved.*

But neither did the one nor the other Part of this Character prevail on *Friendly* to abandon his old Master.° He spent his whole time with him, except only those Hours when he was absent for his Sake, in procuring Evidence for him against his Trial, which was now shortly to come on. Indeed this young Man was the only Comfort, besides a clear Conscience, and the Hopes beyond the Grave, which this poor Wretch had; for the Sight of his Children was like one of those alluring Pleasures which Men in some Diseases indulge themselves often fatally in, which at once flatter and heighten their Malady.

*Friendly* being one Day present while *Heartfree* was, with Tears in his Eyes, embracing his eldest Daughter, and lamenting the hard Fate to which he feared he should be obliged to leave her, spoke to him thus. 'I have long observed with Admiration, thou excellent Man, the Magnanimity with which you go thro' your own Misfortunes, and the steady Countenance with which you look on Death. I have observed that all your Agonies arise from the Thoughts of parting with your Children, and leaving them in a distrest Condition; now, tho' I hope all these Fears will prove illgrounded, yet, that I may relieve you as much as possible from them, be assured, that as nothing can give me more real Misery, than to observe so tender and loving a Concern in a Master, to whose Goodness I owe so many Obligations, and whom I so sincerely love, so nothing can afford me equal Pleasure with my contributing to lessen or to remove it. Be convinced, therefore, if you can place any Confidence in my Promise, that I will employ my little Fortune, which you know to be not entirely inconsiderable, in the Support of this your little Family. Should any Misfortune, which I pray God avert, happen to you before you have better provided for these little ones, I will be myself their Father, nor shall either of them ever know Distress, if it be any way in my Power to prevent it. Your youngest daughter I will provide for, and as for my little Prattler, your eldest, as I never yet thought of any Woman for a Wife, I will receive her as such at your Hands; nor will I ever relinquish her for another.' *Heartfree* flew to his Friend, and embraced him with Raptures of Acknowledgments. He vowed to him that he had eased every anxious Thought of his Mind but one, and that he must carry with him out of the World. 'O *Friendly*, (cried he) it is my Concern for that best of Women, whom I hate myself for having ever censured in my Opinion. O *Friendly*, thou didst know her Goodness, yet, sure her perfect Character none but myself was ever acquainted with. She had every Perfection both of Mind and Body, which Heaven hath indulged to her whole Sex, and enjoyed all in a higher Excellence than Nature ever suffered another to possess a single Virtue. Can I bear the Loss of such a Woman? Can I bear the Apprehensions of what Mischiefs that Villain may have done to her, of which Death is perhaps the lightest?' *Friendly* gently interrupted him as soon as he saw any Opportunity, endeavouring to comfort him on this Head likewise, by magnifying every Circumstance which could possibly afford any Hopes of his seeing her again.

By this kind of Behaviour, in which the young Man exemplified so uncommon an Height of Friendship, he had soon obtained in the

Castle the Character of as odd and silly a Fellow as his Master. Indeed, they were both the By-word, Laughing-stock, and Contempt of the whole Place.

The Sessions now came on at the *Old Baily*.° The Grand Jury at *Hicks's-Hall* had found the Bill of Indictment against *Heartfree*,° and on the second Day of the Sessions he was brought to his Trial; where, notwithstanding the utmost Efforts of *Friendly*, and of the honest old Female Servant, the Circumstances of the Fact corroborating the Evidence of *Fireblood*, as well as that of *Wild*, who counterfeited the most artful Reluctance at appearing against his old Friend *Heartfree*, the Jury found the Prisoner guilty.

*Wild* had now accomplished his Scheme; for as to what remained, it was certainly unavoidable, seeing that *Heartfree* was entirely void of Interest with the GREAT, and was besides convicted on a Statute, the Infringers of which could hope no Pardon.°

The *Catastrophe*, to which our Hero had reduced this Wretch, was so wonderful an Effort of GREATNESS, that it probably made Fortune envious of her own Darling; but whether it was from this Envy, or only from that known Inconstancy and Weakness so often and judiciously remarked in that Lady's Temper, who frequently lifts Men to the Summit of human GREATNESS, only

*— Ut Lapsu graviore ruant;*°

certain it is, she now began to meditate Mischief against *Wild*, who seems to have come to that Period, at which all the Heroes and GREAT MEN of Antiquity have arrived, and which she was resolved they never should transcend. In short, there seems to be a certain Measure of Mischief and Iniquity, which every GREAT MAN is to fill up, and then Fortune looks on him as of no more Use than a Silk-Worm whose Bottom is spun, and deserts him. For Mr. *Blueskin* being convicted the same Day of Robbery, by our Hero, an Unkindness, which tho' he had drawn on himself and necessitated him to, he took greatly amiss; as *Wild* was standing near him, with that Disregard and Indifference which GREAT MEN are too carelessly inclined to have for those whom they have ruined; *Blueskin* privily drawing a Knife, thrust the same into the Body of our Hero with such Violence, that all who saw it concluded he had done his Business.° And indeed, had not Fortune, not so much out of Love to our Hero, as from a fixed Resolution to accomplish a certain Purpose of which we have formerly given a Hint, carefully placed his Guts out of the Way, he must have fallen a Sacrifice to the Wrath of his Enemy, which, as he said, he did not deserve; for had he been contented to have robbed and only submitted to give him the Booty, he might have still continued safe and unimpeached in the Gang; but so it was, that the Knife missing those noble Parts (the noblest of many) the Guts, perforated only the hollow of his Belly, and caused no other Harm than an immoderate Effusion of Blood, of which, tho' it at present weakened him, he soon after recovered.

This Accident, however, was in the End attended with worse Consequences: For as very few People (those greatest of all Men, absolute Princes, excepted) attempt to cut the Thread of human Life, like the Fatal Sisters,° merely out of Wantonness and for their Diversion, but rather by so doing propose to themselves the Acquisition of some future Good, or the avenging some past Evil; and as the former of these Motives did not appear probable, it put inquisitive Persons on examining into the latter. Now, as the vast Schemes of *Wild*, when they were discovered, however GREAT in their Nature, seemed to some Persons like the Projects of most other GREAT MEN, rather to be calculated for the Glory of the GREAT MAN himself, than to redound to the general Good of Society; Designs began to be laid by several of those who thought it principally their Duty to put a Stop to the future Progress of our Hero, and a learned Judge particularly, a great Enemy to this kind of GREATNESS, procured a Clause in an Act of Parliament as a Trap for *Wild*, which he soon after fell into. By this Law it was made Capital in a *Prig* to steal with the Hands of other People. A Law so plainly calculated for the Destruction of all *Priggish* GREATNESS, that it was indeed impossible for our Hero to avoid it.°

### CHAPTER II

*A short Hint concerning popular Ingratitude. Mr.* Wild's
*Arrival in the Castle, with other Occurrences to be found
in no other History.*

IF we had any Leisure, we would here digress a little on that Ingratitude, which so many Writers have observed in all free Governments towards their GREAT MEN; who, while they have been consulting the Good of the Public, by raising their own GREATNESS, in which the whole Body (as the Kingdom of *France* thinks itself in the Glory of their Grand Monarch°) was so deeply concerned, have been sometimes sacrificed by those very People for whose Glory the said GREAT MEN were so industriously at work: And this from a foolish Zeal for a certain ridiculous imaginary Thing called Liberty, to which GREAT MEN are observed to have a great Animosity.°

This Law had been promulgated a very little Time, when Mr. *Wild*, having received from some dutiful Members of the Gang, a valuable Piece of Goods, did, for a Consideration somewhat short of its original Price, reconvey it to the right Owner; for which Fact being ungratefully informed against by the said Owner, he was surprized in his own House, and being over-power'd by Numbers, was hurried before a Magistrate, and by him committed to that Castle, which, suitable as it is to GREATNESS, we do not chuse to name too often in our History, and where many GREAT MEN, at this Time, happened to be assembled.

The Governor, or as the Law more honourably calls him, Keeper of this Castle, having been Mr. *Wild's* old Friend and Acquaintance,° made the latter greatly satisfied with the Place of his Confinement, as he promised himself not only a kind Reception and handsome Accommodation there, but even to obtain his Liberty from him, if he thought it necessary to desire it: But alass! he was deceived, his old Friend knew him no longer, and refusing to see him, ordered the Lieutenant Governor to insist on as high Garnish for Fetters, and as exorbitant a Price for Lodging, as if he had had a fine Gentleman in Custody for Murther,° or as if he had received an Intimation from a certain Place to use all the Severity imaginable to his Prisoner.

To confess a melancholy Truth, it is a Circumstance much to be lamented; that there is no absolute Dependence on the Friendship of GREAT MEN.° An Observation which hath been frequently made by those who have lived in Courts or in *Newgate*, or in any other Place set apart for the Habitation of the said GREAT MEN.

The second Day of his Confinement he was greatly surprized at receiving a Visit from his Wife;° and much more so, when, instead of a Countenance ready to insult him, the only Motive to which he could ascribe her Presence, he saw the Tears trickling down her lovely Cheeks. He embraced her with the utmost Marks of

Affection, and declared he could hardly regret his Confinement, since it had produced such an Instance of the Happiness he enjoyed in her, whose Fidelity to him on this Occasion, would, he believed, make him the Envy of most Husbands, even in *Newgate*. He then begged her to dry her Eyes, and be comforted; for that Matters might go better with him than she expected. 'No, no, (says she) I am certain you will be found guilty *Death*.° I knew what it would always come to. I told you it was impossible to carry on such a Trade long; but you would not be advised, and now you see the Consequence, now you repent when it is too late. All the Comfort I shall have when you are \**nubbed*, is that I gave you good Advice. If you had always gone out by yourself, as I would have had you, you might have robbed on to the End of the Chapter;° but you was wiser than all the World, or rather lazier, and see what your Laziness is come to—to the †*Cheat*, for thither you will go now, that's infallible.° And a just Judgment on you for following your headstrong Will; I am the only Person to be pitied, poor I, who shall be scandalized for your Fault. *There goes she whose Husband was hanged:* Methinks I hear them crying so already.' At which Words she burst into Tears. He could not then forbear chiding her for this unnecessary Concern on his Account, and begged her not to trouble him any more. She answered with some Spirit, 'On your Account, and be d——d to you! No, if the old Cull° of a Justice had not sent me here, I believe it would have been long enough before I should have come hither to see after you: D——n me, I am committed for the ‡*Filing-Lay*, Man, and we shall be both *nubbed* together. I faith, my Dear, it almost makes me Amends for being *nubbed* myself, to have the Pleasure of seeing thee *nubbed* too.' 'Indeed, my Dear, (answered *Wild*) it is what I have always wished for thee; but I do not desire to bear thee Company, and I have still Hopes to have the Pleasure of seeing you go without me; at least I will have the Pleasure to be rid of you now.' And so saying, he seized her by the Waste,° and with strong Arm flung her out of the Room; but not before she had with her Nails left a bloody Memorial on his Cheek: And thus this fond Couple parted.

    *Wild* had scarce recovered himself from the Uneasiness into which

---

\* The Cant Word for *hanging*.
† The *Gallows*.
‡ *Picking Pockets*.

this unwelcome Visit, proceeding from the disagreeable Fondness of his Wife, had thrown him, than the faithful *Achates* appeared. The Presence of this Youth was indeed a Cordial to his Spirits. He received him with open Arms, and expressed the utmost Satisfaction in the Fidelity of his Friendship, which so far exceeded the Fashion of the Times, and said many Things, which we have forgot, on the Occasion; but we remember they all tended to the Praise of *Fireblood*, whose Modesty, at length, put a Stop to the Torrent of Compliments, by asserting he had done no more than his Duty, and that he should have detested himself, could he have forsaken his Friend in his Adversity, and after many Protestations, that he came the Moment he heard of his Misfortune, he asked him if he could be of any Service. *Wild* answered, since he had so kindly proposed that Question, he must say he should be obliged to him, if he could lend him a few Guineas; for that he was very *seedy*. *Fireblood* replied, that he was greatly unhappy in not having it then in his Power, adding many hearty Oaths, that he had not a Farthing of Money in his Pocket, which was, indeed, strictly true; for he had only a Bank-Note which he had that Evening purloined from a Gentleman in the Playhouse-Passage. He then asked for his Wife, to whom, to speak truly, the Visit was intended, her Confinement being the Misfortune of which he had just heard; for, as for that of Mr. *Wild* himself, he had known it from the first, without ever intending to trouble him with his Company. Being informed therefore of the Visit which had lately happened, he reproved *Wild* for his cruel Treatment of that good Creature; then taking as sudden Leave as he civilly could of the Gentleman, he hastned to comfort his Lady, who received him with great Kindness.

### CHAPTER III

*Curious Anecdotes° relating to the History of* Newgate.°

THERE resided in the Castle at the same Time with Mr. *Wild*, one *Roger Johnson*, a very GREAT MAN,° who had long been at the Head of all the *Prigs*, and had raised Contributions on them. He examined into the Nature of their Defence, procured and instructed their Evidence, and made himself, at least in their Opinions, so necessary to them, that the whole Fate of *Newgate* seemed entirely to depend upon him.

   *Wild* had not been long under Confinement, before he began to oppose this Man. He represented him to the *Prigs* as a Fellow, who under the plausible Pretence of assisting their Causes, was in Reality undermining the Liberties of *Newgate*. He at first only threw out certain sly Hints and Insinuations; but having by Degrees formed a Party against *Roger*, he one Day assembled them together, and spoke to them in the following florid Manner.

   'Friends and Fellow-Citizens.°
The Cause which I am to mention to you this Day, is of such mighty Importance, that when I consider my own small Abilities, I tremble with an Apprehension, lest your Safety may be rendered precarious by the Weakness of him who is representing to you your Danger. Gentlemen, the Liberty of *Newgate* is at Stake: Your Privileges have been long undermined, and are now openly violated by one Man; by one who hath engrossed to himself the whole Conduct of your Trials, under Colour of which, he exacts what Contributions on you he pleases: But are these Sums appropriated to the Uses for which they are raised? Your frequent Convictions at the *Old Baily* must too sensibly and sorely demonstrate the contrary. What Evidence doth he ever produce for the Prisoner, which he of himself could not have provided, and often better instructed? How many noble Youths have there been lost, when a single *Alibi* would have saved them! Should I be silent, nay, could your own Injuries want a Tongue to remonstrate, the very Breath, which by his Neglect hath been stopped at the *Cheat*, would cry out loudly against him. Nor is the Exorbitancy of his Plunders visible only in the dreadful Consequences it hath produced to the *Prigs*, nor glares it only in the Miseries brought on them: It blazes forth in the more desirable Effects it hath wrought for himself, in the rich Perquisites° acquired by it: Witness that Silk Night-Gown, that Robe of Shame, which to his eternal Dishonour he publickly wears; that Gown, which I will not scruple to call the Winding-Sheet of the Liberties of *Newgate*. Is there a *Prig* who hath the Interest and Honour of *Newgate* so little at Heart, that he can refrain from Blushing when he beholds that Trophy, purchased with the Breath of so many *Prigs!* Nor is this all. His Wastecoat embroidered with Silk, and his Velvet Cap,° bought with the same Price, are Ensigns of the same Disgrace. Some would think the Rags

which covered his Nakedness, when first he was committed hither, well exchanged for these gaudy Trappings; but in my Eye, no Exchange can be profitable when Dishonour is the Condition. If, therefore, *Newgate*—'

Here the only Copy which we could procure of this Speech breaks off abruptly; however, we can assure the Reader from very authentic Information, that he concluded with advising the *Prigs* to put their Affairs into other Hands. After which, one of his Party, in a very long Speech, recommended him (*Wild* himself) to their Choice.

*Newgate* was divided into Parties on this Occasion; the *Prigs* on each Side writing to one another, and representing their Chief or GREAT Man to be the only Person by whom the Affairs of *Newgate* could be managed with Safety and Advantage. The *Prigs* had indeed very different Interests; for both Parties were permitted by their Leader to have their Share in the Plunder, which the Friends of *Johnson* had already enjoyed, and which those of *Wild* expected on his Exaltation; what may seem more remarkable was, that the Debtors, who were entirely unconcerned in the Dispute, and who were the destined Plunder of both Parties, should interest themselves with the utmost Violence, some on Behalf of *Wild*, and others in Favour of *Johnson*. So that all *Newgate* resounded with WILD *for ever*, JOHNSON *for ever*. And such Quarrels and Animosities happened between them, that they seemed rather the People of two Countries long at War with each other, than the Inhabitants of the same Castle.

*Wild's* Party at length prevailed, and he succeeded to the Place and Power of *Johnson*, whom he presently stript of all his Finery; but when it was proposed, that he should sell it, and divide the Money for the good of the whole; he waved that Motion,° saying, it was not yet Time, that he should find a better Opportunity, that the Clothes wanted cleaning, with many other Pretences, and, within two Days, to the Surprize of many, he appeared in them himself; for which he vouchsafed no other Apology than, that they fitted him much better than they did *Johnson*, and that they became him in a much more elegant Manner.

This Behaviour in *Wild* greatly incensed the Debtors, particularly those by whose Means he had been promoted. They grumbled extremely, and vented great Indignation against *Wild*; when one Day a very grave Man, and one of much Authority among them,° bespoke them as follows:°

'Nothing sure can be more justly ridiculous than the Conduct of those, who, like Children, lay the Lamb in the Wolf's Way, and then lament his being devoured.° What a Wolf is in a Sheepfold, a GREAT Man is in Society. Now, when one Wolf is in Possession of a Sheepfold, how little would it avail the simple Flock to expel him, and place another in his stead? Of the same Benefit to us is the overthrowing one *Prig* in Favour of another. And for what other Advantage was your Struggle? Did you not all know, that *Wild* and his Followers were *Prigs*, as well as *Johnson* and his? What then could the Contention be among such, but that which you have now discovered it to have been? Perhaps some would say, Is it then our Duty tamely to submit to the Rapine of the *Prig* who now plunders us, for Fear of an Exchange? Surely No: But I answer, It is better to shake the Plunder off than to exchange the Plunderer. And by what Means can we effect this, but by a total Change in our Manners? Every *Prig* is a Slave. His own *Priggish* Desires, which enslave him, themselves betray him to the Tyranny of others.° To preserve, therefore, the Liberty of *Newgate*, is to change the Manners of *Newgate*. Let us, therefore, who are confined here for Debt only, separate ourselves entirely from the *Prigs*; neither drink with them, nor converse with them. Let us, at the same time, separate ourselves farther from *Priggism* itself. Instead of being ready, on every Opportunity, to pillage each other, let us be content with our honest Share of the common Bounty, and with the Acquisition of our own Industry. When we separate from the *Prigs*, let us enter into a closer Alliance with one another. Let us consider ourselves all as Members of one Community, to the public Good of which we are to sacrifice our private Views; not to give up the Interest of the whole for the least Pleasure or Profit which shall accrue to ourselves.° Liberty is consistent with no Degree of Honesty inferiour to this, and the Community where this abounds, no *Prig* will have the Impudence or Audaciousness to endeavour to enslave; but, while one Man pursues his Ambition, another his Interest, another his Safety; while one hath a Roguery (a *Priggism* they here call it) to commit, and another a Roguery to defend, they must naturally fly to the Favour and Protection of those, who have Power to give them what they desire, and to defend them from what they fear; nay, in this View it becomes their Interest to promote this Power in their Patrons. Now, Gentlemen, when we are no longer *Prigs*, we shall no longer have these Fears or these Desires. What remains, therefore, for us, but to resolve bravely to lay aside our *Priggism*, our Roguery, in plainer Words, and preserve our Liberty, or to give up the latter in the Preservation and Preference of the former.'

This Speech was received with much Applause; however, *Wild* continued to levy Contributions among the Prisoners, to apply the Garnish to his own Use, and to strut openly in the Ornaments which he had stript from *Johnson*. To speak sincerely, there was more Bravado than real Use or Advantage in these Trappings. As for the Night-Gown, its Outside indeed made a glittering Tinsel Appearance, but it kept him not warm; nor could the Finery of it do him much Honour, since every one knew it did not properly belong to him, nor indeed suited his Degree: As to the Wastecoat, it fitted him very ill, being infinitely too big for him; and the Cap was so heavy, that it made his Head ake. Thus these Clothes, which perhaps (as they presented the Idea of their Misery more sensibly to the People's Eyes) brought him more Envy, Hatred, and Detraction, than all his deeper Impositions, and more real Advantages; afforded very little Use or Honour to the Wearer; nay, could scarce serve to amuse his own Vanity, when it was cool enough to reflect with the least Seriousness. And, should I speak in the Language of a Man who estimated human Happiness without regard to that GREATNESS, which we have so laboriously endeavoured to paint in this History, it is probable he never took (*i.e.* robbed the Prisoners of) a Shilling, which he himself did not pay too dear for.

CHAPTER IV

*The Dead-Warrant arrives for* Heartfree; *on which Occasion* Wild *betrays some human Weakness*.

THE Dead-Warrant,° as it is called, now came down to *Newgate* for the Execution of *Heartfree* among the rest of the Prisoners. And here the Reader must excuse us, who profess to draw natural, not perfect Characters, and to record the Truths of History, not the Extravagancies of Romance, while we relate a Weakness in *Wild*, of which we are ourselves ashamed, and which we would willingly have concealed, could we have preserved at the same Time that strict Attachment to Truth and Impartiality, which we have vowed in recording the Annals of this GREAT Man. Know then, Reader, that this Dead-Warrant did not affect *Heartfree*, who was to suffer a shameful Death by it, with half the Concern it gave *Wild*, who had been the Occasion of it. He had been a little struck the Day before, on seeing the Children carried away in Tears from their Father. This Sight brought the Remembrance of some slight Injuries he had done the Father, to his Mind, which he endeavoured, as much as possible, to obliterate; but when one of the Keepers (I should say, Lieutenants of the Castle) repeated *Heartfree's* Name among those of the Malefactors who were to suffer within a few Days, the Blood forsook his Countenance, and, in a cold still Stream, mov'd heavily to his Heart, which had scarce Strength enough left to return it through his Veins. In short, his Body so visibly demonstrated the Pangs of his Mind, that, to escape Observation, he retired to his Room, where he sullenly gave vent to such bitter Agonies, that even the injured *Heartfree*, had not the Apprehension of what his Wife had suffered shut every Avenue of Compassion, would have pitied him.

When his Mind was thoroughly fatigued, and worn out with the Horrours which the approaching Fate of the poor Wretch, who lay under a Sentence, which he had iniquitously brought upon him, had suggested, Sleep promised him Relief; but this Promise was, alas! delusive. This certain Friend to the tired Body is often the severest Enemy to the oppressed Mind. So at least it proved to *Wild*, adding visionary to real Horrours, and tormenting his Imagination with Fantoms too dreadful to be described. At length starting from these Visions, he no sooner recovered his waking Senses than he cry'd out: 'I may yet prevent this Catastrophe. It is not too late to discover the whole.' He then paused a Moment: But GREATNESS instantly returning to his Assistance, checked the base Thought, as it first offered itself to his Mind. He then reasoned thus coolly with himself: 'Shall I, like a Child, or a Woman, or one of those mean Wretches, whom I have always despised, be frightened by Dreams and visionary Phantoms, to sully that Honour which I have so difficultly acquired, and so gloriously maintained! Shall I, to redeem the worthless Life of this silly Fellow, suffer my Reputation to contract a Stain, which the Blood of Millions cannot wipe away! Was it only that the few, the simple Part of Mankind, should call me a *Rogue*, perhaps I could submit; but to be for ever contemptible to the *PRIGS*, as a Wretch who wanted Spirit to execute my Undertaking, can never be digested. What is the Life of a single Man? Have not whole Armies and Nations been sacrificed to the Humour of *ONE GREAT MAN*°? Nay, to omit that first Class of GREATNESS, the Conquerors of Mankind, how often have Numbers fallen, by a fictitious Plot, only to satisfy the Spleen, or perhaps exercise the Ingenuity of a Member of that second Order of GREATNESS the *Ministerial!* What have I done then? Why, I have ruined a Family, and brought an innocent Man to the Gallows. I ought rather to weep, with *Alexander*, that I have ruined no more, than to regret the little I have done.° He at length, therefore, bravely resolved to consign over *Heartfree* to his Fate, though it cost him more struggling than may easily be believed, utterly to conquer his Reluctance, and to banish away every Degree of Humanity from his Mind, those little Sparks of which composed one of those Weaknesses, which we lamented in the Opening of our History.

But, in Vindication of our Hero, we must beg Leave to observe, that Nature is seldom so kind as those Writers who draw Characters absolutely perfect. She seldom creates any Man so completely GREAT, or completely low, but that some Sparks of Humanity will glimmer in the former, and some Sparks of what the Vulgar call Evil, will dart forth in the latter;° utterly to extinguish which will give some Pain and Uneasiness to both; for I apprehend, no Mind was ever yet formed entirely free from Blemish, unless peradventure that of a sanctified Hypocrite, whose Praises a well-fed Flatterer hath gratefully thought proper to sing forth.

CHAPTER V

*The Arrival of a Person little expected; with other Matters.*

THE Day was now come when poor *Heartfree* was to suffer an igno-minious Death. *Friendly* had, in the strongest Manner, confirmed his Assurance of fulfilling his Promise, of becoming a Father to one of his Children, and a Husband to the other. This gave him inexpress-ible Comfort, and he had, the Evening before, taken his last Leave of the little Wretches, with a Tenderness which drew a Tear from one of the Keepers, joined to a Magnanimity which would have pleased a *Stoic*.° When he was informed that the Coach, which *Friendly* had provided for him,° was ready, and that the rest of the Prisoners were gone, he embraced that faithful Friend with great Passion, and begged that he would leave him here; but the other desired Leave to accompany him to his End; which at last he was forced to comply with. And now he was proceeding towards the Coach, when he found his Difficulties were not yet over; for now a Friend arrived, of whom he was to take a harder and more tender Leave than he had yet gone through. This Friend, Reader, was no other than Mrs. *Heart-free* herself, who ran to him with a Look all wild, staring, and frantic, and, having reached his Arms, fainted away in them without uttering a single Syllable. *Heartfree* was, with great Difficulty, able to preserve his own Senses in such a Surprize at such a Season. And indeed our good-natured Reader will be rather inclined to wish this miserable Couple had, by dying in each other's Arms, put a final Period to their Woes, than have survived to taste those bitter Moments which were to be their Portion, and which the unhappy Wife, soon recovering from the short Intermission of Being, now began to suffer. When she became first Mistress of her Voice, she burst forth into the following Accents: 'O my Husband!—Is this the Condition in which I find you after our cruel Separation! Who hath done this? Cruel Heaven! What is the Occasion? I know thou canst deserve no Ill. Tell me, some Body who can speak, while I have my Senses left to under-stand,—What is the Matter?' At which Words several laughed, and one answered: 'The Matter! Why no great Matter.—The Gentleman is not the first, nor won't be the last: The worst of the Matter is, that if we are to stay all the Morning here, I shall lose my Dinner.' *Heartfree*, pausing a Moment, and recollecting himself, cry'd out: 'I will bear all with Patience.' And then, addressing himself to the commanding Officer, begged he might only have a few Minutes by himself with his Wife, whom he had not seen before, since his Misfortunes. The GREAT Man answered: 'He had Compassion on him, and would do more than he could answer; but he supposed he was too much a Gentleman not to know that something was due for such Civility.' On this Hint, *Friendly*, who was himself half dead, pulled five Guineas out of his Pocket; which the GREAT Man took, and said, he would be so generous to give him ten Minutes; on which one observed, that many a Gentleman had bought ten Minutes with a Woman dearer, and many other facetious Remarks were made, unnecessary to be here related. *Heartfree* was now suffered to retire into a Room with his Wife, the Commander informing him at his Entrance, that he must be expeditious, for that the rest of the good Company would be at the Tree° before him, and he supposed he was a Gentleman of too much Breeding to make them wait.

This tender wretched Couple were now retired for these few Minutes, which the Commander without carefully measured with his Watch; and *Heartfree* was mustering all his Resolution to part with what his Soul so ardently doated on, and to conjure her to support his Loss for the sake of her poor Infants, and to comfort her with the Promise of *Friendly* on their Account; but all his Design was frustrated. Mrs. *Heartfree* could not support the Shock, but again fainted away, and so entirely lost every Symptom of Life, that *Heartfree* called vehemently for Assistance. *Friendly* rushed first into the Room, and was soon followed by many others, and, what was remarkable, one who had unmoved beheld the tender Scene between these parting Lovers, was touched to the quick by the pale Looks of the Woman, and ran up and down for Water, Drops, &c. with the utmost Hurry and Confusion. The ten Minutes were expired, which the Commander now hinted; and seeing nothing offered for the Renewal of the Term (for indeed *Friendly* had unhappily emptied his Pockets) he began to grow very importunate, and at last told *Heartfree, He should be ashamed not to act more like a Man. Heartfree* begged his Pardon, and said, he would make him wait no longer. Then, with the deepest Sigh, cry'd: 'O my Angel!' and embracing his Wife with the utmost Eagerness, kissed her pale Lips with more Fervency than ever Bridegroom did the blushing Cheeks of his Bride; he then cry'd: 'The Great GOD bless thee, and, if it be his Pleasure, restore thee to Life; if not, I beseech him we may presently meet again in a better World than this.' He was breaking from her, when, perceiving her Sense returning, he could not forbear renewing his Embrace, and again pressing her Lips, which now recovered Life and Warmth so fast, that he begged one ten Minutes more to tell her what her Swooning had prevented her hearing. The worthy Commander, being perhaps a little touched at this tender Scene, took *Friendly* aside, and asked him what he would give, if he would suffer his Friend to remain half an Hour? *Friendly* answered, '*Any thing;*

that he had no more Money in his Pocket, but he would certainly pay him that Afternoon.' 'Well then, I'll be moderate,' said he, '—Twenty Guineas.' *Friendly* answered, 'It is a Bargain.' The Commander having exacted a firm Promise, cry'd, 'Then I don't care if they stay a whole Hour together; for what signifies hiding good News?—The Gentleman is repriev'd;'—of which he had just before received Notice in a Whisper. It would be very impertinent to offer at a Description of the Joy this occasioned to the two Friends, or to Mrs. *Heartfree*, who was now again recovered. A Surgeon, who was happily present, was employed to bleed them all.° After which, the Commander, who had his Promise of the Money again confirmed to him, wished *Heartfree* Joy, and, shaking him very friendly by the Hands, cleared the Room of all the Company, and left the three Friends together.

### CHAPTER VI

*In which the foregoing happy Incident is accounted for.*

BUT here, though I am convinced my good-natured Reader may almost want the Surgeon's Assistance also, and that there is no Passage in this whole Story, which can afford him equal Delight; yet lest our Reprieve should seem to resemble that in the *Beggar's Opera*,° I shall endeavour to shew him, that this Incident, which is undoubtedly true, is at least as natural as delightful; for, we assure him, we would rather have suffered half Mankind to be hang'd, than have saved one contrary to the strictest Rules of Writing and Probability.

Be it known then (a Circumstance which I think highly credible) that the GREAT *Fireblood* had been, a few Days before, taken in the Fact of a Robbery, and carried before the same Justice of Peace, who had, on his Evidence, committed *Heartfree* to Prison. This Magistrate, who did indeed no small Honour to the Commission he bore, duly considered the weighty Charge committed to him, by which he was intrusted with Decisions affecting the Lives, Liberties and Properties of his Countrymen; he therefore examined always with the utmost Diligence and Caution, into every minute Circumstance.° And, as he had a good deal balanced, even when he committed *Heartfree*, on the excellent Character given him by *Friendly* and the

Maid; and, as he was much staggered on finding of the two Persons, on whose Evidence alone *Heartfree* had been committed and had been since convicted, one, as he had heard, in *Newgate* for a Felony, and the other now brought before him for a Robbery, he thought proper to put the Matter very home° to *Fireblood* at this time. The young *Achates* was taken, as we have said, in the Fact; so that Denial, he saw, was in vain. He, therefore, honestly confest what he knew must be proved; and desired, on the Merit of the Discoveries he made, to be admitted as an Evidence against his Accomplices. This afforded the happiest Opportunity to the Justice, to satisfy his Conscience in relation to *Heartfree*. He told *Fireblood*, that, if he expected the Favour he solicited, it must be on Condition, that he revealed the whole Truth to him concerning the Evidence which he had lately given against a Bankrupt, and which some Circumstances had induced a Suspicion of; that he might depend on it, the Truth would be discovered by other Means, and gave some oblique Hints (a Deceit entirely justifiable) that *Wild* himself had offered such a Discovery. The very Mention of *Wild's* Name immediately alarmed *Fireblood*, who did not in the least doubt the Readiness of that GREAT Man to hang any of the Gang, when his own Interest seemed to require it. He therefore hesitated not a Moment; but, having obtained a Promise from the Justice, that he should be accepted as an Evidence, he discovered the whole Falshood, and that he had been seduced by *Wild* to depose as he had done.

The Justice having thus luckily and timely discovered this Scene of Villany, *alias* GREATNESS, lost not a Moment in using his utmost Endeavours to get the Case of the unhappy Convict represented to the Sovereign; who immediately granted him that gracious Reprieve,° which caused such Happiness to the Persons concerned; and which, we hope, we have now accounted for to the Satisfaction of the Reader. Indeed, we had Reason to apprehend, it would at first very greatly surprize him, and by that Means lessen the Pleasure of the Critics, a Sort of People, for whom, and for whose Entertainment, we have the tenderest Regard, and to whom we pay all that just Duty and Respect, which, of common Right, they ought to receive from every Author.°

The good Magistrate having obtained this Reprieve for *Heartfree*, thought it incumbent on him to visit him in the Prison, and to sound, if possible, the Depth of this Affair, that if he should appear as innocent as he now began to conceive him, he might use all imaginable Methods to obtain his Pardon and Enlargement.

The next Day therefore after that, when the miserable Scene above described had passed, he went to *Newgate*, where he found those three Persons, namely *Heartfree*, his Wife, and *Friendly*, sitting together. The Justice informed the Prisoner of the Confession of *Fireblood*, with the Steps which he had taken upon it. The Reader will easily conceive the many outward Thanks as well as inward Gratitude which he received from all three; but those were of very little Consequence to him, compared with the secret Satisfaction he felt in his Mind, from reflecting on the Preservation of Innocence, as he soon after very clearly perceived was the Case.

When he entred the Room, Mrs. *Heartfree* was speaking with some Earnestness: As he perceived, therefore, he had interrupted her, he begged she would continue her Discourse, which, if he prevented by his Presence, he desired to depart; but *Heartfree* would not suffer it. He said, she had been relating some Adventures, which perhaps might entertain him to hear, and which he the rather desired he would, as they might serve to illustrate the Foundation on which this Falshood had been built, which had brought on him all his Misfortunes.

The Justice very gladly consented, and Mrs. *Heartfree*, at her Husband's Desire, began the Relation from the first Renewal of *Wild's* Acquaintance with her Husband; but, tho' this Recapitulation was necessary for the Information of our good Magistrate, as it would be useless, and perhaps tedious, to the Reader, we shall only repeat that Part of her Story to which he is a Stranger, beginning with what happened to her, after *Wild* had been turned adrift in the Boat, by the Captain of the *French* Privateer.

## CHAPTER VII

### Mrs. Heartfree *begins to relate her Adventures.*

MRS. *Heartfree* proceeded thus. 'The Vengeance which the *French* Captain exacted on that Villain (*our Hero*) persuaded me, that I was fallen into the Hands of a Man of Honour and Justice; nor, indeed, was it possible for any Person to be treated with more Respect and

Civility than I now was; but, if this could not mitigate my Sorrows, when I reflected on the Condition in which I had been betrayed to leave all that was dear to me, much less could it produce such an Effect, when I discovered, as I soon did, that I owed it chiefly to a Passion, which threatned me with great Uneasiness, as it quickly appeared to be very violent, and as I was absolutely in the Power of the Person who possessed it, or was rather possessed by it. I must however do him the Justice to say, my Fears carried my Suspicions farther than I afterwards found I had any Reason for: He did indeed, very soon acquaint me with his Passion, and used all the gentle Methods, which frequently succeed with our Sex, to prevail with me to gratify it; but never once threatned, nor had the least Recourse to Force. He did not even once insinuate to me, that I was totally in his Power, which I myself saw, and whence I drew the most dreadful Apprehensions, well knowing, that as there are some Dispositions so brutal, that Cruelty adds a Zest and Savour to their Pleasures; so there are others whose gentler Inclinations are better gratified, when they win us by softer Methods to comply with their Desires; yet even these may be often compelled by an unruly Passion to have recourse at last to the Means of Violence, when they despair of Success from Persuasion; but I was happily the Captive of a better Man. My Conqueror was one of those over whom Passion hath a limited Jurisdiction, and tho' he was easy enough to Sin, he was proof against any Temptation to Villany.

'We had been two Days almost totally becalmed, when a brisk Gale rising, as we were in Sight of *Dunkirk*, we saw a Vessel making full Sail towards us. The Captain of the Privateer was so strong, that he apprehended no Danger but from a Man of War, which the Sailors discerned this not to be. He therefore struck his Colours, and furled his Sails as much as possible, in order to lie by and expect her, hoping she might be a Prize.'° Here *Heartfree* smiling, his Wife stopp'd and enquired the Cause. He told her, it was from her using the Sea Terms so aptly: She laughed, and answered, he would wonder less at this, when he heard the long Time she had been on board: And then proceeded, 'This Vessel now came along-side of us, and hailed us, having perceived that, on which we were aboard, to be of her own Country: They begged us not to put into *Dunkirk*, but to accompany them in their Pursuit of a large *English* Merchant-Man, whom we should easily overtake, and both together as easily conquer.

Our Captain immediately consented to this Proposition, and ordered all the Sail to be crowded. This was most unwelcome News to me; however, he comforted me all he could, by assuring me, I had nothing to fear, that he would be so far from offering the least Rudeness to me, that he would at the Hazard of his Life protect me from it. This Assurance gave me all the Consolation, which my present Circumstances and the dreadful Apprehensions I had on your dear Account would admit.' At which Words the tenderest Glances passed on both Sides between the Husband and Wife.

'We sailed near twelve Hours, when we came in Sight of the Ship we were in pursuit of, and which we should probably have soon come up with, had not a very thick Mist ravished her from our Eyes. This Mist continued several Hours, and when it cleared up we discovered our Companion at a great Distance from us; but what gave us (I mean the Captain and his Crew) the greatest Uneasiness, was the Sight of a very large Ship within a Mile of us, which presently saluted us with a Gun, and now appeared to be a third Rate *English* Man of War.° Our Captain declared the Impossibility of either fighting or escaping, and accordingly struck, without waiting for the Broadside which was preparing for us, and which perhaps would have prevented me from the Happiness I now enjoy.' This occasioned *Heartfree* to change Colour, his Wife therefore past hastily to Circumstances of a more smiling Complexion.

'I greatly rejoiced at this Event, as I thought it would not only restore me to the safe Possession of my Jewels, but to what I value beyond all the Treasure in the Universe. My Expectation, however, of both these was somewhat crost for the present: As to the former, I was told, they should be carefully preserved; but that I must prove my Right to them, before I could expect their Restoration; which, if I mistake not, the Captain did not very eagerly desire I should be able to accomplish: And as to the latter, I was acquainted, that I should be put aboard the first Ship, which they met on her Way to *England;* but that they were proceeding to the *West-Indies*.

'I had not been long aboard the Man of War, before I discovered just Reason rather to lament than rejoice at the Exchange of my Captivity (for such I concluded my present Situation to be.) I had now another Lover in the Captain of this *Englishman*, and much rougher and less gallant than the *Frenchman* had been. He used me with scarce common Civility, as indeed he shewed very little to any

other Person, treating his Officers little better than a Man of no great
Good-Breeding would exert to his meanest Servant, and that too on
some very irritating Provocation. As for me, he addressed me with
the Insolence of a *Basha* to a *Circassian* Slave;° he talked to me with
the loose Licence in which the most profligate Libertines converse
with Harlots, and which Women abandoned only in a moderate
Degree detest and abhor. He often kissed me with very rude Familiarity, and one Day attempted further Brutality, when a Gentleman
on board, and who was in my Situation, that is, had been taken by a
Privateer and was retaken, rescued me from his Hands; for which the
Captain confined him, tho' he was not under his Command, two
Days in Irons; when he was released (for I was not suffered to visit
him in his Confinement,) I went to him and thanked him with the
utmost Acknowledgment, for what he had done and suffered on my
Account. The Gentleman behaved to me in the handsomest Manner
on this Occasion; told me, he was ashamed of the high Sense I
seemed to entertain of so small an Obligation, of an Action to which
his Duty as a Christian, and his Honour as a Man, obliged him.
From this Time I lived in great Familiarity with this Man, whom I
regarded as my Protector, which he professed himself ready to be on
all Occasions, expressing the utmost Abhorrence of the Captain's
Brutality, especially that shewn towards me, and the Tenderness of a
Parent for the Preservation of my Virtue, for which I was not myself
more solicitous than he appeared. He was, indeed, the only Man I
had hitherto met, since my unhappy Departure, who did not
endeavour by all his Looks, Words, and Actions, to assure me, he had
a Liking to my unfortunate Person. The rest seeming desirous of
sacrificing the little Beauty they complimented, to their Desires,
without the least Consideration of the Ruin, which I earnestly represented to them, they were attempting to bring on me and my future
Repose.

'I now past several Days pretty free from the Captain's Molesta-
tion, till one fatal Night:' Here perceiving *Heartfree* grew pale, she
comforted him by an Assurance, that God had preserved her Chastity, and again had restored her unsullied to his Arms; she continued
thus: 'Perhaps, I give it a wrong Epithet in the Word *fatal*; but a
wretched Night, I am sure I may call it, for no Woman, who came off
victorious, was, I believe, ever in greater Danger. One Night, I say,
having drank his Spirits high with Punch, in Company with the

Purser, who was the only Man in the Ship he admitted to his Table, he sent for me into his Cabin; whither, tho' unwilling, I was obliged to go. We were no sooner alone together, than he seized me by the Hand, and, after affronting my Ears with Discourse which I am unable to repeat, he swore a great Oath, that his Passion was to be dallied with no longer, that I must not expect to treat him in the Manner, to which a Set of Blockhead Land-Men submitted. *None of your Coquet° Airs, therefore, with me, Madam*, said he, *for I am resolved to have you this Night. No struggling nor squawling, for both will be impertinent. The first Man who offers to come in here, I will have his Skin flea'd off at the Gangway.°* He then attempted to pull me violently towards his Bed. I threw myself on my Knees, and with Tears and Entreaties besought his Compassion; but this was, I found, to no Purpose: I then had Recourse to Threats, and endeavoured to frighten him with the Consequence; but neither had this, tho' it seemed to stagger him more than the other Method, sufficient Force to deliver me. At last, a Stratagem came into my Head, of which my perceiving him reel, gave me the first Hint. I entreated a Moment's Reprieve only, when collecting all the Spirits I could muster, I put on a constrained Air of Gayety, and told him with an affected Laugh, he was the roughest Lover I had ever met with, and that I believed I was the first Woman he had ever paid his Addresses to. *Addresses*, said he, *d——n your Dresses, I want to undress you*. I then begged him to let us drink some Punch together; for that I loved a Can as well as himself, and never would grant the Favour to any Man till I had drank a hearty Glass with him. *O*, said he, *if that be all, you shall have Punch enough to drown yourself in*. At which Words he rung the Bell, and ordered in a Gallon of that Liquor. I was in the mean time obliged to suffer his nauseous Kisses, and some Rudenesses which I had great Difficulty to restrain within moderate Bounds. When the Punch came in, he took up the Bowl and drank my Health ostentatiously, in such a Quantity, that it considerably advanced my Scheme. I followed him with Bumpers, as fast as possible, and was myself obliged to drink so much, that at another time it would have staggered my own Reason, but at present it did not affect me. At length, perceiving him very far gone, I watched an Opportunity, and ran out of the Cabin, resolving to seek Protection of the Sea, if I could find no other: But Heaven was now graciously pleased to relieve me; for in his Attempt to pursue me, he reeled backwards, and falling down the Cabin Stairs, he dislocated his Shoulder, and so bruised himself, that I was not only preserved that Night from any Danger of my intended Ravisher; but the Accident threw him into a Fever, which endangered his Life, and whether he ever recovered or no, I am not certain; for during his delirious Fits, the eldest Lieutenant commanded the Ship. This was a virtuous and a brave Fellow, who had been twenty five Years in that Post without being able to obtain a Ship, and had seen several Boys, the Bastards of Noblemen, put over his Head.° One Day, while the Ship remained under his Command, an *English* Vessel bound to *Cork*,° passed by; myself and my Friend, who had lain two Days in Irons on my Account, went on board this Ship, with the Leave of the good Lieutenant, who made us such Presents as he was able of Provisions, and congratulating me on my Delivery from a Danger to which none of the Ship's Crew had been Strangers, he kindly wished us both a safe Voyage.'

CHAPTER VIII

*In which Mrs.* Heartfree *continues the Relation of her Adventures.*

'THE first Evening after we were aboard this Vessel, which was a Brigantine,° we being then at a little Distance from the *Madeiras*, the most violent Storm arose from the North-West, in which we presently lost both our Masts; and indeed Death now presented itself as inevitable to us—I need not tell my *Tommy* what were then my Thoughts. Our Danger was so great, that the Captain of the Ship, a professed *Atheist*, betook himself to Prayers, and the whole Crew, abandoning themselves for lost, fell with the utmost Eagerness to the emptying a Cask of Brandy, not one Drop of which, they swore, should be polluted with Salt Water. I observed here, my old Friend displayed less Courage than I expected from him. He seemed entirely swallowed up in Despair. But Heaven be praised, we were all at last preserved! The Storm, after about eleven Hours Continuance began to abate, and by Degrees entirely ceased; but left us still rolling at the Mercy of the Waves, which carried us at their own Pleasure to the South-East, a vast Number of Leagues.° Our Crew were all dead drunk with the Brandy which they had taken such Care to preserve from the Sea; but, indeed, had they been awake, their

Labour would have been of very little Service, as we had lost all our Rigging; our Brigantine being reduced to a naked Hulk only. In this Condition we floated above thirty Hours, till in the midst of a very dark Night we spied a Light, which seeming to approach us, grew so large, that our Sailors concluded it to be the Lanthorn of a Man of War; but when we were cheering ourselves with the Hopes of our Deliverance from this wretched Situation, on a sudden, to our great Concern, the Light entirely disappeared and left us in a Despair, encreased by those pleasing Imaginations with which we had entertained our Minds during its Appearance. The rest of the Night we passed in melancholy Conjectures on the Light which had deserted us, which the major Part of the Sailors concluded to be a Meteor. In this Distress we had one Comfort, which was a plentiful Store of Provision: This so supported the Spirits of the Sailors, that they declared, had they but a sufficient Quantity of Brandy, they cared not whether they saw Land for a Month to come; but indeed, we were much nearer it than we imagined, as we perceived at Break of Day: One of the most knowing of the Crew declared we were near the Continent of *Africa;* but when we were within three Leagues of it, a second violent Storm arose from the North, so that we again gave over all Hopes of Safety. This Storm was not quite so outragious as the former, but of much longer Continuance, for it lasted near three Days; and drove us an immense Number of Leagues to the South. We were within a League of the Shore, expecting every Moment our Ship to be dashed in Pieces, when the Tempest ceased all of a sudden; but the Waves still continued to roll like Mountains, and before the Sea recovered its calm Motion, our Ship was thrown so near the Land, that the Captain ordered out his Boat,° declaring he had scarce any Hopes of saving her; and, indeed, we had not quitted her many Minutes, before we saw the Justice of his Apprehensions; for she struck against a Rock, and immediately sunk. The Behaviour of the Sailors on this Occasion very much affected me: they beheld their Ship perish with the Tenderness of a Lover or a Parent, they spoke of her as the fondest Husband would of his Wife; and many of them, who seemed to have no Tears in their Composition, shed them plentifully at her sinking. The Captain himself cried out, *Go thy Ways, charming* Molly, *the Sea never devoured a lovelier Morsel. If I have fifty Vessels, I shall never love another like thee. Poor Slut! I shall remember thee to my dying Day*.°

'Well, the Boat now conveyed us all safe to Shore, where we
landed with very little Difficulty. It was now about Noon, and the
Rays of the Sun, which descended almost perpendicular on our
Heads, were extremely hot and troublesome. However, we travelled
through this extreme Heat about five Miles over a Plain. This
brought us to a vast Wood, which extended itself as far as we could
see both to the right and left, and seemed to me to put an entire End
to our Progress. Here we decreed to rest and dine on the Provision
which we had brought from the Ship, of which we had sufficient for
very few Meals; our Boat being so overloaded with People, that we
had very little Room for Luggage of any Kind. Our Repast was salt
Pork broiled, which the Keenness of Hunger made so delicious to
my Companions, that they fed very heartily upon it. As for myself,
the Fatigue of my Body and the Vexation of my Mind had so thoroughly weakned me, that I was almost entirely deprived of Appetite;
and the utmost Dexterity of the most accomplished *French* Cook
would have been ineffectual, had he endeavoured to tempt me with
Delicacies.° I thought myself very little a Gainer by my late Escape
from the Tempest, by which I seemed only to have exchanged the
Element in which I was presently to die. When our Company had
sufficiently, and indeed very plentifully, feasted themselves, they
resolved to enter the Wood and endeavour to pass it, in Expectation
of finding some Inhabitants, at least Provision; for the Plain which
lay between the Wood and the Sea was extremely barren, nor did it
afford any other Beast or Fowl than Sea Gulls. We proceeded therefore in the following Order; one Man in the Front with a Hatchet to
clear our Way, and two others followed him with Guns to protect the
rest from wild Beasts; then walked the rest of our Company, and last
of all the Captain himself, being armed likewise with a Gun to
defend us from any Attack behind, in the Rear, I think you call it.
And thus our whole Company, being fourteen in Number, travelled
on 'till Night overtook us, without seeing any thing, unless a few
Birds, and some very insignificant Animals. We rested all Night
under the Covert of some Trees, and indeed we very little wanted
Shelter at that Season, the Heat in the Day being the only Inclem-
ency we had to combat with in this Climate. I cannot help telling
you, my old Friend lay still nearest to me on the Ground, and
declared he would be my Protector, should any of the Sailors offer
Rudeness; but I can acquit them of any such Attempt; nor was I ever

affronted by any one, more than with a coarse Expression, proceeding rather from the Roughness and Ignorance of their Education, than from any abandoned Principle, or want of Humanity.'

CHAPTER IX°

*A very wonderful Chapter indeed; which, to those who have not read many Voyages, may seem incredible; and which the Reader may believe or not, as he pleases.*

'WE had now proceeded a very little Way on our next Day's March, when one of the Sailors cried out, *He spied a Tower on our Left*; a second, looking that Way, said *He saw it move*; and indeed so it did towards us. We presently discovered it was an Animal of an enormous Bigness, being of the Elephantine Kind, but so large, that the Elephant is to it in Size but as the Crayfish to the Lobster. The Approach of this vast Animal struck us all with Terror. As for myself, I felt more than I had done during our two Tempests; for I dreaded less being swallowed by the unmerciful Ocean, than being devoured by the Jaws of this Monster, which, with a Voice suitable to his Bulk, now filled all the Wood with his bellowing. It was impossible to escape him by Flight, nor had our Men much time to consider what Means they might use for their Defence. Our two Musqueteers in an instant, therefore, resolved to discharge their several Pieces at his Eyes, the one agreeing to aim at the right, the other at the left. They executed this bold Resolution with such notable Success, that the Beast was immediately deprived of his Sight, the Bullets having both luckily entred in at the Sight of the Eyes; a very fortunate Accident for us, the whole Dimensions of each Eye being very near equal to the Capaciousness of a large Hall. The Beast, which now roared infinitely louder than before, with the Anguish of the Wound fell to the Ground. My Friend persuaded the rest to depart as fast as we could, lest some others, of the same kind, should come to his Assistance, which might prove fatal to us: But the Curiosity of the Sailors was insatiable; they swore they would go up to the Monster, and examine him; for they apprehended he was mortally wounded by the Blow: Whereas in Reality *Windsor Castle*, which our Beast was neither in Size nor Figure much unlike, would have been in as much Danger of being battered down by a Musquet Shot, as this Monster was of being killed by it. But I almost shudder with the Remembrance of what I am now going to relate; for indeed I take it to be the strongest Instance of that Intrepidity, so justly remarked in our Seamen, which can be found on Record. In a Word then, one of our Musqueteers coming up to the Beast as he lay wallowing on the Ground, and perceiving his Mouth wide open, marched directly down his Throat. Had he not declared his Intention to those near him, we should have concluded, that he had been swallowed by the Monster; but as it was, we imagined him little better than *Felo de se*, and gave over all Thoughts of ever seeing him again, when suddenly we heard the hollow Report of a Gun, seemingly at a great Distance. One of the Sailors declared the Sound came from the Inside of the Animal, nor had he sooner said so, than a River of Blood began to issue out at his Mouth, and shortly after the brave Sailor came forth at another Passage, which I must be excused from naming. He informed us, that he had put the Muzzle of his Gun against his Heart, and shot two Bullets into it, which he perceived had done his Business, and indeed the Monster was absolutely dead.

'As soon as the Blood ceased to flow from his Mouth, our whole Company marched rank and file through the Body; but I could by no means be prevailed on to follow them, whether I looked on it as an Indecency, (the Monster being of the Male kind) or was afraid of making my Clothes bloody, or from what other Motive my Aversion arose, is not necessary to determine. Two of our Men, with much Labour, brought forth the Heart. A small Piece of which we broiled; but the Flesh was unsavoury, being much coarser than the worst Neck Beef.° I must not take Leave of the Monster before I observe, that a whole Lion was found in him undigested, and which we concluded he had swallowed a very little Time before we came up with him.

'We now quitted the Monster, and saw, as we advanced through the Wood, several wild Beasts, such as Lions, Wolves, Tygers, and others of the common Kind; but I must not omit a large Reptile we saw, on our third Day's March, of the Colour and Form of a Snake; but so immensely long, that he extended near a Quarter of a Mile; a Length to which his Largeness was disproportionate, being no more than about six times the Size of a moderate Ox. This Serpent would certainly have molested us; but though he stirred as we walked by his middle, he was fortunately asleep as we past by his Eyes. This Day we killed a Bird somewhat resembling a Lark, but infinitely larger; for we guest it could not weigh less than thirty Stone. We drest half the Merrythought for our Dinner, and its Flavour was so excellent, that I myself for the first time eat heartily.

'The next Morning we saw a Fire at a little Distance from us, when we conceived ourselves drawing near some human Habitation; but, on our nearer Approach, we perceived a very beautiful Bird just expiring in the Flames. This was no other than the celebrated *Phœnix*, so much spoke of, and so little known.° We would not suffer such a Rarity to be consumed; we therefore snatched it from the Fire, and, being resolved to taste this elegant Dish, we first picked his Feathers off, and then roasted him; but found the Flesh so far from delicious, that it was greatly distasteful. The Captain then ordered it to be thrown again into the Fire, that it might follow its own Method of propagating its Species.

'Our Pork was now gone, and we had nothing left but the Remainder of the Lark to live on, which indeed would have been sufficient for a Month's Provision, could we have preserved it from tainting; but as we had no Salt, the extreme Heat of the Climate soon made it nauseous both to our Smell and Taste. Death now put on a more dreadful Shape than any he had hitherto worn, and starving appeared to us inevitable; for our Ammunition was all spent, and we could flatter ourselves with no Likelihood of finding the Traces of any human Creature, from whom too, if found, we apprehended much greater Probability of Danger, than of Comfort or Assistance.

'We had now travelled two Days together without any Sustenance, when, coming forth from the Wood, we saw just before us something resembling the famous *Stone-henge* in *Wiltshire*,° and which we found to be a Bed of Pumpkins; but so large that one of them was more than we could have eaten in two Months. We scooped out the Inside with some Tools we had with us, and then crept all of us into the Shell, which afforded us a cool Retreat from the scorching Beams of the Sun. The Food was neither grateful nor nourishing; so that we soon quitted this Place, and arrived at the bottom of a high and steep Hill. I was become so faint with the immoderate Fatigue of my Journey, with the intense Heat of the Climate, and with Hunger, that I threw myself on the Ground, and declared I could go no farther.

One of the Sailors skipt nimbly up the Hill, and, with the Assistance of a speaking Trumpet,° informed us, that he saw a Town a very little Way off. This News so comforted me, and gave me such Strength, as well as Spirits, that, with the Help of my old Friend, and another who suffered me to lean on them, I, with much Difficulty, attained the Summit; but was so absolutely overcome in climbing it, that I had no longer sufficient Strength to support my tottering Limbs, and was obliged to lay myself again on the Ground; nor could they prevail on me to undertake descending through a very thick Wood into a Plain, at the End of which indeed appeared some Houses; but at a much greater Distance than the Sailor had assured us. The little Way, as he had called it, seeming to me full twenty Miles, nor was it, I believe, much less.'

### CHAPTER X

*Containing Incidents very surprizing.*

'The Captain declared, he would, without Delay, proceed to the Town before him; in which Resolution he was seconded by all the Crew; but when I could not be persuaded, nor was I able to travel any farther before I had rested myself, my old Friend protested, he would not leave me, but would stay behind as my Guard; and, when I had refreshed myself with a little Repose, he would attend me to the Town, whence the Captain promised, he would not depart, before he had seen us.

'They were no sooner departed than (having first thanked my Protector for his Care of me) I resigned myself to sleep, which immediately closed my Eye-lids, and would probably have detain'd me very long in his gentle Dominion, had I not been awaked with a Squeeze by the Hand by my Guard; which I at first thought intended to alarm me with the Danger of some wild Beast; but I soon perceived it arose from a softer Motive, and that a gentle Swain was the only wild Beast I had to apprehend.

'He began now to disclose his Passion in the strongest Manner imaginable, indeed with a Warmth rather beyond that of both my former Lovers; but as yet without any Attempt of Force. On my Side Remonstrances were made in more bitter Exclamations and

Revilings than I had used to any, that Villain *Wild* excepted. I told him, he was the basest and most treacherous Wretch alive; that his having cloaked his iniquitous Designs under the Appearance of Virtue and Friendship, added an ineffable Degree of Horrour to them; that I detested him of all Mankind the most, and, could I be brought to yield to Prostitution, he should never enjoy the Ruins of my Honour. He suffered himself not to be provoked by this Language, but only changed his Method of Solicitation from Flattery to Bribery. He unript the Lining of his Wastcoat, and pulled forth several Jewels; these, he said, he had preserved from infinite Danger to the happiest purpose, if I could be won by them. I rejected them often with the utmost Indignation, till at last, casting my Eye, rather by Accident than Design, on a Diamond Necklace, a Thought, like Lightning, shot through my Mind, and, in an instant, I remembered, that this was the very Necklace you had sold the cursed Count, the Cause of all our Misfortunes. The Confusion of Ideas, into which this Surprize hurried me, prevented my reflecting on° the Villain who then stood before me: But the first Recollection presently told me, it could be no other than the Count himself, the wicked Tool of *Wild's* Barbarity. Good GOD, what was then my Condition! How shall I describe the Tumult of Passions which then laboured in my Breast! However, as I was happily unknown to him, the least Suspicion on his Side was altogether impossible. He imputed, therefore, the Eagerness with which I gazed on the Jewels, to a very wrong Cause, and endeavoured to put as much additional Softness into his Countenance as he was able. My Fears were a little quieted, and I was resolved to be very liberal of Promises, and hoped so thoroughly to persuade him of my Venality, that he might, without any Doubt, be drawn in to wait the Captain and Crew's Return, who would, I was very certain, not only preserve me from his Violence, but secure the Restoration of what you had been so cruelly robbed of. But, alas! I was mistaken.' Mrs. *Heartfree* again perceiving Symptoms of the utmost Disquietude in her Husband's Countenance, cry'd out: 'My Dear, Don't you apprehend any Harm.—But, to deliver you as soon as possible from your Anxiety—

'When he perceived I declined the Warmth of his Addresses, he changed at once the Tone of his Features, and, in a very different Voice from what he had hitherto affected, he swore, I should not deceive him as I had the Captain; that Fortune had kindly thrown an

Opportunity in his Way, which he was resolved not foolishly to lose; and concluded with a violent Oath, that he was determined to enjoy me that Moment; and, therefore, I knew the Consequence of Resistance. He then caught me in his Arms, and began such rude Attempts, that I skreamed out with all the Force I could, tho' I had so little Hopes of being rescued, when there suddenly rushed forth from a Thicket, a Creature, which, at his first Appearance, and in the hurry of Spirits I then was, I did not take for a Man; but indeed had he been the fiercest of wild Beasts, I should have rejoiced at his devouring us both. I scarce perceived he had a Musquet in his Hand, before he struck my Ravisher such a Blow with it, that he felled him at my Feet. He then advanced with a gentle Air towards me, and told me in *French*, he was extremely glad he had been luckily present to my Assistance. He was naked, except his middle and his Feet, if I can call a Body so which was covered with Hair almost equal to any Beast whatever. Indeed his Appearance was so horrid in my Eyes, that the Friendship he had shewn me, as well as his courteous Behaviour, could not entirely remove the Dread I had conceived from his Figure. I believe he saw this very visibly; for he begged me not to be frightened, since, whatever Accident had brought me thither, I should have Reason to thank GOD for meeting him, at whose Hands I might assure my self of the utmost Civility and Protection. In the midst of all this Consternation, I had Spirits enough to take up the Casket of Jewels,° which the Villain, in falling, had dropt out of his Hands, and conveyed it into my Pocket, before he recovered himself, which he now began to do. My Deliverer told me, I seemed extremely weak and faint, and desired me to refresh myself at his little Hut, which, he said, was hard by. If his Demeanour had been less kind and obliging, my desperate Situation must have lent me Confidence; for sure the Alternative could not be doubtful, whether I should rather trust this Man, who, notwithstanding his savage Outside, expressed so much Devotion to serve me, which at least I was not certain of the Falshood of, or abide with one whom I so perfectly well knew to be an accomplished Villain. I, therefore, committed my self to his Guidance, though with Tears in my Eyes, and begged him to have Compassion on my Innocence, which was absolutely in his Power. He said, the Treatment he had been Witness of, which, he supposed, was from one, who had broken his Trust towards me, sufficiently justified my Suspicion; but begged me to dry my Eyes, and he would soon convince me, that I was with a Man of different Sentiments. The kind Accents which accompanied these Words, gave me some Comfort, which was assisted by the Repossession of our Jewels by an Accident, so strongly savouring of the Disposition of Providence in my Favour.

'We walked together to his Hut, or rather Cave; for it was underground, on the Side of a Hill; the Situation was very pleasant, and, from its Mouth, we overlooked a large Plain, and the Town I had before seen. As soon as I entered it, he desired me to sit down on a Bench of Turf, which served him for Chairs, and then laid before me some Fruits, the wild Product of that Country, one or two of which had an excellent Flavour. He likewise produced some baked Flesh, a little resembling that of Venison. He then brought forth a Bottle of Brandy, which, he said, had remained with him ever since his settling there, now above thirty Years; during all which Time he had never opened it, his only Liquor being Water; that he had reserved this Bottle as a Cordial in Sickness; but, he thanked GOD, he had never yet had Occasion for it. He then acquainted me, that he was a Hermite;° that he had been formerly cast away on that Coast, with his Wife, whom he dearly loved, but could not preserve from perishing; on which Account he had resolved never to return to *France*, which was his native Country, but to devote himself to Prayer, and a holy Life, placing all his Hopes in the blest Expectation of meeting that dear Woman again in Heaven, where, he was convinced, she was now a Saint, and an Interceder for him. He said, he had exchanged a Watch with the King of that Country, whom he described to be a very just and good Man, for a Gun, some Powder, Shot, and Ball; with which he sometimes provided himself Food, but more generally used it in defending himself against wild Beasts; so that his Diet was chiefly of the vegetable kind. He told me many more Circumstances, which I may relate to you hereafter: But, to be as concise as possible at present, he at length greatly comforted me, by promising to conduct me to a Sea-port, where I might have an Opportunity to meet with some Vessels trafficking for Slaves; and whence I might once more commit myself to that Element, which, though I had already suffered so much on it, I must again trust, to put me in Possession of all I loved.

'The Character he gave me of the Inhabitants of the Town we saw below us, and of their King, made me desirous of being conducted

thither; especially as I very much wished to see the Captain and
Sailors, who had behaved very kindly to me, and with whom, notwithstanding all the civil Behaviour of the Hermit, I was rather
easier in my Mind, than alone with this single Man; but he dissuaded
me greatly from attempting such a Walk, till I had recreated my
Spirits with Rest, desiring me to repose myself on his Couch of
Turf, saying, that he himself would retire without the Cave, where he
would remain as my Guard. I accepted this kind Proposal; but it was
long before I could procure any Slumber: However, at length,
Weariness prevailed over my Fears, and I enjoyed several Hours
Sleep. When I awaked, I found my faithful Centinel on his Post, and
ready at my Summons. This Behaviour infused some Confidence
into me, and I now repeated my Request, that he would go with me
to the Town below; but he answered, it would be better advised to
take some Repast before I undertook the Journey, which I should
find much longer than it appear'd. I consented, and he set forth a
greater Variety of Fruits than before, of which I eat very plentifully:
My Collation being ended, I renewed the Mention of my Walk; but
he still persisted in dissuading me, telling me, that I was not yet
strong enough; that I could repose myself no where with greater
Safety, than in his Cave; and that, for his Part, he could have no
greater Happiness than that of attending me, adding with a Sigh, it
was a Happiness he should envy any other, more than all the Gifts of
Fortune. You may imagine, I began now to entertain Suspicions; but
he presently removed all Doubt, by throwing himself at my Feet,
expressing the warmest Passion for me. I should have now sunk with
Despair, had he not accompanied these Professions with the most
vehement Protestations, that he would never offer me any other
Love but that of Entreaty, and that he would rather die the most
cruel Death by my Coldness, than gain the highest Bliss by becoming the Occasion of a Tear of Sorrow to these bright Eyes, which, he
said, were Stars, under whose benign Influence alone, he could enjoy,
or indeed, suffer Life.' She was repeating many more Compliments
he made her, when a horrid Uproar, which alarmed the whole *Gate*,°
put a Stop to her Narration at present. It is impossible for me to give
the Reader a better Idea of the Noise which now arose, than by
desiring him to imagine I had the hundred Tongues the Poet once
wished for,° and was vociferating from them all at once, by hollow-
ing, scolding, crying, swearing, bellowing, and in short, by every

different Articulation which is within the Scope of the human Organ.

## CHAPTER XI

### *A horrible Uproar in the* Gate.

BUT however great an Idea the Reader may hence conceive of this Uproar, he will think the Occasion more than adequate to it, when he is informed, that our Hero (I blush to name it) had discovered an Injury done to his Honour, and that in the tenderest Point—In a Word, Reader, (for thou must know it, tho' it give thee the greatest Horror imaginable) he had caught *Fireblood* in the Arms of his lovely *Lætitia*.

As the generous° Bull, who having long depastured among a Number of Cows, and thence contracted an Opinion, that these Cows are all his own Property, if he beholds another Bull bestride a Cow within his Walks,° he roars aloud, and threatens instant Vengeance with his Horns, till the whole Parish are alarmed with his bellowing. Not with less Noise, nor less dreadful Menaces did the Fury of *Wild* burst forth, and terrify the whole *Gate*. Long time did Rage render his Voice inarticulate to the Hearer; as when, at a visiting Day,° fifteen or sixteen, or perhaps twice as many Females of delicate but shrill Pipes, ejaculate all at once on different Subjects, all is Sound only, the Harmony entirely melodious indeed, but conveys no Idea to our Ears; but at length, when Reason began to get the Better of his Passion, which latter being deserted by his Breath, began a little to retreat, the following Accents leapt over the Hedge of his Teeth,° or rather the Ditch of his Gums, whence those Hedge-stakes had by a Pattin° been displaced in Battle with an *Amazon* of *Drury*.°

\* '——Man of Honour! doth this become a Friend? Could I have expected such a Breach of all the Laws of Honour from thee, whom I had taught to walk in its Paths? Hadst thou chosen any other Way to injure my Confidence, I could have forgiven it; but this is a Stab in the tenderest Part, a Wound never to be healed, an Injury never to be repaired: For it is not only the Loss of an agreeable Companion, of

---

\* The Beginning of this Speech was lost, for the Reason given before.

the Affection of a Wife, dearer to my Soul than Life itself, it is not this Loss alone I lament: This Loss is accompanied with Disgrace, and with Dishonour. The Blood of the *Wilds*, which hath run with such uninterrupted Purity through so many Generations, this Blood is fouled, is contaminated: Hence flow my Tears, hence arises my Grief. This is the Injury never to be redressed, nor never to be with Honour forgiven.' ' My —— in a Bandbox,'° answered *Fireblood*, 'here is a Noise about your Honour: If the Mischief done to your Blood be all you complain of, I am sure you complain of nothing; for my Blood is as good as yours.' 'You have no Conception,' replied *Wild*, 'of the Tenderness of Honour; you know not how nice and delicate it is in both Sexes; so delicate, that the least Breath of Air which rudely blows on it, destroys it.' 'I will prove from your own Words,' says *Fireblood*, 'I have not wronged your Honour. Have you not often told me, that the Honour of a Man consisted in receiving no Affront from his own Sex, and that of a Woman in receiving no Kindness from ours? Now, Sir, if I have given you no Affront, how have I injured your Honour?' 'But doth not every thing,' cried *Wild*, 'of the Wife belong to the Husband? A married Man therefore hath his Wife's Honour as well as his own, and by injuring her's you injure his. How cruelly you have hurt me in this tender Part, I need not repeat, the whole *Gate* knows it, and the World shall. I will apply to *Doctors Commons*° for my Redress against her, I will shake off as much of my Dishonour as I can by parting with her; and as for you, expect to hear of me in *Westminster-Hall;* the modern Method of repairing these Breaches, and of resenting this Affront.'° 'D——n your Eyes,' cries *Fireblood*, 'I fear you not, nor do I believe a Word you say.' 'Nay, if you affront me personally,' says *Wild*, 'another Sort of Resentment is prescribed.' At which Word, advancing to *Fireblood*, he presented him with a Box on the Ear, which the Youth immediately returned, and now our Hero and his Friend fell to Boxing, tho' with some Difficulty, both being incumbered with the Chains which they wore between their Legs: A few Blows past on both Sides, before the Gentlemen, who stood by, stept in and parted the Combatants; and now both Parties having whisper'd each other, that, if they out-lived the ensuing Sessions and escaped the Tree, the one should give and the other should receive Satisfaction in single Combat; they separated, and the *Gate* soon recovered its former Tranquillity.

Mrs. *Heartfree* was then desired, by the Justice and her Husband

both, to conclude her Story, which she did in the Words of the next
Chapter.

<br>

### CHAPTER XII

#### *The Conclusion of Mrs.* Heartfree's *Adventures.*

'IF I mistake not, I was interrupted just as I was beginning to repeat
some of the Compliments made me by the Hermite.' 'Just as you had
finished them, I believe, Madam,' said the Justice. 'Very well, Sir,'
said she, 'I am sure I have no Pleasure in the Repetition. He concluded then with telling me, Though I was, in his Eyes, the most
charming Woman in the World, and might tempt a Saint to abandon
the Ways of Holiness, yet my Beauty inspired him with a much
tenderer Affection towards me, than to purchase any Satisfaction of
his own Desires with my Misery; if therefore I could be so cruel to
him, to reject his honest and sincere Address, nor could submit to a
solitary Life with one, who would endeavour, by all possible Means,
to make me happy, I had no Force to dread; for that I was as much at
my Liberty as if I was in *France*, or *England*, or any other free
Country. I repulsed him with the same Civility with which he
advanced; and told him, that as he professed great Regard to
Religion, I was convinced he would cease from all further Solicitation, when I informed him, that, if I had no other Objection, my own
Innocence would not admit of my hearing him on this Subject, for
that I was married.—He started a little at that Word, and was for
some time silent; but at length recovering himself, he began to urge
the Uncertainty of my Husband's being alive, and the Probability of
the contrary; he then spoke of Marriage as of a civil Policy only; on
which Head he urged many Arguments not worth repeating, and was
growing so very eager and importunate, that I know not whither his
Passion might have hurried him, had not three of the Sailors well
armed, appeared at that Instant in Sight of the Cave. I no sooner saw
them, than, exulting with the utmost inward Joy, I told him my
Companions were come for me, and that I must now take my Leave
of him; assuring him, that I would always remember, with the most
grateful Acknowledgment, the Favours I had received at his Hands.
He fetched a very heavy Sigh, and, squeezing me tenderly by the

Hand, he saluted my Lips with a little more Eagerness than the *European* Salutations admit of; and told me, he should likewise remember my Arrival at his Cave to the last Day of his Life; adding, "O that he could there spend the whole in the Company of one, whose bright Eyes had kindled—;" but I know you will think, Sir, that we, Women, love to repeat the Compliments made us, I will therefore omit them. In a Word, the Sailors being now arrived, I quitted him, with some Compassion for the Reluctance with which he parted from me, and went forward with my Companions.

'We had proceeded but a very few Paces before one of the Sailors said to his Comrades: "D——n me, *Jack*, who knows whether yon Fellow hath not some good Flip° in his Cave?" I innocently answered, the poor Wretch had only one Bottle of Brandy. "Hath he so," cries the Sailor: " 'Fore *George*° we will taste it;"—and, so saying, they immediately returned back, and myself with them. We found the poor Man prostrate on the Ground, expressing all the Symptoms of Misery and Lamentation. I told him in *French* (for the Sailors could not speak that Language) what they wanted.—He pointed to the Place where the Bottle was deposited, saying, they were welcome to that, and whatever else he had; and added, he cared not if they took his Life also. The Sailors searched the whole Cave, where finding nothing more which they deemed worth their taking, they walked off with the Bottle, and, immediately emptying it, without offering me a Drop, they proceeded with me towards the Town.

'In our Way I observed one whisper another, while he kept his Eye stedfastly fixed on me. This gave me some Uneasiness; but the other answered: "No, d——n me, the Captain will never forgive us. Besides, we have enough of it among the black Women, and, in my Mind, one Colour is as good as another." This was enough to give me violent Apprehensions; but I heard no more of that kind, 'till we came to the Town, where, in about six Hours, I arrived in Safety.

'As soon as I came to the Captain, he enquired what was become of my Friend, meaning the villainous Count. When he was informed by me of what had happened, he wished me heartily Joy of my Delivery, and, expressing the utmost Abhorrence of such Baseness, swore, if ever he met him, he would cut his Throat; but indeed we both concluded, that he had died of the Blow which the Hermite had given him.

'I was now introduced to the Mayor, or chief Magistrate of this

Country, who was desirous of seeing me. I will give you a short Description of him: He was chosen (as is the Custom there) for his superior Bravery and Wisdom. His Power is entirely absolute during its Continuance; but, on the first Deviation from Equity and Justice, he is liable to be deposed, and punished by the People, the Elders of whom, once a Year, assemble, to examine into his Conduct. Besides the Danger which these Examinations, which are very strict, expose him to, his Office is of such Care and Trouble, that nothing but that restless Love of Power, so predominant in the Mind of Man, could make it the Object of Desire; for he is indeed the only Slave of all the Natives of this Country. He is obliged, in Time of Peace, to hear the Complaint of every Person in his Dominions, and to render him Justice. For which purpose every one may demand an Audience of him, unless during the Hour which he is allowed for Dinner, when he sits alone at the Table, and is attended, in the most public Manner, with more than *European* Ceremony. This is done to create an Awe and Respect towards him in the Eye of the Vulgar; but, lest it should elevate him too much in his own Opinion, in order to his Humiliation, he receives every Evening in private, from a kind of Beadle, a gentle Kick on his Posteriors; besides which, he wears a Ring in his Nose, somewhat resembling that we ring our Pigs with, and a Chain round his Neck, not unlike that worn by our Aldermen;° both which I suppose emblematical, but heard not the Reasons of either assigned. There are many more Particularities among these People, which, when I have an Opportunity, I may relate to you. The second Day after my Return from Court, one of his Officers, whom they call SCHACH PIMPACH,° waited upon me, and, by a *French* Interpreter who lives here, informed me, that the Mayor liked my Person, and offered me an immense Present, if I would suffer him to enjoy it (this is, it seems, their common Form of making Love.) I rejected the Present, and never heard any further Solicitation; for, as it is no Shame for the Women here to consent at the first Proposal, so they never receive a second.

'I had resided in this Town a Week, when the Captain informed me, that a Number of Slaves, who had been taken Captives in War, were to be guarded to the Sea-side, where they were to be sold to the Merchants, who traded in them to *America*; that if I would embrace this Opportunity, I might assure myself of finding a Passage to *America*, and thence to *England;* acquainting me at the same time, that he himself intended to go with them. I readily agreed to accompany him. The Mayor, being advertised of our Designs, sent for us both to Court, and, without mentioning a Word of Love to me, having presented me with a very rich Jewel, of less Value, he said, than my Chastity, took his Leave, recommending me to the Care of GOD, and ordering us a large Supply of Provisions for our Journey.

'We were provided with Mules for ourselves, and what we carried with us, and, in nine Days, reached the Sea-shore, where we found an *English* Vessel ready to receive both us and the Slaves. We went aboard it, and sailed the next Day with a fair Wind for *New England*, where I hoped to get an immediate Passage to the *Old:* But Providence was kinder than my Expectation; for the third Day after we were at Sea, we met an *English* Man of War homeward bound; the Captain of it was a very good-natured Man, and agreed to take me on board. I accordingly took my Leave of my old Friend the Master of the shipwrecked Vessel, who went on to *New England*, whence he intended to pass to *Jamaica*, where his Owners lived. I was now treated with great Civility, had a little Cabbin assigned me, and dined every Day at the Captain's Table, who was indeed a very gallant Man, and, at first, made me a Tender of his Affections; but, when he found me resolutely bent to preserve myself pure and entire for the best of Husbands, he grew cooler in his Addresses, and soon behaved in a manner very pleasing to me, regarding my Sex only so far as to pay me a Deference, which is very agreeable to us all.

'To conclude my Story; I met with no Adventure in this Passage at all worth relating, 'till my landing at *Gravesend*, whence the Captain brought me in his own Boat to the Tower.° In a short Hour after my Arrival we had that Meeting, which, however dreadful at first, will, I now hope, by the good Offices of the best of Men, whom GOD for ever bless, end in our perfect Happiness, and be a strong Instance of what I am persuaded is the surest Truth, THAT PROVIDENCE WILL, SOONER OR LATER, PROCURE THE FELICITY OF THE VIRTUOUS AND INNOCENT.'

Mrs. *Heartfree* thus ended her Speech, having before delivered to her Husband the Jewels, which the Count had robbed him of, and that presented her by the *African* Mayor, which latter was of immense Value. The good Magistrate was sensibly touched at her Narrative, as well on the Consideration of the Sufferings she had herself undergone, as for those of her Husband, which he had himself been innocently the Instrument of bringing upon him. That worthy Man, however, much rejoiced in what he had already done for his Preservation, and promised to labour, with his utmost Interest and Industry, to procure the absolute Pardon, rather of his Sentence, than of his Guilt, which, he now plainly discovered was a barbarous and false Imputation.

### CHAPTER XIII

*The History returns to the Contemplation of* GREATNESS.

BUT we have already perhaps detained our Reader too long in this Relation, from the Consideration of our Hero, who daily gave the most exalted Proofs of GREATNESS, in cajoling the *Prigs*, and in Exactions on the Debtors; which latter now grew so GREAT, *i.e.* corrupted in their Morals, that they spoke with the utmost Contempt of what the Vulgar call *Honesty*. The greatest Character among them was that of a Pick-pocket, or, in truer Language, *a File*;° and the only Censure was Want of Dexterity. As to Virtue, Goodness, and such like, they were the Objects of Mirth and Derision, and all *Newgate* was a complete Collection of *Prigs*, every Man being desirous to pick his Neighbour's Pocket, and every one was as sensible that his Neighbour was as ready to pick his; so that (which is almost incredible) as great Roguery was daily committed within the Walls of *Newgate* as without.

The Glory resulting from these Actions of *Wild* probably animated the Envy of his Enemies against him. The Day of his Trial now approached; for which, as *Socrates* did, he prepared himself; but not weakly and foolishly, like that Philosopher, with Patience and Resignation;° but with a good Number of false Witnesses. However, as Success is not always proportioned to the Wisdom of him who endeavours to attain it; so are we more sorry than ashamed to relate, that our Hero was, notwithstanding his utmost Caution and Prudence, convicted, and sentenced to a Death, which, when we consider, not only the GREAT MEN who have suffered it, but the much larger Number of those, whose highest Honour it hath been to merit it, we cannot call otherwise than *honourable*. Indeed those, who have unluckily missed it, seem all their Days to have laboured in vain to attain an End, which Fortune, for Reasons only known to herself, hath thought proper to deny them. Without any further Preface then, our Hero was sentenced *to be hanged by the Neck:* But whatever was to be now his Fate, he might console himself that he had perpetrated what

> —*nec* Judicis *ira, nec ignis,*
> *Nec poterit ferrum, nec edax abolere vetustas.*°

For my own Part, I confess, I look on this Death of *Hanging* to be as proper for a *Hero* as any other; and I solemnly declare, that, had *Alexander the Great* been hanged, it would not in the least have diminished my Respect to his Memory. Provided a Hero in his Life doth but execute a sufficient Quantity of Mischief; provided he be but well and heartily cursed by the Widow, the Orphan, the Poor, and the Oppressed (the sole Rewards, as many Authors have bitterly lamented both in Prose and Verse, of GREATNESS, *i.e. Priggism;*) I think it avails little of what Nature his Death be, whether it be by the Ax, the Halter, or the Sword. Such Names will be always sure of living to Posterity, and of enjoying that Fame, which they so gloriously and eagerly coveted; for, according to our GREAT *Dramatic* Poet:

> —*Fame*
> *Not more survives from good than evil Deeds,*
> *Th' aspiring Youth that fir'd th' Ephesian Dome,*
> *Outlives in Fame the pious Fool who rais'd it.*°

Our Hero now suspected that the Malice of his Enemies would overpower him. He, therefore, betook himself to that true Support of GREATNESS in Affliction, a *Bottle*; by Means of which he was enabled to curse, and swear, and bully, and brave his Fate. Other Comfort indeed he had not much; for not a single Friend ever came near him. His Wife, whose Trial was deferred to the next Sessions, visited him but once, when she plagued, tormented, and upbraided him so cruelly, that he forbad the Keeper ever to admit her again. The Ordinary of *Newgate* had frequent Conferences with him, and greatly would it embellish our History, could we record all which that good Man delivered on these Occasions; but unhappily we could procure only the Substance of a single Conference, which Mr. *Wild* committed to Paper the Moment after it had past.° We shall transcribe it, therefore, exactly in the same Form and Words we received it; nor can we help regarding it as one of the most curious Pieces, which either ancient or modern History hath recorded.

### CHAPTER XIV

*A Dialogue between the Ordinary of* Newgate *and Mr.* Jonathan Wild *the Great: In which the Subjects of Death, Immortality, and other grave Matters are very learnedly handled by the former.*

### Ordinary

GOOD Morrow to you, Sir; I hope you rested well last Night.

### Jonathan

D——n'd ill, Sir. I dreamt so confoundedly of *hanging*, that it disturbed my Sleep.

### Ordinary

Fie upon it. You should be more resigned. I wish you would make a little better Use of those Instructions which I have endeavoured to inculcate into you, and particularly last *Sunday*, and from these Words: *Those who do Evil shall go into everlasting Fire, prepared for the Devil and his Angels,*° I undertook to shew you, First, What is meant by EVERLASTING FIRE; and, Secondly, Who were THE DEVIL AND HIS ANGELS. I then proceeded to draw some Inferences from the whole;* in which I am mightily deceived, if I did not convince you, that you yourself was one of those ANGELS; and, consequently, must expect EVERLASTING FIRE to be your Portion in the other World.

### Jonathan

Faith, *Doctor*, I remember very little of your Inferences; for I fell asleep soon after your naming your Text: But did you preach this Doctrine then, or do you repeat it now, in order to comfort me?

### Ordinary

I do it, in order to bring you to a true Sense of your manifold Sins,

* He pronounced this Word HULL,° and perhaps would have spelt it so.

and, by that Means, to induce you to Repentance. Indeed, had I the Eloquence of *Cicero*, or of *Tully*,° it would not be sufficient to describe the Pains of Hell, or the Joys of Heaven. The utmost that we are taught is, *that Ear hath not heard, nor can Heart conceive.*° Who then would, for the pitiful Consideration of the Riches and Pleasures of this World, forfeit such inestimable Happiness! Such Joys! Such Pleasures! Such Delights! Or who would run the Venture of such Misery, which, but to think on, shocks the human Understanding! Who, in his Senses, then would prefer the latter to the former?

### *Jonathan*

Ay, who indeed! I assure you, *Doctor*, I had much rather be happy than miserable. But† * * * * * * * * * * * * * * * * * *
* * * * * * * * * * * * * * * * * * * * * * * * * * * * *
* * * * *

### *Ordinary*

Nothing can be plainer. St. * * * * * * * * * * * * * *
* * * * * * * * * * * * * * * * * * * * * * * * * * *
* * * * * * * * * * * * * * * * * * * * * * * * * *
* * * * * * * * * * * * * * * * * * * * * * * * * * *
* * * * * * * * * * * * * * * * * * * * * * * * * * *
* * * * * * * * * * * * * * * * * * * * * * * * * * *
* * * * * * * * * * * * * * * * * * * * * * * * * * *
* * * * * * * * * * * * * * * * * * * * * * * * * *
* * * * * * * * * * * * * * * * * * * * * * * * * *
* * * * * * * * * * * * * * * * * * * * * * * * * *
* * * * * * * * * * * * * * * * * * * * * * * * * *
* * * * * * * * * * * * * * * * * * * * * * * * * *
* * * * * * * * * * * * * * * * * * * * * * * * * *
* * * * * * * * * * * * * * * * * * * * * * * * * *
* * * * * * * * * * * * * * * * * * * * * * * * * *
* * * * * * * * * * * * * * * * * * * * * * * * * *
* * * * * * * * * * * * * * * * * * * * * * * * * * *
* * * * * *

---

† This Part was so blotted that it was illegible.

### Jonathan

\* \* \* \* \* \* \* \* \* \* \* \* \* \* \* If   once   convinced
\* \* \* \* \* \* \* \* \* \* no Man \* \* \* \* \* \* \* \* \*
lives of \* \* \* \* \* \* \* whereas sure the Clergy \* \* \* \*
\* \* \* \* Opportunity \* \* \* \* \* \* better   informed \*
\* \* \* \* \* \* \* \* \* \* all Manner of Vice \* \* \* \* \*
\* \* \* \* \*

### Ordinary

\* are \* \* Atheist \* \* \* Deist \* \* \* \* *Ari* \* \* \* \*
\* *cinian*° \* \* hanged \* \* burnt \* roiled \* oasted. \*
\* \* \* \* \* \* \* Dev \* \* \* his An \* \* \* \* \* \* \*ell
Fire \* \* \* \* \* ternal Da \* \*tion.

### Jonathan

You \* \* \* \* to frighten me out of my Wits: But his \* \* \*
is, I doubt not, more merciful than his \* \* \* If I should believe
all you say, I am sure I should die in inexpressible Horrour.

### Ordinary

Despair is sinful. You should place your Hopes in Repentance
and Grace; and though, it is most true, you are in Danger of the
Judgment; yet there is still Room for Mercy, and no Man, unless
excommunicated, is absolutely without Hopes of a Reprieve.

### Jonathan

I am not without Hopes of a Reprieve from the *Cheat* yet:° I
have pretty good Interest; but if I cannot obtain it, you shall not
frighten me out of my Courage, I will not die like a Pimp. D——n
me what is Death? It is nothing but to be with *Plato's* and with
*Cæsars*,—as the Poet says,° and all the other great Heroes of
Antiquity. \* \* \* \* \* \* \* \* \* \* \* \* \* \* \* \* \* \* \* \*
\* \* \* \* \* \* \* \* \* \* \* \* \* \* \* \* \* \* \* \* \* \* \* \*
\* \* \* \* \* \* \* \* \* \* \* \* \*

### Ordinary

Ay, all this is very true; but Life is sweet for all that, and I had
rather live to Eternity, than go into the Company of any such Hea-
thens, who are, I doubt not, in Hell with the Devil and his Angels;

and, as little as you seem to apprehend it, you may find yourself there before you expect it. Where then will be your Tauntings and your Vauntings, your Boastings and your Braggings? You will then be ready to give more for a Drop of Water than you ever gave for a Bottle of Wine.

### Jonathan

Faith, *Doctor*, well minded. What say you to a Bottle of Wine?

### Ordinary

I will drink no Wine with an Atheist. I should expect the Devil to make a third in such Company; for, since he knows you are his, he may be impatient to have his Due.°

### Jonathan

It is your Business to drink with the Wicked, in order to amend them.

### Ordinary

I despair of it; and so I consign you over to the Devil, who is ready to receive you.

### Jonathan

You are more unmerciful to me than the Judge, *Doctor*. He recommended my Soul to Heaven; and it is your Office to shew me the Way thither.

### Ordinary

No: The Gates are barred against all Revilers of the Clergy.

### Jonathan

I revile only the wicked ones, if any such are, which cannot affect you, who, if Men were preferred in the Church by Merit only, would have long since been a Bishop. Indeed, it might raise any good Man's Indignation to observe one of your vast Learning and Abilities obliged to exert them in so low a Sphere, when so many of your Inferiors wallow in Wealth and Preferment.

### Ordinary

Why, it must be confest, there are bad Men in all Orders; but you should not censure too generally. I must own, I might have expected higher Promotion; but I have learnt Patience and Resignation; and I would advise you to the same Temper of Mind, which, if you can attain, I know you will find Mercy; nay, I do now promise you, you will. It is true, you are a Sinner; but your Crimes are not of the blackest Dye: You are no Murtherer, nor guilty of Sacrilege. And if you are guilty of Theft, you make some Atonement by suffering for it, which many others do not. Happy is it indeed for those few who are detected in their Sins, and brought to exemplary Punishment for them in this World. So far, therefore, from repining at your Fate when you come to the Tree, you should exult and rejoice in it; and, to say the Truth, I question whether, to a wise Man, the Catastrophe of many a Man who dies by a Halter, is not more to be envied than pitied. Nothing is so sinful as Sin, and Murther is the greatest of all Sins; it follows, that whoever commits Murther is happy in suffering for it; if therefore a Man who commits Murther is so happy in dying for it, how much better must it be for you, who have committed a less Crime.

### *Jonathan*

All this is very true; but let us take a Bottle of Wine to cheer our Spirits.

### *Ordinary*

Why Wine? Let me tell you, Mr. *Wild*, there is nothing so deceitful as the Spirits given us by Wine. If you must drink, let us have a Bowl of *Punch*; a Liquor I the rather prefer, as it is no where spoken against in Scripture, and as it is more wholsome for the Gravel;° a Distemper with which I am grievously afflicted.

### *Jonathan (having called for a Bowl)*

I ask your Pardon, *Doctor*, I should have remembered, that *Punch* was your favourite Liquor. I think you never taste Wine while there is any *Punch* remaining on the Table.

### *Ordinary*

I confess, I look on *Punch* to be the more eligible Liquor, as well for the Reasons I have before mentioned, as likewise for one other Cause, *viz.* it is the properest for a DRAUGHT. I own I took it a little unkind of you to mention Wine, thinking you knew my Palate.

### *Jonathan*

You are in the right; and I will take a swinging Cup to your being made a Bishop.

### *Ordinary*

And I will wish you a Reprieve in as large a DRAUGHT. Come, don't despair: It is yet Time enough to think of dying, you have good Friends, who very probably may prevail for you. I have known many a Man reprieved, who had less Reason to expect it.

### *Jonathan*

But, if I should flatter myself with such Hopes, and be deceived, what then would become of my Soul?

### *Ordinary*

Pugh! Never mind your Soul, leave that to me; I will render a good Account of it, I warrant you. I have a Sermon in my Pocket, which may be of some Use to you to hear. I do not value myself on the Talent of Preaching, since no Man ought to value himself for any Gift in this World: But perhaps there are not many such Sermons. — But to proceed, since we have nothing else to do till the *Punch* comes. — My Text is the latter Part of a Verse only.

### — *To the* Greeks FOOLISHNESS.°

The Occasion of these Words was principally that Philosophy of the *Greeks* which at that Time had over-run great Part of the Heathen World, had poisoned, and as it were puffed up their Minds with Pride, so that they disregarded all Kinds of Doctrine in Comparison of their own; and however safe, and however sound the Learning of others might be, yet, if it any wise contradicted their own Laws, Customs, and received Opinions, *away with it, it is not for us*. It was *to the* Greeks FOOLISHNESS.

In the former Part therefore of my Discourse on these Words, I shall principally confine myself to the laying open and demonstrating the great Emptiness and Vanity of this Philosophy, with which these idle and absurd Sophists were so proudly blown up and elevated: And here I shall do two Things: First, I shall expose the Matter; and secondly, The Manner of this absurd Philosophy.

And First, for the First of these, namely the Matter. Now here we may retort the unmannerly Word, which our Adversaries have audaciously thrown in our Faces; for what was all this mighty Matter of Philosophy, this Heap of Knowledge, which was to bring such large Harvests of Honour to those who sowed it, and so greatly and nobly enrich the Ground on which it fell; what was it, but FOOL-ISHNESS? An inconsistent Heap of Nonsense, of Absurdities and Contradictions, bringing no Ornament to the Mind in its Theory, nor exhibiting any Usefulness to the Body in its Practice. What were all the Sermons and the Sayings, the Fables and the Morals of all these wise Men, but, to use the Word mentioned in my Text once more, FOOLISHNESS? What was their great Master *Plato*, or their other great Light *Aristotle?* Mere Quibblers and Sophists, idly and vainly attached to certain ridiculous Notions of their own, founded neither on Truth nor Reason. Their whole Works are a strange Medley of the greatest Falshoods, scarce covered over with the Colour of Truth: Their Precepts are neither borrowed from Nature, nor guided by Reason: Mere *Fictions*, serving only to evince the dreadful Height of human Pride. It may be, perhaps, expected of me, that I should give some Instances from their Works to prove this Charge; but as to transcribe every Passage tending to prove what I have here asserted, would be to transcribe their whole Works, and as in such a plentiful Crop, it is difficult to chuse; instead of trespassing on your Patience, I shall conclude this first Head with a small Alteration of the Words of my Text. The Philosophy of the *Greeks* was FOOLISHNESS.

Proceed we now in the second Place, to consider the Manner in which this inane and simple Doctrine was propagated. And here ——

But here, the Punch by entring put a Stop to his Reading at this time: Nor could we obtain of Mr. *Wild* any further Account of the Conversation which past at this Interview.

CHAPTER XV

Wild *proceeds to the highest Consummation of*
*human* GREATNESS.

THE Day now drew nigh, when our GREAT MAN was to exemplify the last and noblest Act of GREATNESS, by which any Hero can signalize himself. This was the Day of Execution, or Consummation, or *Apotheosis*,° (for it is called by different Names) which was to give our Hero an Opportunity of facing Death and Damnation, without any Fear in his Heart, or at least without betraying any Symptoms of it in his Countenance. A Completion of GREATNESS which is heartily to be wished to every GREAT MAN; nothing being more worthy of Lamentation than when Fortune, like a lazy Poet, winds up her Catastrophe° aukwardly, and bestowing too little Care on her fifth Act, dismisses the Hero with a sneaking and private Exit, who had in the former Part of the *Drama* performed such notable Exploits, as must promise to every good Judge among the Spectators, a noble, public and exalted End.

But she was resolved to commit no such Error in this Instance. Our Hero was too much and too deservedly her Favourite, to be neglected by her in his last Moments: Accordingly all Efforts for a Reprieve were vain, and the Name of *Wild* stood at the Head of those who were ordered for Execution.

From the Time he gave over all Hopes of Life, his Conduct was truly GREAT and Admirable. Instead of shewing any Marks of Dejection or Contrition, he rather infused more Confidence and Assurance into his Looks. He spent most of his Hours in drinking with his Friends, and with the good Man above commemorated. In one of these Compotations, being asked, whether he was afraid to die, he answered, *D——n me, it is only a Dance without Music.* Another Time, when one expressed some Sorrow for his Misfortune, as he termed it, he said, with great Fierceness, *A Man can die but once.* Again, when one of his intimate Acquaintance hinted his Hopes, that he would die like a Man, he cocked his Hat in Defiance, and cried out greatly, *Zounds! who's afraid?*

Happy would it have been for Posterity, could we have retrieved any entire Conversation which passed at this Season, especially between our Hero and his learned Comforter; but we have searched many Pasteboard° Records in vain.

On the Eve of his *Apotheosis, Wild's* Lady desired to see him, to which he consented. This Meeting was at first very tender on both Sides; but it could not continue so: For unluckily some Hints of former Miscarriages intervening, as particularly when she asked him, how he could have used her so barbarously once, as by calling her B——? Whether such Language became a Man, much less a Gentleman? *Wild* flew into a violent Passion, and swore she was the vilest of B——s, to upbraid him at such a Season with an unguarded Word spoke long ago. She replied, with many Tears, she was well enough served for her Folly in visiting such a Brute; but she had one Comfort however, that it would be the last time he could ever treat her so; that indeed she had some Obligation to him, for that his Cruelty to her would reconcile her to the Fate he was To-morrow to suffer, and indeed, nothing but such Brutality could have made the Consideration of his shameful Death (so this weak Woman called Hanging) which was now inevitable, to be born even without Madness. She then proceeded to a Recapitulation of his Faults in an exacter Order and with more perfect Memory than one would have imagined her capable of; and, it is probable, would have rehearsed a complete Catalogue, had not our Hero's Patience failed him, so that with the utmost Fury and Violence, he caught her by the Hair and kicked her, as heartily as his Chains would suffer him,° out of the Room.

At length, the Morning came, which Fortune resolutely ordained for the Consummation of our Hero's GREATNESS: He had himself indeed modestly declined the public Honours she intended him, and had taken a Quantity of *Laudanum,*° in order to retire quietly off the Stage; but we have already observed in the course of our wonderful History, that to struggle against this Lady's Decrees is vain and impotent: And whether she hath determined you shall be hanged or be a Prime Minister, it is in either Case lost Labour to resist. *Laudanum*, therefore, being unable to stop the Breath of our Hero, which the Fruit of Hemp-Seed and not the Spirit of Poppy-Seed° was to overcome, he was at the usual Hour attended by the proper Gentlemen appointed for that Purpose, and acquainted that the Cart was ready. On this Occasion he exerted that GREATNESS of Courage, which hath been so much celebrated in other Heroes; and knowing it

was impossible to resist, he gravely declared, *He would attend them*;
he then descended to that Room where the Fetters of GREAT MEN
are knocked off, in a most solemn and ceremonious Manner. Then
shaking Hands with his Friends (to wit, those who were conducting
him to the Tree) and drinking their Healths in a Bumper of Brandy,
he ascended the Cart, where he was no sooner seated, than he
received the Acclamations of the Multitude, who were highly
ravished with his GREATNESS.

The Cart now moved slowly on, being preceded by a Troop of
Horse Guards bearing Javelins in their Hands, through Streets lined
with Crowds, all admiring the great Behaviour of our Hero, who
rode on sometimes sighing, sometimes swearing, sometimes singing
or whistling, as his Humour varied.

When he came to the Tree of Glory, he was welcomed with an
universal Shout of the People, who were there assembled in prodigious Numbers, to behold a Sight much more rare in popular
Cities than one would reasonably imagine it should be, *viz.* the
proper Catastrophe of a GREAT MAN.

But tho' Envy was, through Fear, obliged to join the general Voice
of Applause on this Occasion, there were not wanting some who
maligned this Completion of Glory, which was now about to be
fulfilled to our Hero, and endeavoured to prevent it by knocking him
on the Head as he stood under the Tree, while the Ordinary was
performing his last Office. They therefore began to batter the Cart
with Stones, Brickbats, Dirt, and all Manner of mischievous
Weapons, some of which erroneously playing on the Robes of the
Ecclesiastic, made him so expeditious in his Repetition,° that with
wonderful Alacrity he had ended almost in an Instant, and conveyed
himself into a Place of Safety in a Hackney Coach where he
waited the Conclusion with the Temper of Mind described in these
Verses,

> *Suave Mari magno, turbantibus Æquora ventis,*
> *E Terra alterius magnum spectare Laborem.*°

We must not however omit one Circumstance, as it serves to shew
the most admirable Conservation of Character° in our Hero to his last
Moment, which was, that whilst the Ordinary was busy in his Ejaculations, *Wild*, in the midst of the Shower of Stones, &c. which
played upon him, applied his Hands to the Parson's Pocket, and

emptied it of his Bottle-Screw, which he carried out of the World in his Hand.°

The Ordinary being now descended from the Cart, *Wild* had just Opportunity to cast his Eyes around the Crowd and give them a hearty Curse, when immediately the Horses moved on, and with universal Applause our Hero swung out of this World.

Thus fell *Jonathan Wild* the GREAT, by a Death as glorious as his Life had been, and which was so truly agreeable to it, that the latter must have been deplorably maimed and imperfect without the former; a Death which hath been alone wanting to complete the Characters of several ancient and modern Heroes, whose Histories would then have been read with much greater Pleasure by the wisest in all Ages. Indeed we could almost wish, that whenever Fortune seems wantonly to deviate from her Purpose and leave her Work imperfect in this Particular, the Historian would indulge himself in the Licence of Poetry and Romance, and even do a Violence to Truth, to oblige his Reader with a Page, which must be the most delightful in all his History, and which could never fail of producing an instructive Moral.

### CHAPTER XVI

*The Character of our Hero, and the Conclusion of this History.*

WE will now endeavour to draw the Character of this GREAT MAN,° and by bringing together those several Features as it were of his Mind, which lie scattered up and down in this History, to present our Readers with a perfect Picture of GREATNESS.

*Jonathan Wild* had every Qualification necessary to form a GREAT MAN: As his most powerful and predominant Passion was Ambition,° so Nature had with consummate Propriety, adapted all his Faculties to the attaining those glorious Ends, to which this Passion directed him. He was extremely ingenious in inventing Designs; artful in contriving the Means to accomplish his Purposes, and resolute in executing them: For, as the most exquisite Cunning, and most undaunted Boldness qualified him for any Undertaking, so was he not restrained by any of those Weaknesses which disappoint the Views of mean and vulgar Souls, and which are comprehended in one general Term of Honesty, which is a Corruption of *Honosty*, a Word derived from what the *Greeks* call an *Ass*.° He was entirely free from those low Vices of Modesty and Good-nature, which, as he said, implied a total Negative° of human GREATNESS, and were the only Qualities which absolutely rendered a Man incapable of making a considerable Figure in the World. His Lust was inferior only to his Ambition; but, as for what simple People call Love, he knew not what it was. His Avarice was immense; but it was of the rapacious not of the tenacious Kind; his Rapaciousness was indeed so violent, that nothing ever contented him but the whole; for, however considerable the Share was, which his Coadjutors allowed him of a Booty, he was restless in inventing Means to make himself Master of the meanest Pittance reserved by them. He said, Laws were made for the Use of *Prigs* only, and to secure their Property; they were never therefore more perverted, than when their Edge was turned against these; but that this generally happened through their Want of sufficient Dexterity. The Character which he most valued himself upon, and which he principally honoured in others, was that of Hypocrisy.° His Opinion was, that no one could carry *Priggism* very far without it; for which Reason, he said, there was little GREATNESS to be expected in a Man who acknowledged his Vices; but always much to be hoped from him, who professed great Virtues; wherefore, though he would always shun the Person whom he discovered guilty of a good Action, yet he was never deterred by a good Character, which was more commonly the Effect of Profession than of Action: For which Reason, he himself was always very liberal of honest Professions, and had as much Virtue and Goodness in his Mouth as a Saint; never in the least scrupling to swear by his Honour, even to those who knew him the best; nay, tho' he held Good-nature and Modesty in the highest Contempt, he constantly practised the Affectation of both, and recommended it to others, whose Welfare, on his own Account, he wished well to. He laid down several Maxims, as the certain Methods of attaining GREATNESS, to which, in his own Pursuit of it, he constantly adhered.° As

1. Never to do more Mischief to another, than was necessary to the effecting his Purpose; for that Mischief was too precious a thing to be thrown away.

2. To know no Distinction of Men from Affection; but to sacrifice all with equal Readiness to his Interest.

3. Never to communicate more of an Affair than was necessary, to the Person who was to execute it.

4. Not to trust him, who had deceived him, nor who knew he had himself been deceived by him.

5. To forgive no Enemy; but to be cautious and often dilatory in Revenge.

6. To shun Poverty and Distress, and to ally himself, as close as possible, to Power and Riches.

7. To maintain a constant Gravity in his Countenance and Behaviour, and to affect Wisdom on all Occasions.

8. To foment eternal Jealousies in his Gang, one of another.

9. Never to reward any one equal to his Merit; but always to insinuate, that the Reward was above it.

10. That all Men were Knaves or Fools, and much the greater Number a Composition of both.

11. That a good Name, like Money, must be parted with, or at least greatly risqued, in order to bring the Owner any Advantage.

12. That Virtues, like precious Stones, were easily counterfeited; that Counterfeits in both Cases adorned the Wearer equally, and that very few had Knowledge or Discernment sufficient to distinguish the counterfeit Jewel from the real.

13. That many Men were undone by not going deep enough in Roguery, as in Gaming any Man may be a Loser who doth not play the whole Game.

14. That Men proclaim their own Virtues, as Shopkeepers expose their Goods, in order to profit by them.

15. That the Heart was the proper Seat of Hatred, and the Countenance of Affection and Friendship.

He had many more of the same Kind, all equally good with these, and which were after his Decease found in his Study, as the twelve excellent and celebrated Rules were in that of King *Charles* the first;° for he never promulgated them in his Life time, not having them constantly in his Mouth, as some grave Persons have the Rules of Virtue and Morality, without paying the least Regard to them in their Actions; whereas our Hero, by a constant and steady Adherence to his Rules in conforming every thing he did to them, acquired at last a settled Habit of walking by them, till at last he was in no Danger of inadvertently going out of the Way; and by these Means he arrived at that Degree of GREATNESS, which few have equalled; none, we may say, have exceeded: For, tho' it must be allowed that there have been some few Heroes, who have done greater Mischiefs to Mankind, such as those who have betrayed the Liberties of their Country to others, or have undermined and over-powered it themselves, or Conquerors who have impoverished, pillaged, sacked, burnt, and destroyed the Countries and Cities of their fellow Creatures, from no other Provocation than that of Glory; *i.e.* as the Tragic Poet calls it,

> —*A Privilege to kill,*
> *A strong Temptation to do bravely ill.*°

yet, if we consider it in the Light wherein Actions are placed in this Line,

> *Lætius est, quoties magno tibi constat honestum;*°

when we see him, without the least Assistance or Pretence, setting himself at the Head of a Gang, which he had not any Shadow of Right to govern; if we view him maintaining absolute Power, and exercising Tyranny over a lawless Crew, contrary to all Law, but that of his own Will. If we consider him setting up an open Trade publicly, in Defiance, not only of the Laws of his Country, but of the Common Sense of his Countrymen; if we see him first contriving the Robbery of others, and again the defrauding the very Robbers of that Booty, which they had ventured their Necks to acquire, and which without any Hazard they might have retained: Here sure he must appear admirable, and we may challenge not only the Truth of History, but almost the Latitude of Fiction to equal it.

Nor had he any of those Flaws in his Character, which, though they have been commended by weak Writers, have (as I hinted in the Beginning of this History) by the judicious Reader been censured and despised. Such is the Clemency of *Alexander* and *Cæsar*,° which Nature hath as grossly erred in giving them, as a Painter would, who should dress a Peasant in Robes of State, or give the Nose, or any other Feature of a *Venus*, to a *Satyr*. What had the Destroyers of Mankind, that glorious Pair, one of which came into the World to usurp the Dominion, and abolish the Constitution of his own

Country; the other to conquer, enslave, and rule over the whole World, at least as much as was well known to him, and the Shortness of his Life would give him Leave to visit; what had, I say, such as these to do with Clemency? Who cannot see the Absurdity and Contradiction of mixing such an Ingredient with those noble and great Qualities I have before mentioned? Now in *Wild*, every thing was truly GREAT, almost without Alloy, as his Imperfections (for surely some small ones he had) were only such as served to denominate him a human Creature, of which kind none ever arrived at consummate Excellence: But surely his whole Behaviour to his Friend *Heartfree* is a convincing Proof, that the true Iron or Steel GREATNESS of his Heart was not debased by any softer Mettle. Indeed while GREATNESS consists in Power, Pride, Insolence, and doing Mischief to Mankind;—to speak out,—while a GREAT Man and a GREAT Rogue are synonymous Terms, so long shall *Wild* stand unrivalled on the Pinacle of GREATNESS. Nor must we omit here, as the finishing of his Character, what indeed ought to be remembered on his Tomb or his Statue, the Conformity above mentioned of his Death to his Life; and that *Jonathan Wild* the Great was, what so few GREAT Men are, though all in Propriety ought to be—hanged by the Neck 'till he was dead.

Having thus brought our Hero to his Conclusion, it may be satisfactory to some Readers (for many, I doubt not, carry their Concern no farther than his Fate) to know what became of *Heartfree*. We shall acquaint them, therefore, that his Sufferings were now at an End; that the good Magistrate easily prevailed for his Pardon, nor was contented 'till he had made him all the Reparation he could for his Suffering, tho' the Share he had in bringing the Calamity upon him, was not only innocent, but, from its Motive, laudable. He procured the Restoration of the Jewels from the Man of War, at her Return to *England*, and, above all, omitted no Labour to restore *Heartfree* to his Reputation, and to persuade his Neighbours, Acquaintance, and Customers of his Innocence. When the Commission of Bankruptcy was satisfied, *Heartfree* had a considerable Sum remaining; for the Diamond presented to his Wife was of prodigious Value, and infinitely recompensed the Loss of those Jewels for which the Count had paid, when the GREAT *Wild* procured him to be robbed of the Money. He now set up again in his Trade; Compassion for his unmerited Misfortunes brought him many Customers among those who had any Regard to Humanity; and he hath, by Industry joined with Parsimony, amassed an immense Fortune. His Wife and he are now grown old in the purest Love and Friendship; but never had another Child. *Friendly* married his eldest Daughter at the Age of nineteen, and became his Partner in Trade. As to the youngest, she never would listen to the Addresses of any Lover, not even of a young Nobleman, who offered to take her with two thousand Pounds, which her Father would have willingly produced, and indeed did his utmost to persuade her to the Match: But she refused absolutely, nor would give any other Reason, than that she had dedicated her Days to his Service, and was resolved, no other Duty should interfere with that she owed the best of Fathers, nor prevent her from being the Nurse of his old Age.

Thus *Heartfree*, his Wife, his two Daughters, his Son-in-Law, and his Grandchildren, of which he hath several, live all together in one House; and that with such Amity and Affection towards each other, that they are in the Neighbourhood called *the Family of Love*.°

As to all the other Persons mentioned in this History, in the Light of GREATNESS, they had all the Fate adapted to it, being every one hanged by the Neck, save two, *viz*. Miss *Theodosia Snap*, who was transported to *America*, where she was pretty well married, reformed, and made a good Wife; and the Count, who recovered of the Wound he had received from the Hermit, and made his Escape into *France*, where he committed a Robbery, was taken, and broke on the Wheel.

Indeed whoever considers the common Fate of GREAT MEN must allow, they well deserve, and hardly earn that Applause which is given them by the World; for, when we reflect on the Labours and Pains, the Cares, Disquietudes, and Dangers which attend their Road to GREATNESS, we may say with the Divine, *that a Man may go to Heaven with half the Pains which it costs him to purchase Hell;*° nor is the World so unanimous as they ought to be in conferring this dear-bought Reward. For, while the Majority of Mankind, while Courts and Cities resound the Praises of the said GREAT MEN, there are still some in Cells and Cottages, who view their GREATNESS with a malignant Eye; and dare affirm, that these GREAT MEN, who are always the most pernicious, are generally the most wretched and truly contemptible of all the Works of the Creation.

FINIS

# APPENDIX 1

## 'H. D.', *THE LIFE OF JONATHAN WILD*

# THE

# LIFE

## OF

## *JONATHAN WILD,*

### FROM HIS

## BIRTH to his DEATH.

### CONTAINING

His Rise and Progress in ROGUERY; his first Acquaintance with THIEVES; by what Arts he made himself their HEAD, or GOVERNOR; his Discipline over them; his Policy and great Cunning in governing them; and the several Classes of THIEVES under his Command.

In which all his INTRIGUES, PLOTS and AR-TIFICES are accounted for, and laid open.

*Intermix'd with Variety of diverting* STORIES.

By *H. D.* late Clerk to Justice *R*————

# THE
# PREFACE

THE Account which the Reader will here find, of the most extraordinary ROGUE that ever yet Suffer'd in *England*, was pick'd up, at several Times, from his own Relations and Stories of himself; which are the best Authorities that can be produced for Things which, according to the Iniquity and Nature of them, were transacted with such extreme Caution.

And it is certain, that the greatest Part of his dark Proceedings wou'd still have continu'd a Secret to the World, had it not been, that in his gay Hours, when his Heart was open, he took Pleasure in recounting his past Rogueries, and, with a great deal of Humour, bragg'd of his biting the World; often hinting, not without Vanity, at the poor Understandings of the greatest Part of Mankind, and his own superior Cunning.

And indeed, when we consider that it is not a Man's Grandeur, or high Station in the World, but the strange Adventures of his Life, and his Art and Conduct in the Management of Things, which gives us a Curiosity of looking into his History—— I say, when this is granted, we need make no Apology for collecting these Materials, and offering them to the Publick—for here they will meet with a System of Politicks unknown to *Machiavel*;° they will see deeper Stratagems and Plots form'd by a Fellow without Learning or Education, than are to be met with in the Conduct of the greatest Statesmen, who have been at the Heads of Governments.

And indeed, when Things are rightly compared, it will be found that he had a more difficult Game to play; for he was to blind the Eyes of the World, to find out Tricks to evade the Penalties of the Law; and on the other Side, to govern a Body of People who were Enemies to all Government; and to bring those under Obedience to him, who, at the Hazard of their Lives, acted in Disobedience to the Laws of the Land—This was steering betwixt *Scylla* and *Charybdis*;° and if he had not been a very skilful Pilot, he must long since have split upon a Rock, either on one Side or the other.

To conclude: We have not taken so much Pains to multiply a Number of Stories, which wou'd have swell'd the Bulk of these Sheets, and increas'd the Price, and perhaps tired the Reader; we have only endeavour'd to trace him thro' his several Steps and Gradations, to account for the Policy and Cunning of his Management, and relating only such Facts as have not yet been made publick concerning him.

# THE
# LIFE
OF
## *JONATHAN WILD,*
### From his BIRTH to his DEATH.

*JONATHAN WILD* was born of very honest Parents in the Town of *Wolverhampton* in the County of *Stafford*. His Father was not rich; however, he provided handsomly for his Family while he lived, by his Trade, which was that of a Carpenter: But he dying, and leaving four or five small Children for the Widow to bring up and subsist, 'tis no wonder if their Education was no better taken care of. As for *Jonathan*, he shew'd early Signs of a forward Genius, and, whilst a Boy, would commit a thousand little Rogueries among those of the same or a superior Class, in which he discovered a ready Wit, and a Cunning much above his Years, tho' these Actions did not extend to robbing or any such Crime; but I mean little collusive Tricks which serv'd to impose upon his own Companions, who had a less Faculty of discerning than *Jonathan* had.

At the usual Age, when young *Jonathan* had been instructed to a moderate degree of Learning, such as Writing and Accounts, he was put Prentice to a Buckle-maker, whom he serv'd seven Years honestly enough; when that Time was expired, he carry'd on a little peddling Business himself in the same Way; but *Jonathan* wanted Application, which is generally observ'd to be the Fault of Men of brisk Parts: Work and he were too much at Variance for him to thrive by his Trade; he seem'd to follow it only at a Distance, often playing the Loose, wandering from one Ale-house to another, with the very worst, tho' the merriest Company in the Place; and was particularly fond of the strolling Actors that now and then frequented that Country.

After this manner *Jonathan* liv'd three or four Years, leading a Life of Pleasure, disturb'd with nothing, unless it was now and then at the Noise of a Drum, which he had as great Antipathy to as some Folks to Cheese or a Cat. This was in the height of the late War between *France* and the Confederates,° when the Officers went down into the several Counties for Recruits for *Flanders*, for which kind of Service Mr. *Wild* had perhaps more Aversion than for any other thing in Life; this was not for want of Courage, as we shall prove in the Course of his History; but he thought a

Man of Stratagem might push his Fortune some better Way than by standing to be shot at, and therefore 'twas necessary that he should employ the utmost Cunning to avoid it, which however *Jonathan* could never have done, but by a Trick which he was more beholden to Nature for than Art; this was a Knack of dislocating his Hip-bone, which he could do without Pain, and thereby render himself a Cripple, and repose it in its Place again without Trouble, whenever he pleas'd; this was particularly useful to him, and which he constantly perform'd whenever his unlucky Stars brought him within Sight of a red Coat, which he us'd to pass by in so decrepid and deform'd a Posture as never fail'd to move Pity in the Beholders towards so miserable an Object; and he was no sooner out of sight of 'em, but he walk'd as upright and as firm as any Man.

In the Course of *Jonathan*'s Trading, he visited some Market-Towns to put off his Wares, as other Dealers did, at which time he us'd to hire a Horse of his Neighbour's, (for *Jonathan*'s Stock would not amount to one of his own;) and a certain time when Trade grew bad on his Hands, he sells his whole Cargoe for what he could get, and rides up the Horse to *London*, instead of returning home to *Wolverhampton*; and the Owner heard nothing of his Beast, till 'twas sold, and all the Money spent.

While *Jonathan* was spending, in Gaiety and Pleasure, the little Fortune he had acquired by the Sale of his own Stock, and his Neighbour's Horse, he got acquainted with several Persons of both Sexes who were People of Merit in their Way, by whose Interest, and the Vivacity of his own Parts, he was recommended to an Employment of Trust, in which he acquitted himself very handsomely, considering the Corruption of the Times; but after a while, *Jonathan* finding it rather a Post of Honour than Profit, resign'd, and went down into his own Country again. The Employment I mean, is that of a Bailiff's Follower;° the Qualifications of which are Vigilance, Sagacity, Patience, Quicksightedness, *cum multis aliis*,° which our *Jonathan* had frequent Opportunities of exercising.

One of the first Visiters *Jonathan* had upon his Return to *Wolverhampton*, was Mr. ——, who lent him his Horse; to whom he open'd his Case, letting him know that he was not one Farthing the richer by living in *London*, that he had spent every Groat,° and if he threw him into Prison, he would lose his Money, but that if he would favour him so as to give him Time, he would pay for his Horse at a Shilling in the Pound *per* Month, till the whole was paid; and he should apply himself with Assiduity to his own Business, to enable him to make good these Conditions; which the Creditor considering, came into, and so the Agreement was made.

Mr. *Wild*, pursuant to the above Terms, made two Payments at the Time they became due, but neglecting the third Payment, for a Fortnight or three Weeks, Mr. —— gave *Jonathan* a gentle Dun, telling him at what

time the Month was up, and so forth, but was very much surpriz'd to find
that Mr. *Wild* was so far from making any Excuse for his Omission, that he
told him plainly he should pay him no more Money, and wonder'd at his
Assurance of making Demands on him. *Why*, says the Creditor, *did not
you run away with my Horse, sell him at* London, *and put the Money in your
own Pocket? I did so*, answer'd *Jonathan, but that Affair was settled by an
Agreement between us, that I should pay you so much Money by monthly
Payments, in Consideration thereof; therefore that Cause is at an End. Very
well*, reply'd the Creditor, *why don't you pay me according to that Contract
then? No*, quoth *Jonathan, that Contract is obsolete and of no effect. How so?*
says the Creditor. *Why you'll allow*, says *Jonathan, that Articles of Agreement, or Contracts, not fulfill'd, are broken, and Articles once broken, cannot
subsist afterwards: Now our Articles are broken*, continued he, *for I have
made but two Payments, when there are three due long ago, therefore I owe you
nothing, and nothing I will pay you.*

I mention this Story to shew that *Jonathan* had a Genius for the
Study of the Law; and had not his Practice taken another Turn at first, I
don't know whether, better or worse, as it is practised of late, he might
have been as eminent, and made as great a Figure as some of his
Countrymen.

It was not long after this, that *Jonathan* found the making of Buckles
too mechanick an Employment for him; his Soul was too great to be
confin'd to such servile Work; and what was worse, he easily perceiv'd he
had Occasion for more Money than his Hands could procure him in that
narrow Way of Business; therefore he spurn'd at the Trade, and resolv'd,
some how or other, to transfer the Labour of his Hands to that of the
Head, as being the most likely Means of getting a Livelihood fit for a
Gentleman.

Big with Hopes, he set out for *London* once more; but as if he threw
himself entirely on Fortune, and resolv'd to court her Favours, he begun
his Journey on foot, and with no more than nine Pence in his Pocket; and
the first Day he was so lucky as to meet with the Goddess in the same
Shape the Poets describe her, *viz.* That of a Woman, travelling to *Warwick*,
in her Way to *London*. The Lady was on Horseback, but however she was
so good-natur'd as to let *Jonathan* keep Pace with her for three or four
Miles, till by a little Conversation they grew intimate, and acquainted with
each other's Circumstances: She told *Jonathan* she was an itinerant Doctress, and cur'd People of all Distempers; and that she had been riding
about the Country for the Good of the Publick. *Jonathan* desired her then
to give him her Opinion about his Leg and Thigh, which he presently put
out in the manner before mentioned; the Gentlewoman alighted from her
Horse, and handling *Jonathan*'s Parts, she found his Hip-bone was out of

its Socket, a great Exuberance on the back Part thereof, and his Knee and Foot turn'd almost behind him.

She was amaz'd to see this sudden Alteration, without being sensible of the Cause, and was very much troubled to know what she should do with the poor Fellow in that Condition; but *Jonathan* presently put her out of Pain, desir'd her to mount her Horse, and he would accompany her into Town; and thereupon replaces the Joint, and walks along before her with great Briskness and Agility. When she was thoroughly inform'd of the Trick, she intimated how useful this Deceit might be made to them both, if he would leave it to her Management; and all the Trouble he should be at, was to lie a Bed for a Fortnight, and eat and drink whatever he had a mind to. Upon which she let him into a Secret, that she knew no more of Physick or Surgery than her Horse, and only pretended to it for a Livelihood.

It may be imagin'd, that *Jonathan* was not difficult to be wrought on to such good Purposes, for he never was an Enemy to Eating and Drinking in his whole Life; accordingly the Plan was laid, and *Jonathan* hopp'd into Town in the Evening in the Circumstances of a poor decrepid Beggar-man.

The Doctress and *Jonathan* set up at the best Inn in *Warwick*, ask for a Room, and call the Landlord, telling him, she found a poor miserable object upon the Road, that ask'd Alms of her, which she presently reliev'd; but seeing him a likely young Fellow, tho' lame and infirm, she commiserated his sad Condition, and thought a greater Act of Charity could not be done, than the setting this poor Man upon his Legs, that he might thereby be enabled to get a Livelihood by his Labour and Industry; and therefore, says she, if you have an eminent Surgeon in Town, a Man of Honour and Probity, that will undertake his Cure, I will be at the Expence of it my self, and give him a suitable Reward. The Landlord acquiesced with her Ladiship's Sentiments, prais'd her Goodness to the Skies, and *Jonathan* pray'd aloud for his Benefactress.

One Mr. *B*——, a Surgeon, was sent for, to whom Madam declared her self in like manner; and the Surgeon took a Survey before all the House of the Part affected. He saw the Nature of his Lameness, and therefore only ask'd *Jonathan* how long ago this Misfortune happen'd to him. He answer'd, in a whining Tone, *About eight Years*; and thereupon relates a plausible Story of his falling off a Tree in a Country Village, where no Help was to be met with, and his Mother being a poor Woman had not wherewithal to pay a Doctor, and the like; but pretended to be very much cast down: When the Surgeon, addressing himself to the Gentlewoman, said, *Madam, it would be no less than a Robbery to take your Money, for there's no possibility of serving him; the Bone having been so long misplac'd, has contracted a new Situation, and the Head of the Bone formed a Socket so formidable, that 'twould be unnatural now to remove it thence, so that we must let it rest as it is.* This did not seem to satisfy the Gentlewoman, she was sure, she said, *the Limb might be reduc'd to its proper Place, with due Care, if he would apply Fomentations, and other topical Medicines to the Part, for the Relaxation of the Ligaments, &c. in Preparation for the Reduction.* This was disputed some Time with Warmth, between the Male and the Female Surgeon, till it ended, as often Arguments do, in a Wager of fifty Guineas; and the Lady her self was to take the Matter into her own Hands.

Whereupon the Patient was blooded, and then put into a warm Bed: Stupes were made of a thousand Herbs, and the Fomentation apply'd, or pretended so to be, several times a Day. Mr. *B*—— visited him once in twenty four Hours; and the Gentlewoman continued with him all the while for ten Days together; in which time honest *Jonathan* acted his Part so well that he roar'd himself hoarse, as it is suppos'd, for the Pain he underwent in this extraordinary Operation. At length, one Morning, as Mr. *B*—— the Surgeon, our Quack Doctress, and three or four of the Town, (for the Affair had made some Noise) were coming up Stairs, they heard the Patient, instead of groaning and making other dismal Cries, singing, whistling, and what not; so they all burst into his Chamber, and presently ask'd the Occasion of his Mirth? *Jonathan* told them he never knew so much Pleasure in all his Life-time, for now he said he was as free from Pain as e'er a one in the Room.

The sly Doctress desir'd to be inform'd how and at what time he lost his Pain, and became so easy as he now own'd himself to be? He answer'd, that *about three a Clock that Morning (not having slept for four Nights before) he fell into a Dose, and dream'd that two Angels lifted him out of Bed, and carry'd him thro' several Regions, of which he could give no Account, and set him down upon a fine Bank of Flowers, on the Side of a Rivulet; on the other Side of which were beautiful Walks, pleasant Groves, and curious Waterworks, and in the Center of all, a Pavilion of Ivory, of extraordinary Workmanship, particularly the Sculpture; the Roof was adorn'd with Birds of all kinds inlaid; and on the Inside a Throne of pure Gold, where sate his kind and good Benefactress. At the Sight of her,* continued *Jonathan, I rose up in Haste, thinking to swim the Rivulet, when a Noise like Thunder awaken'd me, and I found my self in this Bed, in perfect Health and Ease.* The cunning Gentlewoman cry'd aloud, *Then went the Bone into its Place.* With that they turned down the Bed-cloaths, and found *Jonathan* a whole Man, to the great Surprize of all the Company.

This extraordinary Cure was look'd upon as a kind of Miracle: Mr. *B*—— own'd it as such, paid the Money, (*viz.* fifty Guineas) and clear'd the Case up to every Body from any Imputation of Deceit. *Jonathan* in two or three Days came Abroad, but limp'd a little; and Madam Doctress gave publick Notice that she would stay a Week in that Town, for the sake of the diseased Poor of the Country, for whom she would make up some Papers of Powders that should cure them of all Disorders, and make it the healthiest Part of the whole Kingdom, for which she would take nothing of them but what the Medicines cost her out of her Pocket, according to the Cant of all Quacks.

The News run, like that of a great Victory gain'd over the *French* and *Spaniards*, and People of all Conditions, Age and Sexes, came into *Warwick*, so that *Jonathan* could not pound Brick-dust fast enough for Sale; the Price of a small Paper of which, with a Mixture of Brimstone and ——, came but to six Pence.

By this Stratagem the Woman's Fame was so rais'd, that when *Jonathan* and she computed their Gains, they found after all Charges were deducted, that they were much about 100 *l.* in Pocket, with which they set out early in the Morning, and arriv'd at *London* safely in two Days following. Here *Jonathan* lived a merry Life as long as the Money lasted, and being seduced by the Pleasures of the Town, had no Thought of getting more till urg'd thereto by Necessity. But now an unlucky Accident happen'd, which seem'd to give an ill turn to his Affairs, for his Lady *Doctress* took it into her Head to fall out with him; whether it be that she was jealous of his having some new Amour, (for *Jonathan* was always a great Man amongst the Ladies) or whether she cou'd not bear his Extravagance, is a piece of History we cannot clear up; but let it be which it will, there arose so furious a Quarrel betwixt them, that Madam the *Quack* arrests *Jonathan* in an Action of Debt; and he being destitute both of Credit and Friends, cou'd meet with no Body who wou'd venture to bail him, so that he was thrown into the *Compter,*° where he lay a considerable Time.

Here *Jonathan* laid the Foundation of all his future Greatness; for it must be observ'd, that the *Compter* is the Place where common Thieves and Pickpockets taken in the City are first carried as soon as they are apprehended: *Jonathan* took care to cultivate an Acquaintance and Intimacy with them all, and as they are an enterprizing Body of Men, there seem'd to be a kind of sympathy betwixt their Natures and that of *Jonathan*, so that they soon crept into one another's Secrets; he became acquainted with all their Tricks and Stratagems, and when the Iron Hand of Justice had laid hold of them, and they were intangled in Difficulties, he often put such Quirks and Evasions in their Heads, and gave them such Advice, as sometimes prov'd of great Advantage to them, so that he became a kind of Oracle amongst the Thieves.

After he had lain a considerable Time in the *Compter*, he wheedled the Female Quack, at whose Suit he lay, and brought her to such Temper that she was prevail'd upon to give him his Liberty. He had now a numerous Acquaintance, with whom he constantly associated; these were the Thieves (as has been before observ'd;) there was no Enterprize they went upon, whether in Town or Country, but they acquainted *Jonathan* with the Particulars of their Success, what Booty they got, and what Hazards they run, so communicative are these Gentlemen to those who keep them Company; yet, at the Beginning, he had so much the Fear of the Gallows before his Eyes, that they cou'd never prevail with him to go with them upon any Adventure, and share in the executive Part.

At first, *Jonathan* drove but a poor pedling Trade, only helping People to Writings which the Thieves cou'd make no Profit of, and which cou'd be of no Use but to the Owners, and in this he at first acted with such extream Caution, for fear of coming within the Penalty of the Laws, that after he had bargain'd with the People, and they were come by his Appointment to pay the Money, and receive the Writings, he led them into a Room contriv'd for that purpose; where pushing back a small Pannel of the Wainscot, a Hand us'd to appear with the Writings in it, and the Parties were to take them out of that Hand, and to put the Money into it, without their seeing the Body which belong'd to it; so that they cou'd not say he had ever taken any of their Money, or receiv'd the stolen Goods; yet the Success and Encouragement he afterwards met with, made him more careless to his great Sorrow.

The first Thing that gave him any Fame, was a Dispute he had with *Cornelius Tilburn*, a noted Quack Doctor;° who being rob'd of some Goods, and hearing of *Jonathan Wild*, apply'd to him for the Recovery of them; but after they had treated some Time they cou'd not agree about the Price; upon the whole, *Tilburn* was vex'd he cou'd not have his Goods again, and thinking *Jonathan* had them, he arrests him in an Action of Trover;° *Jonathan* gave Bail to the Action, and so a Suit of Law was commenced, which was so well defended on *Jonathan*'s side, that *Tilburn* was non-suited,° and Costs were given to *Jonathan*.

This gave him a great Reputation among his good Friends the Thieves, who thought *Jonathan* the best Factor or Agent they cou'd employ, so that his Business so increas'd, that 'tis thought he got two or three hundred Pounds a Year by Commission.

But it is no wonder he shou'd thus by degrees increase in Business and in Fame, for no Man grows great at once. Having now ingross'd the whole Traffick of stolen Goods to himself, he became as useful to the Thieves as they were to him; for now by his Credit they had a safe way of making Money of every Thing which fell into their Hands, whereas before they run as great Hazards of being discover'd and brought to Justice when they went about to dispose of their Goods, as they did in stealing them.

But as the Thieves first set him up only as their Factor, he by degrees made himself their Master and their Tyrant; he divided the City and Suburbs into Wards, or Divisions, and appointed the Persons who were to attend each Ward, and kept them strictly to their Duty; he also call'd them to a very exact Account, and made them produce what they had got, and tho' it were Money he wou'd have his Dividend; and it was no less than Death to *sink* upon him, as he term'd it, for there was scarce any Thing stole which was worth having again but he heard of it, and knew who the Person must be that took it, as well as those who lost it.

This is plain, by what happen'd to a Gentlewoman at *Hackney*,° who us'd to let Lodgings: A Lady, who came attended by a Footman and a Maid, took a Lodging in her House; the first Day they had Possession of it, they broke open a Scrutore belonging to the Gentlewoman of the House, which was full of Chinee° and Muslin, and very dexterously carried off the whole Cargoe; it was a great Loss to the poor Woman, who lamenting with her Neighbours, they advis'd her to go to *Jonathan Wild*, and offer a Sum of Money to recover it; she went accordingly, and when she gave him an Account where she liv'd, and what she had lost, he call'd to his Book-keeper to search the Books, to know if any of their People had been lately out to take the Air at *Hackney*: The Fellow having examin'd, answer'd immediately that *Wapping Moll* had been there, and that *Tawny Bess* was her Maid, and *Harry Smart* her Footman; *Jonathan* appear'd in a Passion, and curs'd them sufficiently, but appointed the Gentlewoman to come again in a little Time, when he procured the Things upon her paying the Money agreed for.

Thus he made them all pay Contribution, whether they made Use of him in disposing of the Things or no: And when the late Act was made, which gives a Pardon to one Felon for convicting another, he became absolute over them all; for if any of them disoblig'd him, or as he call'd it *rebel'd*, he took them up, and thereby got the Reward appointed by Act of Parliament for taking Highwaymen:° On the contrary, when any of his own People were taken, which he had a Mind to save, then he endeavour'd to take some other; then his own Man by claiming the Benefit of the Act became an Evidence. When ever any interloping Traders started up in the Business, that is, People who set up for themselves without paying him any Contribution, or Homage, or holding any Correspondence with him, he did all he cou'd to take them; and if such were otherwise taken up upon Suspicion, or upon any Information, and Evidence was wanting to convict them, nothing was more common than for him to take up one of his own Fellows, whose Life was always in his Power, and make him swear himself into some of the Robberies, of which the others were suspected, whereby their Evidence might obtain some

Credit with a Jury, and *Jonathan* was intitled to the Reward if he was the Person who took them.

And thus by taking some of his own Gang now and then, because they had disoblig'd him, and apprehending others because they were not of his Gang, and hanging them in the manner before described, he was reckoned a very useful Man, and was often call'd upon by the Court to look at the Prisoners, and give them Characters; which seem'd to have great Weight at that time. And sometimes, by ingenious Quirks, or by managing the Juries or Evidences, he has brought off some of his Favourites, who had been taken in the very Facts for which they were commited; as he did once by two Fellows, who having committed a Robbery on the Highway, and several Persons well mounted and arm'd happening to come by immediately, they were pursued and taken, with the Gentlemens Watches and Rings about them; and being forthwith carried before a Justice of Peace, were committed to *Newgate*; within a Day or two of the Sessions, *Jonathan*, whose Wit seldom fail'd him at a Pinch, enquiring the Names of the Prosecutors, went to them, and asking them if they had not been robb'd by such and such Fellows, now in *Newgate?* The Gentlemen answered they had. *Jonathan* pretending a great Spleen to those Fellows, who he said were the greatest Rogues in the whole World, and that he would have hang'd them long ago if he could have found them; and therefore begg'd of the Gentlemen that he might assist them in managing the Prosecution, and he wou'd engage the Rascals shou'd not escape: The Gentlemen, very willing to have Part of the Trouble taken off their Hands, accepted his Offer, knowing Mr. *Wild* to be a Person very well skill'd in those Affairs. Accordingly, they appointed to meet at a Tavern in the *Old-Baily*, on the Morning which was appointed for the Trial of these Highwaymen: When they met, *Jonathan* told them there was a great Croud in the Court, and that they had better stay there till the Trial shou'd begin; which he said wou'd not be till about Three a Clock in the Afternoon. In the mean time a Dinner was bespoke, to be ready at One; and *Jonathan* sent a Man to wait in the Court, with Orders to call them when the Trial came on. *Jonathan* made such good use of his Time, that whether by putting something into the Liquor, or by fair Drinking, is not known; but it is certain he made the Gentlemen very drunk, who pass'd away the Time till Evening without thinking of the Matter; at which time one of them wondring that their Messenger had not call'd them, they sent another to the Court, to know what was doing there; when they found the Court was broke up, and the two Highwaymen were discharg'd, there having no Evidence appear'd against them.

By all the before-mentioned Tricks and Artifices, *Jonathan* pass'd for a Man of so much Understanding and Interest, that the Thieves began to think he could hang or save whom he pleas'd; so that all Malefactors, whether of his own Gang or not, after they were taken, used to flatter themselves that if they cou'd raise any Money for *Jonathan*, he wou'd bring them off; and even after they were condemned, they were of Opinion that his extraordinary Interest might procure them a Reprieve, or have the Sentence chang'd to Transportation.

It is certain that it was one of his Arts to make them believe so; and he used particularly to affect an extraordinary Intimacy with certain Justices of Peace; and as it is said he sometimes drank with those Gentlemen at Taverns, he used to leave word at Home, that if any Body should enquire for him, he was gone to such a Tavern, to meet Justice such-a-one. The Use he made of insinuating this Notion into their Heads was, that if any Information should be given to these Justices, against any of his Friends, he should have timely Notice of it, from them or their Clerks, so that the Party might get out of the way; which was a material Thing towards keeping his People always depending upon him.

The Reader will imagine, by what has been here related, that *Jonathan* must be a Person of no uncommon Parts: —To govern a Commonwealth already fix'd and establish'd, is no more than what may be done by any common Capacity; but to form and establish a Body of such lawless People into what we may call a Form of Government; to erect a Commonwealth like that of the Bees, in which there shou'd be no Drone, in which every Member was oblig'd to go forth and labour, and to bring an Offering to him their King, of Part of the Product of their Cunning and Industry; to be able so many Years to evade the Punishments appointed by the Laws of all Nations, for such Persons as make no Difference betwixt *Meum* and *Tuum*; and to live not only in a Toleration, but even in a kind of Credit, amongst the People he was robbing every Day, and to escape the Plots and Conspiracies of his own treacherous Subjects— I say, to be able to manage all this, must proceed from an admirable Wit and Cunning, and thorough Observation of the Humours and weak Sides of Men.

But to return to our Subject, we have taken Notice in what manner *Jonathan*'s Revenues were rais'd and encreas'd, but as his Subjects were so frequently taken off by untimely Ends, his Royalty wou'd by degrees have declin'd and sunk at last to little or nothing, if he had not by admirable Foresight and Care provided future Thieves both for himself and the Gallows.

The *Mint* in *Southwark*° was the Country where *Jonathan* usually went to raise Recruits when his Army began to grow thin and weak; there I say he constantly beat up for Voluntiers, and most of his best Men came from thence.

He knew it was the Place where Tradesmen who had met with

Misfortunes first retir'd to, that it was the constant Retreat of all those whom Idleness, or Extravagance had render'd obnoxious to the Law—he knew also that People under those Circumstances commonly brought a little Money with them at their first going over, which being soon spent, by reason of their being out of Business to get more, they must of Consequence be reduc'd to extream Necessity, till which time he did not judge them rightly qualified for his Service.

As I was let into this Secret of his Proceedings by a Story from his own Mouth, I shall relate the Method and Way he went to Work with the Gentlemen *Minters.*

*First,* He made himself acquainted with all the People who kept publick Houses, whether Taverns, Ale-Houses, or the Venders of the royal Liquor commonly call'd *Gin;* from these he learn'd from Time to Time what People were newly come over, and if he lik'd the Description of their Persons, and the Account of their Circumstances, he took some Opportunity of getting into Company with them; and *Jonathan*, being facetious as well as frank and open in Conversation, made himself very agreeable to those sort of People, who are call'd *merry Fellows*; besides, *Jonathan* always pretended to compassionate their Misfortunes, and to shew his Generosity would treat them, and make them drunk, and sometimes perhaps lend them small Matters in their extream Necessities— So that he has sometimes confess'd, that by half a Crown well dispos'd, that is lent with a certain Manner of which he was Master; he has sometimes got fifty, and sometimes a hundred Pounds; which it must be confess'd was laying Money out to a very good Advantage.

We shall prove this by an Example—*Jonathan* came acquainted with *A. B.* a broken *Cheesemonger*, who had taken Refuge in the *Mint*; this poor Fellow, being charm'd with the Conversation of the ingenious *Jonathan*, spent the little Money he had saved from the Ruin of his Trade, in keeping him Company; when all was gone, *Jonathan* now and then lent him some small Matter, and observing him to be young, active, and a Fellow of Spirit, work'd upon him, and brought him into his Measures, by representing to him the miserable Prospect he had before him; telling him he deserv'd to be damn'd if such a clever Fellow as he shou'd want good Cloaths on his Back, or Money in his Pocket, and that all the World wou'd despise him; therefore, says he, take my Advice, and *get Money*— The Advice was good and seasonable; for there was nothing in the World the poor Fellow wanted more: But how to do it was the Difficulty—therefore he beg'd his Friend *Jonathan* to give him some Advice in that important Affair; Z——ds, says *Jonathan*, I know a great many clever Fellows, who keep the best Company in Town, and make very smart Figures; and if they have not Six-pence in their Pockets now, they'll have Money enough before they go to Bed, that is, if there be any Money to be had betwixt this and *Bath*, or this and *Tunbridge*.

Now the *Cheesemonger* began to apprehend his Friend *Jonathan*, and in his Necessity and Despair, said he wou'd do any thing; but he had neither Horse nor Arms, nor any means of purchasing them; but *Jonathan*, who did nothing by halves, directed him where good Horses were to be hired for the Use of the Gentlemen of the Snaffle,° and gave him as much Money as wou'd pay for the Hire, for he was too cunning to appear in the Matter himself; he also directed him to go upon the *Epsom* Road, telling him there was no Gentlemen out upon the same Lay that way—and thus our *Cheesemonger* was turn'd into a Gentleman, and equip'd like a Knight Errant in search of Adventures.

After he had loiter'd about the Road for some time, he saw one Man a Horseback coming towards him without any Servant or Attendance, which proved to be a peaceable Citizen; him he ventur'd to stop, and commanding him to deliver, the Citizen surrender'd all the Money he had without any Words, which prov'd to be nine Guineas: As soon as our new Highwayman found himself in Possession of the Money, he made the best of his way Home to his Kennel the *Mint*, without seeking any more Adventures that Day.

He was no sooner alighted, but he found *Jonathan*, who waited to receive him, to whom he very frankly gave an Account of what he had done, and what he had got with all the Circumstances, thinking he had behaved himself very handsomly for a new Beginner; nay, *Jonathan* himself prais'd him, and for his Encouragement took from him but seven Guineas of the nine, leaving him two as a mark of his Favour.

Perhaps some may be of Opinion, that this Dividend was a little unequal, and that he who ventur'd all shou'd have had the greatest Share of the Booty; but it must be consider'd on the other Side, that now he was initiated, he was become the Subject, nay, the Slave of *Jonathan*, who had power of Life and Death over him; and that so far from murmuring at what he took from him, it was *Jonathan*'s Opinion he shou'd think himself oblig'd to him that he did not hang him.

The Fellow continu'd every now and then to make Excursions, sometimes on one Road, sometimes on another, constantly doing Business by himself; and if we may believe *Jonathan*, he always left the Fellow some small Matter of what he got, whether it happen'd to be little or much, but this we must take upon his Credit; but however that be, the *Cheesemonger* was so discontented, that he resolv'd to desert, and see what he cou'd do for himself.

Accordingly, some time after he disappear'd, nor cou'd *Jonathan* find him out by all the Inquiry and Search he cou'd make; *Jonathan* rail'd loudly at him, saying, Thus am I serv'd by a parcel of Rascals when I have put Bread into their Mouths, but I'll hang him if there was not another Rogue left in *England*.—While *Jonathan* was thus enrag'd against the Deserter, some People who had been robb'd upon the *Oxford* Road, came to make Proposals for the Recovery of some Watches and Pocket Books which had been taken from them; *Jonathan* consulted his Books, (for it must be observ'd, he was very exact in minuting down all his Orders) and found that no Gentleman under his Command had been out upon that Road for a Fortnight before; wherefore he was very inquisitive to know what sort of Man the Person was who had committed those Robberies; and according to their Description, and by other Circumstances, he was pretty sure it must be the deserting *Cheesemonger*.

*Jonathan* therefore set out towards *Oxford* well mounted, and well arm'd, intending to renew his Acquaintance with his old Friend, who, according to several Reports, had met with good Luck upon that Road; he jog'd on easily, visiting all the Villages which lay in the By-Roads, both on the Right and Left, going into every Inn, looking into the Stables to see the Horses, and drinking with all the Ostlers and Chamberlains, and enquiring of them what Company was in each House, and what Company they lately had; which was his constant Method when he went in search of a Deserter.

He spent a good deal of Time in this manner to no purpose, when moving on towards *Oxford*, he met a Coach which had been just robb'd, the Coachman giving him warning to take care, and telling him the Place where they had been attack'd, was not above a quarter of a Mile off: Upon this, *Jonathan* enquires the Number of the People who had robb'd them; the Coachman told him it was done by a single Man, and in describing him, confirm'd *Jonathan* it must be his *Cheesemonger:* Upon this Assurance, *Jonathan* sets Spurs to his Horse, and coming to the Spot which had just before been the Scene of Action, he hastes, and takes a View of the Ground like an experienced General; and considering with himself what a Man of any Discipline wou'd do after such an Incident, in order to puzzle and beguile his Pursuers in case any Hue and Cry shou'd be rais'd to pursue him, he spied a Lane upon the right Hand, and wisely concluded with himself, that if the *Cheesemonger* was a Man of Conduct, he must have struck down that Lane, after he had finish'd his Adventure; therefore he doubled his Pace, and after a short Gallop came in sight of a Man in a great Coat, well mounted; he judg'd now that he was come to the end of his Enquiry, and therefore slacken'd his Pace, that he might prepare himself for Battle (for *Jonathan*'s Courage was equal to his Conduct.) The Man before hearing the Tread of a Horse, look'd back; but seeing no more than one Man, he thought it had not the Appearance of a Pursuit, and therefore he never mov'd a Step the faster; and it was at such a Distance, that he did not know the sweet Fiz of *Jonathan. Jonathan*, who was stuck round with Pistols, as thick as an Orange with Cloves, or like the Man in an old Almanack with Darts,° was not idle all this while, but took care to be well cock'd and prim'd, which Part he manag'd under his Great Coat; for he took care to conceal his warlike Appointment, lest it might put the Enemy into a Posture of Defence.

As he approach'd nearer, the Man cast another Look back, and immediately knew it was *Jonathan:* Upon which he faced about manfully, and drawing his Pistol, bid *Jonathan* stand off, for he had done with him. *Jonathan* put on the Fox's Skin, and employing all his Oratory (for he had an excellent Talent at wheedling) begg'd that they might be good Friends, and go and drink together, swearing that he loved Men of Courage, and that he desired nothing but that they might be good Friends as before—But the valiant Cheesemonger told him his Mind in few Words; *Jonathan*, says he, you have led me here into a damn'd Trade, which I am weary of, and now I've got Money in my Pocket I am resolv'd to go over to *Holland*, and try to put my self into some honest Business, by which I may get my Living, without Fear or Danger. *Jonathan*, having a Pistol in his Hand, under his Great Coat, which the other could not see, still continued his Wheedling, and approaching nearer and nearer, that he might have a sure Mark, he of a sudden drew forth his desperate Hand, and let fly a Brace of Bullets in the Face of the valiant Cheesemonger, and drawing forth a sharp Hanger at the same Instant flew upon him like a Tyger, and with one Blow fell'd him to his Horse's Feet, all weltring in his Gore—So have I seen, and with as little Mercy, a gallant Ox fell'd to the Ground by some fierce Butcher; and so, like *Jonathan*, have I seen him bestride the mighty Beast, and strip him of his Skin.

*Jonathan* thus having obtain'd a compleat Victory, and being Master of the Field, immediately fell to plundering—he found fifty odd Guineas in the Fellow's Pockets, with some Moveables of Value, of which having taken *Livery* and *Seisin*,° according to the Law of Arms, he went to the next Town, leading the Horse of the slain in a kind of Triumph, as a Mark of his Victory; and enquiring for the next Justice of Peace, he surrender'd himself, telling him that he had kill'd a Highwayman; and giving a Direction where he had left the Body, the Justice sent and had it taken up, when he was known by some Stage Coachmen and others to be the same that had infested that Road for some time past: *Jonathan* at the same time signifying to the Justice that he was the famous *Wild the Thief-catcher*; the Justice took Bail for him, and *Jonathan* return'd Home to his Wife loaded with Victory and Plunder.

I presume this Story may suffice to let the Reader know by what kind of

Policy this *Machiavel* of Thieves supply'd his Commonwealth with Subjects as fast as they were cut off—Those whom he observ'd to be active, brisk and couragious, he put into his Cavalry; there was another Corps which we may call his Dragoons, because they serv'd sometimes on Horseback, sometimes on Foot, as was most consistent with the Service; these sometimes went forth doubly arm'd, and on the wide extended Common attack'd the Stage Coach in open Day; other whiles they laid Ambuscades, and lying *perdue*° in some Ditch, surpriz'd the heedless Traveller on Foot, and were counted his best Men, being, as the Saying is, *in utrumque parati*;° or having two Strings to their Bow.

But as *Jonathan* was a deep Studier of Nature, he knew that Mens Talents were different, and that he who had not Courage enough to bid a Man stand, upon the Road, might nevertheless make an excellent Pickpocket; and he took care that no Man's Parts should be misapply'd: Nay, it is said that nothing pleas'd him more than to see a Child or Youth of a promising Genius, and that such never wanted his Encouragement; insomuch that a little Boy in a Crowd having at a certain time stole a Pair of silver Buckles out of a Man's Shoes, without being felt, his Mother, not a little proud of her Child's Ingenuity, presented him to *Jonathan*, who gave him half a Crown, with this prophetick Saying, *My Life on't, he'll prove a great Man*—But I must observe, that *Jonathan*'s Prophecy never was fulfill'd, the Youth dying before he came to the Age of Manhood, for he was hang'd before he arriv'd at sixteen.

He had another Sort of Gentlemen under his Command, whom in the Cant or Language of the Profession, he distinguish'd by the Name of *Spruce Prigs*; these were Persons not qualified for the bold and manly Employment of Knocking-down, House-breaking, &c. but being Persons of Address and Behaviour, were dispatch'd to Court on Birth-Nights, to Balls, Operas, Plays and Assemblies, for which Purpose they were furnish'd with laced Coats, brocade Wastcoats, fine Perriwigs, and sometimes equipp'd with handsome Equipages, such as Chariots, with Footmen in Liveries, and also *Valet de Chambres*, the Servants being all Thieves like the Master.

This Body of Gentlemen were generally chosen out of such as had been Footmen, who by waiting at Tables, and frequenting publick Places with their Masters and Mistresses, knew something of the Address and Discourse used among Gentlemen; and the better to qualify them to acquit themselves handsomely at Balls, *Jonathan* sometimes paid a Dancingmaster to teach them to dance; that is, after he lost his own Dancingmaster; the celebrated Mr. *Lun*, who died in his own Profession, *viz.* dancing; being hang'd at *Kingston*, for a Robbery on the Highway; who he sometimes said was a great Loss to the Corporation.

There were another Class of the same Sort of Gentlemen, but who did not strike such bold Strokes as the other; or, as we may say, did not fly at such high Game; these appear'd commonly like young Mercers or Drapers, being always dress'd very clean in plain Cloth, good Wigs, and good Linen, with a Ring or Rings on their Fingers; the Places which they haunted most, were *Sadlers Wells*, and all the Hops° about the Town: They were also great Practicers of the Art of Dancing; and some of them were famous for Hornpipes.

Their Business was to promote Country-Dancing, and while the young Fellows and their Girls were very earnest at their Diversion, they were to assist a Confederate (for nothing cou'd be done without a Partner) to carry off the Silver Swords, and Canes, if there were any; whilst the Dancer himself was to stand his Ground, always pretending to have lost a Cane, or Hat, amongst the rest, and making the greatest Clamor of all.

The genteelest of these Sort of Gentlemen sometimes took handsom Lodgings of two or three Guineas a Week; and being attended by their sham Servants, these Servants were to give out that their Master was just return'd from his Travels; that he was a Peer, or at least a Baronet of a great Estate: And the better to carry on the Bite, they took care to assume the Name of some Person of great Estate, who was actually Abroad— that his Father, or some Relation, being lately dead, was the Occasion of his coming over in Haste, to take Possession of a great Estate; and that His Lordship, or Honour, wou'd not appear, nor have it known he was arriv'd, till he had put himself and all his Servants in Mourning; wherefore a Draper was sent for, and a vast Quantity of fine Cloth was agreed for; not only for his own Family, but he was to give Mourning to all his Relations—The Draper was generally recommended by the Landlord, who thought himself very happy in having such a Customer as His Lordship—As soon as the Cloth came in, it was immediately sent off, being carried away by some Accomplices who waited in the Way, and represented Porters, before the Draper cou'd come for his Money—But if, as it sometimes happen'd, the Draper came himself at the same time with the Cloth, why then His Lordship was so busy in his Closet that he could not speak to him, but he sent him out a Banker's Note, desiring him to give the rest; but if the Draper had not Money enough about him, then he was to go and receive the Whole, and bring His Lordship the rest; but as soon as his Back was turn'd, the whole *Posse* mov'd off, leaving generally an empty Trunk or two to pay for the Lodging.

This Trick has often been play'd in the Streets betwixt the *Temple* and *Somerset-house*, the Situation of those Places being very commodious for making a Retreat by Water.

*Jonathan* one Night at *Southwark*-Fair, was observ'd to sit in one of the

Booths, in a Corner of the Pit, as much out of sight as he cou'd; and being ask'd by an Acquaintance what he was doing there?—See that Beau (says he) in the Side-Box, pointing to a handsom young Fellow, who was very fine, that is one of my People, but the Son of a Whore has hid himself from me these two Months, but I'll frighten him out of his Wits; and if you have a mind for a little Sport, go to the next Tavern, and I'll divert you—We had not been there two Minutes (for I was one of the Company) when *Jonathan* enters, with Sir *Fopling*;° *Jonathan* immediately, with many Oaths and Menaces, began to question him where he had been, and what the D——l was the Reason he had not come near him in all that Time? The Beau, in a very great Fright, swore, and curs'd, and pray'd, all in a Breath, begging *Jonathan* to forgive him, telling him he cou'd not help it, having been in Jail in *Lincolnshire*; where he went upon a very *good Lay*, (that was his Term) for he went down there expecting to marry a Lady of great Fortune; but that miscarrying, that he might not lose his Labour, he *spoke with* a Silver Tankard and some Spoons, for which he was committed; however, he managed it so well, by the Assistance of *nimble Dick*, who personated his Servant, that nothing was found upon him, and so the *Pimps* discharg'd him; not out of good Will, d——n them, says he, but for Want of Proofs. But that he was upon a Lay at that time (if he wou'd let him go) that he was sure of getting a Gold Watch that Night; and swore upon his *Honour* he wou'd bring *Jonathan* some Money the next Day.

Upon these Protestations and Promises, and his paying for a Bottle of Wine, *Jonathan* let him go.—When he was gone, *Jonathan* told us he was an ingenious pretty Fellow, and wou'd live like a Gentleman in any part of the World; for that the last Birth-night he went to Court as fine as any thing there, and no body knowing him, he was taken for some young Man of Fortune, just come to his Estate; his Design being to pick the King's Pocket, but that he was hinder'd and interrupted by a certain Lady, a Citizen's Wife, who wou'd not let him get near enough for the Fondness she had of shewing herself to his M——y; however, it cost her dear, for she lost her repeating Watch by the Bargain.—He told us that he had sav'd the young Fellow's Life once by good Management at his Tryal; for he thought it was pity such a clever Fellow shou'd be cut off so soon, and that he had done a great many handsom Things since that Time: We desir'd to know of *Jonathan* what the young Fellow was originally, he told us he was the Son of a Chairman, who living with a Lady of Quality, she put this young Fellow, when a Boy, into a Livery; that this Lady loving her Pleasures, and being a Woman of Intrigue, the Boy got the Reputation of being a very good Pimp; so that if his Lady had not died, he wou'd have been made a Page, and then perhaps Groom of the Chamber, and then recommended to my Lord for some considerable Post; so that by this

Time he might have been a topping Grandee, if the Death of the Lady had not put an end to his Hopes of rising that way; for after her Decease, being out of Place, he had no Thought or Ambition of going into any way of getting his Bread but by being a Servant; so that being nimble, and light of Body, he practis'd running, thinking to get a running Footman's Place with some Person of Quality, when I (says *Jonathan*) happen'd to meet with him, and thinking it a pity that such Parts shou'd be buried and lost to the World, I took him into my Protection, and I warrant you'll see him *prefer'd one Time or other*.

But tho' it is some Years since this Thing happen'd, I was, not long since, inform'd by *Jonathan* that the Beau is still alive, that he made a considerable Figure at the last Installment at *Windsor*, being the Person who took the Lady *M——n*'s Diamond Buckle; that when her Ladyship applied to *Jonathan* for the Recovery of it, he ask'd her how much she wou'd give; she answer'd twenty Guineas; Z——nds, Madam, says he, you offer nothing, it cost the Gentleman who took it forty for his Coach, Equipage, and other Expences to *Windsor*.

*Jonathan* gave us to understand, that these Gentlemen often visited the *Bath, Tunbridge*, and *Epsom*, not staying long in a Place, but going from one to the other, and always thrusting themselves into the best Company; their Business there was to get Watches and Snuff Boxes, and whenever there happen'd a Crowd on the Walks, or in the long Rooms, then it is these Gentlemen *work*; and if the Things shou'd happen to be miss'd while they are in the Room, the Figure they make carries them off without being suspected; but as has been before observ'd, for fear of Accidents, there must be a Footman, not only for State, but for Use, who to prevent the Consequences of a Search, receives the Booty from the Master as soon as the Work is done, and conveys it to some Place of Safety.

The Footman in his Way is a Person of as great Service to the Commonwealth of Thieves as the Master; he is to insinuate himself into the Acquaintance of all the Servants wherever he goes; from them he is to learn all the Circumstances and Affairs of their respective Masters and Mistresses;—as what Plate they bring with them to those Places of Pleasure, when they remove to Town, or to any other Place, and how they go attended, which are very material Advices; for Intelligence is sent of all these Things to *Jonathan*, who takes care to have them spoke with upon the Road, if it be feasible and safe; the Footman is also to endeavour to corrupt some of the Servants he converses with, and if they are Fellows who love Mirth and good Company, they are often delighted with these Fellows, who study to please; and they are by all means to come acquainted with the Servant Maids who live in good Families, and to make Love to some one of them; by these Means they not only become acquainted with the Situation of the House, and know where all the Plate and other rich Moveables are kept; but if one of the Damsels shou'd happen to be captivated with the Person of Mr. *John*, or Mr. *Thomas*, or whatever Name he takes, she may be wrought upon to let him in at Night, and so a good Prize may be got with little Hazard and Danger.

*Jonathan* told us the World was grown so *peery*, (that was his Term for sharp) that ingenious Men (meaning Thieves) must have Recourse to Stratagems, or else they cou'd not get Bread; for (says he) there are not so many Opportunities of working, as heretofore, there are such a damn'd Number of poor People more than formerly, that are not worth robbing, and those that have made them poor, and got their Money, take so much care to keep it, and are so well guarded, that it is very difficult to come at them; downright robbing, or your chance Jobs are not worth a Farthing; and I may say without Vanity, that if it had not been for the Confederacy I have form'd, the *Business wou'd have come to nothing*; but let them be as cautious and as cunning as they will, we'll be more cunning than they— I'll tell you a Stratagem of some of the Gentlemen, I have the Honour to command—There were a parcel of rich Citizens, who took a singular Pleasure in ringing Bells, one Day in the Week they met and din'd together, and pass'd the rest of the Day in ringing; in Summer Time they travel'd from Place to Place wherever they heard of a good Ring of Bells, in order to divert themselves with ringing, and to try where were the sweetest Bells—One of our Gentry found Means of getting into their Company; and one Night when they were pretty warm with Wine, and boasting of their great Excellence in ringing; our Spark offer'd, that he and five more he wou'd bring shou'd ring with them for two hundred Guineas, provided he was to name the Bells; they took him up immediately, and enter'd into Articles under the Forfeiture of an hundred Pounds to those that shou'd fail, who named *Lincoln* Cathedral, where they agreed to meet by a certain Day.

Our Citizens set out, some in their own Coaches, and some on Horseback with two hundred Guineas for their Wager, and each of them Money besides for Expences; and our Spark with his Confederates met them very punctually—The Citizens immediately strip'd themselves, in order to put on their ringing Dresses, consisting of Drawers, Wastcoats and Caps; and while they were beginning to try the Bells, one of our People convey'd away their Cloaths; when the rest saw him safe out, they stole off, and mounted their Horses, which were ready, and left the Citizens to enjoy all their Musick themselves—This Expedition was worth near three hundred Pounds in Money; for all they carried was in their Breeches Pockets; I say three hundred Pounds, besides Watches, Snuff Boxes, Tobacco Boxes, Cloaths, and Perriwigs.

We own'd to *Jonathan*, that this Affair was well projected, and as well executed: Oh, says he, this is nothing to what has been done; for one of our People once stole a House of six Rooms on a Floor, and an hundred and fifty Pounds a Year Rent.

As this appear'd to be a kind of Rhodomontade, we desir'd Mr. *Wild* to let us know how that cou'd be done; and he being very communicative in his Temper, told us the Story: A Gentleman had fitted up a House in *Queen's-Square*, in a very handsom Manner, expecting to let it to some foreign Minister, or *English* Person of Quality; which as soon as 'twas ready, I equipt a Fellow, who had prov'd himself a Man fit for Business, in a plain neat Suit, gold-headed Cane, Snuff Box, &c. a good Chariot, with two other Rogues for Footmen: This suppos'd Gentleman calls upon the Landlord, and offers to treat with him for the Hire of his House, which he said, if he lik'd his Terms, he would take a Lease of for twenty one Years; whereupon the Bargain was struck, and in few Days the Leases were drawn, the Rent to be paid at half yearly Payments; and the Furniture was promis'd by the Squire to be brought in the *Wednesday* following.

The Week after the Landlord calls at the House to see his new Tenant, in order to promote a more intimate Acquaintance, but finds no Body there but a shabby old Man, and not one piece of Furniture; but on the contrary, two or three of the Marble Chimney Pieces and Slabs taken down: He enquires of the old Man the meaning of it, who told him his Master order'd it, for he did not like the Fashion of 'em, and was pleas'd to have them alter'd. The Landlord swore and storm'd like a Madman, bid him get out of the House, and vow'd neither he nor his Master should have any thing to do there; but at length was pacify'd upon his assuring him his Master design'd nothing but what was honourable, and would make him all the Satisfaction he could desire, and that the next Day at Noon he would come himself and direct what he would have done; whereupon he went away, but not very well pleas'd you may be sure; and returning the next Day as the Fellow had appointed, he meets some Men at the Door, carrying out two Chimney-Glasses, and several Pictures that had been fix'd to the Pannels over the Chimney-Pieces, which he stop'd; but the Squire happening himself to be in the House, but without his Chariot or Footmen, required to know by what Authority he stop the Goods from going where he sent them; *why Sir*, says the Landlord, *are they not my own? What, wou'd you pull my House down before my Face, and send it G— knows where; why is not your own Furniture brought home as you appointed? Sir*, says the Tenant, *I have had two Children sick of the Small Pox, which hinder'd me from moving so soon as I expected, but to-morrow some of my Goods will be here. But what are you doing* replies the Landlord, *with these that you send away. Why*, says he, *I am for fitting up Things according*

*to my own Fancy, and I don't matter the Expence of it; for as I alter the
Chimney-Pieces to another Form, the Glasses must be made to answer them,
and the Frames of the Pictures I shall have made wider, to square with the
Glasses. When I fitted up this House,* says the Landlord, *I thought it might
have serv'd any Man of Quality in the Kingdom. That might be,* said the
Squire again, *I'll have Things done agreeable to my own Humour, for all
that: When your Rent's due I'll pay it; and when my Lease is expired, I shall
leave the House in as good Condition as I have found it.*

The Landlord finding it in vain to oppose him, and withal that he had
promised that some of his Goods would certainly be brought to the House
the next Day; which he hoped would be some Security for what he might
possibly suffer by the Alterations the Tenant was making, he waited till
then, and came again to the House; but was still more provoked, to see
that all the Furniture that was brought, consisted of two old Chairs and a
Table, not worth half a Crown; and they had in the mean time been so
expert in making the Alterations, (as they call'd it,) that they had took
down a very fine new Staircase, and the Wainscot of the best Room.
Whereupon the Landlord, finding himself really trick'd, arrests the Tenant in an Action of 500 *l*. But I got my Gentleman bail'd, and order'd my
Attorney to summon the Plaintiff before a Judge, to shew Cause of
Action; which he failing to do, was oblig'd to take common Bail:° But this
not answering his Purpose, (for in reality the Defendant ow'd him nothing,) the Landlord files a Bill in the *Exchequer*;° upon which the Tenant
prefers a cross Bill,° obliging him to answer to several Points, particularly
the Letting the House to him; which as he could not deny, the Landlord's
Bill was dismiss'd with Costs of Suit; and the Suit at Common Law went
against him also, by Default:° And the Tenant going to work again upon
the Premisses, the Landlord thought fit to make Overtures of Agreement;
*viz*. That upon a Surrender of his Lease, and giving up the Possession of
the House, in the Condition it was then in, he would pay all his Charges,
and release him from all Damages whatsoever: Which, since there was no
more to be got, by my Consent, the Terms were accepted of; and so the
Landlord, besides a Year and a half's Rent, sate down at 400 *l*. Loss.
Which I suppose will make him take a little more Care how he lets his
Houses.

At one time the stealing Shopkeepers Account-Books was grown a
confiderable Branch of Trade; of which *Jonathan* gave us one Instance,
which is worth relating.

A Merchant, a considerable Dealer in Hops, in *Thames-street*, had his
Books stole; and applying to me, offer'd ten Guineas to have them
restor'd: The *Prigs*, says he, were in my *Ken*, that *nim'd* 'em out of his
*Swag*. To explain this Language, it means, that the Thieves were then in

his House, that stole them out of the Shop. But to go on with the Story in plain Terms; *Jonathan* went into the Room where they were, and made the Report; but they sitting in Council, with two or three others of the same Squadron, tho' not in that Detachment,° declared that they thought the Books were really worth twenty; that is, to return to the Owners, which *Jonathan* notify'd to the Merchant: But in short, the Agreement was fifteen. But then arose a Dispute about the Delivery; *Jonathan* propos'd that he should leave the Money behind him, and the Books be brought to his House; which he scrupling, *Jonathan* said to him, *Sir, do you question my Honour? I scorn to do an ill thing by any Man. No, Sir*, answer'd he, *by no means*; and then readily laid down the Money, and went his Way: And before he got home himself, the Books were at his House. Which serves to shew how far *Jonathan*'s Honour was to be depended on.

Within three Weeks the same Gentleman came to *Jonathan*'s House upon the very same Business, for his Shop-Books were gone again; and he would fain have had five Guineas bated this time, because of his having been a Customer before; but *Jonathan* said, 'twas nothing to him: *If the Gentleman*, says he, *will take five Shillings, I shall agree to it*. So, in short, he paid down his Money, like a fair Dealer, and was going home, as before; but *Jonathan* call'd him back, and ask'd him how, and in what part of his Shop, his Counting-house was built? He told him 'twas next the Street, and the Door open'd within-side, behind the Counter. Why, says *Jonathan*, you are quite wrong, you'll never keep your Books, if that's the Case: But I'll come to Morrow my self, and see it, and then I'll advise you what's proper to be done.

The next Day *Jonathan* comes to *Thames-street* (the Books having been sent before) and meets with the Merchant at home: He takes a Survey of the whole Affair, and advises the old Counting-house to be pull'd down, and a new one to be erected at the farther End of the Shop, and to break out a Sky-light over head; this, he said, would be the only Contrivance to make all safe: Which was done according to *Jonathan*'s Model, and yet hardly a Month happen'd before it was again attack'd with the like Success, and cost him the same Sum over again, to get it out of *Jonathan*'s Purgatory.° The Manner of the Adventure is as follows: A Gentleman well dress'd, watch'd his Opportunity, and came into the Shop, and ask'd if Mr. —— was at home? Whereupon he was told that he himself was the Person. Sir, says he, I have two or three Words to speak with you in private; and so walks him towards his Counting-house: The Hop-merchant goes in first, expecting the Gentleman wou'd have follow'd, in order to declare his Business to him there; but instead of that, he only reaches out his Hand to the Desk, upon which the abovementioned Books lay, and takes them away, and at the same instánt shuts to the Door, locks it upon the Hop-Dealer, and walks off very leisurely.

*Jonathan* about this time had one of his best Hands deserted him, and yet the Fellow still did Business, as Mr. *Wild* found by his Books and the Accounts that came in. *Jonathan*'s Clerk minuted down a Gold Watch, a pair of Diamond Ear-Rings, with several other Things of less value, which were *made*, that is, stole in their Language, by this Fellow, and yet he had miss'd several Musters; and *Jonathan*, nor any of his People, had heard one syllable of him for above three Months, any otherwise than that such and such Things were *spoke with*, which he knew must be by the Devil or this Rascal, he said, therefore 'twas time to take him off: Whereupon *Jonathan* was continually upon the hunt for him, but as he kept Company with no other of the Profession, it was a difficult Matter for his Master to get Intelligence of him without his grand Master's Assistance; but whether the Devil did really put it into his Servant *Jonathan*'s Head, or what other way he found it out, I can't say; but true it is, that at length he got certain Information where he then lodg'd.

Mr. *Wild* had my Lord Chief Justice's Warrant in his Pocket, so taking two or three Constables with him, about four in the Morning he beset the House, which was in *Bishopsgate-street*, the Corner of —— *street*, a Publick-House, *Jonathan* headed the Posse, with a Pistol in each Hand, and up Stairs he goes to his Room, tho' not so silently, but that he heard them upon the Stairs, and therefore he gets up, and puts on his Breeches, Shoes, and Stockings; by that time *Jonathan* had wrench'd open the Door (for it was lock'd within side) upon sight of whom, he gave a spring out of the Window, which was one Story high, and came down into a little Yard, from thence leap'd over a Wall into the Street, and ran cross the Way into a Linen-Draper's House, whose Door happen'd to stand open. At that time the Servants of the House were washing below Stairs, to whom the Fellow begs for Protection, for that he was pursu'd by Bailiffs, and if he should be taken, he must be inevitably ruin'd and undone. The poor credulous Women pity'd the Man's Case, and told him, he should stay with them till the Blood-sucking Villains were gone. To return to *Jonathan* and the Constables, as soon as they saw their Man fly out of the Window, you may be sure they were not long behind him; but as much haste as they made down Stairs, they saw not the least Shadow of him, neither in the Yard, or in the Street, which prodigiously surpriz'd them all: But *Jonathan* peer'd about, being satisfy'd, his Motion from the Window was downwards, therefore he must have taken House somewhere, and, at last, spy'd this Linen-Draper's Door open; he goes over, acquaints the Gentleman with what had happen'd, and assures him, the Rogue could be no where but in his House; he said, he had seen no such Person, and that he had not been from the Shop above a Minute. *Sir*, says *Jonathan*, *that was the very time he slipt in, give me leave to search for him*. Which being granted, he went into the Wash-house, where, for a good while, they deny'd they saw any such Person, till being informed he was no Debtor, but a Highwayman and House-breaker, they own'd the Matter, and told Mr. *Wild*, the Man he look'd for was in the Coal-hole under the Stairs; whereupon he takes a Candle, calls all his Mirmidons° about him, and into the Coal-hole he goes, but no Highwayman was there; then he searches round the Cellar, Kitchen, and in short, every Place where he thought a Man could be conceal'd, but no Body was to be seen. *Jonathan* own'd he never was so foil'd in all the Course of his Practice before; he came up and told the Master of the House there was no Body there, the Washer-women were frightned out of their Wits, believing they had seen a Spirit, and all look'd very foolish upon one another, till the Linen Draper gave them to know, that if any Man went down Stairs, he must be there still, for he was sure no Body had come up from thence, he having staid in sight ever since, and then persuaded *Jonathan* to go down again, and look into all the Washing-Tubs, and search every Place over again, for there is, says he, no other Way to get out, but up these Stairs, and so into the Street.

Mr. *Wild* was prevail'd upon at last, and he and the Constables, with his *Guard de Corps*, re-descended, and finding one of the Tubs standing Bottom upwards, they turn'd that up, as the Gentleman had put it into their Heads, and there they found poor *Culprit*. *Jonathan* had no Patience, but flew upon him like a Tyger. *You treacherous Dog*, said he, where are the Diamond Ear-Rings, and Gold Watch you stole at such a Place! G—— D——n me, you Villain, you cheating Son of a Whore, I'll hang you, if there's never another Rogue in *England*, you vile Rascal.

We must remark here, that tho' *Jonathan* in the main us'd to talk up the Gentlemen of his Game, to be generally bright clever Fellows, yet when he was angry with some of them, he would own *there were Scoundrels of the Profession*.

Notwithstanding this Bounce of *Jonathan*'s, the Prisoner understood how to soften this *Matchiaval's* Temper, and thereupon whisper'd him to go up to his Lodging and look behind the Head of the Bed, which *Jonathan* did, telling the People of the House, he must go up Stairs for the Fellow's Cloaths, which he brought down along with him, and in a Hole where the Thief directed him to, he found a Gold-Watch, two silver ones, Rings, and other Things of Value, which he put into his own Pocket, for any Body else would not have known what to have done with them; and the Prisoner being carried before the Justice, was committed on Suspicion of Felony, and the next Sessions no Body appearing against him, he was discharged.

The Success that *Jonathan* went on with in his Business, render'd him famous all over *London*; and he made use of several little Arts to make himself appear considerable to distant Parts of the Kingdom, particularly by some Printers of News-Papers, and Dying-Speeches, whom he prevail'd on to give him a Character therein, in which he was generally stiled THIEF-CATCHER-GENERAL OF GREAT-BRITAIN. His House was handsomly furnished, and set out with Plate, Pictures, &c. and when his Wife appear'd abroad, it was generally with a Footman in a fine lac'd Livery. He kept a Country-House, dress'd well, and in Company affected an Air of Grandeur. A little before his Catastrophe he promis'd me a Haunch or a Side of Venison whenever I pleased to send to him, saying, he had two Parks at his Command well stock'd with Deer.

The Wealth that he was suppos'd to have amass'd by this Business, made several Persons look upon him with Envy; and some well enough acquainted in the Roguish Arts, attempted to set up against him a few Years ago; the Principal were, one *Felt—n*, a superannuated Thief, *Riddlesd—n* an Attorney and Thief, whose chief Merit for the Support of his Pretensions to this Practice, was, his having sacrilegiously and feloniously broke open the Royal-Chapel at *White-hall*, and stole thence the Communion-Plate, and Mr. *H——n*, City Mar——l.° This last, and *Jonathan*, wrote Pamphlets against each other, as it was the Custom then between great Men; but *Jonathan* laying himself too open, *H——n* dropt the Pen, and took up the Cudgels of the Law, with which he bang'd *Jonathan*, so that he thought fit to buy his Peace at the Price of a Sum of Money.

However, none of them all was able to give *Jonathan* any notable Disturbance in his Office; on the contrary, he found means soon after to get *Riddle——n* transported for not complying with the Conditions of his Pardon, to make *Felt—n* run mad, and *H——n* entirely to quit his Pretensions.

Wherefore he turn'd himself again to his Business—and as we were enumerating how many Species of Thieves he had under his Command, we shall resume that Part of our Story.

There were another sort of Gentry under his Command, whose Business it was to loiter about the Streets in the Day-time; and as Servants who go of short Errants to a Chandler's Shop, or Baker's, are apt to leave the Door a jar, (as they call it) they were to whip in, and seize upon the next Thing that was portable, and bring it off. They generally peep'd in, to see that no Body was in the Fore-parlours, and if by chance any Body should surprize them, they were ready to enquire if some Person with a strange Name did not live there; tho' it seldom falls out so, because they generally do their Business in a Minute.

These sort of People sometimes go in Liveries, and sometimes dress'd like Ticket Porters° with Silver Badges either upon their Coats, or about their Necks; one of them some time since whip'd into a House in *King-Street*, near *Long-Acre*, which is divided into Tenements, the People furnishing their own Lodgings, and going directly up two pair of Stairs, from whence he saw a Woman who inhabited it, come down, he easily put back the Lock, and finding nothing in the Room of any Value, except the Bedding, he tied it all up, and was carrying it off, when the Owner happen'd to meet him at the lower end of the Stairs, and asking him where he was carrying that Bedding, he answer'd without Hesitation, that he brought it from Mr. —— the Upholsterer, and was carrying it to such a one, but I find they don't live here; Oh, says the Woman, they live at next Door, thank you Mistress, says the Fellow; and before she got up Stairs, to find it was her own Bedding, he had got into a Hackney Coach, and carried it safe off.

These People sometimes went disguis'd like Chairmen in great Coats and Harness, and a Couple of them meeting together, stole the young Duchess of *Marlborough*'s Chair, as her Grace was visiting at Mrs. *H——n*'s in *Piccadilly*,° her Chairmen and Footmen being gone to a neighbouring Ale-House; one of her Servants thought immediately of applying to Mr. *Wild*, who told him, that if he wou'd leave ten Guineas, he might have the Chair the next Day; the Man made some Difficulty of leaving the Money before-hand, but Mr. *Wild* told him he was a Man of Honour, and scorn'd to wrong him, and indeed his Character was by this Time establish'd as a Man that dealt honourably in his Way; so that the Man ventur'd at last to leave the Money; wherefore Mr. *Wild* bid him direct the Duchess's Chairmen to attend the Morning Prayers at *Lincoln's-Inn-Chapel*, and there they shou'd find the Chair, which the Fellows did accordingly, and they found the Chair, with the Crimson Velvet Cushions and Damask Curtains all safe, and unhurt.

And it must be observ'd, that whenever *Jonathan* oblig'd the Parties to leave the Money before-hand, he very punctually comply'd with the Terms of Agreement, as to the Delivery of the Goods; for one of his common Sayings was, *that Honesty was the best Policy*.

He frequently drew out Detachments of some of his cleverest Fellows, whom he sent out upon Command to Country Fairs; upon which Occasion he generally march'd out himself, for indeed the Service cou'd not be well carried on without him; for the common People seeing *Jonathan* there, were the more careless; because he always gave out, that he came to take some Rogues whom he suspected to be there, and the People had a Notion that his Presence frighten'd away the Thieves; and to countenance this Belief, he went doubly and trebly arm'd, and often wore Armour under his Cloaths, which he took care to shew in all Companies; being attended by three or four, and sometimes half a Dozen terrible looking Fellows by way of *Garde du Corps*, as if all the Thieves in *England* had vow'd to sacrifice him.

This Grimace took very well, for it gave him an Opportunity of protecting and carrying off the Booty which was made in these Fairs; and if any of his Party was in Danger of being taken, these Myrmidons of his, who pass'd for his Body Guard, were to run into the Crowd, and under pretence of assisting the People, who were about to seize such Rogues, were to try to shuffle off, and favour their Escape.

In fine, his Business in all Things was to put a false gloss upon Things; and to make *Fools* of Mankind (which was his own Expression;) yet, when he had a Mind to be merry, to drink his Bottle, and to laugh at the World, he talk'd with too much Freedom of himself, and his own Management, and not without some Vanity; of which there are a thousand Instances: We shall give one, because it is short—A certain Tradesman, a very honest Man, tho' of *Jonathan*'s Acquaintance, going into a Tavern, where he expected to meet some Company, by Mistake went in where *Jonathan* was drinking with some merry Fellows; the Tradesman was about to draw back, but *Jonathan* press'd him to set down and take a Glass with them; the Tradesman was a little angry with *Jonathan* for the following Reason; about a Week before, passing thro' a Country Fair, he saw *Jonathan* a Horseback, and asking him how he did, *Jonathan* damn'd him, and bid him not trouble him with impertinent Questions; therefore, the Tradesman desir'd to know the Reason why *Jonathan* snap'd him up in that rude angry Manner, when he had spoke to him so civilly? Z——ds, says *Jonathan*, you disturb'd me in my Business, for *I had at that Time twenty pair of Hands at Work*.

And indeed, he employ'd Hands in all sorts of Works; so that according to the Author of the *Fable of the Bees*,° he was a great Benefactor to Trade; for as some of our News Papers have observ'd, he kept in Pay many Artists for the altering of Watches and Rings; so he also kept a kind of Magazine, or Armory, of all kind of Instruments us'd in *Thievery*, as Picklocks, Files, Saws, and Engines for forcing Doors, Windows, &c. which he made no Secret of shewing, pretending he found them upon such and such House-breakers whom he had taken and convicted, tho' it is certain he did not suffer them to grow rusty for want of Use; for he never went into a House, but like an Engineer, he wou'd view on which side it might be attack'd with the most Advantage, and he knew better Things, than to send his Men upon Actions without Arms.

Sometimes *Jonathan* spoke in the Stile of a Prince; as when the Son of Mrs. *Knap*, who was murther'd by a Footpad, near *Gray's-Inn-Wall*,° went to him, to desire his Assistance in taking the Murderer, and putting ten

Guineas in his Hand for his Encouragement, with a Promise of forty more when the Work shou'd be done; *Jonathan* answer'd him gravely, he might depend he wou'd produce the Villain; *for*, says he, *I never pardon Murther*—and indeed he was as good as his Word, for he seiz'd the Fellow at the *Jerusalem-Tavern* in *Clerkenwell*, and he was hang'd the Sessions following.

Whilst he went on with this Tide of Success, and seem'd to carry the World before him, an ill Wind arose, which blew from a certain Corner of the Law, and which seem'd to threaten the Overthrow of his Commonwealth—For Sir *W——m T——son*° observing what Mischiefs arose from the Practice of receiving stolen Goods, and returning them again to the Proprietors for such Sums of Money as the Receiver and Proprietor agreed upon, which Money no doubt must be divided betwixt the Receiver and Thief; thought of putting an end to it, by bringing a Bill into the House of Commons, for the *more effectual transporting of Felons, and for preventing Burglaries and Felonies*, in which among other Things was the following Clause.

'And whereas there are several Persons who have secret Acquaintance with Felons, and who make it their Business to help Persons to their stoln Goods, and by that means gain Money from them, which is divided between them and the Felons, whereby they greatly encourage such Offenders: Be it Enacted by the Authority aforesaid, That where-ever any Person taketh Money or Reward, directly or indirectly, under Pretence or upon Account of helping any Person or Persons to any stoln Goods or Chattels, every such Person so taking Money or Reward as aforesaid, (unless such Person do apprehend, or cause to be apprehended, such Felon who stole the same, and cause such Felon to be brought to his Trial for the same, and give Evidence against him) shall be guilty of Felony, and suffer the Pains and Penalties of Felony, according to the Nature of the Felony committed in stealing such Goods, and in such and the same Manner as if such Offender had himself stole such Goods and Chattels, in the Manner and with such Circumstances as the same were stoln.'

We are well informed, that after this Act had pass'd, the R——r° was pleas'd to send for *Wild* to admonish him, and let him know the Danger and Hazard of pursuing the same Course of Life any longer, and recommended to him to detect Rogues and bring them to Justice; promising upon that Condition, to give him all Encouragement, reminding him of what considerable Sums he had got that Way already, by which he might judge that he might get sufficient to keep him by doing good Service to the Publick, and living honestly.

Whether these good Admonitions, or the Fear of this new Law, wrought upon his Conscience, is uncertain; but there was a sudden Damp put upon all his Business, his *Books were shut up* for some Weeks, and he grew so abstemious, that he refused several Sums offer'd him for the Recovery of Things stolen—Yet, he did not break off all Acquaintance and Correspondence with his old Friends and Allies, the Thieves; on the contrary, having the Command of some Money, he gave them some small Matters (just what he pleas'd) for what old *Nick* had sent them in their Way, and deposited the Goods up in a Warehouse.

In the mean time, all *Wild*'s Acquaintance were inquisitive to know what he intended to turn himself to; for they took it for granted, that this new Act had quite cut him out of his former Business; having a Notion that he was too cunning ever to venture himself within the Clutches of the Law—Wherefore he talk'd of a new Project; which was, for setting up a Policy, and opening an Office for taking in Subscriptions for insuring against Robbery; pretending to settle a sufficient Fund, and give good Security for the Performance of Articles; sometimes shewing a manuscript Paper of Proposals, and consulting People whom he supposed to have any Understanding in those Affairs, extolling the great Use and Advantage this Project wou'd be to the Public; not doubting, he said, but that all Trading People, as well as Gentlemen and Noblemen, who kept great Quantities of Plate in their Houses, wou'd for their own sakes encourage so useful an Undertaking; bragging that it was no *South-Sea Bubble*,° and that he could fairly make a great Fortune by it.

Whether he gave out this Report only to amuse People, and to hinder them from enquiring any farther into his Affairs; or whether he was in earnest, and thought to bring it to bear, I can't tell; but the Thing was generally receiv'd as a Banter, or as a Piece of Mr. *Wild*'s Wit, and no farther Steps were taken in it.

It was about this time, that he projected the carrying on a Trade to *Holland* and *Flanders*; and thereupon purchas'd a Sloop, and put in one *Roger J——son*° to command her, who had long been one of *Jonathan*'s clever Fellows. He carry'd over Gold Watches, Rings, Plate, and now and then a Bank or Goldsmith's Note, that had been *spoke with* by the way of the Mail. His chief Trading Port was *Ostend*, where he is particularly well known; from thence he usually travell'd up to *Bruges, Ghent, Brussels*, and other great Towns, where he brought his Toys and Jewels to Market, and then return'd to his Sloop, took in a Lading of Hollands, and other Goods, and came back to the River of *Thames*.

It is not to be expected that *Jonathan* and *Roger* would let any one share in the Profits of such an honourable Profession: It would have been inconsistent with their Practice, who never paid for any thing, to pay Custom; that would have been reflected upon as idle and foolish: No, the Cargoe came generally safe to Land the first Night; and at a certain House within forty Miles of *Newington-Buts*, most Part of the dark Business was acted; where Councils were secretly held, and Projects form'd. But I hope from what has happen'd, some Persons who are well known, will have Prudence to take Warning, since I can assure them that their Actions are sifting into by Persons of no small Penetration, and whom they are not entire Strangers to.

But to return from this Digression, *Roger* drove on the Business abovementioned but two Years, which was owing to an Accident that he himself was the Occasion of: It happen'd, that by some Negligence or other, two Pieces of *Holland* were lost in the shipping them for *England*, which, when he arriv'd, he stop'd out of his Mate's Wages, making him pay for the whole Loss. This so provok'd the Mate, that he went immediately and gave Information of *Jon——n*'s running such Quantities of Goods. Whereupon the Vessel was exchequer'd in the River, and he was oblig'd to stand a Trial with the King, in which he was cast in 700 *l.* Damages; and so his Trade was put an End to in that particular Way.

This Stop brought *Jonathan* again to Consideration; he soon miss'd his Returns from *Ostend*, and having three Wives living, and always a Seraglio of Mistresses, no less than half a dozen at a time, to maintain, according to his Rank; and being frequently importun'd and teaz'd by People who had been robb'd, to help them to their Goods, he ventur'd to dabble a little again; but with great Caution, and for none but such as he took to be Men of Honour; every now and then bringing in an Offering to the Gallows of some idle Rascal who did not mind his Business, and who, according to his Notions, was fit for nothing but hanging.

Finding no bad Consequence to proceed from his new Practice, it made him bolder and bolder, so that he began to think he might go on as before, and that he should be conniv'd at; in a small time carrying on his Trade with very little Caution, he went publickly down to the late Instalment at *Windsor*, accompanied by his Lady Madam *Wild*, attended by a Couple of Footmen in laced Liveries; and the Detachment, he commanded down upon that Occasion, made as good a Figure, both for Dress and Equipage, as any People there.

As there was a very great Booty brought off safe from that Expedition, Mr. *Wild* had more than ordinary Court made to him by People of Fashion of both Sexes, who sollicited hard to have their Jewels, Watches, &c. return'd upon a reasonable Composition; and his open Way of treating upon this Occasion was the most impudent thing he ever did in Contempt of the late Act—He proceeded so far as to break off with several People, because they wou'd not come up to his Terms; and he considerably advanced the Price of stolen Goods; for whereas at first he took no more for any thing of Plate than its Value in Weight, now he wou'd make People pay something for the Fashion also, otherwise they should never have them; intending to send them over to *Holland*, where they might come to a better Market—

Yet no Prosecution follow'd all these daring Proceedings; which made him think, no doubt, that he could do any thing; yet he had not long ago a narrow Escape, as we shall shew by the following Relation.

*Jonathan*, sitting one Day at an Inn in *Smithfield*, observ'd a large Trunk in the Yard, and imagining there might be some Things of Value therein, he immediately went home, and order'd one *Rann*, a notorious Acquaintance,° to habit himself like a Porter, and to endeavour to *speak with it: Rann* obeys his Master's Commands, and accordingly succeeds. The Trunk belong'd to Mr. *Jarvis*, a Whip-maker in that Neighbourhood, who was sending it down to a Dealer in the Country. There was in it a great Quantity of rich Linen, and other Things for a Wedding. Upon Mr. *Jarvis*'s applying to *Wild*, after many Delays, he had most of the Goods again for ten Guineas. But soon after *Wild* and *Rann* falling out, he got him hang'd: And the Day before his Execution, he sent for Mr. *Jarvis*, and related to him the above Particulars: but Mr. *Jarvis* dying soon after, *Jonathan* had the good Luck to hear no more of the Matter.

But now it being decreed by Providence, that *Jonathan* should reign no longer, he was infatuated to do a Thing which brought on his Destruction—Certain Persons having Information where a considerable Quantity of rich Goods lay, supposed to be stoln, obtained a Warrant for the Seisure of them; which was accordingly done: Tho' *Jonathan* did not go and claim the Goods as his own, he had the Assurance to take out an Action, in the Name of *Roger Johnston*, to whom he pretended the Goods belong'd, and arrested the Person or Persons who seiz'd them. Thus he pretended to recover those Goods by Law, for possessing which (if they were found upon him) the Law would hang him—

A Proceeding so bare-faced and impudent, put certain Persons upon finding out Means of bringing so sturdy a Rogue to Justice; *Jonathan* was threaten'd loud, which occasion'd a Report all over the Town, that he was fled from Justice; upon which occasion, he publish'd a bullying Advertisement in some of the News Papers, offering a Reward of ten Guineas to any Person who shou'd discover the Author of such a scandalous Report; at the same Time he run into all publick Places to shew himself, and let the World see that he was not run away as was reported—Yet, in the midst of all this blustering he was seiz'd and committed to *Newgate*.

There are some other Circumstances in this Story, but as we had it only from his own Mouth, that he was malicious against the Persons concern'd, and endeavour'd to asperse them, we shall say no more of it.

How far *Roger John—n* was concern'd with *Wild* at the time of his

Apprehension, I leave the World to judge, when immediately upon his being committed to *Newgate*, an Express was sent over, and *John—n*, with another of the Trade, came down to *Ostend*, and appear'd like Persons of Quality, told the News to all about him, and swore he'd hang both *Jonathan* and the B—— who calls her self his Wife; so he takes a Packet and hires her for *Dover*: But as he has not appear'd publickly in *London*, we may very well suppose that the hanging of them was the least Part of his Business.

We can't forbear observing something remarkable in the Fate of this Fellow; first, that he had Opportunities of escaping after he knew that a Prosecution was design'd against him; and *secondly*, that the Fact for which he died, was committed whilst he was a Prisoner in *Newgate*; for he was so blind, as to imagine, that the taking but ten Guineas for the Recovery of the Lace, when the Woman offer'd fifteen or twenty, and refusing to accept of any thing for his own Trouble, and also that palliating Speech he made her, that he did these Things only *to serve poor People who had been wrong'd*, wou'd have been Circumstances in his Favour when he shou'd come to be tried; not considering that he directly by this Action incurr'd the Penalty of the Act of Parliament before quoted; which is a Proof, that all his former Cunning and Sagacity forsook him, when he wanted it most, and makes good that Saying—*Quem Jupiter vult perdere, dementat prius*—Jupiter first takes away the Understanding of him whom he has a Mind to destroy.°

I believe no Malefactor ever stood his Ground so long, committing every Day acts of Felony in Sight of the World; so that I've heard him compute, that in fifteen Years he had receiv'd near ten thousand Pounds for his Dividend of stoln Goods return'd, living all this while in Riot and Voluptuousness.

But Vengeance at length overtook him, and from the Minute of his being seiz'd, his Sense and Resolution fail'd; nor was he spirited up by the Hopes of a Reprieve, which some People endeavour'd to flatter him with, and industriously spread such a Rumour about, whilst they were trembling, lest it shou'd be so; because, he and they are suppos'd to be no Strangers to each others Practices.

We shall not trouble the Readers with any Thing which has already been made Publick, concerning this extraordinary Fellow, who has made so much Noise in the World; therefore we shall conclude, with observing that whoever had seen him in the Gaiety of his Life, when all his Rogueries were successful; and had also been Witness of his deplorable State of Mind after his Condemnation, might have drawn a Lesson of Morality from it, which perhaps might have been of use to an Atheist.

I say to have seen one remarkable for the Gaiety of his Temper, for a vast Depth of Cunning, as well as Hardness and personal Courage, so chang'd at the Apprehensions of his approaching Death, and the great Account which is to follow; to have seen him under the greatest Distractions and Horrors of Mind, that human Nature is capable of suffering, wou'd be convinc'd, that *Virtue only can give true Tranquillity, and nothing can support a Man against the Terrors of Death, but a good Conscience.*

FINIS.

# APPENDIX 2

## EXTRACT FROM THE PREFACE TO
### *MISCELLANIES*

I COME now to the Third and last Volume, which contains the History of *Jonathan Wild*. And here it will not, I apprehend, be necessary to acquaint my Reader, that my Design is not to enter the Lists with that excellent Historian, who from authentic Papers and Records, *&c.* hath already given so satisfactory an Account of the Life and Actions of this Great Man. I have not indeed the least Intention to depreciate the Veracity and Impartiality of that History; nor do I pretend to any of those Lights, not having, to my Knowledge, ever seen a single Paper relating to my Hero, save some short Memoirs, which about the Time of his Death were published in certain Chronicles called News-Papers, the Authority of which hath been sometimes questioned, and in the Ordinary of *Newgate* his Account, which generally contains a more particular Relation of what the Heroes are to suffer in the next World, than of what they did in this.°

To confess the Truth, my Narrative is rather of such Actions which he might have performed, or would, or should have performed, than what he really did; and may, in Reality, as well suit any other such great Man, as the Person himself whose Name it bears.

A second Caution I would give my Reader is, that as it is not a very faithful Portrait of *Jonathan Wild* himself, so neither is it intended to represent the Features of any other Person. Roguery, and not a Rogue, is my Subject; and as I have been so far from endeavouring to particularize any Individual, that I have with my utmost Art avoided it; so will any such Application be unfair in my Reader, especially if he knows much of the Great World, since he must then be acquainted, I believe, with more than one on whom he can fix the Resemblance.

In the third Place, I solemnly protest, I do by no means intend in the Character of my Hero to represent Human Nature in general. Such Insinuations must be attended with very dreadful Conclusions; nor do I see any other Tendency they can naturally have, but to encourage and soothe Men in their Villainies, and to make every well-disposed Man disclaim his own Species, and curse the Hour of his Birth into such a Society. For my Part, I understand those Writers who describe Human Nature in this depraved Character, as speaking only of such Persons as *Wild* and his Gang; and I think it may be justly inferred, that they do not find in their own Bosoms any Deviation from the general Rule. Indeed it would be an insufferable Vanity in them to conceive themselves as the only Exception to it.

But without considering *Newgate* as no other than Human Nature with its Mask off, which some very shameless Writers have done, a Thought which no Price should purchase me to entertain, I think we may be excused for suspecting, that the splendid Palaces of the Great are often no other than *Newgate* with the Mask on. Nor do I know any thing which can raise an honest Man's Indignation higher than that the same Morals should be in one Place attended with all imaginable Misery and Infamy, and in the other, with the highest Luxury and Honour. Let any impartial Man in his Senses be asked, for which of these two Places a Composition of Cruelty, Lust, Avarice, Rapine, Insolence, Hypocrisy, Fraud and Treachery, was best fitted, surely his Answer must be certain and immediate; and yet I am afraid all these Ingredients glossed over with Wealth and a Title, have been treated with the highest Respect and Veneration in the one, while one or two of them have been condemned to the Gallows in the other.

If there are then any Men of such Morals who dare to call themselves Great, and are so reputed, or called at least, by the deceived Multitude, surely a little private Censure by the few is a very moderate Tax for them to pay, provided no more was to be demanded: But I fear this is not the Case. However the Glare of Riches, and Awe of Title, may dazzle and terrify the Vulgar; nay, however Hypocrisy may deceive the more Discerning, there is still a Judge in every Man's Breast, which none can cheat or corrupt, tho' perhaps it is the only uncorrupt Thing about him. And yet, inflexible and honest as this Judge is, (however polluted the Bench be on which he sits) no Man can, in my Opinion, enjoy any Applause which is not thus adjudged to be his Due.

Nothing seems to me more preposterous than that, while the Way to true Honour lies so open and plain, Men should seek false by such perverse and rugged Paths: that while it is so easy and safe, and truly honourable, to be good, Men should wade through Difficulty and Danger, and real Infamy, to be *Great*, or, to use a synonimous Word, *Villains*.

Nor hath Goodness less Advantage in the Article of Pleasure, than of Honour over this kind of Greatness. The same righteous Judge always annexes a bitter Anxiety to the Purchases of Guilt, whilst it adds a double Sweetness to the Enjoyments of Innocence and Virtue: for Fear, which all the Wise agree is the most wretched of human Evils, is, in some Degree, always attending on the former, and never can in any manner molest the Happiness of the latter.

This is the Doctrine which I have endeavoured to inculcate in this History, confining myself at the same Time within the Rules of Probability. (For except in one Chapter, which is visibly meant as a Burlesque on the extravagant Accounts of Travellers, I believe I have not exceeded it°).

And though perhaps it sometimes happens, contrary to the Instances I have given, that the Villain succeeds in his Pursuit, and acquires some transitory imperfect Honour or Pleasure to himself for his Iniquity; yet I believe he oftner shares the Fate of my Hero, and suffers the Punishment, without obtaining the Reward.

As I believe it is not easy to teach a more useful Lesson than this, if I have been able to add the pleasant to it, I might flatter myself with having carried every Point.

But perhaps some Apology may be required of me, for having used the Word *Greatness*, to which the World have affixed such honourable Ideas, in so disgraceful and contemptuous a Light. Now if the Fact be, that the Greatness which is commonly worshipped is really of that Kind which I have here represented, the Fault seems rather to lie in those who have ascribed it to those Honours, to which it hath not in Reality the least Claim.

The Truth, I apprehend, is, we often confound the Ideas of Goodness and Greatness together, or rather include the former in our Idea of the latter. If this be so, it is surely a great Error, and no less than a Mistake of the Capacity for the Will. In Reality, no Qualities can be more distinct: for as it cannot be doubted but that Benevolence, Honour, Honesty, and Charity, make a good Man; and that Parts, Courage, are the efficient Qualities of a Great Man, so must it be confess'd, that the Ingredients which compose the former of these Characters, bear no Analogy to, nor Dependence on those which constitute the latter. A Man may therefore be Great without being Good, or Good without being Great.

However, tho' the one bear no necessary Dependence on the other, neither is there any absolute Repugnancy among them which may totally prevent their Union so that they may, tho' not of Necessity, assemble in the same Mind, as they actually did, and all in the highest Degree, in those of *Socrates* and *Brutus*; and perhaps in some among us. I at least know one to whom Nature could have added no one great or good Quality more than she hath bestowed on him.

Here then appear three distinct Characters; the Great, the Good, and the Great and Good.

The last of these is the *true Sublime* in Human Nature. That Elevation by which the Soul of Man, raising and extending itself above the Order of this Creation, and brighten'd with a certain Ray of Divinity, looks down on the Condition of Mortals. This is indeed a glorious Object, on which we can never gaze with too much Praise and Admiration. A perfect Work! the *Iliad* of Nature! ravishing and astonishing, and which at once fills us with Love, Wonder, and Delight.

The Second falls greatly short of this Perfection, and yet hath its Merit.

Our Wonder ceases; our Delight is lessened; but our Love remains; of which Passion, Goodness hath always appeared to me the only true and proper Object. On this Head I think proper to observe, that I do not conceive my Good Man to be absolutely a Fool or a Coward; but that he often partakes too little of Parts or Courage, to have any Pretensions to Greatness.

Now as to that Greatness which is totally devoid of Goodness, it seems to me in Nature to resemble the *False Sublime* in Poetry; whose Bombast is, by the ignorant and ill-judging Vulgar, often mistaken for solid Wit and Eloquence, whilst it is in Effect the very Reverse. Thus Pride, Ostentation, Insolence, Cruelty, and every Kind of Villany, are often construed into True Greatness of Mind, in which we always include an Idea of Goodness.

This Bombast Greatness then is the Character I intend to expose; and the more this prevails in and deceives the World, taking to itself not only Riches and Power, but often Honour, or at least the Shadow of it, the more necessary is it to strip the Monster of these false Colours, and shew it in its native Deformity: for by suffering Vice to possess the Reward of Virtue, we do a double Injury to Society, by encouraging the former, and taking away the chief Incentive to the latter. Nay, tho' it is, I believe, impossible to give Vice a true Relish of Honour and Glory, or tho' we give it Riches and Power, to give it the Enjoyment of them, yet it contaminates the Food it can't taste, and sullies the Robe which neither fits nor becomes it, 'till Virtue disdains them both.

. . . I come now to return Thanks to those Friends who have with uncommon Pains forwarded this Subscription:° for tho' the Number of my Subscribers be more proportioned to my Merit, than their Desire or Expectation, yet I believe I owe not a tenth Part to my own Interest. My Obligations on this Head are so many, that for Fear of offending any by Preference, I will name none. Nor is it indeed necessary, since I am convinced they served me with no Desire of a public Acknowledgement; nor can I make any to some of them, equal with the Gratitude of my Sentiments.

I cannot, however, forbear mentioning my Sense of the Friendship shewn me by a Profession of which I am a late and unworthy Member, and from whose Assistance I derive more than half the Names which appear to this Subscription.°

It remains that I make some Apology for the Delay in publishing these Volumes, the real Reason of which was, the dangerous Illness of one from whom I draw all the solid Comfort of my Life, during the greatest Part of this Winter.° This, as it is most sacredly true, so will it, I doubt not, sufficiently excuse the Delay to all who know me.

Indeed when I look a Year or two backwards, and survey the Accidents which have befallen me, and the Distresses I have waded through whilst I have been engaged in these Works,° I could almost challenge some Philosophy to myself, for having been able to finish them as I have; and however imperfectly that may be, I am convinced the Reader, was he acquainted with the whole, would want very little Good-Nature to extinguish his Disdain at any Faults he meets with.

But this hath dropt from me unawares: for I intend not to entertain my Reader with my private History: nor am I fond enough of Tragedy, to make myself the Hero of one.

However, as I have been very unjustly censured, as well on account of what I have not writ, as for what I have; I take this Opportunity to declare in the most solemn Manner, I have long since (as long as from *June* 1741) desisted from writing one Syllable in the *Champion*,° or any other public Paper; and that I never was, nor will be the Author of anonymous Scandal on the private History or Family of any Person whatever.

Indeed there is no Man who speaks or thinks with more Detestation of the modern Custom of Libelling. I look on the Practice of stabbing a Man's Character in the Dark, to be as base and as barbarous as that of stabbing him with a Poignard in the same Manner; nor have I ever been once in my Life guilty of it.

It is not here, I suppose, necessary to distinguish between Ridicule and Scurrility; between a Jest on a public Character, and the Murther of a private one.

My Reader will pardon my having dwelt a little on this Particular, since it is so especially necessary in this Age, when almost all the Wit we have is applied in this Way; and when I have already been a Martyr to such unjust Suspicion. Of which I will relate one Instance. While I was last Winter° laid up in the Gout, with a favourite Child dying in one Bed, and my Wife in a Condition very little better, on another, attended with other Circumstances, which served as very proper Decorations to such a Scene, I received a Letter from a Friend, desiring me to vindicate myself from two very opposite Reflections, which two opposite Parties thought fit to cast on me, *viz.* the one of writing in the *Champion*, (tho' I had not then writ in it for upwards of half a Year) the other, of writing in the *Gazetteer*, in which I never had the Honour of inserting a single Word.

To defend myself therefore as well as I can from all past, and to enter a Caveat against all future Censure of this Kind; I once more solemnly declare, that since the End of *June* 1741, I have not, besides *Joseph Andrews*, published one Word, except *The Opposition, A Vision. A Defence of the Dutchess of Marlborough's Book. Miss Lucy in Town*, (in which I had a very small share.)° And I do farther protest, that I will never hereafter

publish any Book or Pamphlet whatever, to which I will not put my Name.°
A Promise, which as I shall sacredly keep, so will it, I hope, be so far
believed, that I may henceforth receive no more Praise or Censure, to
which I have not the least Title.

And now, my good-natured Reader, recommending my Works to your
Candour, I bid you heartily farewell; and take this with you, that you may
never be interrupted in the reading these Miscellanies, with that Degree
of Heart-ach which hath often discomposed me in the writing them.

# APPENDIX 3

## ADVERTISEMENT TO THE 1754 EDITION

### ADVERTISEMENT
### FROM THE PUBLISHER TO THE READER

THE following Pages are the corrected Edition of a Book which was first published in the Year 1743.

That any personal Application could have ever been possibly drawn from them, will surprize all who are not deeply versed in the black Art (for so it seems most properly to be called) of deciphering Mens Meaning when couched in obscure ambiguous or allegorical Expressions: This Art hath been exercised more than once on the Author of our little Book, who hath contracted a considerable Degree of Odium from having had the Scurrillity of others imputed to him. The Truth is, as a very corrupt State of Morals is here represented, the Scene seems very properly to have been laid in *Newgate*: Nor do I see any Reason for introducing any Allegory at all; unless we will agree that there are, without those Walls, some other Bodies of Men of worse Morals than those within; and who have, consequently, a Right to change Places with the present Inhabitants.

To such Persons, if any such there be, I would particularly recommend the Perusal of the third Chapter of the fourth Book of the following History, and more particularly still the Speech of the Grave Man in Pages 195, 196 of that Book.°

# APPENDIX 4

## NOTE ON MONEY

In the eighteenth century the pound sterling was the unit of currency as it is in Britain today, but it was divided differently. There were twenty shillings in a pound, twelve pence in a shilling, and two halfpence, or four farthings, in a penny. The unit of five shillings was a crown, and two shillings and sixpence half a crown. Many larger transactions were carried out in guineas: a guinea was a gold coin with the value of one pound and one shilling.

It is impossible to offer an accurate estimate of what an eighteenth-century pound would be worth today, since direct comparisons of income and expenditure cannot be drawn, but the figures can be placed in some perspective by taking into account contemporary estimates that a servant might receive somewhere between £6 and £10 a year (plus board and 'perks'), a London labourer might earn 10 shillings a week or £25 a year, and a tradesman with a family and servants might expect to live comfortably on something like £350 a year.

# TEXTUAL NOTES

THERE were two major editions of *Jonathan Wild* in Henry Fielding's lifetime, in 1743 and 1754 (the 'second edition' published in 1743 uses the original text, with a new title-page). The 1754 edition was overseen by Fielding, and he made a large number of changes, some simply alterations of spellings and grammar, but others working cumulatively to alter the tone of the book. In particular the 1754 edition, in line with the disclaimer in the publisher's Advertisement (see Appendix 3) that satire on any individual was intended, downplays the emphasis on the 'Great Man' analogy by replacing many of the small capitals with italics, and makes some of the specific satirical points more general. In addition, Book II Chapter xii, 'Of PROVERBS', and Book IV Chapter ix, 'A very wonderful chapter indeed'—Mrs Heartfree's account of the more lurid part of her travels—were omitted in 1754. A full list of differences between the 1743 and 1754 editions is given in Hugh Amory's Documentary Appendix A: Collation of Substantive Sources, 1742–62, in *M3*, 252–94, and his Textual Introduction (pp. 197–224) explains these changes in scrupulous detail. The list below therefore is a selective one, containing all changes of roughly a line or longer, and any other changes which significantly alter or add to the sense of Fielding's narrative. Individual examples of the replacement of 'GREAT', 'GREATNESS' or 'GREAT MAN' by '*Great*', *Greatness*' or '*Great Man*' or 'great', 'greatness' or 'great Man', have not been noted.

4. 28 Book II Chapter xii: omitted in 1754, and subsequent chapters in Book renumbered.

5. 21 *Elogiums on Constables,* &c. *And new* ] *New.*

6. 2 Book IV Chapter ix: omitted in 1754, and subsequent chapters in Book renumbered.

8. 7–14 who, as he was . . . of ancient Heroes. ] to whom tho' Nature had given the greatest and most shining Endowments, she had not given them absolutely pure and without Allay. Tho' he had much of the Admirable in his Character, as much perhaps as is usually to be found in a Hero, I will not yet venture to affirm that he was entirely free from all Defects; or that the sharp Eyes of Censure could not spy out some little Blemishes lurking amongst his many great Perfections.

8. 30–9. 8 Now, tho' the Writer . . . he was to establish it. ] It seems therefore very unlikely that the same Person should possess them both; and yet nothing is more usual with Writers, who find many Instances of Greatness in their favorite Hero, than to make him a Compliment of Goodness into

the Bargain; and this, without considering that by such means they destroy the great Perfection called Uniformity of Character. In the Histories of *Alexander* and *Cæsar*, we are frequently, and indeed impertinently reminded of their Benevolence and Generosity, of their Clemency and Kindness. When the former had with Fire and Sword over-run a vast Empire, had destroyed the Lives of an immense Number of innocent Wretches, had scattered Ruin and Desolation like a Whirlwind, we are told, as an Example of his Clemency, that he did not cut the Throat of an old Woman, and ravish her Daughters, but was content with only undoing them. And when the mighty *Cæsar*, with wonderful Greatness of Mind, had destroyed the Liberties of his Country, and with all the Means of Fraud and Force had placed himself at the Head of his Equals, had corrupted and enslaved the greatest People whom the Sun ever saw; we are reminded, as an Evidence of his Generosity, of his Largesses to his Followers and Tools, by whose Means he had accomplished his Purpose, and by whose Assistance he was to establish it.

9. 35 MR. *Jonathan Wild*, or *Wyld* ] IT is the Custom of all Biographers, at their Entrance into their Work, to step a little backwards (as far, indeed, generally as they are able) and to trace up their Hero, as the Antients did the River *Nile*, till an Incapacity of proceeding higher puts an End to their Search.

WHAT first gave Rise to this Method, is somewhat difficult to determine. Sometimes I have thought that the Hero's Ancestors have been introduced as Foils to himself. Again, I have imagined it might be to obviate a Suspicion that such extraordinary Personages were not produced in the ordinary Course of Nature, and may have proceeded from the Author's Fear that if we were not told who their Fathers were, they might be in Danger, like Prince *Prettyman*, of being suppposed to have had none. Lastly, and perhaps more truly, I have conjectured that the Design of the Biographer hath been no more than to shew his great Learning and Knowledge of Antiquity. A Design to which the World hath probably owed many notable Discoveries, and indeed most of the Labours of our Antiquarians.

BUT whatever Original this Custom had, it is now too well established to be disputed. I shall therefore conform to it in the strictest Manner.

MR. *Jonathan Wild*, or *Wyld*, then

10. 23 *Edward* served ] *Edward* had a Grandson who served

11. 16–18 *Grace* was married . . . And *Honour* ] *Grace* was married to a Merchant of *Yorkshire*, who dealt in Horses. *Charity* took to Husband an eminent Gentleman, whose Name I cannot learn; but who was famous for so friendly a Disposition, that he was Bail for above a hundred Persons in one Year. He had likewise the remarkable Humour of walking in *Westminster-Hall* with a Straw in his Shoe. *Honour*

11. 22 *Ralph Hollow* ] *Scragg Hollow*, of *Hockley-in-the-Hole*,

11. 38 Intention. ] Intention, giving us warning as it were, and crying:

*—Venienti occurrite morbo.*

14. n. * Thievery. ] * This Word in the Cant Language signifies Thievery.

15. 10–11 whose Daughter, the Sister of this Gentleman . . . *Snap*, ] the Daughter of which *Geoffry* had inter-married with the *Wilds*. Mr. *Snap* the younger,

15. 24 10 *l.* ] 10 *l* or indeed 2 *l.*

17. 5 *Prigs*, that these ] *Prigs* * [Footnote: * Thieves], that in Reality it recommended them to each other: For a wise Man, that is to say a Rogue, considers a Trick in Life, as a Gamester doth a Trick at Play. It sets him on his Guard; but he admires the Dexterity of him who plays it. These therefore,

17. 12–13 the Friendship founded upon them. ] the Friendship founded upon them. Mutual Interest, the greatest of all Purposes, was the Cement of this Alliance, which nothing, of consequence, but superior Interest was capable of dissolving.

18. 21–2 buried in Oblivion; ] lost in a low Situation;

19. 6 better to be a prime Minister, or a common Thief? ] better to be a great Statesman, or a common Thief?

19. 36–7 a complete Ministerial Tool, or perhaps a prime Minister himself? ] a complete Tool of State, or perhaps a Statesman himself?

21. 22–3 the Fortunes of thousands? ] the Fortunes of Thousands, perhaps of a great Nation?

21. 27 having gently jogged him, ] having first picked his Pocket of three Shillings, then gently jogged him,

21. 33 BEING met the next Morning ] THE Count missed his Money the next Morning, and very well knew who had it; but, as he knew likewise how fruitless would be any Complaint, he chose to pass it by without mentioning it. Indeed it may appear strange to some Readers, that these Gentlemen, who knew each other to be Thieves, should never once give the least Hint of this Knowledge in all their Discourse together; but, on the contrary, should have the Words Honesty, Honour, and Friendship, as often in their Mouths as any other Men. This, I say, may appear strange to some; but those who have lived long in Cities, Courts, Gaols, or such Places, will perhaps be able to solve the seeming Absurdity.

WHEN our two Friends met the next Morning,

22. 29–30 a Million of Money ] a Hundred Pound

23. 1–15 as a further Pawn; . . . As, therefore, ] as a further Pawn.

THE Maid still remained inflexible, till *Wild* offered to lend his Friend a Guinea more, and to deposite it immediately in her Hands. This Reinforcement bore down the poor Girl's Resolution, and she faithfully promised to open the Door to the Count that Evening.

THUS did our young Hero not only lend his Rhetoric, which few People care to do without a Fee, but his Money too, a Sum which many a good Man would have made fifty Excuses before he would have parted with, to his Friend, and procured him his Liberty.

BUT it would be highly derogatory from the GREAT Character of *Wild*, should the Reader imagine he lent such a Sum to a Friend without the least View of serving himself. As, therefore,

23. 30 *Sneaking-Budge* ] *Sneaking-Budge* * [Footnote: * Shoplifting.]

27. 14 *Prig* ] * *Prig* [Footnote: * *A Thief.*]

27. 25 he laid his Hand to his Sword. ] he laid his Hand to his Pistol.

27. 35, 28. 7, 28.16 Sword ] Hanger

28. 9 the Sword ] your Blood

29. 1 Times ] Weeks

29. 7–17 the naked Breast to appear, and . . . red Stuff. ] the naked Breast to appear. Her Gown was a Sattin of a whitish Colour, with about a dozen little Silver Spots upon it, so artificially interwoven at great distance, that they looked as if they had fallen there by Chance. This flying open, discovered a fine yellow Petticoat beautifully edged round the Bottom with a narrow Piece of half Gold-Lace, which was now almost become Fringe; beneath this appeared another Petticoat stiffened with Whalebone, vulgarly called a Hoop, which hung six Inches at least below the other; and under this again appeared an under Garment of that colour which Ovid intends when he says,

—*Qui Color albus erat nunc est contrarius albo.*

29. 19–20 red Stuff . . . Under-Petticoat. ] yellow Stuff, which seemed to have been a Strip of her Upper-Petticoat.

30. 26 Apprentice to a Tallow-Chandler ] Clerk to an Attorney

32. 28–9 the debauching a Wife . . . or betraying, ] the debauching a Friend's Wife or Daughter, belying or betraying the Friend himself,

33. 2 Advantage. ] Advantage. He would often indeed say, that by the contrary party Men often made a bad Bargain with the Devil, and did his Work for nothing.

34. 20 *Doe* ] *Doe* * [Footnote: * This is a fictitious Name which is put into every Writ; for what Purpose the Lawyers best know.]

36. 22 *seedy* ] * *seedy* [Footnote: * poor.]

37. 7 reputable ] profitable

38. 20 whence, tho' he might ] whence (as he tells us in the Apology for his Life afterwards published * [Footnote: * Not in a Book by itself, in Imitation of some other such Persons, but in the Ordinary's Account, &c. where all the Apologies for the Lives of Rogues and Whores which have been published within these twenty Years should have been inserted.]) tho' he might

38. 32 Gentleman; who ] Gentleman at whom it was levelled, tho' it was not addressed to him. He

40. 10 because Men call him a Man of Honour ] because Men, I mean those of his own Party, or Gang, call him a Man of Honour

43. 7–8 when I consider . . . extirpate, then indeed ] when I consider whole Nations rooted out only to bring Tears into the Eyes of a Great MAN, not indeed because he hath extirpated so many, but because he had no more Nations to extirpate, then truly

44. 11 *Prime Ministers,* and *Prigs.* ] *Statesmen,* and *Prigs\** [Footnote: \* Thieves.]

45. 6 Pocket. ] Pocket. This Loss however he bore with great Constancy of Mind and with as great Composure of Aspect. To say truth, he considered the Money as only lent for a short Time, or rather indeed as deposited with a Banker.

45. 18 Action. ] Action; nor had he any more than two Shillings in his Pocket when he was attacked.

46. 16–19 his School-Fellow . . . accosted *Wild* ] his Companion, and indeed intimate Friend at School. It hath been thought that Friendship is usually nursed by Similitude of Manners; but the contrary had been the Case between these Lads: for whereas *Wild* was rapacious and intrepid, the other had always more Regard for his Skin than his Money; *Wild* therefore had very generously compassionated this Defect in his School-Fellow, and had brought him off from many Scrapes, into most of which he had first drawn him, by taking the Fault and Whipping to himself. He had always indeed been well paid on such Occasions; but there are a Sort of People, who, together with the best of the Bargain, will be sure to have the Obligation too on their Side; so it had happened here: for this poor Lad considered himself in the highest Degree obliged to Mr. *Wild,* and had contracted a very great Esteem and Friendship for him; the Traces of which, an Absence of many Years had not in the least effaced in his Mind. He no sooner knew *Wild* therefore, than he accosted him

47. 28–31 and the Obligations . . . who receives it. ] and the many Obligations he had received from him.

50. 26–7 six more; ] six more, making *Bagshot* Debtor for the whole ten;

52. 8–10 Brilliant, worth about five hundred Pounds . . . four thousand Pounds, ] Brilliant, worth about three hundred Pounds, and ordered a Necklace, Ear-rings, and Solitaire of the Value of three thousand more

52. 31–2 four hundred Pounds, which ] its full Value, and this

53. 9 four thousand five hundred Pounds ] two thousand eight hundred Pounds

55. 26–7 that Purse ] a Purse containing Bank Notes for 900 £.

58. 2 *Harwich.* ] *Dover.*

59. 9–11 rob those Subjects . . . and to reduce them ] rob those Subjects of their Liberties, who are content to sweat for the Luxury, and to bow down their Knees to the Pride of those very Princes? What but this can inspire them to destroy one half of their Subjects in order to reduce the rest

60. 37–61. 1 the four thousand Pound Note ] the Count's Note

61. 13 a Bank-Note ] a Bank-Note of 500 £.

61. 15–16  looking at the Back of it . . . and presently recollected ] looking at the
Number, immediately recollected

61. 37  The young Lady, ] Miss *Straddle*, for that was the young Lady,

62. 15–19  The Lady readily consented; and Mr *Wild* . . . then returned to his
Friend, ] The Lady readily consented: and advanced to embrace Mr. *Wild*,
who stept a little back and cry'd: "Hold, *Molly*; there are two other Notes of
200 £. each to be accounted for, where are they?" The Lady protested with
the most solemn Asseverations that she knew of no more; with which when
*Wild* was not satisfied, she cry'd: "I will stand Search." "That you shall,
answered *Wild*, and stand Strip too." He then proceeded to tumble and
search her, but to no Purpose, till at last she burst into Tears and declared
she would tell the Truth (as indeed she did;) she then confessed that she
had disposed of the one to *Jack Swagger*, a great Favourite of the Ladies,
being an *Irish* Gentleman, who had been bred Clerk to an Attorney, afterwards whipt out of a Regiment of Dragoons, and was then a Newgate-
Sollicitor and a Bawdy-House Bully; and as for the other, she had laid it all
out that very Morning in Brocaded Silks, and Flanders-Lace. With this
Account *Wild*, who indeed knew it to be a very probable one, was forced to
be contented; and now abandoning all further thoughts of what he saw was
irretrievably lost, he gave the Lady some further Instruction and then,
desiring her to stay a few Minutes behind him, he returned to his Friend,

62. 37–63. 3  However, he said . . . he would find out Miss *Straddle*, and
endeavour ] However, he told *Fierce* that he must certainly be mistaken in
that Point, of his having had no Acquaintance with Miss *Straddle*; but
added that he would find her out, and endeavour

64. 6–7  Apprentices, and loose ] Apprentices, Attorneys Clerks, and loose

64. 13  Eyes; between which, Jars and Animosities almost perpetually
arose. ] Eyes. The former were called *Cavaliers* and *Tory Rory Ranter Boys*,
&c. The latter went by the several Names of *Wags*, Round-Heads, Shake-
Bags, Old-Nolls, and several others. Between these continual Jars arose;
insomuch that they grew in time to think there was something essential in
their Differences, and that their Interests were incompatible with each
other, whereas, in Truth, the Difference lay only in the Fashion of their
Hats.

65. 33–4  the Note of four thousand five hundred Pound ] the Count's Note

68. 22  CHA. EASY. ] CHA. EASY.
*P.S.* I hope good Mrs. Heartfree and the dear little ones are well.

70. 3  MRS. *Heartfree*, who had ] THIS was a Degree of Impudence beyond
poor Mrs. *Heartfree*'s Imagination. Tho' she had

72. 30–1  Weaknesses in vulgar Life . . . to which ] Weaknesses in vulgar Life,
to which

73. 19–20  from him; adding, that if she had not Resolution enough ] from him,
for that the Moment he had lodged her safe in *Holland*, he would return,

procure her Husband his Liberty and bring him to her. I have been the unfortunate, the innocent Cause of all my dear *Tom's* Calamity, Madam, said he; and I will perish with him, or see him out of it. Mrs. *Heartfree* overflowed with Acknowledgments of his Goodness; but still begged for the shortest Interview with her Husband. *Wild* declared that a Minute's Delay might be fatal; and added, tho' with the Voice of Sorrow rather than of Anger, that if she had not Resolution enough

74. 16 modern. ] modern; a Resolution, which plainly proved him to have these two Qualifications so necessary to a Hero, to be superior to all the Energies of Fear or Pity.

76. 34–5 overwhelm him; which was indeed ] overwhelm him? nay this was indeed the fair Side of his Fortune, as it was

78. 1 80. 26 CHAP. XII ... Veracity before. ] omit. Subsequent chapters renumbered.

82. 5–6 Flattery should ... Bishop, ] Flattery, or half a dozen Houses in a Borough-Town, should denote a Judge, or a Bishop,

82. 11–14 to a Man uninspired, great Fortitude of Mind ... rather than the reverse; ] to a Mind uninspired, a Man of vast natural Capacity and much acquired Knowledge may seem by Nature designed for Power and Honour, rather than one remarkable only for the want of these, and indeed all other Qualifications;

82. 23 Swimmer ] Swimmer, and it being a perfect Calm,

83. 36 an Oar ] a Pair of Scullers

84. 3 an Oar ] Scullers

84. 21 Money. ] the Assistance of Money, or rather can most easily procure Money for the Supply of their Wants.

84. 34–6 Situation ... Conduct of our Hero; ] Situation;

85. 19–21 as Men are apt ... from malign Events; ] as the Mind is desirous (and perhaps wisely too) to comfort itself with drawing the most flattering Conclusions from all Events;

85. 27–8 she had acquainted him ... so doing. ] she had herself positively acquainted him she had her Husband's express Orders for so doing, and that she was gone to *Holland*.

87. 4 *Nanny* ] *Nancy*

89. 35–7 and which, if we understand ... Proofs of a supreme Being ] and to which the Road, if we understand it rightly, appears to have so few Thorns and Briers in it, and to require so little Labour and Fatigue from those who shall pass through it, that its Ways are truly said to be Ways of Pleasantness, and all its Paths to be those of Peace. If the Proofs of Christianity

90. 28 Stories ] Characters

91. 13 his Stock ] his Coat

91. 16 *Solomon's*, ] *Solomon*, or, if he was, did not, any more than some other Descendants of wise Men, inherit the Wisdom of his Ancestor,

92. 38  Neck ] Coat

93. 2  Dependence. ] Dependance, thus falling, as many Rogues do, a Sacrifice not to his Roguery, but to his Conscience.

95. 12–15  He determined . . . He went to *Newgate*, ] But however necessary this was, it seemed to be attended with such insurmountable Difficulties, that even our Hero for some time despaired of Success. He was greatly superior to all Mankind in the Steadiness of his Countenance, but this Undertaking seemed to require more of that noble Quality than had ever been the Portion of a Mortal. However at last he resolved to attempt it, and from his Success, I think, we may fairly assert, that what was said by the Latin Poet of Labour, that it *conquers all things*, is much more true when applied to Impudence.

   WHEN he had formed his Plan, he went to *Newgate*,

95. 20–1  on the other's Wife . . . Commands; and his Motive ] on the other's Wife; and his Motive

96. 22  WILD having thus, ] *Heartfree* however was soon curious enough to enquire how *Wild* had escaped the Captivity which his Wife then suffered. Here likewise he recounted the whole Truth, omitting only the Motive to the *French* Captain's Cruelty, for which he assigned a very different Reason, namely his Attempt to secure *Heartfree*'s Jewels. *Wild* indeed always kept as much Truth as was possible in every Thing; and this he said was turning the Cannon of the Enemy upon themselves.

   WILD having thus,

98. 8–9  possible, and promising to use all honest Means . . . took his Leave of his Friend for the present. ] possible, which he did with admirable Dexterity  This Method of getting tolerably well off, when you are repulsed in your Attack on a Mans Conscience may be styled the Art of Retreating in which the Politician as well as the General hath sometimes a wonderful Opportunity of displaying his great Abilities in his Profession.

   WILD having made this admirable Retreat, and argued away all Design of involving his Friend in the Guilt of Murther, concluded however that he thought him rather too scrupulous in not attempting his Escape; and then promising to use all such Means as the other would permit, in his Service, took his Leave for the Present.

98. 27  and much less [tho' much greater

99. 34–6  Honour, to which the other . . . utmost Fidelity; he dispatched him ] Honour; he dispatched him

102. 1–2  And if he could be . . . pleased. ] He asserted indeed, and swore so heartily, that had not *Wild* been so thoroughly convinced of the impregnable Chastity of the Lady, he might have suspected his Success; how ever, he was, by these means entirely satisfied of his Friend's Inclination towards his Mistress.

102. 7–8  of *Culprit*, nor a Reprieve to the Prisoner condemned, ] of a Prisoner at the Bar, nor the Sound of a Reprieve to one at the Gallows,

103. 3 Lady, and the truly ardent Passion ] Lady, who was thought to be possessed of every Qualification necessary to make the Marriage State happy; and from the truly ardent Passion

103. 31, 33 Sir *John* ] *Jack Strongbow*

105. 1–2 Batchelor; but that ] Batchelor; I have no Reason to complain of your Necessities: but that

112. 35 the Goodness of God is ] Almighty Goodness is by its own Nature

116. 20 *Elogiums on Constables*, &c. *And new Instances* ] *New Instances*

116. 35 The Constable ] One of the Officers

117. 7, 14 Constable ] Officer

117. 37 Command. ] Command; and this he swore to have been done after *Heartfree* had Notice of the Commission, and in order to bring it within that time, *Fireblood* as well as *Wild* swore that Mrs. *Heartfree* lay several Days concealed at *Wild*'s House before her Departure for *Holland*.

118. 5 for his Friend. ] for his Friend, which indeed, through the Humanity of the Keeper, he did at a cheap Rate.

121. 9 *Tuum.* ] *Tuum* which would cause endless Disputes, did not the Law happily decide them by converting both into *Suum*.

124. 10 Hero, however . . . Secret; for, he ] Hero received *Fireblood*'s Information with a very placid Countenance. He

124. 21–3 like Gunpowder, which, whoever uses . . . executing his mischievous Purpose ] like Gunpowder, must be used with Caution; since both are altogether as liable to blow up the Party himself who uses them, as to execute his mischievous Purpose

128. 35 observed in all ] observed to spring up in the People in all

129. 28–9 for Murther or as if . . . imaginable to his Prisoner. ] for Murther, or any other genteel Crime.

132. 20–1 the *Old Baily* must too sensibly ] the *Old Baily*, those Depredations of Justice, must too sensibly

133. 9 Party, ] Party, as had been before concerted,

133. 12 Side writing to one another, and representing ] Side representing

133. 15–18 for both Parties . . . Exaltation; what may seem ] for whereas the Supporters of *Johnson*, who was in Possession of the Plunder of *Newgate*, were admitted to some Share under their Leader; so the Abettors of *Wild* had, on his Promotion, the same Views of dividing some Part of the Spoil among themselves. It is no Wonder therefore they were both so warm on each Side. What may seem

133. 23 And such Quarrels ] And the poor Debtors re-echoed *the Liberties of Newgate*, which in the Cant Language signifies *Plunder*, as loudly as the Thieves themselves. In short, such Quarrels

134. 34 enslave; but ] enslave; or if he should, his own Destruction would be the only Consequence of his Attempt. But

137. 30 *The Arrival . . . with other* ] *Containing various*

141. 30–6 of the Reader. Indeed, we had Reason . . . every Author. ] of the Reader.

149. 23–5 Provision; for the Plain . . . than Sea Gulls. ] some Provision.

150. 4–7 CHAP. IX . . . *as he pleases* ] omit. Subsequent chapter numbers amended.

150. 9–153. 1 when one of the Sailors . . . skipt nimbly ] when one of the Sailors having skipt nimbly

155. 25–6 Pocket, before he recovered . . . began to do. ] Pocket.

156. 6 WE walked together ] WE left the Villain weltering in his Blood, tho' beginning to recover a little Motion, and walked together

165. 36–7 which Mr. *Wild* committed . . . after it had past. ] which was taken down in Short-hand by one who overheard it.

172. 19 Pride. ] Pride; in one Word FOOLISHNESS.

172. 24–5 a small Alteration . . . Text. The ] asserting what I have so fully proved; and what may indeed be inferred from the Text, That the

172. 30–1 put a Stop to his Reading at this time: ] waked Mr. *Wild* who was fast asleep, and put an End to the Sermon;

176. 19 instructive Moral. ] instructive Moral.
NARROW Minds may possibly have some Reason to be ashamed of going this Way out of the World, if their Consciences can fly in their Faces, and assure them they have not merited such an Honour; but he must be a Fool who is ashamed of being hanged who is not weak enough to be ashamed of having deserved it.

180. 19–20 *Jonathan Wild* the Great was, . . . hanged ] *Jonathan Wild the Great* after all his mighty Exploits was, what so few GREAT Men can accomplish—hanged

180. 36–8 Jewels for which . . . Money. ] Jewels which Miss *Straddle* had disposed of.

181. 30–7 *Hell;* nor is the World . . . the Creation. ] *Hell.* To say the Truth the World have this Reason at least to Honour such Characters as that of *Wyld*; that while it is in the Power of every Man to be perfectly Honest, not one in a thousand is capable of being a complete Rogue; and few indeed there are who if they were inspired with the vanity of Imitating our Hero would not after much fruitless Pains be obliged to own themselves Inferior to Mr. *Jonathan Wild* the GREAT.

# EXPLANATORY NOTES

## ABBREVIATIONS

All references to classical texts are taken from the relevant volume in the Loeb Classical Library (Cambridge: Harvard University Press) unless otherwise stated.

| | |
|---|---|
| *Amelia* | Henry Fielding, *Amelia* (1751), ed. Martin C. Battestin (Oxford: Oxford University Press, 1983). |
| M. and R. Battestin | Martin C. Battestin with Ruthe R. Battestin, *Henry Fielding: A Life* (London: Routledge, 1989, repr. 1993). |
| Beattie | J. M. Beattie, *Policing and Punishment in London, 1660–1750: Urban Crime and the Limits of Terror* (Oxford: Oxford University Press, 2001). |
| *Beggar's Opera* | John Gay, *The Beggar's Opera* (1728), ed. Edgar V. Roberts (Lincoln: University of Nebraska Press, 1969). |
| Brewer | *Brewer's Dictionary of Phrase & Fable* (London: Cassell, 1870; 14th edn. rev. Ivor H. Evans, 1989). |
| Cannon | *The Oxford Companion to British History*, ed. John Cannon (Oxford: Oxford University Press, 1997). |
| *Champion* | *Champion*, 1739–40, in Henry Fielding, *Contributions to the Champion and Related Writings*, ed. W. B. Coley (Oxford: Clarendon Press, 2003). |
| *Covent-Garden Journal* | Henry Fielding, *The Covent-Garden Journal, and a Plan of the Universal Register Office*, ed. Bertrand A. Goldgar (Oxford: Clarendon Press, 1988). |
| *David Simple* | Sarah Fielding, *The Adventures of David Simple* (1744), ed. Linda Bree (Harmondsworth: Penguin, 2002). |
| *Eovaai* | Eliza Haywood, *The Adventures of Eovaai, Princess of Ijaveo: A Pre-Adamitical History* (1736), ed. Earla Wilputte (Peterborough, Ont.: Broadview Press, 1999). |
| *Familiar Letters* | Sarah Fielding, *Familiar Letters between the Principal Characters in David Simple and Some Others* (2 vols., London, 1747). |
| Grose | *A Classical Dictionary of the Vulgar Tongue by Captain Francis Grose edited with a Biographical and Critical Sketch and an Extensive Commentary by Eric Partridge* |

|  | (London: Scholartis Press, 1931; London: Routledge & Kegan Paul, 3rd edn. 1963). The text of Grose is the 1796 edition. |
| HF | Henry Fielding |
| *History of Charles XII* | *The History of Charles XII. King of Sweden, by Mr. de Voltaire, trans. from the French* (London, 1733). |
| Howson | Gerald Howson, *Thief-Taker General: The Rise and Fall of Jonathan Wild* (London: Hutchinson, 1970). |
| Jacob | Giles Jacob, *New Law Dictionary* (London, 1725). |
| Johnson | Samuel Johnson, *A Dictionary of the English Language* (1755), ed. Anne McDermott on CD-Rom (Cambridge: Cambridge University Press, 1996). |
| *Joseph Andrews* | Henry Fielding, *Joseph Andrews and Shamela* (1741–2), ed. Douglas Brooks-Davies, rev. with new introduction by Thomas Keymer (Oxford: Oxford University Press, 1999). |
| JW | the fictional Jonathan Wild |
| *M1* | Henry Fielding, *Miscellanies, Volume One* (1743), ed. Henry Knight Miller (Oxford: Clarendon Press, 1972). |
| *M2* | Henry Fielding, *Miscellanies, Volume Two* (1743), ed. Bertrand A. Goldgar and Hugh Amory (Oxford: Clarendon Press, 1993). |
| *M3* | Henry Fielding, *Miscellanies, Volume Three* (1743), ed. Bertrand A. Goldgar and Hugh Amory (Oxford: Clarendon Press, 1997). |
| *NCD* | *New Canting Dictionary* (London, 1725). |
| *OED* | *Oxford English Dictionary* on CD-Rom (Oxford: Oxford University Press, 1998). |
| *Pamela* | Samuel Richardson, *Pamela: Or, Virtue Rewarded* (1741), ed. Thomas Keymer and Alice Wakely (Oxford: Oxford University Press, 2001). |
| *Paradise Lost* | John Milton, *Paradise Lost* (2nd edn., 1674), in *Milton: Poetical Works*, ed. Douglas Bush (Oxford: Oxford University Press, 1966, repr. 1969). |
| Partridge | Eric Partridge, *A Dictionary of the Underworld* (1949, 3rd edn. 1968). |
| Pope | *The Poems of Alexander Pope: A One Volume Edition of the Twickenham Pope*, ed. John Butt (London: Methuen, 1963, repr. 1965). |
| Rawson | Claude Rawson, *Henry Fielding and the Augustan Ideal under Stress* (London: Routledge & Kegan Paul, 1972; repr. Atlantic Highlands, NJ: Humanities Press, 1991). |
| Ribeiro | Aileen Ribeiro, *Dress in Eighteenth-Century Europe, 1715–1789* (New Haven: Yale University Press, 2002). |

| | |
|---|---|
| *Select Trials* | *Select Trials at the Sessions-House in the Old-Bailey* (4 vols., London, 1742; repr. in facsimile, 2 vols., New York: Garland, 1985). |
| SF | Sarah Fielding |
| *Shamela* | Henry Fielding, *Joseph Andrews and Shamela*, ed. Douglas Brooks-Davies, rev. with new introduction by Thomas Keymer (Oxford: Oxford University Press, 1999). |
| *Spectator* | *The Spectator* (1711–14), ed. Donald F. Bond (Oxford: Oxford University Press, 5 vols., 1965). |
| Swift | *The Basic Writings of Jonathan Swift*, sel. Claude Rawson (New York: Random House, 2002). |
| *Tatler* | *The Tatler* (1709–11), ed. Donald F. Bond (3 vols., Oxford: Oxford University Press, 1987). |
| *Tom Jones* | Henry Fielding, *The History of Tom Jones: A Foundling*, ed. Martin C. Battestin and Fredson Bowers (Oxford: Oxford University Press, 1977). |
| Tilley | Morris Palmer Tilley, *A Dictionary of the Proverbs in England in the Sixteenth and Seventeenth Centuries* (Ann Arbor: University of Michigan Press, 1950). |
| *Vernoniad* | *The Vernoniad* (1741), in Henry Fielding, *Contributions to the Champion and Related Writings*, ed. W. B. Coley (Oxford: Clarendon Press, 2003). |
| *Voyage to Lisbon* | Henry Fielding, *The Journal of a Voyage to Lisbon* (1755), ed. Tom Keymer (Harmondsworth: Penguin, 1996). |

7 *The Life . . . the Great*: in 1743 and 1754 the title-page read *The Life of Mr. Jonathan Wild the Great*, while the title above Book I Chapter i read *The History of the Life of the Late Mr. Jonathan Wild the Great*. The title-page version is the title by which the novel is usually known, and so, although Hugh Amory chose the Book I title for the Wesleyan edition of the novel, the title-page version has been used throughout here.

*Shewing . . . Great Men*: the idea expressed throughout this chapter that the lives of prominent individuals or 'great men' are worth reading because they provide examples of behaviour to imitate or avoid was a commonplace of the time. In the introductory Discourse to *The History of Charles XII*, Voltaire wrote of 'those Princes who have made no figure either in peace or war; who have neither been remarkable for great virtues, nor vices; their lives furnish so little matter either for imitation, or instruction, that they are not worthy of notice' (*History of Charles XII*, p. v). 'Greatness' is given a particular political emphasis from the outset by the capitalization of the term. As Jonathan Swift wrote, in 'On Poetry: A Rhapsody' (1733?),

> To Statesmen would you give a Wipe,
> You print it in *Italick Type*.
> When Letters are in vulgar Shapes,
> 'Tis ten to one the Wit escapes;
> But when in CAPITALS exprest,

The dullest Reader smoaks a Jest.
(Swift, *Works* (Dublin, 1735), ii. 437, lines 95–100)

In the 1754 edition HF altered many of the references to great man, great men, and greatness from small capitals to italic or Roman print—see Textual Notes p. 227.

7 *not only . . . usefully instructed*: most literary work in the eighteenth century claimed that it intended to fulfil the dictum of the classical poet and critic Horace that 'Poets aim at giving either profit or delight, or at combining the giving of pleasure with some useful precepts of life . . . The man who has managed to blend profit with delight wins everyone's approbation, for he gives his reader pleasure at the same time as he instructs him' (*On the Art of Poetry*, lines 333–4, 343–4, in Aristotle/ Horace/Longinus, *Classical Literary Criticism*, trans. T. S. Dorsch (Harmondsworth: Penguin, 1965), 90–1). In the Preface to the *Miscellanies* HF wrote that Wild suffered the fate he deserved, and 'As I believe it is not easy to teach a more useful Lesson than this, if I have been able to add the pleasant to it, I might flatter myself with having carried every Point' (*MI*, 11, see Appendix 2).

*a consummate Knowledge . . . perplexed Mazes*: compare HF's claim that the 'Merit' of his sister Sarah Fielding's novel *The Adventures of David Simple* resided in 'a vast Penetration into human Nature, a deep and profound Discernment of all the Mazes, Windings and Labyrinths, which perplex the Heart of Man' (Preface to 2nd edition, 1744, reproduced in *The Adventures of David Simple*, ed. Linda Bree (Penguin: Harmondsworth, 2002), 462).

*Plutarch, Nepos, Suetonius*: writers of famous works of biography in classical times: Plutarch (*c*.46–*c*.120) wrote *Parallel Lives*, forty-six portraits of great men of earlier times, presented in pairs of Greek and Roman figures sharing some resemblance; Cornelius Nepos (*c*.110–*c*.24 BC) wrote *Lives of Famous Men*, a collection of biographical studies of which twenty-five survive; Gaius Suetonius Tranquillus (*c*.70–*c*.130) wrote *The Lives of the Caesars*, a set of twelve imperial biographies.

8 *an Aristides or a Brutus, a Lysander or a Nero*: a carefully balanced quartet, consisting of a negative and a positive example of a Greek and Roman leader respectively. Aristides (*c*.530–*c*.468 BC), an Athenian statesman known as 'the Just', was the subject of praise in biographies by both Plutarch and Nepos. Marcus Junius Brutus (*c*.85–42 BC) was one of the subjects of Plutarch's *Lives*, as an example of a virtuous Roman senator and war leader; HF cites him in the Preface to the *Miscellanies* as an example of a man both great and good (*MI*, 12). The Greek political leader and naval commander Lysander (d. 395 BC) was heavily criticized by both Plutarch and Nepos, for avarice and treachery among other vices. The life and 'shameful and criminal deeds' of the notoriously cruel and decadent Nero Claudius Caesar (37–68) was recounted by Suetonius in *The Lives of the Caesars*.

*Weakness of modern . . . Greatness of ancient Heroes*: HF is alluding to the ongoing debate, peaking in the late seventeenth and early eighteenth century, about the comparative merits of the Moderns and their counterparts in the classical, or Ancient, world. See for example Jonathan Swift's satire, *A Full and True Account of the Battel fought Last Friday between the Antient and the Modern Books in St. James's Library* (written in 1690s, published 1704).

*to confound the Ideas of Greatness and Goodness . . . Goodness in removing it from them*: the satiric comparison between 'greatness', represented mostly by Jonathan Wild, and 'goodness' in the form of Heartfree, runs throughout the narrative. In the Preface to the *Miscellanies* HF argues seriously and at length that it is 'a great Error, and no less than a Mistake of the Capacity for the Will' to 'confound the Ideas of Goodness and Greatness together, or rather include the former in our Idea of the latter . . . In Reality, no Qualities can be more distinct' (*M1*, 11; see Appendix 2). The poems 'Of True Greatness' and 'Of Good-nature' open the first volume of *Miscellanies*, and much of 'A Journey from this World to the Next' (*M2*, 1–128) explores the same comparison. HF's definition of 'Great' in 'A modern Glossary' was: 'Applied to a Thing, signifies Bigness; when to a Man, often Littleness, or Meanness' (*Covent-Garden Journal*, 4, 14 January 1752, p. 36). The ironic association of 'greatness' and 'wickedness' was not original: *The Whole Duty of Man* (1658), a widely used handbook of morality in the late seventeenth and eighteenth centuries, was one of many sources to suggest that 'there is nothing so horrid, which a Man that eagerly seeks greatness will stick at; Lying, Perjury, Murder, or anything will down with him, if they seem to tend to his advancement' (1702 edition, Sunday VII. 3, p. 163); and an anonymous correspondent to *Mist's Weekly Journal* wrote of Alexander that 'we often mention with Wonder, the extensive Conquests of the *Macedonian* Youth, but never condemn his unbounded and destructive Ambition' (*A Collection of Miscellany Letters, selected out of Mist's Weekly Journal* (2 vols., 1722), i. 257).

9 *for Instance . . . by whose Assistance he was to establish it*: Plutarch describes, as an example of 'savagery', in Thebes that some Thracians broke into the house of Timocleia, a respectable woman; when their leader tried to rape her she tricked him into looking down a well and pushed him in. When Alexander heard of this he was impressed with her dignity and said she and her children could go free (Plutarch, 'Alexander', s. 12). Caesar 'pardoned many of those who had fought against him, and to some he even gave honours and offices besides' (Plutarch, 'Caesar', s. 57).

*a Great Man*: from the 1720s to the 1740s the term 'Great Man' was strongly connected with the figure of Sir Robert Walpole, chief minister of Britain from 1721 to 1742, and was frequently used by critics of Walpole to allude to him without mentioning his name; see among many examples Eliza Haywood's account of the villainous Ochihatou in *The*

*Adventures of Eovaai* (1736, reissued in 1741 as *The Unfortunate Princess; or, The Ambitious Statesman*), which begins 'This great Man was born of a mean Extraction', and the reference to 'a certain Great Man' in contemporary politics in *An Apology for the Life of Mr. T.— C.—, Comedian* (1740), issued anonymously and once attributed to HF. Walpole, a man of relatively humble background who achieved great wealth and power while continuing to cultivate his image as a non-establishment figure, was widely attacked throughout his period in office by a fragmented political opposition and by most of the prominent literary figures of the day, including Alexander Pope, Jonathan Swift, John Gay, and latterly HF; in addition to particular political and party concerns they resented what they saw as his corrupt activities. Walpole was widely believed to have used his extensive powers of patronage exclusively to enrich himself, his family and supporters, including pro-government writers. Walpole subscribed for ten sets of the *Miscellanies* on royal paper at two guineas each.

9 *Giving . . . Purpose*: then, as now, biographies of famous people often began with a history of the subject's family, and much attention was paid to illustrious ancestors—for example, section 2 of Plutarch's 'Alexander' establishes that Alexander was descended from the hero Heracles. In 1754 HF inserted a lengthy comment on the practice, and concluded 'it is now too well established to be disputed. I shall therefore conform to it in the strictest Manner.' HF might have been parodying particularly the pamphlet *Memoirs of the Family of Walpole* (1732), later incorporated into *A Brief and True History of Sir Robert Walpole and his Family* (1738), in which 34 of the pamphlet's 78 pages were devoted to Sir Robert's ancestors.

*Wild . . . Name*: HF spelt the name 'Wyld' in the Prospectus to the *Miscellanies*. Wild's early biographers mostly spelt his name 'Wild' or 'Wilde', and his father's name 'John Wyld or Wyldie' (Howson, 10). Thanks to his illiteracy, the fictional JW spells his own name even more haphazardly (see III. vi). Spelling variations in names were however common at this time: HF's own family spelt their name variously as Fielding, Feilding and ffielding.

10 *Hengist . . . Purses*: according to John Milton's account which later appeared in *A Complete History of England* (1706), a copy of which HF owned, Hengist the Saxon invaded Britain after 458, invited the Britons to a feast, and—to the watchword of '*Nemet eour Saxes*, that is, *Draw your Daggers*'—slaughtered 300 of them (i. 32). HF's Anglo-Saxon adaptation is accurate.

*Henry . . . Inventor*: Hubert de Burgh (*c*.1175–1243) was chief minister to Henry III from 1219 to 1232. He was one of many figures from history used by the Opposition as an analogy with Walpole in the ability to line his own pockets at the expense of the state. See e.g. *Fog's Journal*, 14 September 1734, reprinted in *Gentleman's Magazine*, 4 (September 1734), 485, in which Hubert de Burgh, described as Henry's 'prime minister', is condemned as a covetous cheat.

*Edward . . . Companion*: the character of Sir John Falstaff, a rogue befriended by Prince Henry and then rejected when the prince becomes Henry V (Shakespeare, *1*, *2 Henry IV* and *Henry V*), is said to be distantly based on a real-life Sir John Oldcastle; but the fictional Falstaff took on a life of his own: 'The Life of Sir John Falstaff' is the opening narrative in *A General History of the Lives and Adventures of the most Famous Highwaymen, Murderers, Street-Robbers &c.* by 'Capt. Charles Johnson' (1734). In 1754 HF revised the text here to improve the chronology, making it Edward's grandson who served Falstaff, but since Henry V came to the throne in 1413 the timing from Langfanger is still implausible.

*Civil Wars*: armed conflict between royalist and parliamentary forces lasted from 1642 to 1651; Charles I, who had come to the throne in 1625, was executed in 1649.

*Hind*: James (not John, as mentioned below) Hind (executed 1652) was a famous highwayman and thief; many accounts of his life survive, including in *Lives and Adventures of the most Famous Highwaymen*.

11  *contrary to the Law of Arms . . . Murder*: that is, executed by legal process rather than killed by military action. Trial by jury had been well established in England since medieval times.

*James*: 1743 has 'Edward' here, which was corrected by Hugh Amory in preparing the present text: Amory suggests HF had become confused with the earlier Edwards in the family. However, he also points out that Walpole's grandfather was called Edward, and an allusion of some kind may be intended. JW's father is named Jonathan, as Sir Robert's father was named Robert.

*soliciting . . . Newgate*: Newgate prison, 'the most famous and forbidding prison in the land' (Cannon), occupied the gatehouse which spanned the junction of Holborn and Newgate streets in the city of London and housed those accused of a wide variety of crimes while they awaited trial (prison sentences were not a usual form of punishment, though debtors were effectively sentenced to spend their lives in prison unless they could pay off their creditors). Edward was an attorney, exploiting prisoners while claiming to act on their behalf. HF criticized attorneys' activities in Newgate through the character of Murphy in *Amelia* (1751): see for example Murphy's suggestions that witnesses be bribed (I. x).

*eminent . . . Captives*: the 'Ordinary of Newgate' was the chaplain of the prison, who was responsible for giving the prisoners religious instruction, and preparing condemned prisoners for death. The office was widely satirized and criticized in the eighteenth century; Peter Linebaugh's description of the holders of the office in the eighteenth century, in 'The Ordinary of Newgate and his *Account*' in *Crime in England: 1550–1800*, ed. J. S. Cockburn (London: Methuen, 1977), 248–9, suggests that criticism may have been justified.

*Geoffry Snap Gent. . . . Fortune*: a snap was 'a greedy Fellow' (Johnson), a sharper or swindler, or a 'bite' or capture (*NCD*); snapt meant 'taken or caught' (Grose). Mr Snap is a bailiff, appointed by the high sheriff who represented royal authority in London and the county of Middlesex bordering it to the north. Bailiffs paid a fee in return for their appointment, and recovered this and gained additional income through 'every means—including robbery, murder, blackmail and the arresting of innocent people for wholly fictitious debts' (Howson, 12); debtors were kept in bailiffs' private prisons before going to court, and during this period were at the bailiff's mercy for such matters as food and visits, all of which were subject to heavy charges. HF criticized bailiffs elsewhere, notably in *Amelia*, where Mr Bondum 'was reckoned an honest and good Sort of Man in his Way, and had no more Malice against the Bodies in his Custody, than a Butcher hath to those in his' (VIII. i).

11  *Thomas . . . American Colonies*: that is, he was transported as a convicted criminal, to America, probably to Maryland or the Carolinas.

*Gentleman . . . Horses*: probably a horse-thief. Men of the large northern county of Yorkshire had a reputation for shrewdness and sharp practice; 'to come Yorkshire over one' is to bamboozle or overreach someone (Brewer).

*eminent . . . Alley*: a number of stock-jobbers and brokers had been evicted from the Royal Exchange in 1698; they conducted their often disreputable business in nearby Exchange Alley. In 1754 HF revised this section to indicate that Charity married an 'eminent Gentleman . . . who was famous for so friendly a Disposition, that he was Bail for above a hundred Persons in one Year. He had likewise the remarkable Humour of walking in *Westminster-Hall* with a Straw in his Shoe.' (False witnesses identified themselves by wearing straws in the buckles of their shoes while they waited by the courts for employment (Howson, 141).)

*Honour . . . all who would accept of them*: orange-sellers at the theatre generally had a reputation for being loose in their morals, as in real life Nell Gwyn, mistress of Charles II, or in fiction Shamela's mother in HF's 1741 burlesque of Richardson's *Pamela* (1740): *Shamela*, 314.

*Alma Mater*: 'bounteous mother', a title given by the Romans to several goddesses, especially to Ceres, the goddess of corn and harvests, and Cybele, the goddess of Nature and natural growth.

12  *Astyages . . . Asia*: the dream is described in Herodotus, *The Histories*, 1. 108. Astyages tries to have his baby grandson killed, but fails, and the prophecy comes true (1. 109–30).

*Hecuba . . . Flames*: this dream of Hecuba, Queen of Troy, is described by Cicero in *De Divinatione*, 1. 21 in a quotation from an unknown poet. Urged to have the baby, Paris, killed, Hecuba instead abandoned him on nearby Mount Ida; years later Paris eloped with Helen, wife of Menelaus, King of Sparta, prompting the Greeks' siege of Troy.

*Mercury . . . Acquaintance*: Mercury was the god of thieves; Priapus was the god of fertility, and was often depicted with enormous genitals. The fact that Jonathan Wild Snr had no acquaintance with Priapus might imply that he is not the father of JW; the real-life Jonathan Wild was one of five children (Howson, 10) whereas HF's Jonathan seems to be an only child. The quibble over pronunciation echoes the discussion as to how to pronounce the name of Richardson's Pamela, which the Pedlar, telling Pamela's history, mentions in *Joseph Andrews* (IV. xii); a similar quibble over the pronunciation of Attalus, King of Pergamum, is raised by Parson Adams (*Joseph Andrews*, II. iv).

*Birth . . . 1665*: traditionally the birth of heroes was accompanied by significant external events; Alexander, for example, was said to have been born on the day when the temple of Artemis at Ephesus was destroyed by fire (Plutarch, 'Alexander', 3). In fact no one single day is associated with the outbreak of the Plague, which spread rapidly through the city of London in the early months of 1665. The real Jonathan Wild was born in Wolverhampton about 1682 (*Select Trials*, ii. 228), and was baptized there on 6 May 1683 (Howson, 10). The fictional JW's birthdate of 1665 places the main action of the novel in the early 1690s but the narrative is not chronologically consistent.

*House . . . Covent-Garden*: a round-house was 'the constable's prison, in which disorderly persons, found in the street, are confined' (Johnson); Covent Garden, where the fruit and vegetable market was held by day, housed a large number of brothels and was notorious for disorderly behaviour at night.

*Titus Oates*: Oates (1649–1705) was notorious as a liar and criminal. Once an Anglican priest, he embraced Catholicism in 1677, and his false evidence of a Catholic plot designed to overthrow the Protestant establishment in 1678 resulted in the execution of innocent people. He was exposed, and found guilty of perjury in 1685, but was later pardoned.

*Th . . . Wild*: presumably young Jonathan finds them easy to pronounce because they are the first letters of the word 'thief'.

13  *of his own Head*: on his own initiative.

*making his Exercise*: the eighteenth-century school curriculum for sons of gentlemen consisted largely of Bible study and working through formal exercises in Latin and Greek texts and grammar.

*Gradus ad Parnassum . . . Parnassus*: a popular Latin dictionary used in schools in the late seventeenth and early eighteenth centuries, containing quotations, epithets, and synonyms. Parnassus was a mountain in central Greece, anciently sacred to Apollo and the Muses; its name became a symbol for achievement in literature, especially poetry.

*Gradus . . . Gallows*: 'patibulum' is Latin for 'gibbet'.

*learned . . . him*: Mist's *Weekly Journal*, 12 June 1725, noted the real JW's fondness for the classics in translation, and his notion, derived from Tacitus, that the Roman period was 'fine Times to get Money'.

14  *Achilles . . . Money*: Homer states that Achilles had once caught Isus and

Antiphus as they looked after their sheep on Mount Ida and had tied them up with willow twigs, but afterwards accepted ransom and released them (*Iliad*, 11. 104–6). JW ignores the fact that the story is told on the occasion of the violent death of the two young men at the hands of Agamemnon.

14 *Priggism*: this and a similar use in IV. iii are the only cited passages in the *OED* under 'priggism' meaning professional thievery or roguery.

*Nestor . . . Eleans*: as the Greek army faces disaster Nestor contrasts his present decline with a long-ago successful raid against the Eleans, during which he and his men rounded up an extensive 'booty . . . fifty herds of cattle, as many flocks of sheep, as many droves of swine, as many roving herds of goats, and chestnut horses, one hundred and fifty, all mares and many of them had foals at the teat' (*Iliad*, 11. 670–81).

*Story . . . severe*: King Evander tells of 'half-human' Cacus, offspring of Vulcan, who, 'his wits wild with frenzy, that no crime or craft might prove to be left undared or untried', stole four bulls and four heifers, dragging them to his cave by their tails to prevent their hooves leaving revealing tracks. Hercules heard one of the cows lowing, wrenched away the stone protecting Cacus' cave, and 'seizes him in a knot-like embrace, and, close entwined, throttles him till the eyes burst forth, and the throat is drained of blood' (*Aeneid*, 8. 185–267).

*Alexander . . . Parallels*: such parallels were often drawn in the early eighteenth century, including by Alexander Pope in *Essay on Man*:

> Look next on Greatness; say where Greatness lies?
> 'Where, but among the Heroes and the Wise?'
> Heroes are much the same, the point's agreed,
> From Macedonia's madman to the Swede;
> The whole strange purpose of their lives, to find
> Or make, an enemy of all mankind! (IV. 217–22)

Alexander the Great, one of the most famous military rulers of the classical world—'that Mad-man Alexander', as HF calls him in the *Champion*, 17 November 1739, in one of many critical references— was widely regarded as a criminal conqueror. Charles XII of Sweden (1682–1718), an expansionist ruler who attacked Denmark, Russia, Norway and Poland at various times, and who was killed in battle, was a controversial figure, for a time highly praised by English Jacobites and Tories, and condemned by Whigs including HF; details of his life were well known in England through Voltaire's biography (1731, see note to p. 7). In 1740 HF was responsible for the translation of Gustavus Adlerfeld's *The Military History of Charles XII, King of Sweden*. He also described Charles as 'the last Hero, except the present *Persian* Madman, who hath infested, or I hope will, infest the Earth' (*Champion*, 3 May 1740). HF satirizes Alexander's heroism in 'A Dialogue between Alexander the Great and

Diogenes the Cynic' (*M1*, 226–35) and pairs Alexander and Charles XII in the Palace of Death in 'A Journey from this World to the Next' (*M2*, 23). The reference to Charles XII here is anachronistic: since the fictional JW had been born in 1665, his schooldays would have taken place before Charles was born. See Introduction, pp. xxi–xxiii.

*Czar's Retreat . . . Country*: possibly referring to the retreat of Peter the Great after Charles XII's victory at Narva (1700) in the Great Northern War (1700–21). According to Defoe's account it was Peter who invited the hard-working inhabitants of other countries 'to come and settle in his Dominions' (Daniel Defoe, *An Impartial History of the Life and Actions of Peter Alexowitz, the Present Czar of Muscovy* (London, 1723), 132).

*Spanish . . . Play*: Mateo Alemán's picaresque novel, *The Life of Guzmán de Alfarache, or the Spanish Rogue*, had been popular since its first English translation, by James Mabbe as *The Rogue*, in 1622. HF may be referring to any one of a number of later, freer, translations or abridgements, including the anonymous early eighteenth-century *The Spanish Rogue; or, The Life of Guzman de Alfarache* (printed for Thomas Smith, n.d.), or *The Life of Guzman d'Alfarache; or, The Spanish Rogue* (1707). The novel in its various versions contains similar situations and incidents to some in *Jonathan Wild*, including the fact of a rogue-hero, his cuckoldry and imprisonment, his being robbed by a woman during amorous caresses, and his finding that a casket of fake jewels has been substituted for true gems. Thomas Otway's farce *The Cheats of Scapin*, adapted from Molière's play *Les Fourberies de Scapin* (1671) and first performed in 1676, remained popular until well into the eighteenth century, including in ballad-opera versions. In both works the rogue-hero is an attractive figure. A report in *Mist's Weekly Journal* suggests that the real Jonathan Wild possessed and valued '*The English Rogue*' among other books including *Machiavel, The Lives of the Highwaymen* and Tacitus (12 June, 1725).

15 *well warranted*: properly authorized, given authority; also possibly having plenty of warrants for the arrest of La Ruse. The phrase is repeated on p. 251.

*La Ruse*: 'la ruse' in French means 'cunning'; 'faire une ruse' is to commit an act of trickery.

*Seconds*: supporters; the word was used for those supporting the 'men of honour' fighting a duel.

*the Law . . . mistaken*: HF accurately describes the situation whereby debtors for small sums could be apprehended and then required to meet expenses which multiplied their debt many times over, and made discharge increasingly difficult. HF frequently criticized the laws relating to debt, which he argued 'do put it in the Power of every proud, ill-natur'd, cruel, rapacious Creditor to satisfy his Revenge, his Malice, or his Avarice this Way on any Person who owes him a few Shillings more than he can pay him' (*Champion*, 19 February 1740). In the second edition HF made the point even more forcibly by adding after the reference to a debt of £10, 'or even 2 *l*.'.

15 *on his Parole*: in full, on his parole of honour, that is, on his word of honour that, if released, he would return to custody under stated conditions.

16 *Whisk and Swabbers*: whist—the word means 'silent', emphasizing the way in which it was thought proper to play—is a card-game for four players, divided into pairs. It was widely played among the lower classes in the seventeenth century and became fashionable in the early eighteenth, as part of a wider craze for gambling. 'Whisk and swabbers' was a form of the game which favoured players holding the ace of hearts, knave of clubs, ace and deuce of trumps.

*Cousin-German*: marriage of first cousins had been acceptable to the church since the sixteenth century, but could still arouse social disapproval. In fact Jonathan and Laetitia are related not by blood but by marriage, since Jonathan's father's brother married Laetitia's father's sister. HF's reference first to Jonathan's uncle's marriage to Editha Snap being without issue and then to Laetitia's mother being Mr Snap's 'second Lady' may indicate some confusion in his mind between the two marriages.

*Men . . . can*: freemasonry developed in the seventeenth century and by the early eighteenth century was well established: in 1717 a 'grand lodge' was formed in London, with a new constitution and ritual, and system of secret signs, including those by which members could recognize each other.

*in the Fact*: legal term for 'in the act'.

17 *pack the Cards*: arrange or shuffle the cards for the purposes of cheating.

*Prigs*: cant term for 'thieves', as HF's note to the 1754 edition confirmed.

18 *I have often . . . himself did*: in the *Champion* HF quotes approvingly 'Sir *William Temple*'s Observation, that the World hath produced a thousand equal to *Alexander*, but scarce one capable of writing an *Iliad*' (27 November 1739).

*the same Genius . . . a Thief*: the main article in *Mist's Weekly Journal*, 12 June 1725, concerns 'the Life of that celebrated Statesman and Politician, the late Mr. *Jonathan Wild*' and argues 'a Person may be a Rogue, and yet be a great Man'. 'H.D.' promises that in reading Wild's biography his readers 'will meet with a System of Politicks unknown to *Machiavel* . . . [and] deeper Stratagems and Plots form'd by a Fellow without Learning or Education, than are to be met with in the Conduct of the greatest Statesmen, who have been at the Heads of Governments' (see p. 185).

*Tower-Hill . . . Tyburn*: aristocrats found guilty of major crimes were usually beheaded on the block at Tower Hill; common criminals were hanged from the gallows at Tyburn, near where Marble Arch now stands at the west end of Oxford Street.

19 *Pewter* ... *Silver Dish*: in the early eighteenth century ordinary people ate and drank from pewter plates and mugs; use of silver was the prerogative of the wealthy.

*prime Minister*: although a number of chief ministers in other European countries might be described as 'Prime Minister', in Britain 'the title of first prime minister is usually given to Sir Robert Walpole, though the term was derogatory and he denied it' (Cannon, s.v. prime minister). For example, in one of her learned notes to 'The History of Ochihatou, Prime Minister of Hypotofa', a blatant satire on Walpole, Haywood writes that 'our Author might have saved himself the Trouble of particularizing in what manner *Ochihatou* apply'd the Nation's Money; since he had said enough in saying, he was a *Prime Minister*, to make the Reader acquainted with his Conduct in that Point' (*Eovaai*, 64). HF used the term 'Prime Minister' to refer to Walpole, as in the *Champion*, 8 May 1740.

*it was better* ... *Heaven*: a version of Satan's assertion, 'Better to reign in hell than serve in heav'n' (*Paradise Lost*, 1. 263), given fashionable contemporary resonance.

*the Highroad*: that is, being a highwayman. Among the criminal fraternity highwaymen were admired for their bravery and a common name for a highwayman was a 'gentleman of the road'.

*shuffle* ... *Cards*: changing the position of the cards in a pack in order to prevent other players from knowing the order of the cards, here with fraudulent intent.

*Westminster-Hall*: until the late nineteenth century the early Medieval Hall housed the chief law court of England.

20 *a nearer Connection* ... *more Favour with the Great than he usually meets with*: HF's comparison had been made by John Gay in *The Beggar's Opera* (1728), at the end of which the Beggar comments that 'Through the whole piece you may observe such a similitude of manners in high and low life, that it is difficult to determine whether (in the fashionable vices) the fine gentlemen imitate the gentlemen of the road, or the gentlemen of the road the fine gentlemen' (III. xvi).

*Cant Dictionary*: cant, the language of the underworld, first appeared in Britain in the early sixteenth century and cant dictionaries began to appear by the end of the century. Several were circulating in the early eighteenth century, notably 'B.E.', *A New Dictionary of the Terms Ancient and Modern of the Canting Crew* (1699), and the anonymous *A New Canting Dictionary* (1725). However, 'bridle cull' does not appear in either of these dictionaries, while in *NCD* 'buttock and file' is only defined as 'buttock', 'a whore', and 'file', 'a pick-pocket', usually accompanied by a partner who distracts the victim. 'Mill Ken' appears with the definition 'House-breaker', 'Bridle Cull' with the definition 'Highwayman' and 'Buttock and File' as 'Pick-pocket Whore' in the list of cant terms contained in Charles Hitchin's pamphlet *The Regulator; or, A Discovery of the Thieves, Thief-taker, and* Locks,—*in and about the City of London, with the Thief-taker's Proclamation: Also an Account of all the* Flash Words *now in Vogue among the Thieves, etc.* (1718) reprinted in *Select Trials*, ii. 233–6.

20 *Palaces and Pictures*: Walpole's massive rebuilding and expansion programme at his estate at Houghton, Norfolk, and his acquisition of a large collection of pictures to fill it, was much criticized. Ochihatou, Eliza Haywood's Walpole figure, for example, 'proceeded to seize the publick Treasure into his own Hands, which he converted not to Works of Justice or Charity, or any Uses for the Honour of the Kingdom, but in building stately Palaces for himself . . .' (*Eovaai*, 64–5). HF satirized Houghton more openly in his narrative poem *The Vernoniad* (1741), where Mammon represents Walpole: 'A huge dark Lantern hung up in his Hall, | And Heaps of ill-got Pictures *hid* the Wall' (lines 57–8), to which HF added a mock-learned note that the poet probably 'endeavours to satyrize the Clumsiness and Want of Taste, which is so often apparent in the Expences of Great Men'.

21 *B——y . . . Pimp*: that is, 'Bawdy-house . . . Court-Pimp'. One of the accusations made against Walpole was that he encouraged George II's links with his mistresses, both during and after Queen Caroline's lifetime.

22 *promise Mountains in futuro*: 'promise mountains' or 'promise golden mountains' was proverbial; 'in futuro' means in, or for, the future.

*plain Spanish*: Spanish snuff. The maid has bought the snuff with threepence from the guinea she was asked to change for La Ruse.

23 *in præsenti*: at present. In 1754 Jonathan's offer, and the arrangement with the serving maid, are revised, so that, the maid first declaring she would not break her trust for a hundred pounds, she remains inflexible until JW offers a guinea rather than eighteen pence.

*two Acts . . . themselves*: payment for tickets for boxes, the best seats at the theatre, was collected at the end of the second act, offering an opportunity to evade payment by leaving after seeing the first two acts free. In *The Beaux' Stratagem* (1707) Archer, one of the two impoverished beaux, talks of being 'obliged to sneak into the sidebox, and between both houses steal two acts of a play, and because we han't money to see the other three, we come away discontented' (George Farquhar, *The Beaux' Stratagem*, IV. ii. 20–3, in *The Recruiting Officer and Other Plays*, ed. William Myers (Oxford: Oxford University Press, 1995), 299).

*Sneaking-Budge*: HF adds a note 1754 defining this as 'shoplifting', having by then defined the same term more broadly in *Amelia* I. iii. as 'a Cant Term for Pilfering'. *NCD* defines a Sneaking Budge as 'one that robs alone, and deals chiefly in petty Larcenies'.

*in the Funds*: in 'the stock of the national debt, considered as a mode of investment' (*OED*).

*Beau*: fop, dandy. The beau was a frequent object of HF's satiric condemnation: see, for example, 'Of True Greatness' where a beau is 'The Lady's Play-thing, and the Footman's Sport; . . . This little, empty, silly, trifling Toy' (lines 222, 227), to which HF adds a note, 'These Verses attempt (if possible) to imitate the Meanness of the Creature they describe' (*M1*, 27), and the ignominious figure of Beau Didapper in *Joseph Andrews* (IV. vii–xv).

24 *Father . . . America*: that is, he was transported as a criminal for a seven-year term. Individuals found guilty of capital crimes, and if unable to plead 'benefit of clergy'—a mechanism which had originated in the medieval arrangement whereby the clergy were tried by ecclesiastical not lay courts, but which by the early eighteenth century amounted to a condemned person escaping the gallows by proving he or she could read —could have their death sentence commuted to transportation to 'the American plantations', probably Maryland, Virginia, or the Carolinas; this was technically a voluntary act, since the individual's agreement was required in order to make transportation legal. In his subsequent description HF parodies the fashion for the aristocracy and wealthy gentry to send their sons on the 'Grand Tour' of the courts of Europe to finish their education. The Grand Tour was frequently the butt of satire, including by Alexander Pope who records that his Grand Tourist 'saunter'd Europe round, | And gather'd ev'ry Vice on Christian ground' (*The Dunciad* (1743), IV. 311–12).

*Leagues*: a league was an irregular measurement of distance, usually in England about 3 miles.

*Hemisphere*: Europe, Asia, and Africa were widely known as the Eastern, and America the Western, hemisphere.

25 *Hazard-Table*: hazard was a game of chance played with dice, which 'speedily makes a Man or undoes him; in the twinkling of an Eye either a Man or a Mouse' (Charles Cotton, *The Compleat Gamester*, 5th edn. (1726), 119).

*Bob Bagshot*: Bagshot Heath, to the west of London near Windsor—and therefore on a route frequently travelled by the wealthy and powerful on their way to and from the king's residence at Windsor Castle—was a notorious haunt of highwaymen. The criminal gang in *The Beggar's Opera* includes 'Robin of Bagshot, alias Gorgon, alias Bluff Bob, alias Carbuncle, alias Bob Booty' (I. iii), a clear allusion to Walpole.

*Case of Pistols*: a case usually contained a pair of pistols.

*Corps de Reserve . . . Occasion*: reinforcement, to be used if required.

*one Misfortune never comes alone*: proverbial; its most famous version is in *Hamlet*, 'When sorrows come, they come not single spies | But in batallions' (IV. v. 78–9).

26 *golden Snuff-Box*: snuffboxes, like watches and handkerchiefs, were
desirable booty because popular—both men and women took snuff—as
well as valuable and easily stolen. In *The Beggar's Opera* Crook-Finger'd
Jack is praised for his industry in acquiring, among other items, 'Sixteen
snuffboxes, five of them of true gold' (I. iii).

*First secure . . . the rest*: see for example the *Weekly Journal*'s account of
the real-life JW as 'a right Modern Whig' who lives up to the motto '*Keep
what you get, and get what you can*' (*Mist's Weekly Journal*, 19 June 1725).

*is not . . . Hire?*: quoting Christ's pronouncement that 'the labourer is
worthy of his hire' (Luke 10: 7). The whole of JW's speech here, with its
multiplicity of biblical and classical references and rhetorical devices,
parodies the style of tracts and sermons on moral topics popular at the
time. Its content, including the references to architecture and works of
art, may allude to Walpole gaining benefits from the labours of others.

*Verses . . . themselves*: probably Christ's Sermon on the Mount: 'Behold
the fowls of the air: for they sow not, neither do they reap, nor gather into
barns; yet your heavenly Father feedeth them. Are ye not much better
than they?' (Matthew 6: 26.)

*Aristotle . . . Cattle*: distorting Aristotle's arguments that a healthy state
depends on 'the union of natural ruler and natural subject for the sake of
security (for one that can foresee with his mind is naturally ruler and
naturally master, and one that can do these things with his body is subject
and naturally a slave; so that master and slave have the same interest)'
(Aristotle, *Politics*, 1. 1. 4).

*well said . . . Earth*: 'we are but ciphers, born to consume earth's fruits'
(Horace, *Epistles*, 1. 2. 27).

28 *Toy-Shop*: a shop where trinkets and small ornamental articles were sold.
In *Amelia*, Booth is tricked into leaving the safety of his lodgings by the
claim that Amelia has been taken ill at Mrs Chevenix's toy-shop, one of
the most famous and fashionable in London (VIII. i).

*in . . . Deshabille*: dressed in a deliberately negligent or careless style.
Formal evening wear during this period was very ornate; by contrast,
during the day it was fashionable to receive visitors at home in a simpler
'undress' (the word HF used in place of 'deshabille' in 1754)—although
not quite the form of undress that Laetitia displays here. The hair would
be 'powdered' (that is, sprinkled with flour until it was white or grey) for
formal occasions. A clout was a small, worthless, piece of cloth or handkerchief. Jumps were tight underbodices, less rigid than stays but still
providing support for the breasts. Many women wore a lace-edged handkerchief, a diagonally folded square of a light material such as muslin or
linen, draped round the neck with the ends knotted in front or secured
under or over the bodice of the dress. White satin with spots was fashionable as a pattern, but, despite the claim that the spots were artificially (that
is, ingeniously, with much art) interwoven, their 'Chance' appearance
indicates that they were probably stains. It was usual for skirts to open at

the front to reveal the under-petticoat. Both were given form and shape by the hoop, a controversial structure of whalebone which first became fashionable early in the century and which was growing ever bigger by the 1740s, but which was not intended to be visible. Stuff was a coarse woollen fabric. The whole particularized account of dress may be a satiric allusion to Samuel Richardson's lingering accounts of Pamela's clothes, see for example *Pamela*, Letter 24. In 1754 HF revised the description of Laetitia's appearance in several significant details—see Textual Notes.

29 *pretty Feet . . . Under-Petticoat*: fashionable shoes of the period were often made of silk, but the fastenings here suggest the original buckles or other fastening had perished. HF may be alluding to the red ribbon insignia of the Bath, the order of knighthood that Walpole persuaded the King to revive in 1725 and in which he was immediately invested before quitting it in 1726 for the older and more prestigious Order of the Garter whose insignia was a blue ribbon. In 1754 HF changed 'red' to 'yellow'.

*Tea-Table . . . called for*: a servant would bring in a small, light table on which the tea would be made. Tea-drinking had been introduced into England in the seventeenth century but tea was expensive and the drink remained a luxury.

30 *She then . . . Devil with her*: in *Shamela* HF had satirized what he saw as Richardson's Pamela's hypocritical preoccupation with her virtue, defined strictly as her virginity: 'I would have you know, Madam,' says Shamela, 'I value my Vartue more than I do any thing my Master can give me; and so we talked a full Hour and a half, about my Vartue'; and later 'I thought once of making a little Fortune by my Person. I now intend to make a great one by my Vartue' (*Shamela*, Letter 10).

*Dress . . . Readers*: 'If Dress is their only Title, sure, even the Monkey, if as well dressed, is on as high a Footing as the Beau', 'An Essay on Conversation' (*M1*, 140). Pumps were light slip-on shoes used particularly for dancing, and 'adopted out-of-doors by some of the more foppish men' (Ribeiro, 30). Pinchbeck plate was an alloy of copper and zinc imitating gold, named after Christopher Pinchbeck (d. 1732), the London watch- and toy-maker who invented it; the first usage of the word cited in the *OED* is in HF's play *The Intriguing Chambermaid* (1734). Plush was silk, cotton, or wool, prepared with a nap longer and softer than that of velvet and used for rich garments including footmen's liveries. The fashion for breeches to end above the knee lasted to the early 1730s, after which below the knee was the norm. A rich waistcoat was an essential component of the three-piece suit—coat, waistcoat, and breeches—usually in the same or at most complementary colours. Dimity was a stout cotton fabric woven with raised stripes or fancy figures. A fashionable man's hat would be cocked, that is, turned up at the brim on three sides; the brim was usually edged with brain or lace; the fashionable wore their hats small, almost as 'an afterthought' (Ribeiro, 29) and stuck jauntily on one side of the head.

31  *in Red*: that is, as soldiers, who wore red coats.

*Sir ... Milton*: Newton (1642–1727 – and therefore still living in the period in which the novel is ostensibly set) was recognized as the greatest of all physical scientists; Shakespeare (1564–1616) and John Milton (1608–74) were widely regarded as the finest English dramatist and poet respectively. Shakespeare's reputation had been enhanced by the first serious attempts to publish authoritative editions of his plays, under the editorship of Nicholas Rowe (1709), Alexander Pope (1723–5) and Lewis Theobald (1733–4); and Joseph Addison devoted no fewer than eighteen editions of the hugely influential journal the *Spectator* (on Saturdays from 5 January to 3 May 1712) to *Paradise Lost* as 'the greatest Production, or at least the noblest Work of Genius, in our Language' (No. 321, Saturday 8 March 1712). In *Amelia* HF described Shakespeare as 'The greatest Genius the World hath ever produced' (VI. v) and Milton (1608–74) as in the first rank of poets alongside Homer and Virgil (VIII. v).

*but half a Yard of Ribbon in his Hat*: ribbon on a man's hat was an indication that he was a member of the army.

32  *Carriage*: conduct, behaviour.

*Virgil ... pater*: The recurrent identifying adjective is a standard epic convention, found in both Homer and Virgil. Pius (good, dutiful) and pater (father) were regularly attached to the name of Aeneas, the hero of Virgil's *Aeneid*, except where Aeneas fell short of the high standards required by the description, as in the episode where he fails to follow his destiny (which is to sail to Italy so that his descendants can found the Roman Empire), instead dallying in Carthage with Dido (Book 4).

33  *an usual*: his usual.

*the Watch*: the body of men appointed by each city ward and funded by individual citizens, who were responsible for keeping order in the streets overnight. Criticism of their effectiveness was commonplace, before and after an overhaul of the system through the Watch Act of 1737.

34  *Pike ... thereout*: one of HF's favourite analogies. For example, 'The great Man received the Money, not as a Gudgeon doth a Bait, but as a Pike receives a poor Gudgeon into his Maw. To say the Truth, such Fellows as these may well be likened to that voracious Fish, who fattens himself by devouring all the little Inhabitants of the River' (*Amelia*, XI. v). The same image is used by Gay in *Beggar's Opera* Air 43 (III. ii) in describing gamesters: 'Like pikes, lank with hunger, who miss of their ends, | They bite their companions, and prey on their friends.'

*little Slips ... Request*: that is, Mr Snap or his fellow-bailiffs serve writs for actions for debt. In 1754 HF added a note to explain John Doe as 'a fictitious Name which is put into every Writ; for what Purpose the Lawyers best know'. John Doe and Richard Roe were sham names used to indicate unknown or unidentified plaintiffs and defendants.

35  *Justice of Peace*: Justices of the Peace were 'those that are appointed by

the King's Commission to keep the Peace of the County where they dwell' (Jacob); their duties included hearing accusations and deciding what action should be taken.

36 *seedy*: in 1754 HF added a note to define 'seedy' as 'poor'. *NCD* has 'poor, Moneyless, exhausted'.

*Dinner*: the main meal of the day, traditionally eaten at or just after noon. It was however gradually becoming the fashion to eat dinner later in the afternoon. 'In my own Memory the Dinner has crept by Degrees from 12 a Clock to Three, and where it will fix no Body knows'—*Tatler* 263, Thursday 14 December 1710 (iii. 332).

37 *reputable*: in 1754 HF changed the word to 'profitable'.

*rolled*: revolved.

*Ireland . . . Potatoes*: through the late seventeenth and early eighteenth centuries Ireland was Britain's 'principal colony', though the relationship between the two countries was often troubled. Depending on HF's chronology here, the gentleman might have taken part in the campaign of 1689–90, culminating in the notorious Battle of the Boyne, in which the Irish and their allies, under the ousted Stuart King James II, were heavily defeated by William III and his troops. The first documentary reference to the cultivation of potatoes in Ireland is in 1606. They were grown initially as a garden vegetable, and in the late seventeenth century were just beginning to become the staple agricultural crop that Ireland later depended upon so heavily.

*set him*: set down a sum as stake or wager with him.

38 *Conv——n . . . Room*: the convocations of Canterbury and York, constituting the ruling body of the Church of England, had been prorogued, or suspended, by the government in 1717, effectively preventing all except the most formal meetings taking place. The situation did not change until the 1850s.

39 *resented it properly*: showed his anger or resentment at the injury in the manner of a gentleman, effectively by challenging his accuser to a duel or seeking 'proper Satisfaction'.

*on the Road . . . express it*: highwaymen were often known as the 'gentlemen of the road'. See note to p. 19.

*a Word . . . by it*: the following declamation reflects the highly contested nature of the concept of 'honour', in response to a growing sense that the traditional association of 'honour' with the aristocratic code, including its use to justify actions of violence and revenge, was becoming outdated in the modern world. In HF's 'Dialogue between Alexander the Greek and Diogenes the Cynic', while Alexander equates 'Glory and Honour', Diogenes argues that 'true Honour . . . results from the secret Satisfaction of our own Minds, and is decreed to us by Wise Men and the Gods; it is the Shadow of Wisdom and Virtue, and is inseparable from them' (*MI*, 229). In his satirical 'Modern Glossary' (*Covent-Garden Journal*, 14 January 1752) HF defines honour as 'duelling'.

39  *the Lie's . . . injured*: playing rather obscurely on the term 'to give one the lie', that is, to accuse someone to his face of telling a falsehood.

   *Cardinal Virtues*: justice, prudence, temperance, and fortitude were known as the cardinal or 'natural' virtues as distinguished from the 'theological' virtues of faith, hope, and charity.

40  *Estate*: state.

41  *Rapping*: NCD defines 'Rapper' as 'swinging great Lye'.

   *Whippers-in*: the huntsmen's assistants who kept the hounds from straying by driving them back into the pack with whips.

42  *great Minds . . . Prosperity*: here and elsewhere HF's argument alludes to the view of nature propounded by the philosopher Thomas Hobbes: 'Seeing all *delight* is *appetite*, and presupposeth a *further* end, there can be *no contentment*, but in *proceeding*: and therefore we are not to marvel, when we see, that as men attain to more riches, honour, or other power; so their appetite continually groweth more and more; and when they are come to the utmost degree of some kind of power, they pursue some other, as long as in any kind they think themselves behind any other . . . *Felicity*, therefore, by which we mean continual delight, consisteth *not* in *having* prospered, but in *prospering*' ('Human Nature, or the Fundamental Elements of Policy' (1640) in *The English Works of Thomas Hobbes*, ed. William Molesworth (11 vols., London: John Bohn, 1839–45), iv. 33.

   *noble . . . Feeding*: recalling Hamlet's comment about his mother's behaviour to his father, 'Why, she would hang on him | As if increase of appetitite had grown | By what it fed on' (Shakespeare, *Hamlet*, i. ii)

   *it happens . . . made*: HF visited Bath, a city he knew well, in the autumns of 1741 and 1742, and would have been familiar with the surrounding hills. He may also be recalling famous lines in Alexander Pope's *An Essay on Criticism* (1711), where the labours of learning are compared to travelling through the Alps:

   > So pleas'd at first, the towring *Alps* we try,
   > Mount o'er the Vales, and seem to tread the Sky;
   > Th'Eternal Snows appear already past,
   > And the first *Clouds* and *Mountains* seem the last:
   > But *those attain'd*, we tremble to survey
   > The growing Labours of the lengthen'd Way,
   > Th'*increasing* Prospect *tires* our wandring Eyes,
   > Hills peep o'er Hills, and *Alps* on *Alps* arise! (lines 225–32).

43  *Sic, sic juvat*: 'Thus, thus it pleases me', part of Queen Dido's lament as, rejected by Aeneas, she kills herself: 'sic, sic iuvat ire sub umbras', 'Thus, thus I go gladly into the dark' (*Aeneid*, 4. 660).

   *one . . . Diversion*: probably alluding to Charles XII, who in the severe winter of 1709 'resolved to brave the seasons . . . and ventured to make long marches with his troops during the excessive severity of the weather . . . two thousand of his men were starved to death almost before his eyes . . . this once flourishing army was reduced to four and twenty thousand men ready to perish for hunger' (*History of Charles XII*, 158).

*wrecked*: probably a variant either of 'wreaked' or 'wracked'—that is, spoiled or destroyed—or of 'racked', which was adopted by Arthur Murphy in the 1762 edition.

*another . . . Vassals*: alluding to Julius Caesar, whose successes prompted 'plans for greater deeds and a passion for fresh glory . . . nothing else than emulation of himself, as if he had been another man, and a sort of rivalry between what he had done and what he purposed to do' (Plutarch, 'Caesar', 58. 2).

*whole Nations . . . extirpate*: alluding to an anecdote about Alexander the Great widely cited in the eighteenth century (including by Swift in 'A Tritical Essay upon the Faculties of the Mind' (1707)) but the classical source of which is difficult to identify precisely. Something similar is told in many versions, including by Plutarch: 'Alexander wept when he heard Anaxarchus discourse about an infinite number of worlds, and when his friends inquired what ailed him, "Is it not worthy of tears," he said, "that, when the number of worlds is infinite, we have not yet become lords of a single one?" ' (*Moralia*, 'On Tranquillity of Mind', 466 D). See Rawson, 194 and 221, for a full discussion.

*I am almost . . . World*: in *Covent-Garden Journal*, 19 (7 March 1752), HF talks of the reigns of great men as 'great tragical Farces in which one Half of Mankind was with much Humour put to Death and Tortures, for the Diversion of the other Half'.

*Greatness . . . Benefit of Society*: JW here expresses a commonplace of early eighteenth-century mercantilist thought.

44 *procure a Gang . . . center in myself*: analogies were often made between Walpole's relationship to his henchmen and a gangleader's to his criminal gang; see for example the satirical 'Speech of Bob Booty to his Gang' published in *Common-Sense* and reprinted in *Gentleman's Magazine* (1739), 138–9, in which Booty/Walpole harangues the members of his gang about the lack of success of their activities and the need for loyalty.

45 *this Gentleman . . . Action*: that is, he played as part of a syndicate, and had left his winnings behind to be shared out.

46 *Good-natured*: praise of 'good nature' runs throughout *Miscellanies*. In 'Of Good-nature' HF wrote

> What by this Name, then, shall be understood?
> What? but the glorious Lust of doing Good?
> The Heart that finds it Happiness to please,
> Can feel another's Pain, and taste his Ease.
> The Cheek that with another's Joy can glow,

Turn pale, and sicken with another's Woe;
Free from Contempt and Envy, he who deems
Justly of Life's two opposite extremes.
Who to make all and each Man truly blest,
Doth all he can, and wishes all the rest? (lines 23–32, *M1*, 31)

And in 'An Essay on the Knowledge of the Characters of Men' HF defines good nature as 'that benevolent and amiable Temper of Mind which disposes us to feel the Misfortunes, and enjoy the Happiness of others; and consequently pushes us on to promote the latter, and prevent the former; and that without any abstract Contemplation on the Beauty of Virtue, and without the Allurements or Terrors of Religion' (*M1*, 158). In 1743 HF returned to his play *The Good-Natur'd Man*, begun as early as 1729, in hopes of presenting it on stage, but felt it needed too much revision to be completed in the necessary time. The plot has very little in common with that of *Jonathan Wild* but it does concern the eventual triumph of a good-natured man over his moral opposite (in this case a greedy, unloving, and unethical head of a family).

46 *Jeweller*: encomiums on the virtues of honest trade were frequent in the period. In *The Vernoniad* HF shows the Walpole-figure, Mammon, as naturally hostile to merchants and traders 'whom I must envy; for their Wealth | Is by just Means acquired, but mine by Stealth' (lines 101–2). The lines are accompanied by a note explaining why there is bound to be animosity between Mammon and trade. '*First*, that Poverty, which is so detestable in *Mammon*'s Sight, is the Mother of Industry, on which all Trade and Merchandize is founded. *Secondly*, it is the Nature of Trade to circulate and spread Riches universally, whereas the Delight of *Mammon* is to engross and amass them into one private Heap. *Thirdly*, *Mammon* as the God of Riches, must be supposed likewise ambitious of Power; it is therefore reasonable to conceive the Cause of his Antipathy to a Set of Men, who from an honest Pride which attends Riches, when the Effects of Merit and procured by Industry might be more sparing of their Sacrifices, and less humble to his *Honour* than the Wretches, who, (their Wealth however great not being equal to their Luxury) would submit at any Rate to receive his Riches and his Bounty.'

In making Heartfree a jeweller HF may have had particularly in mind George Lillo (*c*.1693–1739), author of one of the most popular plays of the early eighteenth century, *The London Merchant; or, The History of George Barnwell* (1731) and a jeweller by trade. In his obituary notice of Lillo, HF wrote that 'he had the spirit of an old Roman, join'd to the Innocence of a primitive Christian; he was content with his little State of life, in which his excellent Temper of Mind gave him an Happiness beyond the Power of Riches' (*Champion*, 26 February 1740).

*a Kind of Foil to the noble and great Disposition of our Hero*: greatness and goodness are consistently compared in *Miscellanies*; more generally argument by contrast was a common rhetorical device of the time, and one often used by HF, as with Tom Jones and Blifil in *Tom Jones*.

47  *that Sort . . . World*: HF wrote of Abraham Adams, 'As he had never any Intention to deceive, so he never suspected such a Design in others' (*Joseph Andrews*, I. iii), and in defending Amelia from the charge of dullness of apprehension in failing to see Colonel James's designs upon her, concluded 'it is not Want of Sense, but Want of Suspicion by which Innocence is often betrayed' (*Amelia*, VIII. ix).

*Play . . . Pit*: the theatre was a popular entertainment for all classes in London. By convention, the wealthy and privileged occupied the boxes (which cost five shillings per person) and the lower classes the upper gallery (at one shilling), with young gentlemen and families in the pit, now the stalls (at three shillings): in *Covent-Garden Journal* HF refers to 'Shopkeepers Wives and Daughters' in the pit at the theatre (4 April 1752). Admission fees were good value, since the programme often consisted of a full-length play plus a shorter 'after-piece'.

49  *Marry come up*: a traditional expression of indignant or amused surprise or contempt, deriving from 'May Mary come up to my assistance, or to your discomfort' (Brewer).

*Sirrah*: another traditional expression, used to address men or boys, expressing contempt or assuming authority over the addressee.

*the Difference between committing . . . charge myself with*: the real-life Jonathan Wild achieved great success by exploiting legal loopholes by which only those who actually committed a theft could be prosecuted. His chief practice was to return stolen goods to their owners, taking a small reward from the owner (and a much larger sum from the thieves) for so doing.

50  *Skirts*: in the early eighteenth century men wore coats with 'skirts' that extended, flared and often with side-pleats, to the knee.

*become*: that is, become bail, surety that the prisoner would appear in court to stand trial.

*impose . . . Heartfree*: at a time when London was expanding fast, and many more people spent some part of the year there, it was relatively easy to set up a false identity in such matters as obtaining lodgings and setting up accounts with tradesmen. Taking lodgings and then absconding with the contents—'The Lodging Lay'—was a well-known crime.

53  *Note*: written promise to pay the sum owed at a specified time.

*thousand Pound . . . to Heartfree*: since the total cost of the jewels is specified as £4,500, in claiming payment of £5,500 Heartfree is charging interest of more than 22 per cent on the deal. Either this was a mistake by HF, or he afterwards felt it was inappropriate, because he adjusted the figures in 1754 so that the jewels cost £3,300 overall and Heartfree sought payment of £3,800, an interest rate of 15 per cent.

54  *Molly Straddle*: possibly an allusion to Walpole's mistress Maria (or

Molly) Skerrett, whom he married after his wife's death in 1738. 'Molly' is also however a type name for a disreputable female or prostitute, given added colour by Defoe's Moll Flanders (1722) and her real-life counterpart Moll King.

54 *Bridges-Street*: a narrow street onto which a side-door from the front boxes at Drury Lane theatre exited, and where, as an outraged correspondent complained, 'the Insolence of the Pick-Pockets is grown to such a Height, that Ladies going out that Way are not only in Danger of being robbed, but even murdered' (*Common Sense*, 94, 18 November 1738).

*the Rummer and Horshoe*: the Rummer and Horseshoe (or Horshoe or Horshue) was a popular tavern in Drury Lane. A rummer is a large drinking glass. A horseshoe was often nailed to a door as a lucky mascot and was very common on London inn signs.

*in Imitation of Penelope ... knit again by Night*: in Homer's *Odyssey* Penelope, left alone for years without her husband, Odysseus, and pressed to remarry, declared that she must first weave a winding-sheet for her father-in-law Laertes. Each night, in secret, she undid the work she had done by day (19. 134–56).

*Clocks*: ornamental patterns embroidered onto the side of stockings were very popular. Early in the century the patterns were often bright in colour to attract attention, but 'The brighter colours, especially red and blue, were increasingly limited after about 1740 to the lower classes' (Ribeiro, 44, 162). When Richardson's Pamela decides to return to her humble station she exchanges her mistress's fine white stockings for 'two Pair of ordinary blue Worsted Hose, that make a smartish Appearance, with white Clocks' (*Pamela*, letter 20).

55 *perfect Mastery of his ... Muscles ... on the Stage*: a strong tribute to Wild's abilities. It was a contemporary commonplace that 'Every Passion gives a particular Cast to the Countenance and is apt to discover itself in some Feature or other' (*Spectator*, 86, 8 June 1711).

*predominant Passions*: at a time when reason was highly prized, the opposition of reason and passion, the need to balance the two, and the fear that men could be ruled by a single predominant passion to disastrous effect, was widely explored. In *Essay on Man* Pope described the opposition between the passions, 'to urge, and Reason, to restrain':

> Nor this a good, nor that a bad we call,
> Each works its end, to move or govern all:
> And to their proper operation still,
> Ascribe all Good; to their improper, Ill. (II. 54, 55–8)

In *Amelia* HF explored at length, through the tribulations of his hero, Booth, 'the Miseries in which Men of Sense sometimes involve themselves by quitting the Directions of Prudence, and following the blind Guidance of a predominant Passion' (*Amelia*, I. i).

*applied*: administered as remedy.

*and Comp.*: and company, and others, playing on the common usage of the term as unnamed others in a commercial partnership or company.

56 *coquette*: flirty; the word would more usually be 'coquettish'.

*one of those beautiful Necklaces ... Drollic Story*: Bartholomew Fair, which took place at Smithfield, to the north of Newgate, in August each year, offered a variety of entertainments including drolls: farces or burlesques played by live actors or puppets. Sybil Rosenfeld's *The Theatre of the London Fairs in the Eighteenth Century* (Cambridge: Cambridge University Press, 1960), 37–42, records performances, in 1732, of both *The History of King Henry the VIII and Anne Bullen*, which contained prominent roles for Anne Boleyn and her daughter, the future Queen Elizabeth, and *The Envious Statesman; or, The Fall of Essex*, featuring Queen Elizabeth. There is no record of any performance of John Weston's *The Amazon Queen; or, The Amours of Thalestris to Alexander the Great* (1667) which retold the classical story of Thalestris as taking 300 of her Amazon women to Alexander the Great in hopes of creating a race of Alexanders, though the 1733 season featured *Love and Jealousy; or, The Downfall of Alexander the Great*, an adaptation of Nathaniel Lee's Restoration tragedy *The Rival Queens*. HF's own play *The Miser* was also performed there in 1733, as was *A Cure for Covetousness; or, The Cheats of Scapin*, a ballad-opera version of the play mentioned in I. ii as JW's boyhood favourite. (*The Cheats of Scapin*, in various forms, was one of the most popular drolls of the 1730s and early 1740s.)

*Derdæus Magnus*: Deards the Great, referring to William Deard or Deards (d. 1761), a toy- and trinket-seller, and pawnbroker, in the Strand, whom HF sued in 1739 (M. and R. Battestin, 253) and whom he often alluded to in his work, for example as 'an eminent Toyman, who is well known to deal in immaterial Substance' ('A Journey from this World to the Next', M2, 9).

58 *Harwich*: a port town 100 miles or so to the east of London, from where a traveller would normally embark for Holland. In 1754 HF replaced Harwich with Dover, the main embarcation point for sea crossings to France; later JW and Mrs Heartfree embark from Harwich for Holland.

*the following ... Greatness!*: the formal soliloquy reflecting on a large philosophical or ethical topic was a commonplace of drama from the time of Shakespeare.

61 *the four thousand Pound Note*: In II. iii Heartfree is said to have been paid £1,000 cash, and a note for £4,500. HF is here assuming that there was more than one note, one for £4,000 which Heartfree kept in a separate pocket-book, and—as becomes apparent later in the chapter—another note or notes which were stolen from Wild by Molly Straddle. HF overhauled the whole section in 1754 to make the financial situation clearer and more consistent.

*the Old Baily*: the famous court-house next to Newgate prison, popularly named after the nearby street of Old Bailey. Individuals charged with felony in the City of London, the County of Middlesex to the north-west of the City, and some other outlying parts of London, including the real-life Jonathan Wild, were tried there.

62 *to flinch*: to turn aside from her duty, that is, not to do what Wild wants her to do now.

*give an Information on Oath*: accuse under oath before a magistrate or a court.

*prevent him of his Company*: prevent his accompanying him.

63 *Witnesses . . . to his Character*: character witnesses were very influential in eighteenth-century trials, since prosecutions were brought by private individuals and a person accused of a felony was not allowed to be represented by an attorney so found it difficult formally to rebut charges.

*Mr. James Sly . . . offer himself as an Evidence*: an accomplice could receive a pardon in return for giving evidence against the principal offenders. Only by the middle of the eighteenth century was corroboration required for such evidence. The real-life Jonathan Wild extended his power over his own gang by use of the kind of tactic described here.

*the Gate-house*: gatehouses were apartments over the gate of a city or palace, often strongly built and hence easily adaptable to become prisons, as with Newgate. The prison formally called 'the Gatehouse' was just to the west of Westminster Abbey.

*Mr. Ketch*: Jack Ketch was the executioner from *c.* 1663 until his death in 1686, and was notorious for his barbarity and bungling, particularly over the executions of William Lord Russell in 1683 and the Duke of Monmouth in 1685. His name became synonymous with that of 'hangman'.

*Politicks . . . Pollitricks*: in 'Essay on the Knowledge of the Characters of Men' HF wrote of politicians as 'the crafty and designing Part of Mankind, [who] consulting only their own separate Advantage, endeavour to maintain one constant Imposition on others'; and argued that, 'as it is impossible that any Man endowed with rational Faculties, and being in a State of Freedom, should willingly agree, without some Motive of Love or Friendship, absolutely to sacrifice his own Interest to that of another; it becomes necessary to impose upon him, to persuade him, that his own Good is designed, and that he will be a Gainer by coming into those Schemes, which are, in Reality, calculated for his Destruction. And this, if I mistake not, is the very Essence of that excellent Art, called *The Art of Politics*' (*MI*, 155). HF's Shamela had used the term 'Pollitricks' (*Shamela*, Letter 12).

64 *Of Hats*: this chapter is clearly indebted to Jonathan Swift's account of the 'two struggling Parties' in Lilliput, the Tramecksan and Slamecksan, who were distinguished from each other because one wore high and one wore low heels on their shoes (*Gulliver's Travels*, I. 4); in the early eighteenth century the two major political factions in Sweden were known as

the 'Hats' or 'Caps' and the 'Night-Caps', the former urging war and the latter peace—a fact which attracted much satiric attention in England around 1740 when peace and war were at issue; the imagery also recalls an incident in which George II was said to have kicked his hat overboard during his return from Hanover late in 1736.

*Misunderstanding*: dissension, disagreement.

*gentle, but forcible Manner*: clearly intended to satirize the kind of oration Walpole might give to his henchmen. See note to p. 44.

*There is something very mysterious in this Speech*: HF liked to include mock-learned footnotes, as for example with his long poem *The Vernoniad* (1741), where both the poem and its extensive commentary formed a single comic and satiric whole. Eliza Haywood used the same technique in *Eovaai* (*passim*).

*that chapter written by Aristotle . . . mentioned by a French Author . . . lost Works of that Philosopher*: allusions to non-existent works of literature as now-lost achievements of classical scholars were commonplace; HF made use of the same conceit in *The Vernoniad*, which was introduced as 'from the original *GREEK*. Of HOMER. Lately found at *CON-STANTINOPLE*' (556). Aristotle's 'Chapter on Hats' is mentioned twice in Molière's *Le Médecin malgré lui*; both references were retained in HF's popular adaptation, *The Mock Doctor*, first performed in 1732 and revived in 1740 (pp. 14–15); in the play Walpole is satirized as a 'mock doctor' figure.

*Galerus . . . Hat . . . Dog-fish*: galerus, galerum, and galea (deriving from the Greek γαλεη) are Latin for hat, leather hood or cap, and galeos (γαλεος) means dogfish. Kυνεη is the skin of a dog, and by extension a helmet made of dogskin. 'The most expensive hats were produced from beaver-skins, which made a glossy and impermeable fabric . . . rigid enough to be shaped into the three-cornered style which was the form of the formal hat throughout the eighteenth century' (Ribeiro, 30). Rabbitskin would offer an alternative.

*Ajax . . . Master of the Art*: in Sophocles' tragedy *Ajax* Teucer says that Ajax won the drawing of lots to fight the Trojans' champion Hector by throwing into the helmet containing marked tokens from each contender a hard token that was bound to be chosen first, while some of the others threw in pieces of earth that would crumble or stick to the helmet (lines 1283–7). The scholiast – that is, the ancient commentator on the work— links this story to that of Cresphontes, who, after the conquest of the Peloponnese, with Temenus and Aristodemus' two sons, agreed to cast lots for the cities of Argos, Lacedaemon, and Messene. Cresphontes wanted Messene, and so instead of the required stone he put a lump of earth in the pitcher of water as his lot. It dissolved, so that the other two lots would be drawn (Apollodorus, *Library*, 2. 8. 4). This could be seen as 'cheating in Hats' since the pitcher was a dogskin helmet.

64 *Achilles . . . Dog's Eyes*: *Iliad*, 1. 159. The Loeb edition translates the reference as 'dog-face'.

*Old Hat*: 'a woman's privities; because frequently felt' (Grose).

65 *move*: remove.

66 *the Note of four thousand five hundred Pound . . . demanded of the Endorser*: Heartfree has paid for the jewels with the Count's promissory note, which he has endorsed. The Count has disappeared and cannot be held to account for the promissory note, which has therefore 'bounced'; as a result Heartfree is liable for the money.

*Proprietor*: present owner.

*an honest Quaker . . . Bail for any Man*: Quakers had conscientious objections to taking formal oaths and so instead made affirmations, formal and solemn declarations which had the same legal effect as oaths. HF described the hypocritical behaviour of another 'honest Quaker' in *Tom Jones*, VII. x.

67 *content*: satisfy, pay in full.

68 *Rubbers*: a rubber or rubbers is a set of (usually three) games at whist, the third played as a deciding game if each side has won one of the first two. The first *OED* use of 'rubbers' is given as *David Simple* (1744).

*Peter Pounce*: first introduced in *Joseph Andrews* as Lady Booby's agent, who by the 'charitable Methods' of paying servants' wages late and at a discount, 'together with lending Money to other People, and even to his own Master and Mistress, . . . had, from nothing, in a few Years amassed a small Sum of twenty thousand Pounds or thereabouts' (*Joseph Andrews*, I. x). The character was based on the notorious miser Peter Walter (1664?–1746) of Stalbridge Park, near HF's family estate at East Stour in Dorset. HF knew and disliked him; he satirized him in several of his works including as '*Great Peter*, or *Peter, the Great*' in 'A Journey from this World to the Next', 1. 1 (*M*2, 9).

*Vaux-hall*: the famous pleasure-gardens on the south bank of the Thames, managed by HF's friend Jonathan Tyers, and fashionable throughout the period. A scene of *Amelia* is set in Vauxhall Gardens; the narrator remarks, 'The extreme Beauty and Elegance of this Place is well known to almost every one of my Readers; and happy is it for me that it is so; since to give an adequate Idea of it, would exceed my Power of Description' (*Amelia*, IX. ix).

*Cha. Easy*: Sir Charles Easy is a leading character in Colley Cibber's *The Careless Husband* (1705). *NCD* defines 'easy' as 'facile, supple, pliant, manageable'.

69 *that Assurance . . . Epithet of Good*: 'la bonne assurance', or impudence. In the *Covent-Garden Journal*, 53 (4 July 1752) HF refers to 'la bonne assurance' as 'that Assurance, which the French alone call good, and which it is very probable, they alone may call Philosophy'.

*a pitiful Parson . . . after having opposed him at an Election*: in *Amelia* HF shows a nobleman offering to reward a worthy young man recommended by parson Dr Harrison only on condition that Dr Harrison supports the nobleman's candidate, ' "a mere Stranger, a Boy, a Soldier of Fortune . . . of a very shallow Capacity, and no Education" ', at a forthcoming election (*Amelia*, IX. ii).

*a Prime Minister . . . the Place . . . was disposed of before*: in an era when 'places' or appointments at all levels of public service were made by the Prime Minister on the basis of personal recommendation or patronage the minister wielded enormous patronage and could confirm or deny appointments as he chose. HF was always sceptical about the will of the powerful to keep their promises.

*Composition*: a compromise settlement of the debt, by agreement between the Count and his creditors.

*Z——ds!*: Zounds, a euphemistic abbreviation of the traditional oath 'By God's wounds'.

70 *his little Family*: that is, his children.

*Drawcansir-like . . . because they dare*: Drawcansir, a character in *The Rehearsal* (1672) by George Villiers, Duke of Buckingham, makes many extravagant claims including: 'I drink, I huff, I strut, look big and stare; | And all this I can do, because I dare' (*The Rehearsal*, IV. i. 222–3). SF alluded to the same couplet in *David Simple* (II. vii). HF took the name 'Sir Alexander Drawcansir' for his narrative persona in the *Covent-Garden Journal*.

71 *that Passion . . . which the Gentlemen of this our Age agree to call Love*: in the 'Modern Glossary' HF defines love as 'A Word properly applied to our Delight in particular Kinds of Food, sometimes metaphorically spoken of the favourite Objects of all our *Appetites*' (*Covent-Garden Journal*, 4 (14 January 1752)). Thomas Hobbes had argued that human beings are moved by impulses 'called APPETITE, or DESIRE; the latter, being the general name; and the other oftentimes restrained to signify the desire of food, namely *hunger* and *thirst* . . . That which men desire, they are also said to LOVE: . . . So that desire and love are the same thing', *Leviathan*, I. vi (Hobbes, *Works*, iii. 39–40).

*the Dominical Day*: Sunday.

*Buttock*: the joint of beef or steak nowadays mostly known as rump.

*one of those Eating-Houses . . . young Gentlemen*: that is, a bagnio or brothel. Covent Garden was notorious for its brothels, and the corruption of innocent young women by brothelkeepers was a commonplace morality tale of the period; see for example plate 1 in William Hogarth's picture-sequence *The Harlot's Progress* (1731).

72 *his Cups*: his drinking of intoxicating liquor, his drunken revelry.

*Discovery*: disclosure. Laetitia knows that Jonathan has had Heartfree's jewels and by revealing this she could spoil all his designs.

73 *Holland . . . to prevent her*: once Heartfree was formally declared

bankrupt all his property would have to be realized to meet his debts and it would be illegal for Mrs Heartfree to leave the country with the jewels, and she could be prevented from leaving. If she was already in Holland however she could not be extradited back to England – a fact well known in the 1740s, since the government had spent years in the early 1720s trying in vain to bring one of the South Sea Company directors back from Holland to face charges over the 'South Sea Bubble', an early stock-market disaster in which HF's father with many others lost extensive investments.

73  *Chariot and six*: a light four-wheeled carriage, which, drawn by six horses, would move at considerable speed.

74  *Goodwin Sands*: a series of sandbars off the coast of Kent, at one of the narrowest points in the English Channel, notorious as a danger to shipping.

75  *Kiss —— &c.*: that is, kiss my arse; said to be one of Walpole's favourite expressions (*Champion*, p. lxxxviii). See Shamela's account of an exchange with Squire Booby, 'I have a great Mind to kick your A——. You, kiss —— says I' (*Shamela*, Letter 6), and 'kiss my A—— again' in *The Vernoniad* (line 114), to which HF adds a mock-scholarly note: 'The Hiatus is indeed highly to be lamented. It is doubtless a Place of great Obscurity'.

*Privateer*: that is, a privately owned vessel authorized to attack and take prize of ships from a hostile nation during time of war.

*a War with France*: since JW was born in 1665, and is about the same age as his schoolfellow Heartfree (who is said to be 25), then this action would be taking place some time around 1690. England was at war with France from 1689 to 1697, in the War of the League of Augsburg, but it may well be the later War of the Spanish Succession (1702–13), in which HF's father fought a number of army campaigns, that HF has in mind.

*crowded*: unfurled, for the purposes of increasing the speed of the ship.

*struck*: lowered the sail and/or hauled down his flag as a sign of surrender.

*the Boat*: that is, a smaller boat carried by the ship, the lifeboat.

*understood French . . . perfectly well*: it was usual for a gentlewoman to learn French. HF's sisters' school curriculum in Salisbury, for example, required the girls to learn French as well as reading, writing, and dancing.

76  *the Laws of War*: which would require him to treat his prisoner-of-war with respect.

78  *A Chapter . . . Learning*: the proverbs contained in this chapter are taken, with only slight changes, from the list of 'Moral Sentences' on pp. 85–103 of *Joe Miller's Jests; or, The Wit's Vade Mecum* (5th edition, published in July 1742). (Amory's text gives the original 'Joe Miller' text; the present edition restores HF's 1743 wording.) The miscellany of jokes,

anecdotes, and proverbs was first compiled by John Mottley, historian and playwright, in 1739, using the name of Joe Miller, an actor who died in 1738; successive editions added length, and the Moral Sentences listed here were new to the 5th edition. HF parodies the proverbs by offering a commentary in close imitation of the commentary of Francis Bacon (1561–1626) on the proverbs of Solomon, in *The Advancement of Learning* (1605), a new edition of which had been published by Andrew Millar, publisher of *Joseph Andrews*, in 1740.

*Erasmus on this Occasion*: Erasmus' *Adagia* (1508), a collection of proverbs, remained popular into the eighteenth century.

*the incomparable Publisher . . . not very material*: 'Elijah Jenkins' was a pseudonym used by Mottley; the title page of *Joe Miller's Jests* refers to Jenkins (Mottley) as the 'lamentable friend' of Miller. Edmundus de Crull alludes to the notoriously unscrupulous bookseller Edmund Curll (1675–1747); in fact Curll had no connection with *Joe Miller's Jests*.

*as the learned Lord Bacon says . . . Number of Examples*: a direct quotation from Bacon, *The Advancement of Learning*, Book II.

*Sir Clement Cotterel in a strange Place*: Sir Clement Cottrell (1686–1758, Sir Clement Cottrell Dormer from 1741) was the Master of the Ceremonies at court, responsible for organizing the King's formal activities; the office of Master of the Ceremonies had been held by the Cottrell family for generations.

79 *nine of them . . . one Man*: an old expression of contempt at the expense of tailors, whose occupation was not conducive to the development of physical prowess.

*in the Play-house . . . Taylor*: in *Joseph Andrews* (III. x) the Poet claims that those who hissed his play off the stage were ' "All Taylors, Sir, all Taylors" '.

*never out of his Books*: never out of his books of account, that is always in his debt.

*Grace . . . Ordinary*: the short prayer of grace could be said before or (as here) after a meal. 'Ordinary' means both a public meal provided at a fixed price, and an ecclesiastical officer, such as a bishop, with jurisdiction in legal cases.

80 *Debauching . . . and afterwards marrying her*: HF may have had in mind here William Pulteney, who gave up his opposition to the government when he became Earl of Bath in summer 1742; however even without any specific application it is appropriate to HF's satire of politicians' behaviour. 'Debauching' did not necessarily have a sexual connotation, but could refer to more general corruption.

*Right Honourable . . . Honest Woman*: Members of Parliament were referred to as 'Honourable'; 'Right Honourable' was a prefix to the title of earls, viscounts, and barons, as well as some civic and other dignataries. Marrying a woman has long been described as 'making an honest woman of her'.

80 *Thus ... Proportion of an Example*: another direct allusion to Bacon, *Advancement of Learning*, Book II. See note to p. 78.

*He that is born to be hang'd ... somewhat musty*: 'He that is born to be hanged will never be drowned' and 'He that is born to be drowned will never be hanged' are both proverbial (Tilley). Shakespeare's Hamlet is told by Rosencrantz not to fear his future advancement, 'when you have the voice of the King himself for your succession in Denmark'. 'Ay sir,' replies Hamlet, 'but "While the grass grows"—the proverb is something musty' (*Hamlet*, III. ii. 331–4).

81 *a Coffee-House Door near St. James's*: fashionable gentlemen gathered at coffee-houses for sustenance, conversation, and to read newspapers and journals. St James's Palace was the London base of the court, and St James's, the area around it, was one of the smartest areas in the West End of London. Its streets, however, as all the rest of the streets in London, would be filthy and, in wet weather, muddy.

*Nec Deus ... without him*: the quotation, its meaning in English accurately rendered by HF, forms part of Horace's instructions on how drama should be presented on stage (*The Art of Poetry*, lines 191–2). HF discusses the relationship between realism and the supernatural in fiction at greater length in *Tom Jones* VIII. i and later the narrator refers back to 'that supernatural Assistance with which we are entrusted, upon Condition that we use it only on very important Occasions' (XVII. i).

*many Occurrences ... Hemisphere*: possibly referring to a comet which appeared in the sky over England in February–March 1742; though a very similar phrase—'some Phœnomena which have lately appeared in this Hemisphere'—is used in 'An Essay on the Knowledge of the Characters of Men' (*M1*, 176) to refer to human behaviour.

*Naturam ... Gentlemen read*: 'You may drive out Nature with a pitchfork, yet she will ever hurry back' (Horace, *Epistles*, I. 10. 24). HF may have been quoting from memory, since the line should read 'Naturam expelles furca, tamen usque recurret'.

*Embassadors*: 'Our authors write almost indiscriminately embassador or ambassador, embassage or ambassage, yet there is scarce an example of ambassy, all concurring to write embassy' (Johnson).

*Solomon ... designed them so*: the Old Testament King Solomon (fl. tenth century BC) was noted for his wisdom. The relationship between God, Nature, and man was a regular topic for discussion; see for example the essay in *Spectator*, 404, 13 June 1712 (possibly by Pope), which begins 'Nature does nothing in vain; the Creator of the Universe has appointed every thing to a certain Use and Purpose, and determined it to a settled Course and Sphere of Action, from which, if it in the least deviates, it becomes unfit to answer those Ends for which it was designed'.

82 *second Causes ... the End by the Means*: the idea that man cannot always understand the significance of events in God's overall design is a

conventional one. HF may be alluding to Jonathan Swift's account in *The Battel of the Books* of certain minor gods, Jupiter's 'ministring Instruments in all Affairs below' who 'are call'd by mortal Men, *Accidents*, or *Events*; but the Gods call them, *Second Causes*' (Swift, 130).

*Exaltation*: both to a position of authority, dignity, power, station and wealth; and to the gallows.

84 *Deal*: port on the south-east coast of England, just north of Dover.

*Havre de Grace*: the French port now called Le Havre.

*Borrowing . . . his Approbation*: see 1. viii above.

*Stage-Coach*: horse-drawn coach travelling at specified times and between specified locations, and taking up paying passengers; the eighteenth-century equivalent of a train or long-distance bus.

*as God permitted it to perform the Journey*: notices advertising stagecoach journeys often finished their description of the timetable with the formulaic phrase 'if God permit' (see reproductions in Joan Parkes, *Travel in England in the Seventeenth Century* (Oxford: Oxford University Press, 1925), 88–9.

86 *a Story of Crœsus . . . stupid and motionless*: the story as told here does not appear in Herodotus. HF may be thinking of an episode said to have been witnessed by Croesus in which Cambyses, having defeated King Psammenitus of Egypt, parades before Psammenitus first his daughter as a slave and then his son on his way to execution. Psammenitus merely bows his head. But when he sees an elderly friend reduced to begging, he weeps. When asked why, he tells Cambyses, 'my private grief was too great for weeping; but the misfortune of my companion called for tears— one that has lost wealth and good fortune and now on the threshold of old age is come to beggary' (Herodotus, *The Histories*, 3. 14).

*Child*: term of affection, not necessarily to a child, but often used to a boy in service, or an apprentice.

*her false Pretence to his Commands*: her false claim that she was acting by his commands.

87 *Nanny*: both Nanny and 'Nancy', to which this was amended in 1754, are diminutive forms of the name Anne.

*the following Soliloquy*: a formal speech or oration of consolation made at a moment of grief or loss—in classical terms a *consolatio*—was a feature of fiction and essays of the period and appears throughout HF's work: see for example Allworthy's formal speech when he believes he is about to die (*Tom Jones*, V. vii), Abraham Adams's exhortation to Joseph to be comforted in losing Fanny (*Joseph Andrews*, III. xi), Mrs Bennet's account of her father's formal speech to her sister and herself on the day of their mother's funeral (*Amelia*, VII. ii) and the essay 'Of the Remedy of Affliction for the Loss of our Friends' (*M1*, 212–25). In each case, 'Reason is to be called to our Assistance' against the violence of passion, 'and we should use every Suggestion which it can lend to our Relief' ('Remedy', *M1*, 218).

88 *Toys adapted to all Ages . . . Throne*: follows similar thinking to Pope's in *Essay on Man* (1711):

> Behold the child, by Nature's kindly law,
> Pleas'd with a rattle, tickled with a straw,
> Some livelier play-thing gives his youth delight,
> A little louder, but as empty quite:
> Scarfs, garters, gold, amuse his riper stage;
> And beads and pray'r books are the toys of age:
> Pleas'd with this bauble still, as that before;
> 'Till tir'd he sleeps, and Life's poor play is o'er! (II. 275–82)

*jointed Baby*: doll or puppet.

89 *Where is To-morrow? . . . Is sure to none*: lines 373–5 in Edward Young's hugely popular poem *The Complaint; or, Night Thoughts on Life, Death & Immortality*, the first part of which, Night the First, was published in May 1742. HF may be quoting from memory: the lines as published read: 'Where is To-morrow? In another world. | For numbers this is certain; the Reverse | Is sure to none.'

*if it could be chimerical . . . Eye of Man*: HF expresses a similar idea in *Champion*, 22 January 1740, in discussing the 'transporting . . . Thought' that man is looked on with favour by God: 'If this be a Dream, it is such a one as infinitely exceeds all the paultry Enjoyments this Life can afford'.

*if we understand the Road . . . Briers in its Way*: the idea of life as a journey, involving crossroad choices between easy and difficult routes (though often, unlike here, the easy route is that of vice, the difficult that of virtue), is a commonplace of classical literature and was popularized by John Bunyan in *The Pilgrim's Progress* (1678, 1684). In 'A Journey from this World to the Next' HF writes of 'two large Roads leading different Ways, and of very different Appearance; the one all craggy with Rocks, full as it seemed of boggy Grounds, and every where beset with Briars, so that it was impossible to pass through it without the utmost Danger and Difficulty; the other, the most delightful imaginable, leading through the most verdant Meadows, painted and perfumed with all kinds of beautiful Flowers . . . the bad Road was the way to *Greatness*, and the other to *Goodness*' (I. v, *M2*, 25).

90 *Enthusiasm*: ill-regulated or misdirected religious emotion. Those who held extravagant and visionary religious opinions were widely known at the time as Enthusiasts.

*the Return of the Writ*: the formal endorsement of the writ by the Sheriff; once this has been obtained Heartfree must be imprisoned pending his trial.

*as Socrates did . . . prepare for Death*: when Socrates' friend Crito tells him that a ship, the arrival of which will signal his execution, is expected that day Socrates replies, 'If this is the will of the gods, so be it' (Plato, *Crito*, 43C–44A).

91 *sowed in his Stock*: 'sowed' was an alternative form of 'sewn'; a stock is a close-fitting neckcloth fastened at the back, widely worn by men from the 1720s (Ribeiro, 29). In 1754 HF replaced 'Stock' with 'Coat' as the hiding place for the money.

*the Premium commonly taken for the Remittance*: before banks were widely established people wanting to transfer money from one place to another without carrying it themselves would have to arrange for a bill of exchange, or an agent to carry the money, either option involving additional expense.

*Marybone*: now Marylebone, in the early eighteenth century one of the centres of London's criminal and gambling world.

92 *the Commission of Murther . . . never passed undiscovered or unpunished*: 'murder will out' is proverbial: the earliest dated reference in *OED* is to 'Mordre wol out, that se we day by day' in Geoffrey Chaucer's 'The Nun's Priest's Tale' (Chaucer, *The Canterbury Tales* (*c*.1386), ed. F. N. Robinson (London: Oxford University Press, 2nd edition 1966, repr. 1970), line 3052).

*God's Revenge against Murther*: the sentiment is conventional but the precise phrase is taken from John Reynolds, *The Triumphs of Gods Revenge against the crying and execrable Sinne of (willfull and premeditated) Murther*, originally published between 1621 and 1635 and still popular in the 1740s; HF owned a copy of the first complete edition (1635). The volume describes thirty lurid murders and equally lurid reprisals or punishments, generally demonstrating that murder will always be discovered and punished. A modernized version appeared in serial form in the *London Evening Post* from September 1739.

*the Tongue of a Viper . . . Slanderer*: HF argued elsewhere that slander and libel were analogous to murder; see for example the Preface to *Miscellanies*, 'Indeed there is no Man who speaks or thinks with more Detestation of the modern Custom of Libelling. I look on the Practice of stabbing a Man's Character in the Dark, to be as base and as barbarous as that of stabbing him with a Poignard in the same Manner' (*M1*, 14).

*the Purse of the Oppressor*: that is, the ability of the oppressor to bribe opponents.

*Neck*: that is, the gentleman's stock, where Wild had suggested he keep his money; revised to 'Coat' in 1754, to be consistent with the changed place of hiding the money (see note to p. 91).

93 *Black-Book*: a book recording the names of persons who have rendered themselves liable to punishment: Brewer cites a 1726 reference to a university proctor listing in a black book the names of students who would not get their degree, but the term seems to have been used more generally

from the mid-seventeenth century, including in Richard Brome's *The Weeding of the Covent Garden; or, The Middlesex Justice of Peace* (1658), IV. i, and Thomas Killigrew's *The Pilgrim* (1664), IV. iv. In *The Beggar's Opera* Peachum has a 'black-list' (I. iv. 4) which serves the same purpose as JW's black-book.

93 *the Achates of our Æneas . . . the Hæphestion of our Alexander . . . Fireblood*: Achates was the faithful servant of Aeneas in Virgil's *Aeneid*, and Hephaestion the close friend of Alexander the Great. Nathaniel Lee's play *The Rival Queens* (1710) includes Alexander and Hephaestion among its characters; Colley Cibber's *Rival Queens*, a satire on Lee's version, was frequently performed in the early eighteenth century, including in 1738. The name 'Fireblood' is a pun on Hephaestion, since Hephaestus is the Greek God of fire, and also alludes to 'Blueskin' Blake, a known henchman of the real-life Jonathan Wild. (See Introduction, p. xxiii.)

*that Weakness . . . Men of Heroic Disposition*: among many examples are the Old Testament warrior Samson who was betrayed by Delilah (Judges 16: 15–21), and the Roman triumvir Antony whose story, popularized in a number of plays including Shakespeare's *Antony and Cleopatra* (*c.*1607) and Dryden's *All for Love; or, The World Well Lost* (1677), shows his infatuation for Cleopatra costing him his power and his life. In *The Beggar's Opera* Peachum tells Macheath that 'The greatest heroes have been ruined by Women' (II. v).

94 *the very next Sessions*: 'Sessions', at which outstanding cases were tried, were held between eight and ten times a year at the Old Bailey. There were Sessions of the Peace, to deal with misdemeanours and lesser offences, Sessions of Oyer & Terminer to deal with felonies, and Sessions of Gaol Delivery which were supposed to clear Newgate of remaining prisoners; in practice there was considerable leeway as to which Session a prisoner would be tried at.

*How apt . . . do themselves*: proverbial since classical times. See for example Seneca, *De Ira*, 'those whom they have injured they also hate' (2. 33. 1), and Tacitus, *Agricola*, 'It is a principle of human nature to hate those whom you have injured' (42. 3).

95 *Statute of Bankruptcy*: the process by which a person is declared a bankrupt, at which point all his possessions are forfeit to meet his debts.

97 *it were to be wished . . . advancing their most noble Projects*: probably an allusion to the Licensing Act of June 1737, which required all new plays to be approved by the Lord Chamberlain and enabled politically sensitive material to be censored. HF's hugely popular plays and burlesques, especially *Pasquin* and *The Historical Register for the Year 1736*, which satirized Walpole, his government, and the self-seeking nature of politicians generally, had helped to prompt the Act, which effectively terminated HF's career as a dramatist. Fears in the late 1730s that the Act would be

extended to include printed books were not fulfilled, but plays remained subject to censorship until 1968.

*Socrates refused . . . when it was open*: Plato's *Crito* consists of a dialogue between Socrates and his friend Crito, in which Crito is trying to persuade Socrates to escape, but is eventually convinced by Socrates' arguments that escape, though possible, would be wrong for a number of reasons, notably because it would be breaking the laws of the country. See also Xenophon, *Memorabilia*, 4. 8. 1–10, which describes Socrates' cheerful and serene submission to his sentence of execution.

98 *a Treaty of Marriage . . . Smithfield or St. James's*: Smithfield, just north of Newgate, was the main meat market of the City of London as well as the site of Bartholomew Fair. A 'Smithfield match' was proverbial for a marriage contracted purely as a monetary bargain. St James's was the London centre of the court (see note to p. 81).

99 *He had likewise established . . . might have them again*: HF here describes, with only slight exaggeration, the system that the real-life Wild established: he set up a succession of offices near the Old Bailey, where people came to report the theft of their goods. He charged a small 'search fee'; once he had 'discovered' the thieves and the stolen property, the owner of the goods would make a payment to the thieves (much of which they passed on to Wild) for the return of their goods, sometimes with a small 'tip' of gratitude to Wild.

*the great Bubble-boy himself*: probably another satirical allusion to the toyman William Deards (see note to p. 56). A bubble is a cheat or deception; a link with 'bauble' might also be intended.

*the Keeper and Turnkeys of Newgate*: the keeper, who had an official residence on site, was in charge of the prison; the deputy keeper was the head turnkey, and the turnkeys were the assistant keepers or prison officers.

100 *that Epistolary kind of Writing . . . Academy of Compliments*: *Academy of Compliments* was the title of many volumes, including *The Academy of Complements; or, A New Way of Wooing. Wherein is a variety of love-letters very fit to be read of all young Men and Maids, that desire to learn the Way of Complements*, first published in 1685 and often reprinted. In his Preface to Sarah Fielding's *Familiar Letters* HF speaks slightingly of volumes of 'Love-Letters' as among those 'with which the Moderns have very plentifully supplied the World' (*Familiar Letters*, 1. vi). For 'Beaus' see note to p. 23.

101 *some Flourishes of his own Eloquence . . . found in their Writings*: in the Preface to *Voyage to Lisbon* HF wrote: 'Some few embellishments must be allowed to every historian: for we are not to conceive that the speeches in Livy, Sallust, or Thucydides, were literally spoken in the very words in which we now read them' (10). Sallust—Gaius Sallustius Crispus (86–34 BC)—was a Roman politician and historian.

101  *those inimitable Harangues . . . said Hurgos are not so extremely eminent*:
     a Hurgo was a 'great Lord' in the Lilliput of *Gulliver's Travels* (I. i). In
     1738 Parliament banned journal accounts of its debates; in order to cir-
     cumvent this, the *Gentleman's Magazine* began to present its accounts of
     parliamentary proceedings as 'Debates in the Senate of Magna Lilliputia'
     (later 'Debates in the Senate of Lilliput'), with the 'House of Hurgos'
     representing the House of Lords. HF's suggestion that the quality of the
     speeches had improved in transit was probably well founded; from 1740
     to 1743 reports were being written by Samuel Johnson who did not
     attend Parliament but arranged for reporters to make notes of the
     speeches. Boswell records that the debates were first written up by Wil-
     liam Guthrie, and revised by Johnson; 'after some time, when . . . the
     speeches were more and more enriched by the accession of Johnson's
     genius, it was resolved that he should do the whole himself, from the
     scanty notes furnished by persons employed to attend in both houses of
     Parliament. Sometimes, however, as he himself told me, he had nothing
     more communicated to him than the names of the several speakers, and
     the part which they had taken in the debate' (James Boswell, *Life of
     Johnson* (1791), ed. R. W. Chapman (Oxford: Oxford University Press,
     1953, repr. 1985), 85).

102  *Culprit*: a recent coinage in the early eighteenth century, meaning a pris-
     oner at the bar, or an accused person, rather than a guilty person – from
     the law-French 'culpable; prist', meaning the Crown was ready to prove
     the prisoner guilty. In 1754 HF replaced 'Culprit' with 'Prisoner at the
     Bar'.

     *Caudle Cup*: caudle was a warm drink of boiled oatmeal and water or
     milk, mixed with wine or ale and sweets or spices, given to invalids,
     women in childbirth (as probably here), and their visitors.

     *a whole Number . . . third only*: possibly using the language of the lottery,
     where an individual could buy a share in a ticket or 'number'.

     *Most Histories . . . but the same*: marriage was the conventional ending of
     dramatic comedies, from Shakespeare onwards, and of the prose
     romances that were popular in the late seventeenth and early eighteenth
     century; the two most popular novels published in the years before
     *Jonathan Wild*, *Pamela* and *Joseph Andrews*, both closed with the wedding
     of the chief characters. At the end of his play *The Good-Natur'd Man*—
     which HF was working on in 1743 and which notably does not end with
     the marriages of the main characters – Sir George Boncour suggests that
     recent events would make 'a good subject for a comedy' but his brother
     replies that 'a catastrophe would be wanting; because you know it is a
     constant rule, that comedies should end in a marriage' (*The Fathers; or,
     The Good-Natur'd Man* (1778), v. v). When HF opened *Amelia* (1751)
     with the announcement that 'The various Accidents which befel a very
     worthy Couple, after their uniting in the State of Matrimony, will be the
     Subject of the following History' (*Amelia*, I. i), he was staking claim to

what was still a very unusual literary topic. Salisbury Plain, near where HF was brought up, was well known as a large flat and open area of land.

103 *Dialogue matrimonial*: the matrimonial dialogue was one of the conventional literary forms of the early eighteenth century. HF as an experienced dramatist was very used to writing such dialogue, often with a satirical edge, as in the bickering between Sir Owen Apshinken and Madam Apshinken his wife (widely seen as representing George II and Queen Caroline) in *The Welsh Opera* (1731), or between Boncour and Mrs Boncour in *The Good-Natur'd Man*.

104 *for better and worse*: echoing the traditional form of the marriage ceremony, in which the bride and groom agreed to take each other 'for better, for worse, for richer, for poorer, in sickness and in health . . .'.

105 *made your Convenience of me*: taken advantage of, made a tool of, me.

107 *what a B——ch you are*: one account of the real-life JW recorded that his wife 'so provok'd him to Wrath, that he swore by the Lord, he would mark her for a Bitch, and thereupon drawing his Sword, he smote off one of her Ears' (*Select Trials*, ii. 232). The epithet 'bitch', which generally implied a lewd or sensuous female, was a stronger term of abuse then than now. In *Joseph Andrews*, when Mrs Tow-wouse finds the maid Betty in bed with Mr Tow-wouse, and calls her, among other things, 'a monosyllable, beginning with a B—, . . . a Word extremely disgustful to Females of the lower sort', Betty declares angrily that ' "I will never be called *She-Dog*, by any Mistress in *England*" ' (I. xvii). Grose records that 'bitch' is 'the most offensive appellation that can be given to an English woman, even more provoking than that of whore'.

108 *converse with*: not only 'talking with', but implying a general intimacy, possibly leading to 'criminal conversation', the legal term for adultery.

109 *the Sweets of Matrimony*: in his revisions to Sarah Fielding's *David Simple* in 1744 HF inserted a statement that the innocent David 'never once reflected . . . that to prevent a Husband's Surfeit or Satiety in the Matrimonial Feast, a little Acid is now and then very prudently thrown into the Dish by the Wife' (I. viii, n. 18).

*his serene Consort*: the honorific epithet 'serene' was frequently applied to a reigning prince, especially of Germany. George I, who reigned during Jonathan Wild's adult lifetime, and George II, King at the time of the publication of *Jonathan Wild*, were also electors of Hanover, where their family originated.

*Corvinus . . . Camilla*: classical names were often used for exemplary purposes, as here, without any allusion to specific individuals or moral positions.

*that Desire, according to my Lady Betty Modish, of curing each other of a Smile*: in Act III of Colley Cibber's popular play *The Careless Husband* (1705), Lady Betty says of her suitor Lord Morelove, 'I want to Cure him of that Laugh now' (p. 32).

110  *the Boy Hymen . . . Cupid out of Doors*: in classical myth Hymenaeus was
     the god who led the marriage procession, often carrying a torch and a
     crown of flowers; Cupid was the god of love.

     *the Liberties of the Fleet*: the Fleet was the best known of London's
     debtors' prisons; it was named after the run of water which flowed into
     the Thames between Ludgate Hill and Fleet Street, then an open sewer,
     and a byword for filth, as celebrated by Pope in *The Dunciad* (1728, 1742/
     3). Outside the prison was an area known as 'the Liberties', once owned
     by monasteries and still allowed certain exemptions and privileges.
     'Prisoners for debt . . . may be removed by *Habeas corpus* to the Fleet;
     and enjoy the rules, or liberty to walk abroad, and to keep a house within
     the liberties of this prison . . . The rules comprehend all Ludgate-hill,
     from the Ditch to the Old Bailey on the north side of the hill, and to
     Cock-alley on the south side of the hill: both sides of the Old Bailey,
     from Ludgate-hill eastward to Fleet Lane, all Fleet-lane, and the east side
     of the ditch or market, from Fleet-lane to Ludgate-hill' (John
     Noorthouck, *A New History of London* (1773), 642).

     *appeared to the Commission of Bankruptcy against him*: the Commissioners
     examined bankrupts, and had power to sell or otherwise dispose of their
     estates 'for the Satisfaction of the Creditors' (Jacob, 'Commission of
     Bankrupts').

111  *attach*: arrest, seize by authority of a writ of attachment.

     *Honey-Moon*: 'the first month after marriage, when there was nothing
     but tenderness and pleasure' (Johnson).

     *Great Men . . . Persons*: under English law Members of Parliament during
     parliamentary sessions, and peers of the realm at all times, had immunity
     from arrest or imprisonment for many crimes. HF satirized this law as 'a
     Law called NOLI ME TANGERE' in the *Champion*, 17 July 1740.

     *Works of Supererogation*: a theological expression for good works beyond
     what is required by God; by extension, general acts beyond the bounds of
     duty.

     *Fury*: in classical mythology the three Furies were the goddesses of
     vengeance, punishing transgressors without mercy.

112  *bloodying . . . Ghost*: an allusion to what had become dramatic clichés,
     most notably exemplified in Shakespeare's *Macbeth*, where both Macbeth
     and Lady Macbeth are horrorstruck at having literal or metaphorical
     blood on their hands (II. ii, v. i), and Macbeth sees the ghost of Banquo,
     one of his victims, in judgement on him (III. iv, IV. i).

     *God's Revenge against Murther*: John Reynolds, *The Triumphs of Gods
     Revenge against . . . Murther* (see note to p. 92) consisted of thirty stories
     of lurid murders and equally lurid punishments for them.

     *what a ravishing Thought! . . . engaged to reward me!*: HF expressed
     similar thoughts in the *Champion*, 22 January 1740: 'What a glorious?
     What a rapturous Consideration must it be to the Heart of Man to

think the Goodness of the Great God of Nature concerned in his Happiness?'

113 *Constable*: an officer appointed by the parish or city ward, with responsibility to keep the peace, prevent bad behaviour and calm disturbances, and authority to interfere in disturbances, and arrest and imprison suspects.

*Writ de Homine Replegiando . . . Capias in Withernam*: the lawyer argues that JW should be released by means of a writ of homine replegiando or replevin ('an ancient Writ for bailing a Man out of Prison'—Jacob), the law officer should record or return the new situation, and a process called a capias in withernam, literally a taking in reprisal, should be instituted to imprison Heartfree until he produces the missing goods or person, in this instance probably the latter, his wife. The argument does not succeed since the Justice still leans toward committing JW for trial.

114 *Digression and Sub-digression*: a favourite rhetorical conceit, previously used to great effect by Swift, who in *A Tale of a Tub* (1704) offered a number of digressions including 'A Digression in Praise of Digressions' (Section 7). In his *Apology for the Life of Mr. Colley Cibber* (1740) Cibber (a figure frequently ridiculed by HF—see note below) wrote that 'I shall make no Scruple of leaving my History, when I think a Digression may make it lighter' (5); the statement was satirized in the parody *An Apology for the Life of Mr. T— C—, Comedian* (1740), once attributed to HF, where the narrator, having declared that 'I shall also make *Digressions* in my Memoirs . . . for *Digressions* it seems are in this Kind of Writing what Eggs are in a Pudding, they *lighten* the Composition, and tender it more palatable and digestive' (3), later claims to be 'making a Digression in a Digression' (8).

115 *the Stage of the World . . . Drury Lane principally in this*: the traditional analogy of the world as a stage, most famously described by Shakespeare in *As You Like It*: 'All the world's a stage, | And all the men and women merely players . . .' (II. vii) was developed by HF and other early eighteenth-century satirists who compared Walpole to various figures in the theatre, including specifically the impresario of Drury Lane, Colley Cibber. In *The Historical Register for the Year 1736* Pistol (who 'is run mad, and thinks himself a great Man', boasts of being a 'Prime Minister Theatrical' (II. i)), while the playwright Medley makes the analogy even more explicit: '. . . I told you before my Rehearsal, that there was a strict Resemblance between the States Political and Theatrical; there is a Ministry in the latter as well as the former, and I believe as weak a Ministry as any poor Kingdom cou'd ever boast of; Parts are given in the latter to Actors, with much the same Regard to Capacity as Places in the former have some Times been, in former Ages I mean; and tho' the Publick damn both, yet while they both receive their Pay, they laugh at the Publick behind the Scenes; and if one considers the Plays that come from one Part, and the Writings from the other, one would be apt to think the same

Authors were retain'd in both' (II. i). In *Eurydice Hissed* (1737) Pillage is at the same time Prime Minister and theatre manager casting a farce.

115 *Puppet-show ... assigning to each the Character which the Great Man is pleased they shall move in, or rather in which he himself is pleased to move them*: the analogy between a senior politician pulling the strings of others and a puppeteer was a common one. In *The Vernoniad* Aeolus tells Mammon:

> The World's thy Puppet-shew, and Human *Things*
> Dance, or hang by, as thou dost touch the Strings.
> In gay and solemn Characters they shine,
> In Robes or Rags: for all the Skill is thine.
> Behind the Curtain, in a various Note,
> Thou bawlest or thou squeakest through each Throat.
> Each Puppet's drest, as to thy Will seems good,
> The Robes thou giv'st them—and the rest is wood.
> (lines 253–60)

HF adds in a scholarly note that '*Those who* DANCE *the* WOODEN FIG-URES *of Men, when they draw the String of that particular Member which they would move, presently*, according to the String which is touched, *the Neck is twisted, the Head nods, the Eyes roll, or the Hands perform the* MINISTERIAL *Purpose*' (p. 581). Puppet shows were popular in the early eighteenth century, as were hybrid plays in which actors acted as puppets: in *The Author's Farce* (1730) HF offered real actors 'strutting and squeaking about the stage as life-size puppets' (M. and R. Battestin, 83). A travelling puppet show of the more traditional kind is described in *Tom Jones* (XII. v). In 1748 HF became for a short time the operator of his own puppet show.

116 *two very Great Men ... Diversion of the Spectators*: possibly an allusion to a reported public scuffle between Walpole and his close political ally Lord Townshend, who was also his brother-in-law.

*Nemo mortalium omnibus horis sapit*: 'none among mortals is wise all the time', cited by Pliny in *Natural History*, 7. 40. 131, as a proverb. HF used the same quotation in *Joseph Andrews*, III. v, and *Tom Jones*, XII. xiii.

*Ira furor brevis est*: 'Anger is short-lived madness' (Horace, *Epistles*, I. 2. 62).

117 *a Legacy to the Parish*: abandoned children were by law a charge on the parish in which they were left.

*a Warrant for Felony against him*: anyone found guilty of committing a felony—a very serious crime—was liable to suffer the death penalty. Under an Act of 1732, a bankrupt removing or embezzling money or effects to the value of £20 or more with an intent to defraud his creditors 'shall be deemed and adjudged to be guilty of Felony, and shall suffer as Felons without Benefit of Clergy, or the Benefit of any Statute made in relation to Felons' (5 Geo. II, c. 30).

*Mittimus*: warrant ordering a prison-keeper to receive into custody and hold in safekeeping the person specified in the warrant.

118 *Newgate . . . the Press-Yard for his Friend*: Newgate prison had many cells, tunnels, and passages, all of which held prisoners in dark, dirty, and overcrowded conditions. The Common Side was the worst part of the prison where those without money were sent and 'where you are to have Thieves and Villains for your Associates, and to be perpetually Tormented and Eat up by Distempers and Vermin' (*The History of the Press Yard* (1717), 3). The Press Yard, though so-called because it had once been the place where torture had been carried out, and still the place from where the condemned prisoners started their journey to the gallows at Tyburn, was in the Master Side, the better part of the gaol, where the sun was occasionally visible and there was some fresh air. It was overshadowed by, and legally considered part of, the keeper's residence; the keeper charged exorbitant prices for such items as private rooms, good food, and maid service. According to the author of the *History of the Press Yard* a shared cell required an entrance fee of twenty guineas and a weekly rental of eleven shillings. In the early chapters of *Amelia* Booth is incarcerated in a prison which is probably Newgate and manages to achieve some comfort there.

*forty Shillings in the Pound, if he would*: then as now, a bankrupt could reach agreement with his creditors to pay his debts at a compromise rate of a number of shillings for every pound owed. The accusation here is that Heartfree could pay his debts twice over if he chose to.

119 *Injustice*: revised to 'Justice' in 1754.

*a Calamity . . . never to be healed*: HF's hyperbole satirizes the increasing emphasis placed on female chastity, especially in literature through Richardson's hugely successful *Pamela* (1740), which HF had satirized directly in *Shamela* (1741), and *Joseph Andrews* (1742). HF himself later controversially created in Tom Jones and Booth heroes who were far from sexually chaste, and he showed a tolerance, very unusual for his time, towards lapses in female chastity, as in his portrayal of Molly Seagrim and Mrs Waters in *Tom Jones*.

*chaste . . . Epithet*: it was a commonplace of Augustan satire that married women could safely indulge themselves in sexual intrigues—Mrs Peachum, for example, says that once a young woman has made her fortune through marriage 'she hath nothing to do but to guard herself from being found out, and she may do what she pleases' (*Beggar's Opera*, i. viii)—and in that sense Laetitia is now chaste; HF may also be alluding to Laetitia's and Jonathan's decision to abstain from sexual activity with each other.

120 *Parish-Officers . . . eternal Oblivion*: because any bastard child whose parents were unable to care for it, or were unknown, became the responsibility of the parish, parish officers were very keen to identify the father of any child. Here, because there is no such assurance, they commit Theodosia to Bridewell, a house of correction.

120  *less criminal . . . to solicit her to it*: a rare example at this period of serious
     criticism of the double standard by which men were expected to be
     sexually active before and outside marriage, while a woman's chastity was
     regarded as her 'honour' and vital to her respectability. See also note to
     p. 119.

     *a Pair of Scissars for his Purse*: purses were not part of skirts or breeches,
     but were often attached to other clothes by strings or ribbons, which
     could be cut.

     *five Shillings . . . Gallows*: in fact a range of rewards were payable, includ-
     ing £40 for the conviction of highwaymen and forgers as well as thieves.
     In 1720 a reward of £100 was added to the £40 already available, for the
     conviction of men or women who committed robberies in London. The
     real-life JW collected these rewards on many occasions.

121  *Blueskin*: Joseph 'Blueskin' Blake (the reason for the nickname is
     unknown) was a member of the real-life Jonathan Wild's gang. Born in
     1698, he was gaoled regularly as a thief from childhood, but was usually
     protected by Wild. In 1723 he threw in his lot with the notorious crim-
     inal Jack Sheppard, who was never under Wild's control. When Blueskin
     was arrested again, Wild would not help him escape the gallows; and
     Blueskin tried to cut his throat with a penknife. Blueskin was hanged in
     November 1724, but his attempt to kill Wild created doubts in people's
     minds about Wild, and was one of the factors that led to his eventual
     downfall (see *Select Trials*, ii. 162–7). The anonymous *Blueskin's Ballad*,
     written at the time of Blueskin's execution, possibly by Swift or Gay,
     was first performed in the comedy *The Harlequin Sheppard*, which re-
     enacted the assault and Blueskin's end, before the end of November
     1724.

     *Meum and Tuum*: mine and yours. 'H.D.' used the same conceit in his
     account of Wild (see p. 195), and Swift had used it previously (1710) in
     the Introduction to *A Tale of a Tub* (Swift, 36). In 1754 HF extended the
     joke by adding 'which would cause endless Disputes, did not the Law
     happily decide them by converting both into *Suum*'.

     *Surprizes*: not only sudden attacks, but also seizures of people or things.

122  *the chief Magistrate is always chosen for the public Good . . . Wealth, or
     Pleasure, or Humour*: HF's firm belief that magistrates were often
     incompetent and/or self-serving, is reflected in many of his works
     including his account of Parson Adams's appearance before the country
     magistrate in *Joseph Andrews* (II. xi) and Booth's experiences in *Amelia*
     (I. i). By the time of *Amelia* HF was a magistrate himself, and his
     attempts to reform the office were widely held to have contributed to the
     breakdown in his health leading to his death in 1754.

     *without a Head, you know, you cannot subsist*: the analogy between body
     and state or other collective organization appears, for example, in Shake-
     speare (*Coriolanus*, I. i) where the common people regard themselves as
     the belly of the state, and in Pope's *Essay on Man*, where the foot, head,

eye, ear, and mind constitute 'parts of one stupendous whole | Whose body, Nature is, and God the soul' (I. 267–8).

*The Ribbon, or the Bawble . . . Right Honourable*: alluding to the insignia of titles conferred on individuals on the recommendation of the chief ministers of state (see note to p. 29). Specific references to Walpole may be implied, both as recommending titles for political reasons, and as having himself in 1742 accepted the title of Earl of Orford. Right Honourable is a title of general respect, but is specifically applied to peers below the rank of Marquess, to Privy Councillors, and to certain civic dignatories including the Lord Mayors of London, York, and Belfast, and the Lords Provost of Edinburgh and Glasgow.

123 *Feather*: a general sign of rank, feathers were worn by the Knights of the Garter.

*Information*: the act of informing against, charge, accusation.

124 *in the cart at Tyburn*: criminals travelled to the gallows at Tyburn through the streets in a cart, and were sometimes hanged from it.

*a Copy of his Countenance*: 'a mere outward show or sign of what one would do or be; hence, pretence' (*OED*).

*severe Secret*: OED tentatively suggests that 'severe' applied to secret means 'strictly kept'; its only citation is HF's play *The Universal Gallant* (1735), 'I beg this thing may be kept a severe secret'.

*Castle*: HF is using the term metonymically; one part of Newgate was called 'the Castle'.

125 *possessed*: convinced.

*Ordinary . . . a very sagacious as well as worthy Person*: the real-life Ordinaries (see note to p. 11) in the early years of the eighteenth century were Paul Lorraine (1700–19), Thomas Purney (1719–27), and James Guthrie (1727–46). As an extension of the task of attending to the spiritual needs of condemned criminals, the Ordinary often published the dying speeches of the condemned, actually or supposedly drawn from their conversations with them; Purney produced *The Behaviour and Dying Speeches* of Wild and three other criminals executed at the same time, though illness may have prevented him from carrying out his duties from 30 April 1725 (on 22 May *Mist's Weekly Journal* reported that Wild was 'attended in the condemn'd Hold by the Reverend Mr. Nicholson, Lecturer of St. Sepulchre'), and he was away from London on 24 May, the day of Wild's death (*The Works of Thomas Purney*, ed. H. O. White (Oxford: Blackwell, 1933), p. xxiii). HF's subsequent satire of the Ordinary is consistent with general concerns expressed in the early eighteenth century about the quality of the individual appointed to the position. The author of *The History of the Press Yard* (1717) criticizes 'the great Want there was of an able Spiritual Guide for these poor Creatures, who instead of having the Doctrines of Faith and Repentance truly inculcated into them, very often went out of the World, destitute of proper Helps'

(p. 49). 'The Complaint of Jonathan Wild', reproduced in *Select Trials* (ii. 282–4) describes the prison,

> Where some in Tears lament, and others swear,
> While *Purney*, sniv'ling, spells a godly Prayer;
> Or while his Deputy, with holy Qualms,
> Devoutly hums o'er one of *Sternhold*'s Psalms. (lines 5–8)

Daniel Defoe's Moll Flanders not only gains no consolation from the Ordinary, but is shocked to see 'the poor Creature preaching Confession and Repentance to me in the Morning and . . . drunk with Brandy and Spirits by Noon' (*The Fortunes and Misfortunes of the Famous Moll Flanders* (1722), ed. G. A. Starr (Oxford: Oxford World's Classics, 1981, repr. 1987), 277.

125 *no Conjurer*: far from clever (a common phrase in the early eighteenth century).

*he believed a sincere Turk would be saved*: a common point of religious contention. Parson Adams argues 'that a virtuous and good *Turk*, or Heathen, are more acceptable in the sight of their Creator, than a vicious and wicked Christian, tho' his faith was . . . perfectly Orthodox', a belief which his hearer says 'the Clergy would be certain to cry down' (*Joseph Andrews*, I. xvii).

*prevail on Friendly to abandon his old Master*: the virtuous apprentice was a conventional figure seen as highly worthy of praise; see for example Trueman in Lillo's *The London Merchant*, and the industrious apprentice in Hogarth's famous series of plates *Industry and Idleness* (1747).

127 *The Sessions . . . at the Old Baily*: see note to p. 94.

*The Grand Jury at Hicks's Hall . . . Heartfree*: a jury of freeholders met before each Sessions to hear accusations against the accused; if they found there was a case to be answered they would confirm the formal indictment and commit the accused for trial. Hicks's Hall, in St John's Street, Clerkenwell, founded by and named after Baptist Hicks, first Viscount Campden (1551–1629), was where the justices of Middlesex held their sessions from 1612 until 1778. People committed here would be tried at the Old Bailey.

*entirely void of Interest . . . no Pardon*: those condemned to death of some crimes might be reprieved through the intervention on their behalf of some influential person; however the law did not allow reprieve for those convicted of bankrupt fraud.

*Ut Lapsu graviore ruant*: 'that he may be hurled down in more headlong ruin'. The phrase comes from Claudian's *Against Rufinus*, in which the fate of the evil Rufinus is seen as an affirmation that the gods do care for the world: 'No longer can I complain that the unrighteous man reached the highest pinnacle of success. He is raised aloft that he may be hurled down in more headlong ruin' (I. 21–3). HF refers to the opening of

*Against Rufinus* again in *Amelia* in the context of Booth's doubts over the larger issue of Fortune v. Providence (I. iii).

*Blueskin privily drawing a Knife . . . done his Business*: in the real-life incident on which this account is based Blueskin tried to cut Wild's throat with a penknife. See note to p. 121.

128 *the Fatal Sisters*: in classical mythology, the three Fates, or goddesses of Destiny, were depicted as sisters spinning thread and measuring out, at whim, the lifespan of all men. They presided over birth, marriage, and death respectively.

*a Clause in an Act of Parliament . . . impossible for our Hero to avoid it*: referring to Sir William Thomson (1676–1739), the City Recorder; section 4 of 'An Act for the further preventing Robbery, Burglary, and other Felonies and for the more effectual Transportation of Felons' (4 George I, c. 11), which he helped to frame, and which became law in 1719, was widely seen from the outset as intended to stop Wild's activities. 'H.D.' reproduces the clause in full (see page 213) and adds that the Recorder warned Wild that it made his activities vulnerable to prosecution. The whole Act became known as Jonathan Wild's Act: in 1741 HF reported as one of a list of 'Casualties in our Time' that James Smith and Hannah Harrison had been committed 'for Felony, against *Jonathan Wild's* Act, *i.e.* for helping Persons to stolen Goods without apprehending the Felons' (*The History of Our Own Times*, i, 1–15 January 1741, ed. Thomas Lockwood (Delmar, NY: Scholars' Facsimiles and Reprints, 1986), 30).

129 *their Grand Monarch*: Louis XIV of France (reigned 1643–1715) was known as Le Grand Monarque.

*Liberty, to which Great Men are observed to have a great Animosity*: 'Liberty' was a rallying cry of the opposition to the government in the 1730s and early 1740s, as in HF's poem 'Liberty' addressed to his friend the opposition politician George Lyttelton, reprinted in *Miscellanies* (*M1*, 36–41).

*Keeper of this Castle . . . Acquaintance*: the Keeper was appointed by the sheriffs of London and Middlesex to manage the prison. William Pitt, 'Citizen and grocer', was Keeper 1707–32; Thomas Bold, 'bailiff of Southwark', was Keeper 1738–44. The large fee Keepers paid for their office—William Pitt is said to have paid £4,500—were warranted by the very large sums they could expect to receive from prisoners or their friends to obtain anything better than the most basic conditions in the prison. Thomas Baston claimed that Keepers of Newgate connived with 'an Officer they have among them, call'd a *Thief-Catcher*' in criminal practices 'so that this Prison . . . is a Sanctuary, and great Encouragement to Felons' (Baston, *Thoughts on Trade and a Public Spirit* (1716), 207). HF owned a copy of this volume.

*as high Garnish . . . Custody for Murther*: garnish was money extorted from prisoners either as fees to improve their conditions—here to avoid having to wear heavy fetters—or, by custom, to buy drinks for the other prisoners. 'You know the custom, sir. Garnish, Captain, garnish,' Lockit tells Macheath when he arrives in Newgate (_Beggar's Opera_, II. vii). HF was outraged by the system: in _Amelia_ he describes how Booth, who needs to have the term explained to him, is unable to pay and is therefore left to the mercy of the other prisoners (_Amelia_, I. iii); and in the course of his own legal activities he worked hard to secure the appointment of an honest constable, William Pentlow, to the Keepership of New Prison, Clerkenwell, to encourage reform. By the early 1750s the corruption and cruelty of the garnish system were becoming unacceptable and the _Gentleman's Magazine_ recorded in 1752 that 'The Sheriffs of _London_ have ordered that no debtor in going into any of the goals of _London_ and _Middlesex_, shall, for the future, pay any garnish, it having been found for many years a great oppression' (22: 239).

129 _no absolute Dependence ... Great Men_: the topic of one of the most famous airs in _The Beggar's Opera_, sung by Macheath to the popular tune of 'Lillibulero' (the original lyrics of which celebrated a late seventeenth-century Irish promise to cut Englishmen's throats):

> The mode of the court so common are grown
> That a true friend can hardly be met;
> Friendship for interest is but a loan,
> Which they let out for what they can get. (Air 54, III. iv)

Issues concerned with the importance of friendship, and its uneasy relationship to dependence on those with power and influence, are explored again and again in HF's work, most extensively in _Amelia_, and also in Sarah Fielding's _David Simple_ and its sequel _Volume the Last_ (1753).

_a Visit from his Wife_: reminiscent of the visit of Polly Peachum and Lucy Lockit (both of whom consider themselves to be the wives of Macheath) to Macheath in _The Beggar's Opera_. HF later showed, in the heroine of _Amelia_ (1751), a dutiful wife visiting her husband in Newgate and making every effort to get him released; in _The Countess of Dellwyn_ (1759) Sarah Fielding told a similar story of Mrs Bilson, who when her husband was imprisoned in Newgate, insisted on going to live with him there until she could earn enough money to get him released.

130 _found guilty Death_: echoing the phrasing of the legal verdict: see for example, '_John Chance_ deposed, That he and the Prisoner committed the Fact. Guilty, _Death_' (_Select Trials_, ii. 268).

_to the End of the Chapter_: to the end, throughout.

_that's infallible_: that cannot fail to happen.

_Cull_: 'A man.—_Cull_ is likewise frequently used to signify a Fool' (the Marshal's 'List of _Flash Words_', _Select Trials_, ii. 234).

_Waste_: waist.

131 _Anecdotes_: secret, private, or previously unpublished narratives. The more modern meaning of an anecdote as a narrative of a single event, often as a matter of gossip, is not recorded in _OED_ until the 1760s.

*the History of Newgate*: the struggle for power over the prisoners of Newgate, and its outcome, as described in this chapter, reflects to some extent a real-life situation in Newgate (see note below), but also has wider contemporary political resonances. In 1742 Walpole was finally brought down by his long-standing parliamentary rival William Pulteney. Walpole had been deeply unpopular and many, including HF, had placed confidence in Pulteney's promises of reform and improvement. 'Pulteney was one of the first politicians to head a sustained appeal to public opinion, only to raise hopes which he dashed. With a great reputation as a debater, he was increasingly mistrusted by his allies . . . His failure to effect reform or root out corruption after Walpole's fall was thought by many to reveal factiousness and self-seeking and he was accused of avarice' (Cannon). In this context Johnson is the Walpole figure, with Wild representing Pulteney. This shift in direction is typical of HF's methodology in his plays, where his political satire often shifts between characters and situations.

*Roger Johnson, a very great Man*: the real-life Roger Johnson knew Wild, and had a position in Newgate somewhat resembling that described, but not in Wild's lifetime. Johnson was born *c*.1695. In 1718 he was condemned to death for 'the Kid Lay' ('when you see a Boy or a Porter with a Bundle, [you] desire him to go of an Errand for you, telling him you'll take Care of his Goods the while; but, as soon as he's out of Sight, you make off with the Booty'—*Select Trials*, ii. 234), but reprieved; and he then went into business with Wild, acting as captain of a ship which they used for smuggling. When Wild himself was arrested Johnson was implicated in various Wild activities; however he seems to have remained mostly at liberty until 1729. Later, back in Newgate, he eventually 'became more or less responsible for the discipline of the prison. He used to hold rehearsal trials at which prisoners would have to answer questions likely to be made against them at the Old Bailey. Under his rule, Newgate became quite an orderly place' (Howson, 289–90). By this time prisoners were largely responsible for managing their own affairs and elected officers to lead them. Contemporaries concluded that Johnson 'did as it were govern the whole Goal . . . *Roger*'s Word was a Law, and the rest of the Prisoners stood in fear of him' (*A Full and Particular Account of the Life and Notorious Transactions of Roger Johnson* (1740), 25). He was finally released under an amnesty and died in 1740.

132 *Friends and Fellow-Citizens*: a typical beginning to a dramatic set-piece speech: see for example Brutus' 'Romans, countrymen, and lovers!' and Mark Antony's 'Friends, Romans, countrymen' (Shakespeare, *Julius Caesar*, III. ii).

*Perquisites*: the benefits beyond wages that an individual gains from a position, often—as here—in the form of articles that have served their primary purpose and are left to the individual to 'pick up' for his or her own use.

132 *Velvet Cap*: caps and turbans were widely worn to cover men's heads, shaved in order to be comfortable under wigs.

133 *waved that Motion*: in debating terms, to put aside that proposition for the present, with the notion of reserving it for discussion at a later opportunity.

134 *a very grave Man, and one of much Authority among them*: recalling *Aeneid*, 1. 148–53. John Dryden's translation of the passage, as quoted by HF in the *Champion*, 15 January 1740, is as follows:

> As, when in Tumults rise th'ignoble Crowd,
> Mad are their Motions, and their Tongues are loud;
> And Stones and Brands in rattling Vollies fly,
> And all the rustick Arms that Fury can supply:
> If then some grave and pious Man appear,
> They hush their Noise, and lend a listning Ear;
> He sooths with sober Words their angry Mood,
> And quenches their innate Desire of Blood.

*bespoke them as follows*: in the Advertisement attached to the 1754 edition—stated to be by the publisher but possibly written by HF—readers are recommended to 'the Perusal of the third Chapter of the fourth Book . . . , and more particularly still the speech of the Grave Man' (see Appendix 3). It is possible that HF is alluding to the staunch Tory and Jacobite William Shippen (1673–1743), who frequently opposed Walpole in Parliament and who, on the opposition Whig motion against Walpole in 1741, walked out, declaring that ' "he would not pull down Robin on republican principles"' (Romney Sedgwick, *The History of Parliament: The House of Commons, 1715–1754* (London: HMSO, 1970, s.v. Shippen). 'Bespoke them' means 'spoke to them'.

*lay the Lamb in the Wolf's Way, and then lament his being devoured*: proverbial, but probably recalling 'Misplaced Confidence', one of Aesop's *Fables*.

*His own Priggish Desires . . . the Tyranny of others*: Plato's *Republic*, Book 9, concerning 'The Tyrannical Character: Its essential similarity to the Criminal Type', includes the argument that tyrannical characters 'are always either masters or slaves, but the tyrannical nature never tastes freedom or true friendship' (s. 576).

*Let us consider ourselves all as Members . . . which shall accrue to ourselves*: see note to p. 122.

135 *Dead-Warrant*: warrant for carrying out the death sentence.

137 *Have not whole Armies and Nations been sacrificed to the Humour of one great man*: in 'Of True Greatness' HF writes

> Shall ravag'd Fields, and burning Towns proclaim
> The Hero's Glory, not the Robber's Shame?
> Shall Thousands fall, and Millions be undone
> To glut the hungry Cruelty of one? (lines 73–6, *M1*, 22)

'Humour' was changed to 'Honour' in 1754.

*I ought rather to weep . . . the little I have done*: another reference to the famous anecdote; see note to p. 43.

*any Man so completely great . . . in the latter*: HF expands on this idea in *Tom Jones* where he warns readers 'not to condemn a Character as a bad one, because it is not perfectly a good one' (x. i), and where he presents in Tom a hero who is far from perfect. His presentation of such 'mixed' characters made him the undeclared target of much of Samuel Johnson's famous *Rambler* essay of 31 March 1750 which, in contending that mixed characters offered readers a bad example, argues that 'It is . . . not a sufficient Vindication of a Character, that it is drawn as it appears; for many Characters ought never to be drawn.'

138 *Stoic*: one who practises repression of emotion and patient endurance. Stoicism was a school of Greek philosophy founded by Zeno (335–263 BC) characterized by the austerity of its ethical doctrines, which were often praised in the eighteenth century.

*the Coach, which Friendly had provided for him*: felons would normally be taken on the journey from Newgate to Tyburn in an open cart, which left them vulnerable to the shouts and missiles of watching crowds. According to *Parker's Penny Post* the real Jonathan Wild, who was 'convey'd in a Cart, without a Hat', was pelted 'by Dirt and Stones' so that he 'suffer'd much', while 'the Blood flew . . . plentifully' from another felon in the same cart through cuts he received from stones aimed at Wild (26 May 1725).

139 *the Tree*: that is, the gallows at Tyburn.

140 *to bleed them all*: drawing blood was widely practised in eighteenth-century medicine as a restorative measure.

*lest our Reprieve should seem to resemble that in the Beggar's Opera*: at the end of Gay's hugely popular play the condemned highwayman Macheath is arbitrarily reprieved because 'an opera must end happily . . . to comply with the taste of the town' (*Beggar's Opera*, III. xvi).

*This Magistrate . . . every minute Circumstance*: this behaviour, which differs markedly from that of most other magistrates in HF's writing (from Squeezum in *Rape upon Rape* to Thrasher in *Amelia*), exemplifies HF's belief here that it is not the law that is at fault, but the corrupt way the law is operated.

141 *very home*: very directly, point blank.

*the Sovereign; who immediately granted him that gracious Reprieve*: the fate of every convict sentenced to death at the Old Bailey was decided at a meeting of ministers and other officials, often in the presence of the King, and always making their decisions under his personal authority, on the basis of a verbal report from the city recorder along with written petitions from the convict's friends or relatives. A reprieve was usually the result of personal appeal or other intervention; it did not necessarily result in a full pardon, since some other punishment could be substituted; but a high proportion of condemned men and women went on to be pardoned.

141 *the Critics . . . every Author*: given the relatively small group of literate people who visited the theatre and read new books in London, and the importance of word-of-mouth in a work's success, all attendees could be considered as critics; but this may allude particularly to the group of professional or semi-professional writers who reviewed new works in journals and pamphlets, and with whom authors and playwrights conducted an ongoing battle. HF omitted the reference in 1754.

143 *struck his Colours . . . a Prize*: see note to p. 75. The idea here is for the ship to come to near standstill to wait for the other ship, hoping to capture her.

144 *a third Rate English Man of War*: ships of the British Navy were divided into six rates, according to the number of guns carried, a first rate ship being the biggest.

145 *a Basha to a Circassian Slave*: a basha or bashaw or pasha was a Turkish governor; such men were known to have great power and to keep slaves in harems and so were something of a byword for exotic licentiousness.

146 *Coquet*: the masculine form, gradually falling out of regular use by the 1740s, of 'coquette'.

*Gangway*: the narrow platform between the upper decks at the back and the front of the ship.

147 *a virtuous and a brave Fellow . . . put over his Head*: HF frequently criticizes the injustices caused as a result of military and naval appointments being made through patronage and/or by purchase; see also, for example, the 'worthy lieutenant' of nearly 60 years old who had distinguished himself in battle but 'had seen vast Numbers preferred over his Head, and had now the Mortification to be commanded by Boys, whose Fathers were at Nurse when he first entered into the Service' (*Tom Jones*, VII. xii).

*Cork*: a small fishing port in Southern Ireland.

*Brigantine*: small vessel equipped for both sailing and rowing, and therefore often employed for purposes of piracy or reconnoitring.

*Leagues*: a maritime league was usually 3 nautical miles.

148 *Boat*: lifeboat.

*Go thy Ways . . . to my dying Day*: in *Amelia* HF presented a very similar scene of a storm at sea, ending in the captain's vain efforts 'to save his dear *Lovely Peggy* . . . which he swore he loved as dearly as his own Soul' (III. iv).

149 *the utmost Dexterity of the most accomplished French Cook would have been ineffectual, had he endeavoured to tempt me with Delicacies*: at a time when English food focused on roast beef and pudding the French were noted for their more sophisticated cuisine.

150 *Chapter IX*: omitted in the 1754 text. HF described this in the Preface to
the *Miscellanies* as 'a Burlesque on the extravagant Accounts of Travellers' (*M1*, 11). Travellers' tales were popular at a time when exotic parts
of the world were still largely undiscovered by Western travellers, whose
exaggerated claims merged into the outright fictions of authors such as
Defoe in *The Adventures of Robinson Crusoe* (1719) and Swift in *Gulliver's
Travels* (1726). HF might also have had in mind Lucian's *A True Story*:
after castigating the 'charlatanry' of Homer and others who have written
of 'imaginary travels and journeys . . . telling of huge beasts, cruel men,
and strange ways of living' Lucian declares 'I am writing about things
which I have neither seen nor had to do with nor learned from others—
which, in fact, do not exist at all and, in the nature of things, cannot exist'
(1. 4).

151 *Neck Beef*: beef taken from the neck of the cow was known as of coarse,
inferior quality.

152 *the celebrated Phœnix . . . known*: a mythical bird of gorgeous plumage,
fabled to be the only one of its kind, and to live five or six hundred years,
after which it burns itself on a pyre, to emerge from ashes with renewed
youth, to live through another cycle of years.

*the famous Stone-henge in Wiltshire*: a spectacular archaeological site, consisting of over 70 standing stones, most of them set in a horseshoe shape,
with capping stones up to 22 feet above ground.

153 *a speaking Trumpet*: 'a conical tube with a wide mouth, used for increasing the force and carrying power of the voice' (*OED*).

154 *reflecting on*: fixing the mind or attention on.

155 *Casket of Jewels*: in fact the Count had already taken the jewels individu-
ally from the lining of his waistcoat (see p. 154).

156 *Hermite*: several of HF's fictions include a hermit figure—a man who has
withdrawn from the world in disillusion—who helps the hero or heroine
in distress, see for example The Man of the Hill in *Tom Jones* (VIII. x–
xv). The figure of the hermit was significant in eighteenth-century
thought, representing reaction against the increasing commercialization
and commodification of urban life.

157 *the whole Gate*: the whole of Newgate.

*the hundred Tongues the Poet once wished for*: the Sibyl, guiding Aeneas on
his visit to the underworld, shows him a horrific scene of the wicked
undergoing torture in hell: 'All dared a monstrous sin, and what they
dared attained. Nay, had I a hundred tongues, a hundred mouths and
voice of iron, I could not sum up all the forms of crime, or rehearse all
the tale of torments' (Virgil, *Aeneid*, 6. 624–7).

158 *generous*: including the now obsolete meanings of high-born, of good
breed or stock.

*his Walks*: his haunts, the place where he grazed.

158 *a visiting Day*: a day formally designated for receiving visitors, a regular social event for the leisured classes.

*the Hedge of his Teeth*: a phrase used by Homer in *Iliad*, 9. 409, and *Odyssey*, 10. 328.

*Pattin*: pattens were overshoes made with wooden soles raised on iron rings, which protected the rather flimsy leather or fabric shoes of the period from the mud.

*Amazon of Drury*: a mock-heroic term denoting a combative woman of Drury Lane, an area of London associated with actresses and prostitutes. Amazons were of renewed interest in the early 1740s: Abbé C. Guyon's *Histoire des Amazons* appeared in 1740 and an excerpt, translated by Samuel Johnson, appeared in *Gentleman's Magazine*, 11 (April 1741), 202–8.

159 *My —— in a Bandbox*: 'My Arse in a Bandbox'—'that won't do' (Partridge, but dating only to later in the eighteenth century). A bandbox is a very light flimsy box; the 1811 *Dictionary of the Vulgar Tongue* has 'my arse on a bandbox', that is, deriving from the idea of a bottom with something very inappropriate to sit on. Bandboxes were used by clergymen to keep their clerical bands etc. in so a coarse juxtaposition may have been intended (Brewer).

*Doctors Commons*: originally the common or dining table of the Association of College of Doctors of Civil Law in London, and hence the buildings occupied by them on St Bennet's Hill, just south of St Paul's Cathedral. Divorce suits were among the various ecclesiastical and civil law cases heard there.

*modern Method . . . of resenting this Affront*: that is, by prosecuting Fireblood for damages for adultery, or 'criminal conversation'.

161 *Flip*: 'a liquor much used in ships, made by mixing beer with spirits and sugar' (Johnson).

*'Fore George*: 'St George' was the battlecry of English soldiers, invoking their national saint, and from this arose such expressions as 'before George' or 'fore George' (Brewer).

162 *Aldermen*: each of the twenty-six wards of the City of London was led by an alderman elected for life; the Lord Mayor was chosen from among the aldermen.

*Schach Pimpach*: probably King of Pimps; 'schach' was one of the several ways of spelling 'shah' in the seventeenth and eighteenth centuries.

163 *Gravesend . . . to the Tower*: the River Thames was navigable for small and medium size boats as far as London, and the Tower of London—not much more than a mile from Newgate—was a popular landing stage.

164 *File*: a pickpocket, one of those 'who generally go in Company with a Rogue, called a *Bulk* or *Bulker*, whose Business 'tis to jostle the Person against the Wall, while the *File* picks his Pocket' (*NCD*).

Socrates ... *Patience and Resignation*: Xenophon describes Socrates' equanimity in preparing for his trial, including his remark to Hermogenes that 'Perhaps God in his kindness is taking my part and securing me the opportunity of ending my life not only in season but also in the way that is easiest' (*Socrates' Defence to the Jury*, 7). See also note to p. 97.

165 —*nec ... vetustas*: the original quote is from the closing paragraphs of Ovid's *Metamorphoses*, where the poet calls for his own literary immortality by claiming it is something 'which neither the wrath of Jove, nor fire, nor sword, nor the gnawing tooth of time shall ever be able to undo' (15. 871–2). HF adapts the sentiment to JW's circumstances by replacing 'Iovis'—of Jove—with 'Judicis'—of the judge. HF quotes the original accurately in 'Of the Remedy of Affliction for the Loss of our Friends' (*MI*, 217).

*our great Dramatic Poet ... rais'd it*: referring ironically in this context not to Shakespeare but to Colley Cibber, since the lines quoted are Cibber's at the end of Act III in his version of Shakespeare's *Richard III*. In *The Historical Register for the Year 1736* (1737) HF had ridiculed the attempts of Ground-Ivy (Cibber) to improve Shakespeare's *King John* ('Shakespeare was a pretty Fellow, and said some things which only want a little of my licking to do well enough' (III. i)). 'Th'aspiring Youth' is Herostratus, who burned the temple of Diana in order to gain fame.

*The Ordinary of Newgate ... after it had past*: the Ordinary often published his own account of his last interviews with condemned criminals— see for example Thomas Purney, *The Ordinary of Newgate His Account of the Behaviour, Last Dying Speeches and Confessions of the Four Malefactors Who Were Executed at Tyburn ... the 24th of May, 1725* (1725) which included JW (though in fact Purney was unlikely to have heard Wild's dying speech—see note to p. 125). In the introduction to *Miscellanies* (see p. 219) 'The Ordinary's Account' is also included in *Select Trials* (ii. 284–8). HF said that one of the few 'Papers' relating to JW he had seen was the account of the Ordinary of Newgate. The account bears little resemblance to the dialogue that follows here.

166 *Those who do Evil ... Devil and his Angels*: an adaptation of the famous passage in Matthew 25 in which Jesus says the day will come when he will separate people as a shepherd separates the sheep from the goats; the virtuous will inherit the kingdom of heaven; but to the rest he will say, 'Depart from me, ye cursed, into everlasting fire, prepared for the devil and his angels ... And these shall go away into everlasting punishment' (25: 41, 46).

*Hull*: the hull is the husk, or outer covering, of a fruit or vegetable, or a boat without sails or oars; to hull is 'to float; to drive to and fro upon the water without sails or rudder' (Johnson).

167 *the Eloquence of Cicero, or of Tully*: Tully and Cicero are both names for the Roman orator Marcus Tullius Cicero (106–43 BC).

*that Ear hath not heard, nor can Heart conceive*: 'But as it is written, Eye hath not seen, nor ear heard, neither have entered into the heart

of man, the things which God hath prepared for them that love him'
(1 Corinthians 2: 9).

168 *Atheist . . . cinian*: all terms of abuse by High Church clergy who criticized those with more liberal views, of which there were an increasing
number in the eighteenth century. Deists, Arians (named after Arius
(*c.*250–336), who preached in Alexandria), and Socinians (named after
Laelius and Faustus Socinus, two Italian Renaissance theologians) all saw
God as in some way the supreme bring, but denied the divinity of Christ.

*Hopes of a Reprieve . . . yet*: the real Wild had 'some Expectations of a
Reprieve' (*Select Trials*, ii. 285*)*.

*nothing . . . as the Poet says*: in Edward Young's *The Revenge* (1721)
Alonzo, a type of the Great Man or conqueror, says, 'Death joins us to
the great Majority: | 'Tis to be born to *Plato's* and to *Caesar*' (Act IV;
reprinted in *The Poetical Works of Edward Young* (1741), ii. 285, a copy of
which HF owned).

169 *since he knows you are his . . . have his Due*: 'the Devil will have his due' is
proverbial.

170 *the Gravel*: a disease involving pain and difficulty passing urine.

171 *To the Greeks Foolishness*: the full text is 'For the Jews require a sign, and
the Greeks seek after wisdom: But we preach Christ crucified, unto the
Jews a stumblingblock, and unto the Greeks foolishness' (1 Corinthians
1: 22–3). The passage was often used as the basis for sermons arguing the
inadequacy of heathen philosophers, but the Ordinary here, by omitting
the Christian context, distorts the meaning of the phrase he uses. HF
parodies a number of familiar oratorical techniques associated with
sermons, a very popular literary genre at the time.

173 *Apotheosis*: rise to glory; literally, deification, transformation into a god.
In *An Enquiry into the Causes of the late Increase of Robbers* (1751) HF
argues non-satirically against the practice of public hanging in general,
partly because 'The Day appointed by Law for the Thief's Shame is the
Day of Glory in his own Opinion. His Procession to *Tyburn*, and his last
Moment there, all are triumphant; attended with the Compassion of the
meek and tender-hearted, and with the Applause, Admiration, and Envy
of all the bold and hardened' (xi, p. 121).

*Catastrophe*: the final event in a play, denouement. In *Tom Jones* HF
criticized plays in which a happy ending was achieved only because characters behaved inconsistently, and commented on the likelihood of their
rather making a 'heroic Figure' at the gallows (VIII. i). See also note to
p. 140.

174 *Pasteboard*: a substitute for thin wooden board made by pasting sheets of
paper together—possibly the material used for records of the Ordinaries
of Newgate and similar pamphlets.

*as heartily as his Chains would suffer him*: condemned criminals were often
bound by chains and fetters. One account of the real Wild's journey to

Tyburn says that 'his not having his Hands tied all the Way' was an 'Indulgence' (Applebee's journal, quoted by Howson, 275).

*Laudanum*: a drug of which opium was the chief ingredient; in small quantities it was used as a painkiller and general soporific, but its lethal properties were known. The incident here is based on events the night before the real-life Wild's execution. The Ordinary of Newgate recorded that JW 'endeavoured to prevent his Execution by drinking *Laudanum*; but the Largeness of the Draught, together with his having fasted before, instead of destroying him immediately, was the Cause of his not dying by it' (*Select Trials*, ii. 286).

*the Fruit of the Hemp-Seed and not the Spirit of Poppy-Seed*: the strong rope used for hanging was made of the woven fibres of the hemp plant. Laudanum was derived from the seeds of the opium poppy.

175 *his Repetition*: the Ordinary would have a certain number of biblical verses to say or 'repeat' to the condemned man in order to carry out his designated function of preparing him for the afterlife.

*Suave Mari . . . spectare Laborem*: 'Pleasant it is, when over a great sea the winds trouble the waters, to gaze from shore upon another's great tribulation' (Lucretius, *De Rerum Natura*, 2. 1–2).

*Conservation of Character*: in *Tom Jones* HF describes 'what dramatic Critics call Conservation of Character', which 'requires a very extraordinary Degree of Judgment, and a most exact Knowledge of human Nature': he criticizes 'modern Authors of Comedy' whose 'Heroes generally are notorious Rogues, and their Heroines abandoned Jades, during the first four Acts; but in the fifth, the former become very worthy Gentlemen, and the latter, Women of Virtue and Discretion: Nor is the Writer often so kind as to give himself the least Trouble, to reconcile or account for this monstrous Change and Incongruity. There is, indeed, no other Reason to be assigned for it, than because the Play is drawing to a Conclusion; as if it was no less natural in a Rogue to repent in the last Act of a Play, than in the last of his Life; which we perceive to be generally the case at *Tyburn*, a Place which might, indeed, close the Scene of some Comedies with much Propriety, as the Heroes in these are most commonly eminent for those very Talents which not only bring Men to the Gallows, but enable them to make an heroic Figure when they are there' (VIII. i). See Introduction, pp. xxvi–xxix.

176 *carried out of the World in his Hand*: none of the accounts of the real-life Wild record this detail; however, an anecdote about Paul Lorrain, Ordinary of Newgate in the early years of the century, describes how 'one Wretch more harden'd than the rest, made an Attempt upon Mr. *Lorrain*'s Pocket just before he was turn'd off' (*A Trip through London*, 8th edn. (1728), 51). Another possible source, as discussed in the Introduction (p. xxix), is *The History of Charles XII*. After describing in gruesome detail the death of Charles XII when cannon shot pierced his temple, Voltaire continues, 'He was dead in an instant; but he had the force in

that instant to put his hand to the guard of his sword, and lay in that posture' (p. 318).

176  *the Character of this great Man*: the kind of summing up which frequently closed the biographies of the period and earlier. See, for example, the summary of Charles XII's character in *History of Charles XII*, 139–40.

*his most powerful and predominant Passion was Ambition*: alluding once more to earlier 'great men' such as Alexander, Julius Caesar, and Charles XII of Sweden. See for example notes to pp. 14 and 43.

177  *a Corruption of Honosty . . . an Ass*: the Greek word for ass is όνος. HF used a very similar play on the same words in the *Vernoniad* in another allusion to Walpole (n. 24).

*Negative*: negation, to which the word was changed in 1754.

*Hypocrisy*: throughout *Miscellanies* HF reserves some of his strongest moral criticisms for hypocrisy, and hypocrisy in its various forms is a particular focus of 'An Essay on the Knowledge of the Characters of Men' (*M2*, 153–78). 'Thus while the crafty and designing Part of Mankind, consulting only their own separate Advantage, endeavour to maintain one constant Imposition on others, the whole World becomes a vast Masquerade, where the greatest Part appear disguised under false Vizors and Habits' (p. 155).

*several Maxims . . . to which . . . he constantly adhered*: maxims and wise sayings of the hero are standard features of the biographies of great men; there may also be a connection with the real-life Wild: the *Life* included in *Lives . . . of the most Famous Highwaymen* (see note to p. 10) indicates a few of the 'Maxims by which he supported himself in this dangerous capacity' (p. 467).

178  *the twelve excellent and celebrated Rules . . . of King Charles the first*: these 'Twelve Good Rules' were framed and displayed in many taverns in the eighteenth century. They derived from a broadside illustrating the execution of Charles I and were said to have been 'found in the study of King Charles the First of Blessed Memory', though there is no firm evidence of this. The rules were (1) Urge no healths; (2) Profane no divine ordinances; (3) Touch no state matters; (4) Reveal no secrets; (5) Pick no quarrels; (6) Make no comparisons; (7) Maintain no ill opinions; (8) Keep no bad company; (9) Encourage no vice; (10) Make no long meals; (11) Repeat no grievances; (12) Lay no wagers (Brewer).

179  *—A privilege to kill, | A strong Temptation to do bravely ill*: in the opening scene of Nathaniel Lee's *Sophonisba* (1676) King Massinissa rejects ambition as

> The Lust of Power.
> Like Glory, Boy, it licenses to kill;
> A strong Temptation to do bravely ill;
> A Bait to draw the Bold and Backward in,
> The dear-bought Recompence of highest Sin.

The phrase 'Privilege to kill' occurs in *Mustapha* by Roger Boyle, 1st Earl of Orrery (*Dramatic Works* (1739), i. 384).

*Lætius est . . . honestum*: Lucan, *The Civil War*, 9. 404. The original, part of Cato's speech to his soldiers praising their courage and willingness to endure hardship, reads 'Laetius est, quotiens magno sibi constat, honestum'—'virtue rejoices when it pays dear for its existence'; HF's replacement of 'sibi' by 'tibi' alters the sense to 'virtue rejoices when you pay dear for its existence'.

*the Clemency of Alexander and Cæsar*: see note to p. 9.

181 *the Family of Love*: a favourite phrase of both HF and Sarah Fielding: it is used for example in HF's *The Author's Farce* (1. 7) and the *Champion* (26 February 1740), and extensively in SF's *David Simple* (1744) and its sequel *Volume the Last* (1753). The phrase originally alluded to a sect which flourished in the sixteenth and seventeenth and lingered into the eighteenth centuries, who maintained that all people were of one family and that religion consisted essentially of love, there is no indication that this specialist use was intended by either Fielding.

*we may say with the Divine . . . it costs him to purchase Hell*: possibly a reference to Robert South, 'this we may with great Boldness venture to affirm, that if Men would be at half the Pains to provide themselves *Treasure in Heaven*, which they are generally at to get Estates here on Earth, it were impossible for any Man to be damned' ('A Discourse preached at Christ-Church, *Oxon.*' in *Twelve Sermons preached at several Times*, 5th edn. (1722), 541).

## APPENDIX 1

title page *H.D. . . . Justice R——*: this account, published within months of Wild's death, purports to be by the clerk to Sir Robert Raymond, Lord Chief Justice of the King's Bench from March 1725. It has been suggested that Sir Robert may have presided over Wild's trial; but the Session books for the period do not mention his name (Howson, 258). It has also been suggested that 'H.D.' might be a pseudonym for Daniel Defoe (1660–1731), who was in London writing a variety of factual and fictional works in the 1720s. However scholars are now doubtful about this. P. N. Furbank and W. R. Owens, *Defoe De-Attributions: A Critique of J. R. Moore's Checklist* (London: Hambledon, 1994), 138–9, conclude that Defoe was probably not the author, while Defoe's latest biographer feels only that 'It is tempting to think that Defoe was the author' (Maximilian E. Novak, *Daniel Defoe, Master of Fictions: His Life and Ideas* (Oxford: Oxford University Press, 2001), 642). It was printed by T. Warner, of Paternoster Row, who printed and sold innumerable pamphlets, including Wild's own *An Answer to a Late Insolent Libel*, replying to *A True Discovery of the Conduct of Receivers and Thief-Takers, in and about the City of LONDON*, written by his early mentor and rival Charles Hitchen in 1718; see note to p. 210 below.

185 *Machiavel*: Niccolò Machiavelli (1469–1527), Italian statesman and author of the classic prose text about politics and the state *The Prince* (1532), recognized throughout Europe as a master of pragmatic, not to say devious, politics.

*betwixt Scylla and Charybdis*: one of the many trials Odysseus successfully undergoes in his return from the siege of Troy is to steer his ship between two great rocks on one of which is the multi-headed monster Scylla, and on the other Charybdis, 'who sucks down the black water' (*Odyssey*, 12. 104).

186 *the late War between France and the Confederates*: the War of the Spanish Succession (1702–13) was fought to prevent Louis XIV from assimilating Spain and its possessions in the Netherlands and Italy into an enlarged French monarchy. Despite a series of early victories by the 'Confederates'—Britain, the United Provinces, Austria, Prussia, Hanover, and other German states—the war eventually reached stalemate on land and sea, and it was concluded by the Treaty of Utrecht (1713) when France's aims were no longer feasible.

187 *Bailiff's Follower*: see note to p. 11.

*cum multis aliis*: along with many other things.

*Groat*: a groat was worth fourpence, but the coins ceased to be in general circulation from 1662, and thereafter the word was used more generally to mean a small sum.

191 *the Compter*: Wild was committed to the Compter in Wood Street, which lies between Cheapside and London Wall, in 1710; the Compter was a debtors' prison but 'Most people arrested in the City were taken there for a night or two before going to Newgate, and there was a section reserved for "Rats" – that is, drunks, street-walkers, vagabonds, stray children and other "nuisances" picked up in the night by the Marshals or the Watch' (Howson, 15).

192 *Cornelius Tilburn, a noted Quack Doctor*: Howson links Tilburn to another of Wild's exploits, in which 'Jonathan Wild appear'd on his Recognizances at Guild-Hall to take his Tryal, but the Quack Doctor not appearing, nor any of his Evidences, he was discharged of the Prosecution' (*Original Weekly Journal*, 16 May 1719).

*Action of Trover*: 'an action at law to recover the value of personal property illegally converted by another to his own use' (*OED*).

*Tilburn was non-suited*: that is, the judge stopped the case or suit, because in his opinion Tilburn as plaintiff had failed to bring sufficient evidence to make his legal case.

193 *Hackney*: now very much part of the East End of London, but then a village within walking distance to the east of the city.

*Chinee*: probably Chinese satin or silk, which had begun to be imported in the late seventeenth century and which was highly valued.

*the late Act . . . Highwaymen*: under an Act of 1691 an informer who succeeded in convicting a highwayman would receive a reward of £40; this system was extended to cover coiners in 1695 and burglars in 1706. If the informer was an accomplice of those found guilty he or she would also be given a free pardon. In 1720 all streets in London and other cities were declared 'highways' under the 1692 statute, and a royal proclamation in the same year offered £100 over and above the £40 reward for the conviction of robbers who committed offences within 5 miles of Charing Cross, and for murderers (Beattie, 231, 378).

195 *The Mint in Southwark*: one of the last remaining sanctuaries for insolvent debtors, so called because Henry VIII had kept a mint there.

197 *Gentlemen of the Snaffle*: a gentleman of the snaffle is 'a highwayman that has got booty' (*OED*).

199 *Orange . . . with Darts*: the soft skin of oranges was pierced with cloves for use in flavouring food and drink; almanacks, which were very popular, frequently contained a picture of a person, often an old man, pierced with twelve diagrammatic arrows indicating how specific parts of the body related to signs of the Zodiac.

*Livery and Seisin*: more correctly 'livery of seisin', 'the delivery of property into the corporal possession of a person' (*OED*), that is, the material handover of goods.

200 *lying perdue*: lying 'in ambush, in wait, in order to surprise or attack' (*OED*).

*in utrumque parati*: literally, prepared for other things.

201 *Hops*: a hop was 'a dancing party, esp. of an informal or unceremonious kind' (*OED*). *OED* gives first usage of this in 1731.

202 *Sir Fopling*: Sir Fopling Flutter was the larger-than-life 'prince of fops' in George Etherege's popular play *The Man of Mode* (first performed 1676).

206 *to take common Bail*: bail 'is used in our Common Law for the Freeing or Setting at Liberty of one arrested or imprisoned upon any Action, either Civil or Criminal, on Surety taken for his Appearance at a Day and Place certain' (Jacob).

*a Bill in the Exchequer*: a formal claim for the money in the Court of the Exchequer, which dealt with some financial claims.

*a cross Bill*: a counterpetition.

*the Suit at Common Law went against him also, by Default*: because the Court of Exchequer verdict went against him the earlier common law suit fell.

207 *Squadron . . . Detachment*: military terms for small bodies of men separated from the main force or army.

*Purgatory*: literally, place of temporary suffering or purification.

209 *Mirmidons*: a myrmidon, originally one of a warlike race of men inhabiting Thessaly, whom Achilles led to the siege of Troy, had become 'an

unscrupulously faithful follower or hireling . . . often applied con-
temptuously to a policeman, bailiff, or other inferior administrative
officer of the law' (*OED*).

210  *one Felt——n, a superannuated Thief, Riddlesd——n an Attorney and
     Thief, . . . and Mr. H——n, City Mar——l*: little is known about
     Edward Felton, who is listed in the London rolls of 1719 as a thieftaker,
     and who on one occasion charged Wild unsuccessfully with assault
     (Howson, 135). A 'William Rigelsden' is listed in the 'List of the Persons
     discover'd, apprehended, and convicted' by him that Wild presented at
     his trial in 1725: Rigelsden is said to have been caught with Elizabeth
     Shirley 'For breaking into a Dwelling-house, adjoining to the Banquet-
     ing-house, *White-hall*; and from thence breaking into the Banquetting-
     house, and stole from the Communion-table a silver Candlestick' (*Select
     Trials*, ii. 216, 218); Riglesden and Riddlesden are identified as the same
     person later in the account, which states that Riddlesden, an attorney,
     was transported for the theft of the candlestick, returned to England, was
     transported again, and 'we have not yet heard of his being hang'd' (ii.
     266). Charles Hitchen, appointed Under City Marshal in 1712 and
     known as 'the Marshal', first employed Wild and then in 1718, alarmed
     by Wild's success, tried to discredit him by writing a hostile pamphlet, to
     which Wild replied; in 1727 he was convicted of attempting to commit
     sodomy and although he survived his punishment—a fine, a period in the
     pillory, and imprisonment—he was dismissed from his post and died
     shortly afterwards in extreme poverty (Howson, 49–56, 288). A very
     detailed account of Hitchen's relationship with Wild is given in *Select
     Trials* (ii. 236–59).

211  *Ticket Porters*: a ticket porter was 'a member of a body of porters in the
     City of London who were originally licensed by the Corporation, orig.
     called *street-porters*' (*OED*).

     *the young Duchess of Marlborough . . . Mrs. H——n's in Piccadilly*: Lady
     Henrietta Godolphin had become second Duchess of Marlborough on
     the death of the first Duke, John Churchill, in 1722. The anecdote is
     presented in *Select Trials*, ii. 260–1, as taking place in 1715. Mrs *H——n*
     is unidentified.

212  *the Author of the Fable of the Bees*: Bernard de Mandeville (1670–1733)
     wrote moral and satirical verse and pamphlets. His *The Fable of the Bees;
     or, Private Vices, Public Benefits* (1714, 1723) famously rejected optimistic
     views of human nature, and argued that the prosperity, and smooth run-
     ning, of society depends not upon mutual support but upon personal
     acquisitiveness and the love of luxury.

     *Mrs. Knap . . . Gray's-Inn-Wall*: the incident is described in *Select Trials*,
     ii. 262–4, as taking place in 1716.

213  *Sir W——m T——son*: Sir William Thomson, who became City
     Recorder (the Recorder being 'a person with legal knowledge appointed
     by the mayor and aldermen to "record" or keep in mind the proceedings
     of their courts and the customs of the city' (*OED*)) in 1714, was widely

seen to be behind the clause accurately quoted here, included in the 'Transportation Act' of 1718 and assumed to be aimed at curbing Wild's activities. Thomson was also active in the eventual arrest and conviction of Wild in 1725 (Howson, 92, 238–40). See note to p. 128.

*R——r*: Recorder; see note above.

214 *South Sea Bubble*: five years after its collapse, a byword for a fraudulent and unprofitable trading venture.

*one Roger J——son*: Roger Johnson, who worked with Wild (see note to p. 131).

216 *one Rann, a notorious Acquaintance*: Jeremiah Rann or Rand was clearly a confederate of Wild's; *Select Trials* recounts this anecdote in very similar terms (ii. 280). Rann appears on Jonathan Wild's list of those he has brought to justice, in Rann's case in May 1722 'For assaulting and robbing a *Clock-maker*'s Servant of a Clock, who lives in *Lombard street* (*Select Trials*, ii. 217).

217 *Quem Jupiter . . . Mind to destroy*: proverbial, originating in one of the *Fragments* of Euripides.

## APPENDIX 2

219 *a single Paper . . . what they did in this*: Wild's death was important news at the time, and there were many reports in contemporary newspapers, including in *Mist's Weekly Journal*, 22 and 29 May, and 12 and 19 June 1725. In addition there were a large number of pamphlets, including 'H. D.' 's account (see Appendix 1). Thomas Purney, *The Ordinary of Newgate His Account of the Behaviour, Last Dying Speeches and Confessions of the Four Malefactors who were executed at Tyburn . . . the 24th of May, 1725* (1725), may be a forgery, as Purney's biographer suggests, but it was accepted at the time to be as factual as the Ordinary's reports usually were. The Ordinary's account was reproduced in *Select Trials* (ii. 284–8) of which a new edition was published in 1742.

220 *one Chapter . . . have not exceeded it*: Book IV Chapter IX, omitted in the 1754, and most subsequent, editions.

222 *Subscription*: *Miscellanies* was published by subscription, that is, individuals paid in advance for the volumes and the author met printing and other costs out of the subscription income. The average eighteenth-century subscription list might include about 250 names; HF attracted 427.

*a Profession . . . Subscription*: HF had been called to the bar in 1740. There are a large number of names of members of the legal profession on the subscription list.

*dangerous Illness . . . this Winter*: HF's wife Charlotte had been unwell in 1742–3. She died in November 1744.

223 *Accidents . . . these Works*: HF had suffered a number of professional setbacks and personal sadnesses since the Licensing Act of 1737 effectively ended his career as a playwright. In 1738 he and his siblings had had

to sell the much-loved family estate of East Stour; early in 1741 he was briefly imprisoned for debt (M. and R. Battestin, 295–6); later that year his father Edmund died in disgrace and penniless (M. and R. Battestin, 297–301); in 1742 his eldest child, Charlotte, died at the age of 5, while HF was himself ill (M. and R. Battestin, 340).

223 *long since . . . the Champion*: *the Champion; or, The British Mercury*, a current-affairs journal with a broadly Opposition stance in political matters, began publication in November 1739. HF was a partner with two one-sixteenth shares in the venture, the editor of the journal (under the guise of 'Captain Hercules Vinegar'), and at the outset one of its major contributors. From mid-1740 he began to withdraw from active participation in the project, and in March 1742 the other partners voted him out of the partnership.

*last Winter*: that is, the winter of 1741–2. See note to p. 222.

*declare . . . Share*: during this period HF also translated, with William Young, Aristophanes' play *Plautus* (May 1742). His anonymous collaborator in the ballad-opera *Miss Lucy in Town* might have been the actor David Garrick.

224 *I will never hereafter . . . my Name*: HF withdrew this promise in his Preface to the second edition of *David Simple* (1744).

## APPENDIX 3
225 *Pages 195, 196 of that Book*: pages 134–5 of the present edition.

# GLOSSARY

*ab effectu* from the outcome

**abroad** away from home

**Accident** unforeseen incident, event

**Ambuscade** ambush

**animadvert** comment (often critically)

*Arcana* mysteries

**awful** full of awe, timorous, reverential

**balance (ballance)** 'waver, deliberate, hesitate' (*OED*)

**bate** 'decrease in amount, weight or estimation' (*OED*)

**beadle** parish constable responsible for punishing petty offenders

**beat up** recruit

**Beau** fop, dandy

**bite** 'deceive, overreach, take in' (*OED*)

**blow up** destroy, ruin

**Bounce** 'the loud burst of noise produced by an explosion' (*OED*) and so figuratively an outburst of rage

**Brickbat** fragment of brick

**Brigantine** small vessel equipped for sailing and rowing, and therefore often employed for purposes of piracy or reconnoitring

**Brilliant** 'a diamond of the finest cut and brilliancy' (*OED*)

**brisk** quick and active

**broken** ruined, bankrupt

**bubbled** deluded with bubbles, that is, cheated

**Bumper** cup or glass of wine filled to the brim

**Can** vessel designed to hold liquid

**Carriage** conduct, behaviour

**Catastrophe** final event or conclusion (of a series of events or a narrative), generally unhappy

**catechize** give detailed instruction (usually in religion)

**Chair** Sedan chair, a closed carriage on poles, designed to hold one person carried by two men

**Chairman** one of the two men who carry a **chair** (q.v.)

**Character** trait or characteristic; or 'description . . . of a person's qualities' (*OED*)

**Chef d'Oeuvre** masterpiece

**chimerical** imaginary, fanciful, visionary

**Chimney-Glass** the looking glass normally placed over a chimney piece or mantelpiece

**Closet** small inner room

**cog a Die** fraudulently control or direct the fall of the dice

**collusive** 'fraudulently concerted or derived' (*OED*)

**Colour** outward appearance, show

**Complexion** the balance of the four bodily 'humours', cold and hot, moist and dry, making up the physical constitution of an individual

**Compotations** group drinking bouts

**Confabulation** familiar conversation, chat

**Conversation** informal chat, but also more generally association or connection, sometimes with an implication of sexual intimacy

**Coquet (Coquette)** flirt

**Cousin-German** first cousin, or more generally near relation

**Cruize** naval tour of the sea looking for ships to take as prizes

**cunning** intelligent, clever, skilful, artful, sly

**Deal** timber cut from fir or pine

**depasture** graze

**discover** find out; also demonstrate, reveal

**Discoveries** revelations

**Draught** 'a Quantity of Liquor drank at once' (Johnson)

**Drawer** the person drawing liquor for customers in an alehouse

**Dun** importunate creditor or agent employed to collect a debt; also the demand for payment

**efficient** essential, that which makes something what it is

**eligible** appropriate, deserving to be chosen

**Elogium** explanatory inscription

**Engineer** a constructor of military engines

**Enlargement** release from confinement

**Ensign** sign, emblem, badge of office

**Equipage** carriage and horses with attendant servants

**Evidence** a giver of evidence, informer

**executive** carrying into practical effect

**Exercitation** exercise, exertion

**exquisite** carefully elaborate, brought to a high degree of perfection

**Exuberance** 'excrescence, protuberance' (*OED*)

**fang** grasp, catch in a snare

*felo de se* one who deliberately puts an end to his own existence, or commits an unlawful act which results in his own death

**Figure** importance, distinction

**Fiz** (phiz) from physiognomy, 'face, countenance, expression or aspect of face' (*OED*)

**flea** flay

**florid** full of the flowers of rhetoric, that is, of fine words and phrases

**Fomentations** flannels soaked in hot water

**Footpad** a highwayman who robs on foot rather than on horseback

**Frigidity** deficiency of fire or spirit

**grateful** agreeable, acceptable

**Guard de Corps** from *guard du corps*, bodyguard

**hackney Coach** four-wheeled coach, drawn by two horses and able to seat six people, available for hire

**Hanger** short sword

**hardly** boldly, daringly, hardily

**Hermite** hermit

**Hind** skilled farmworker

**Hollands** Hollands gin, 'a grain spirit manufactured in Holland' (*OED*)

**horrible** exciting, or fit to excite, horror

**impeach** bring a charge or action against, give accusatory evidence against

**impertinent** not pertinent, a waste of time

**Inanity** lacking substance, being void of interest

**indifferent** neutral, disinterested

**Insignia** 'distinguishing marks of office or honour' (Johnson)

*in Specie* in cash, in actual coin

**instalment** 'formal induction into an office or dignity' (*OED*)

**in the gross** generally, without going into particulars

**Lay** originally a wager or adventure, and by extension a scam, or scheme to steal

**Livery Man** liveried servant

**Long-boat** the largest boat belonging to a sailing vessel

**louring** frowning, scowling

**Mechanic(k)** workman in a manual trade (with an implication of lowness)

**Merchant-man** merchant ship

**Merrythought** the portion of a bird that, when carved, includes the wishbone

**Meteor** any luminous body seen temporarily in the sky, including a fireball or shooting star

**Musquet** musket, a handgun used by infantrymen in the eighteenth century

**Muster** assembling of (often military) men for inspection or review

**Nab** broad-brimmed hat

**Natural** 'one naturally deficient in intellect; a half-witted person' (*OED*)

**nice** precise, fine, fastidious, delicate

**Night-Cellar** 'a cellar serving as a tavern or place of resort during the night for persons of the lowest class' (*OED*)

**Night-gown** long loose wrap-over garment like a modern dressing-gown, worn informally in the morning and evening

**obnoxious to** exposed to (something harmful)

**outragious** extravagant, excessive

**Packet** boat 'plying at regular intervals between two ports for the conveyance of mails, also of goods and passengers' (*OED*)

**Parsimony** carefulness in saving money (without the present derogatory sense)

**Parties** pairs, teams, factions in a contest

**Parts** abilities, capacities, talents

**play the whole Game** 'cheat' (Grose)

**Post-horse** a horse kept at a post-house or inn for hire to travellers

**Philogyny** love of women

**popular** populous

**prefer** offer preferment; advance in status, rank, or fortune

**presently** immediately

**Prig** thief

**Priggism** professional thievery or roguery

**prodigious** unnatural, abnormal

**Profession** declaration, promise

**Professor** one given to affirming openly and often

**providentally** by special intervention of Providence

**purling** rippling, undulating, murmuring

***Quomodo*** manner or means; literally, 'in what way'

**rampant** aggressively lustful

**regale** entertain

**Rejoinder** reply, in rhetoric or law a formal answer to a proposition or accusation

**rhodomontade** 'vainglorious brag or boast' (*OED*)

**Sally** outburst or transport of passion

**salute** greet with a kiss

**scandalize** insult, make a scandal of

**Scrutore** escritoire or writing desk

**seedy** poor

**sensible** perceptible to the senses

**sensibly** with intense emotion

**simple** silly

**Smirk** 'a finical, spruce fellow' (*NCD*, Grose)

**Sneaker** small bowl

**sneaking** mean, low; also a cant word for stealing or pilfering

**Solitaire** 'a precious stone, usually a diamond, set by itself' (*OED*)

**Spark** 'a lively, showy, splendid, gay man' (Johnson)

**Spleen** 'violent ill-nature or ill-humour, irritable or peevish temper' (*OED*)

**spoil** despoil, strip of arms/armour

**Stage-Coach** horse-drawn coach travelling at specified times and between specified locations, and taking up paying passengers

**Stupes** pieces of 'tow, flannel, or other soft substance, wrung out of hot

liquor and medicated, for
fomenting a wound or ailing
part' (*OED*)

**Sugar-Plumb** small flavoured
sweetmeat made of boiled sugar, by
extension a sop or bribe

**tinsel** specious, showy ('tinsel'
was originally a kind of shiny
cloth)

**topical** 'that belongs to or is applied
to a particular part of the body'
(*OED*)

**Toy-Shop** a shop where trinkets and
small ornamental articles are sold

**Under-Actors** actors taking minor
roles

**Water-work** ornamental fountain or
cascade

*The Oxford World's Classics Website*

## www.worldsclassics.co.uk

- Browse the full range of Oxford World's Classics online

- Sign up for our monthly e-alert to receive information on new titles

- Read extracts from the Introductions

- Listen to our editors and translators talk about the world's greatest literature with our Oxford World's Classics audio guides

- Join the conversation, follow us on Twitter at OWC_Oxford

- Teachers and lecturers can order inspection copies quickly and simply via our website

## www.worldsclassics.co.uk

**American Literature**

**British and Irish Literature**

**Children's Literature**

**Classics and Ancient Literature**

**Colonial Literature**

**Eastern Literature**

**European Literature**

**Gothic Literature**

**History**

**Medieval Literature**

**Oxford English Drama**

**Poetry**

**Philosophy**

**Politics**

**Religion**

**The Oxford Shakespeare**

---

A complete list of Oxford World's Classics, including Authors in Context, Oxford English Drama, and the Oxford Shakespeare, is available in the UK from the Marketing Services Department, Oxford University Press, Great Clarendon Street, Oxford OX2 6DP, or visit the website at www.oup.com/uk/worldsclassics.

In the USA, visit www.oup.com/us/owc for a complete title list.

Oxford World's Classics are available from all good bookshops. In case of difficulty, customers in the UK should contact Oxford University Press Bookshop, 116 High Street, Oxford OX1 4BR.